THE SECRET HANGMAN

Peter Diamond, the Bath detective, is having woman trouble. His boss wants him to find a missing person, the daughter of one of her friends, and a 'Secret Admirer' wants to set up a meeting with him. Then there is sexy Ingeborg Smith, the ex-journo detective constable, distracting the murder squad from their duties. No one ignores Ingeborg.

Murder becomes a possibility when a woman's body is found hanging from a swing in Sydney Gardens and a second ligature mark is found around her neck. More hangings are discovered and soon Diamond is certain that a secret hangman is at work in the city.

Is it the mounting pressure of this gruesome case that propels Diamond into the arms of the Secret Admirer? The hunt for the killer, through abandoned mine-workings and the deserted city by night, galvanizes the entire squad and forces Diamond to face his own demons as well as the secret hangman.

THE SECRET HANGMAN

Peter Lovesey

WINDSOR

PARAGON

First published 2007
by
Sphere
This Large Print edition published 2007
by
BBC Audiobooks Ltd by arrangement with
Little, Brown Book Group

Hardcover ISBN: 978 1 405 61722 2
Softcover   ISBN: 978 1 405 61723 9

British Library Cataloguing in Publication Data available

Printed and bound in Great Britain by
Antony Rowe Ltd., Chippenham, Wiltshire

1

To Detective Superintendent Peter Diamond

Dear Mr Diamond,

This is so difficult. Several tries have ended in the bin already. Please be kind and read to the end before making up your mind.

I'm a woman of—let's say a few years younger than you. Like you, I was married for a time but now I'm back to the single life and I can't say I enjoy it even though I'm left with my own house and enough to live on. What else? I went through university in the days when it was difficult to get in. I like a lot of the things you enjoy, like old black-and-white films, rock music and the occasional glass of beer. I'm lucky enough to be in good health. People tell me I'm good company. Figure-wise, I could still get into some of the clothes I had as a student if I'd kept them, but I keep up with fashion, so I'm always buying new things. You don't have to be a detective to see where this is leading, so I'm going to stop wittering on about myself. I just wanted you to know I'm not the Wicked Witch of the West.

You'll be wondering how I know so much about you and I'd better come clean and say I read about you in the paper a couple of years ago and cut the piece out because I liked your picture and the things you were saying. It was a feature article with a photo. I just loved the way you talked about your life in the police. You give it to them straight whether they're chief constables or cub reporters from the Daily Grind. Since then I've followed you through several

1

cases and it's obvious you're in the top bracket as a detective.

What do I want now I've plucked up the courage to write? I just wonder if you'd like to meet some time for a drink and a chat? My generation of women isn't used to making the first move, not face to face, and even writing it down like this is a big effort—which is why I'm hiding behind a made-up name and no address.

I'll be in the Saracen's Head this Thursday between seven and eight. If you come in, I'll introduce myself.

In anticipation—and thanks, anyway, for reading this far,

Your secret admirer

Lady, if you knew anything about me you wouldn't bother, Peter Diamond thought. He sighed and shook his head.

He dropped the letter into the bin with the other junk mail. The envelope was about to follow, but didn't. He'd noticed it was the self-seal kind and the seal wasn't too good because the flap had come apart easily without tearing anything. He tried sealing the thing again and it wouldn't hold—just as if someone had opened it already.

No stamp. No address. Just his name on the envelope and *By hand* written where the stamp should have been. She must have delivered it to the front desk, and that gave him an uncomfortable thought. Suppose the entire nick knew he'd got a secret admirer.

Now he picked the letter out of the bin, replaced it in the envelope and put it in his jacket pocket. Later, he'd put it through the office

2

shredder.

A worse thought: some joker on his own team had done this as a hoax. They were waiting to see his reaction.

Well, he wouldn't give them that satisfaction. Bugger it, he'd check *their* reactions. He got up and took his usual route between the desks towards the door at the far end, appearing nonchalant while alert to any suggestion of a snigger. At one point he stopped and swung round as if he'd forgotten a file and needed to go back.

No one was paying him any attention.

Two, at least, had their eyes on Ingeborg, the novice detective, as she bent over a filing cabinet. Keith Halliwell, the longest-serving DI—and well capable of practical joking—was on the phone. The civilian staff were fingering their keyboards.

Yet he doubted if Halliwell would stoop to this. Halliwell had been with him that ill-fated morning when he attended a crime scene in Royal Victoria Park and made the worst of all discoveries. Keith of all people knew better than to trespass on his personal life.

The hoax theory withered and died.

He moved on and kept going through the building as far as the canteen. Picked up a mug of tea and a sticky bun and parked himself at a table at the quiet end. He was used to being alone.

Not for long. Assistant Chief Constable Georgina Dallymore, the closest thing he had to a boss, appeared from nowhere carrying a glass of water and sat opposite him.

'Peter, you look peaky.'

Peaky. That was a word from the past. He'd last heard it used by one of his aunts forty years ago to

3

explain why she wouldn't sample his mother's Victoria sponge.

'I'm OK,' he said to Georgina.

'Overwork?'

'Hardly.'

'Something personal?'

'I said I'm OK.'

The boss gave him a sympathetic look. She'd given him looks like that ever since Steph was murdered, as if she expected him at any moment to bury his face in her bosom and sob uncontrollably. She said, 'An MP report has come in.'

'That's all we need,' he said, rolling his eyes upwards.

She frowned. 'What's wrong?'

'Politicians, that's what's wrong. We don't want them breathing down our necks.'

'Not members of parliament,' she said in the despairing tone of a schoolmistress to the kid who never listened. Diamond had an inbuilt resistance to abbreviations. 'Missing person.'

He thought about that for a while before saying, 'Got you.'

'A woman in Walcot with a partner and two small daughters was out on Tuesday night and hasn't been home since.'

'Tuesday? That's only yesterday.'

'It's very unlike her,' Georgina went on as if she hadn't heard. 'She's in the habit of speaking to her mother on the phone every day at the same time.'

'The mother reported it. Not the partner?'

'He's relaxed about it. Says she must have needed space and she'll come back when she's ready.'

'He's probably right. And you want it checked?'

'Please, Peter.'

'Isn't it rather quick? One night away isn't much. She's not a fourteen-year-old.'

Georgina's chest expanded, an ominous sign well known in Manvers Street nick. 'I happen to have spoken to her mother. She's in my choir. A level-headed woman. She wouldn't fuss without reason.'

He understood now. Georgina was a devoted singer. How good her voice was, he didn't know. She had joined, and left, several of Bath's many choirs over the past four years. Even so, there is a fellowship among singers, a kind of freemasonry as Diamond viewed it, that meant they helped each other when they could. She was going to insist on a routine check.

'Who's looking after the kids?' he asked.

'The partner.'

'Are they his?'

'I believe not.'

'His name?'

'Corcoran. Ashley Corcoran. More importantly, hers is Delia Williamson.' She handed him a scrap of paper with some details she'd got from her friend in the choir.

Missing persons are a constant of police work. Over four thousand join the list every week in Britain. Rebellious teenagers, runaway spouses, middle-aged dropouts, feeble-minded old people. The index grows steadily, but a good proportion return. Some give cause for real concern. A few are never heard of again.

He returned upstairs and told DC Ingeborg Smith to find out what she could about Delia

5

Williamson.

'Are you thinking this is a domestic, guv?' Ingeborg asked, mustard-keen as usual. She had everything on computer at the speed of a texting teenager. As a former investigative journalist, she was used to meeting deadlines.

'I'm keeping an open mind. When you visit the partner—this Corcoran—make sure a man is with you.'

'I can handle it.'

'With a bloke at your side, Inge. I don't want two female detectives knocking on his door.'

She drew a sharp breath, and then bit back what she was going to say and settled for less. 'It says here Corcoran is cooperating.'

'They do at the beginning. That's an order.'

He looked at the printout she'd given him. Delia Williamson was thirty-three, dark-haired and wore glasses. The two daughters, aged eight and six, were from a previous relationship. 'Get the name of the father,' he told her. 'Everything you can on him.'

*   *   *

At home in Weston that evening, he felt in his pocket for a pen and discovered that letter from the secret admirer. He'd forgotten to shred it. No need. He'd tear it into small pieces and dispose of them with the rubbish.

But he didn't.

Here in the black hole that was his private life, with only domestic chores and television to keep self-pity at bay, he thought about the effort it must have taken to write that letter and deliver it to the

6

nick. He unfolded it and read it again. The woman hadn't said if she was bereaved or divorced. *I'm back to the single life and I can't say I enjoy it.*

'You and me both,' he said.

Even so, he wasn't going to be suckered into walking into a pub to meet a stranger who'd read about him in the paper. It would be worse than a date set up by one of those agencies that make money out of lonely people. At least they show you a video-clip to help you decide.

Three years had gone by since he'd found Steph gunned down in Royal Victoria Park. He'd loved her with a passion no one else would understand. She had been warm, amusing, honest, wise, sexy, brave and, in his eyes, beautiful. She'd made him the luckiest man in the world—until that February morning. He'd repeatedly told himself he would find his own way through the grief. For Steph's sake he wouldn't let the sadness show. She would have expected him to hold up, and he had, so far as anyone could tell. Finding her killer had helped fill the gap in those early months. Work, work, work had been the therapy since. Slack times were black times.

He could just about remember the newspaper interview this woman must have seen. It had been in the *Bath Chronicle* six months after the murder, when the investigation seemed to be going nowhere. He hadn't kept a copy. His mind had been on other things. They must have printed that trivia about the black-and-white films and the rock music, or where would she have got it from? But what was he doing, talking to the press about music and movies six months after Steph had died?

7

He could check in the newspaper files, but he'd be wasting his time. The letter was of no importance. He wouldn't be meeting the woman.

He glanced down the page and smiled at that sentence: *I just wanted you to know I'm not the Wicked Witch of the West*. She had a sense of humour, whoever she was. He stuffed it back into his pocket. Then he sorted through the heap of dusty videos on the floor and picked out *The Postman Always Rings Twice*. The original version, with John Garfield and Lana Turner. It would see him through until bedtime.

2

A woman's body was found next morning in Sydney Gardens. It was hanging from the crossbar of a swing in the children's play area.

'Are you up to this?' Georgina asked Diamond.

'What do you mean—up to this?' he said. But he knew exactly what she meant: a woman dead in a park.

He took Keith Halliwell. From the Beckford Road entrance they were able to drive right up to the play area along an asphalt path generally used only by pedestrians. The swings, chute, seesaw, roundabout and sandpit were enclosed by a metal fence, so police tape hadn't been needed. A uniformed constable manned the gate. Already some gawpers were standing outside as if it was the first day of a sale. Two were young mothers with kids in strollers. People amazed him sometimes. He asked them to move along.

The dead woman was suspended from the yellow swings meant for the older children. Dark-haired, she was dressed in jeans, dark blue sweater and Adidas trainers.

'Get this screened off now,' he told the sergeant at the scene.

He went right up to the corpse and looked at the face without shifting the hair that lay over one eye. She had turned a bluish red, as if she'd struggled, he thought. People who choose to hang themselves don't know what they're in for. They hardly ever do it right. Mid-thirties, he estimated. The nose had the pressure marks of glasses. He glanced at the hands. No wedding ring. 'I might know who this is,' he told Halliwell.

Halliwell gave him a concerned look, recalling the last time he'd recognised the victim.

But he was calm. 'A woman went missing from Walcot this week, name of Williamson.'

'Was she—'

'Dark hair, glasses, in her thirties.' He looked around, raising his voice for the others. 'Did anyone find a bag or a suicide note?'

Heads were shaken.

'Strange choice,' he said to Halliwell. 'The hangings I've seen have all been in private. If I'm right about the victim, she's a mother of two. Fancy choosing a play park.'

Halliwell, practical as always, pointed out that a swing had certain advantages for a would-be suicide. The crossbar was a good height and the seat of the swing was well placed for stepping off.

'What I meant,' Diamond said, 'is that a mother might give a thought to being found here by young kids.'

9

'We don't know for certain that she's a mother, guv.'

'We don't know for certain that she hanged herself. Where's the doc? Did anyone call the police surgeon?'

Dr Hindle had already been by, the constable told Diamond. She'd advised leaving the body in situ. A forensic pathologist was on his way from Bristol.

'Why? Is there something fishy?'

'She didn't say, sir.'

'Sally Hindle, you said? I'll give her a bell. And while we're waiting, chase up those bloody screens, man. Let's show this poor woman some respect.'

Sally Hindle was a local GP who earned extra for dealing with police-related medical matters. The title of police surgeon meant no special skill in forensic medicine. 'I simply certified that death had occurred,' she told Diamond from her surgery. 'No, I had no reason to doubt that she hanged herself, but I don't advise moving her until the pathologist gives his consent.'

She was right, and they had to wait. Some canvas screens arrived and were erected. The police photographer took his shots and the crime scene people tried to make sense of footprints in abundance. Now that the swing was enclosed there was a sense of intimacy, as if they were in a room with the corpse.

Diamond stepped outside and phoned Ingeborg and asked her to come to the park and bring a picture of Delia Williamson.

'Have you found her, guv?'

Always with Inge, the ex-journo, questions he

10

wasn't able to answer and she needn't have asked.

'Just get in your car and drive here.'

'Try and stop me.'

Her eagerness to please was a pain at times, but he was glad to have her on the team. So were the others. She was a real babe.

He joined Halliwell again. 'Two young kids, if I'm right. She'd have to be desperate.'

'Wouldn't anyone?' Halliwell said. 'To top themselves, I mean.'

'Extra desperate.'

'True.'

After a long pause Diamond said, 'You know what I'm thinking, don't you, Keith?'

Halliwell hesitated. He'd worked with this boss for most of his CID career, but he still wasn't sure how frank he ought to be. 'Like, em, you've been through a bad patch yourself?'

Diamond frowned. 'What?'

'But you were never as desperate as this.'

'Sometimes I don't know which world you inhabit, Keith. What I'm thinking is we'd better not assume anything until the pathologist has been by.'

Halliwell backtracked fast. 'I get you now.'

Ingeborg arrived in ten minutes. She put her head around the screen and said, 'Oh, poor soul. Haven't you cut her down yet?'

Another pointless question. The body was rotating in the breeze.

'Just show us the picture,' Diamond said.

Ingeborg had brought two photos, a head-and-shoulders shot taken in a booth and an outdoor one of the mother and her two small daughters. Beyond any doubt the dead woman was Delia

11

Williamson. Diamond looked at the smiles of the children and felt his stomach clench. Someone would have to break it to those little girls that their mother was dead. They would ask questions and that same someone would have the choice between merciful lying and the appalling truth.

Ingeborg said, 'Guv.'

'Mm?'

'Do you want me to speak to the family?'

'No,' he said. 'Not your job.'

She took a closer look at the body. 'Armani jeans.'

'Yep, I read the label.'

'And the sweater is cashmere.'

This he hadn't spotted. 'So she wasn't short of a bob or two.'

The pathologist turned up eventually. This Dr Bertram Sealy was new to Diamond but not new to the game. He'd brought a flask of hot coffee and poured himself a cup before stepping around the screen. The smell was tantalising. 'Do you have a gofer I can borrow?' he asked.

There were times when Diamond was hard on his staff, but he didn't think of them like that. He let the remark pass. People come out with insensitive things in stressful situations. Instead, he beckoned to Ingeborg and introduced her.

'You're CID?' Dr Sealy said to her with approval. 'I thought you all chewed gum and shaved your heads. Do me a favour, my beauty. The boot of my car is unlocked. Inside you'll find an essential tool of the trade, my blue plastic milk crate. Would you mind fetching it?'

Ingeborg obeyed, but only after a look that said she didn't like being patronised.

12

Dr Sealy winked at Diamond while Ingeborg opened the boot and bent over it for the crate. 'It's not a job that appeals to everyone, mine. I make the best of it.'

Diamond stared through him.

Sealy screwed the cup back on his flask. 'Make yourself useful and hold this for me, would you? Got to put on my surgical gloves.'

Diamond kept his hands behind his back. It was Halliwell who stepped forward for the flask.

The purpose of the crate was made clear. Sealy needed to step up and he wasn't going to risk standing on the seat of one of the swings. He asked Ingeborg to place the crate upside down on the ground behind the suspended body. With a hand resting on her shoulder he stepped up level with the woman's neck. He spent some time studying the marks made by the plastic cord. When he'd finished he made sure Ingeborg gave him a hand down. Then he asked her to move the crate to the front, all the while watching as if he'd never seen a woman in his life. Once again, he steadied himself by grasping and squeezing her shoulder. Almost as an afterthought he turned his attention to the corpse and used an electronic thermometer with a digital read-out to measure the temperature in the nostrils. Then he stepped down, smiled at Ingeborg and took out a notebook to record his reading. He invited the photographer to stand on the crate and take some close-ups. While this was going on, he examined the dead woman's hands.

Finally he stepped away. 'I've done. When you bring her down, I want the cord cut a foot above the head and left in place round the neck.'

13

'Any first impressions?' Diamond asked.

'Some remarkable features.' He turned for another look at Ingeborg. 'And the corpse is not without interest.'

If he'd expected a reaction from Diamond, he got none.

'I wouldn't have expected the cyanosis to be so marked.'

'The purple colour of the face?'

'And there's something else. She has two sets of ligature marks, overlapping in places, but diverging at the side of the neck where she is suspended.'

'Two sets of marks?'

'Be my guest, Mr Diamond. Step on the crate.'

Diamond wasn't built for step-ups. Ingeborg said, 'All right, guv,' and steadied his arm with a willingness that showed where her loyalty lay.

His face was six inches from the dead woman's neck.

Sealy said, 'See the brownish horizontal line below the knot, going right round, like a collar? That's the one that interests me.'

'So what does this mean—that she was strangled first, and strung up?'

'Don't rush your fences, Inspector.'

'Superintendent.'

'Oops,' said Sealy, and made a mock salute.

'Someone could have faked the suicide to cover up a murder?'

'I'd have thought a superintendent would know we men of science like to assemble all the facts before reaching an opinion.'

'Pompous twit,' Diamond muttered.

Sealy was making more notes.

14

Diamond stepped off the crate and waited for him to finish.

Without looking up from the notebook Sealy asked, 'How do you spell your name?'

'The usual way.'

'You're a bit of a card, then?'

That old joke fell flat.

But Sealy wanted to run with it. 'The king, the ace or the joker?'

Diamond said nothing. Why encourage him?

'If it isn't a card you are,' Sealy said, 'you must be a gem. Diamond ... gem ... Follow me? In which case you might be interested in a little-known service they provide in America. You look reasonably fit to me, Mr Diamond, but of course we all have to make provision for what lies ahead. The one certainty, as they say. You may have decided already what you want done with your mortal remains. Even if you have, I suggest you think about this, a beautiful prospect for a man lucky enough to bear the name you do. There's a firm in California who will take a cadaver and subject it to intense heat and pressure for eighteen weeks, reducing it to carbon atoms. The end product is a small, but exquisite, one-carat diamond.'

The only one to smile was Sealy.

'And if you're quick'—he looked at his watch—'I can do the PM ... p.m.' He took back his vacuum flask and strutted towards his car as if he'd knocked out the heavyweight champ.

Diamond arranged with Halliwell to oversee the removal of the body to an undertaker's van already parked nearby. The duty of observing the post-mortem also fell to Halliwell.

15

Diamond said, 'Ingeborg.'

'Guv?' She was about to pick up the crate and return it to Dr Sealy's car.

'Leave that.'

'But he's going to forget it.'

'Yes.'

*   *   *

Ingeborg had recently treated herself to one of those bug-shaped Fords known as a Ka, comfortable once Diamond had persuaded his bulk into the passenger seat and drawn the belt across. He asked her to drive him to the house in Walcot.

'Tell me about the men in this lady's life.'

'The one I met is Ashley Corcoran, her partner. He's cool.'

Aware that the last word had refinements he hadn't kept up with, Diamond said, 'Which is . . . ?'

'In control. No panic. He strikes me as responsible, if a little too laid back,' she told him. 'He's great with the kids. He collects them from school every day. Reads to them at bedtime.'

'What's his job?'

'Composing theme music for television. He's got a Steinway piano and all kinds of synthesisers and stuff.'

'Swish place, then?'

'A converted warehouse close to the river. Made me envious.'

'But he wasn't too worried about his partner's disappearance?'

'He said she'd be back. She'd always valued her

16

freedom and he respected that, or some such.'

'Leaving him with her kids?'

'No problem, apparently.'

'So was he annoyed with Delia's mother for reporting her missing?'

'He just smiled and said she's a worrier.'

'With good reason, it turns out. Did you sense anything suggesting this man could be violent?'

'Absolutely not.'

They were already across Pulteney Bridge. Ingeborg was a nifty driver.

'And what did you discover about the other guy, the father of the girls?'

'Not a lot. Only his first name, which is Danny.'

'Not much to go on.'

'Ashley Corcoran said he'd never asked. I can believe that's true.'

'He *is* cool. What are the girls called, then? They must have a surname.'

'Williamson. They use the mother's name.' She turned right, off Walcot Street, and drove into the cobbled yard that fronted Ashley Corcoran's stylish residence.

'By the way,' he told her as he got out, 'leave the questions to me.'

*   *   *

There's money in television. The Corcoran residence had a varnished oak door with coach-lamps either side. The chime was the opening of Beethoven's Fifth. In the moment before it was answered, Diamond took stock. This was a unique situation that had to be handled right. He'd be breaking the news, but not all the news. He'd be telling Corcoran that his partner had been found dead, hanging from a swing, no more. No suspicion that anyone else was involved. The man's reaction would be worth noting. Any possible sign of guilt would be subtle, not to be missed. Even a glimmer of relief at this stage would tell Diamond he was speaking to a murderer.

The door was opened by a long-haired man in a black kaftan and white jeans. He was rubbing his eyes as if he'd just woken.

Then he recognised Ingeborg. 'Oh, you.'

Diamond showed his warrant card and asked if they could come in.

A hand through the hair, matted brown hair that looked as if it could do with a wash. 'Is it about Delia?'

Diamond nodded. 'So shall we speak inside?'

The interior was open plan, a vast space with toys for all the family: giant teddies, an exercise bike, plasma television, a music system and the grand piano. Corcoran led them across the wood floor to an area with a large Afghan rug surrounded by sofas.

'This is bad news, I take it. Is it the worst?'

'I'm afraid so.' Diamond sketched the circumstances. He said he couldn't say for certain that the woman in the park was Delia Williamson, but she closely resembled the photos.

People given news of sudden death are often reduced to one-word questions—When? Where? How?—and this was how it played with Ashley Corcoran. No hint of foreknowledge. He was cool, as Ingeborg had said, yet anxious to hear precisely what had been discovered.

18

'I'll be asking you to identify her later,' Diamond said. 'Probably not today.'

'Is she still . . . ?'

'Being driven to Bristol by now.'

'Whatever for?'

'The post-mortem.'

'I see.' Still cool.

'There are two daughters, I'm told.'

'At school until three thirty.' Corcoran raked a hand through his hair. 'Oh, God, I'll have to tell them.'

'That had better wait until we're a hundred per cent certain. What about their father. Where's he?'

'I said I'll tell them. They treat me as their dad.'

'Yes, but he's got to be informed.'

'I guess you're right.' Corcoran's thoughts were played out on his face. 'This changes everything.'

'Has he been seeing his daughters?'

'He's written them off.'

'I gather you don't know his surname or present address?'

'Danny? No idea.'

'Would Delia have it written down somewhere?'

'Can't say. Far as I know, she hasn't heard from him in years.' He opened his hands in appeal. 'Listen, I can keep the girls, can't I?'

'They'll need someone else, at least while things are sorted out. Their grandmother sounds like a caring person. She was the one who notified us that Delia was missing.'

'Amanda's OK,' he said. 'A worry-guts, that's all.'

Diamond moved the conversation on. 'Is it possible Delia left a suicide note somewhere in

19

the house? Nothing was found in the park.'

'I haven't seen one.'

'Have you looked? I understand you weren't too concerned that she went missing.'

He shifted in his seat. 'That makes me sound uncaring. I didn't dream she'd do anything like this.'

'Was there an argument before she left?'

'No. We were fine.'

'But she lives here. Has she gone missing before?'

'We don't keep tabs on each other.' Corcoran sighed. 'Look, I'm a musician. I'm on a deadline for a new TV drama. I work unsocial hours, right? I find night-time is the most creative. We don't see so much of each other when I'm working.'

'Are you saying you didn't notice she was gone?'

He shrugged. 'The first I knew was when Amanda called me yesterday afternoon.'

'Excuse me butting in, guv,' Ingeborg said, unable to stay silent, 'but what about the girls? How did they get to school in the morning?'

Corcoran said, 'We have a Filipino girl who helps out. She comes in at seven and sees them off with a packed lunch. Then she comes back and does some housework until midday.'

Diamond asked, 'And what's Delia doing in the morning?'

'She sleeps in.'

'Doesn't she have a job?'

'Waitress, in Tosi's, the Italian restaurant just up the street from here.'

Diamond's spirits took a plunge. A simple case was suddenly complicated by Italian waiters and restaurant customers. 'Full-time?'

'Six evenings a week.'

He looked around at the expensive furnishings. 'Did she need the money?'

'She didn't want to be kept, as she put it.'

'From what you were saying earlier, am I right in thinking she had her own room? If so, could we take a look at it?'

A gallery extended around three sides of the upper level and the bedrooms led off it. Delia had a walk-in dressing room and en-suite bath and shower. The bed was queensize with an empire-style arrangement of drapes on the wall at the head. The quilt had been thrown back and a nightdress tossed across the pillows. Underclothes were scattered on top of a basket inside the door. These signs of occupation made Delia Williamson seem more real than the corpse in the park.

'I respected her privacy,' Corcoran said. 'This is the first time I've looked in here since she went missing, except on the afternoon her mother phoned. I put my head round the door in case she was ill, or something.'

'We all kiss goodbye to privacy when we die.' Diamond pulled open a drawer of the bedside cupboard and told Ingeborg. 'See what you can find.'

Almost at once she handed him two birth certificates. The children's names were Sharon and Sophie. More importantly, the full name of their father was Daniel Geaves.

*   *   *

They traced Geaves to an address in Freshford, a village between Bath and Bradford on Avon best known to Diamond for its pub, named logically enough the Inn at Freshford. He'd been there a couple of times with Steph.

Ingeborg did the driving again. Unfortunately the man they had come to see was not at home. The cottage he rented looked as if it hadn't been used for some days, and the neighbour said she hadn't seen him all week. Diamond had a hunch, he told Ingeborg, that someone at the inn might have some information.

What he didn't tell her was that his hunches rarely amounted to anything. His real purpose in going in was a late lunch of fish and chips. The landlord said Danny came in sometimes, but never stayed long. He'd take his drink and a packet of crisps to an empty table. He usually had a paper with him and did the crossword.

Afterwards they took their drinks outside and sat on the wall of the packhorse bridge listening to the ripple and gurgle of the Avon. Across a green field, the steep side of the Limpley Stoke Valley was covered in lush foliage. 'Not bad, eh?' he said. 'Better than watching your friend Dr Sealy doing a post-mortem.'

'Give me a break, guv. He's no friend of mine. He's pathetic.'

'I can't disagree with that.'

Ingeborg took a sip of lager and stared down at the waterweeds rippling in the flow. 'I don't know if it's me, but the blokes who seem to fancy me are the ones I'd rather avoid.'

He was reminded of his secret admirer. For one mad moment he considered taking the letter from his inside pocket and showing it to Ingeborg, but the moment slipped by.

*　　　*　　　*

Back in Manvers Street what passed for an incident room was more like the quiet room in a silent order. Halliwell was hand-feeding a pigeon on the window ledge.

'What progress?' Diamond said, trying to energise someone.

Halliwell turned and said, '*What* progress?'

One of the civilian computer operators said, 'There's something on your desk, Mr Diamond.'

'Desk work. That's not progress,' he said. 'That's punishment.' He went into his office to look.

He'd never had anything so organised as an in-tray. Items for attention were heaped on his desk. On top now was a parcel with *THIS WAY UP* written in large letters and his name underneath. No address. It was wrapped in brown paper fastened with Sellotape and was about the size and shape of a box file. One end had been unsealed. Nothing suspicious about that: every package was security-checked downstairs. More damned paperwork, he guessed, though why it was done up as a parcel he couldn't fathom. He picked the thing up and was relieved to find it didn't weigh too heavily. He put it to one side and looked to see what else had come in.

Three pages of minutes from a meeting he'd managed to miss of the Police and Community Consultative Group. A reminder from Georgina that the overtime figures for last month hadn't been presented yet. A request from the new boy, Paul Gilbert, for the firearms course. He was riding for a fall, that lad.

The rest of the heap could wait. He reached for the parcel and tore it open. Inside was a cardboard box and when he lifted the lid he found several layers of loosely crumpled red tissue paper. He removed them.

A chocolate cake.

'What on earth?'

'Is it your birthday, guv?'

He looked up. Ingeborg, Halliwell, Leaman, Gilbert and the civilian staff had gathered in the doorway.

'Is this anything to do with you lot? Because I can tell you it isn't anywhere near my birthday.'

'We're being nosy, that's all,' Halliwell said.

'Security tipped you off, is that it?'

'Someone thinks you deserve a treat, that's obvious,' Ingeborg said. 'Is there a note with it?'

He lifted out the cake—which looked to have a black cherry filling—and went through the tissue paper and the wrappings. No message.

'It looks yummy,' Ingeborg said. 'Do you like chocolate?'

'I can take it or leave it.' He added in an afterthought, 'If I had a knife I'd offer some around.'

'Got one in my drawer,' Halliwell said almost too quickly.

'A cake knife?'

'A flick-knife confiscated from a nine-year-old. It'll do.'

'Get it then.'

'You don't have to, guv,' Ingeborg said. 'It was meant for you personally. You should take it home.'

24

'And eat all of this myself? What kind of guts do you take me for?'

Halliwell did the slicing. Everyone agreed the cake went down a treat. It was rich and light-textured.

'I don't know when I last had chocolate cake,' Diamond said.

'You've obviously got a secret admirer,' Ingeborg said. 'Oops, get the boss some water.'

He was choking on the crumbs.

3

Next morning Diamond turned to the back page of the post-mortem report, expecting it to tell him all he wanted in words he could understand. What's the point of a summary if it doesn't save you wading through pages of medical jargon? Dr Sealy had put it in a nutshell all right. The trouble was that he'd stated only what everyone knew, that Delia Williamson had been strangled with a ligature and later suspended from the swing. What use was that?

He phoned the hospital and was given Sealy's mobile number. Rightly or not, he pictured the little pipsqueak taking the call at home, reclining on a sun-lounger in the garden.

'How much later?' he asked. 'Was she strangled in the park and then strung up?'

'Unlikely.'

'We agree on that, then. Did you find any medical evidence to back this up?'

Sealy sounded as if he was speaking through

clenched teeth. 'That's what an autopsy is for. If you'd bothered to read my findings, you wouldn't ask.'

'Tell me, then.'

'The trouble with you policemen is that you only bother with the conclusion, and then you want it all in one-syllable words. In my description of the external findings on page two, which you seem to have ignored, I mention indications of hypostasis on the right side of the back and buttocks.'

'Hypo . . . ?'

' . . . stasis. It wasn't pronounced, but it was there. You have to allow for secondary gravitation, and that diminishes the effect.'

'We're talking about pressure marks?'

'Essentially, yes. They show up as pale areas after a couple of hours or so in one position. If the body was suspended directly after being killed I wouldn't expect to find hypostasis where I did.'

'The right side, you said. As if she was lying on her side for some time?'

'I would say so.'

'Curled up in a car boot, perhaps?'

'Speculation.'

'She'd have to be transported to the park. A car is the obvious way to do it.'

'You tell me,' Sealy said.

'No, I'm asking.'

'Not my job, squire. She could have been brought there on the back of an elephant for all I know.'

'What about the time of death?' Diamond asked with little expectation of an answer. Even the friendliest of pathologists can be guaranteed

26

to baulk at that one.

'How long have you been in the job, Mr Diamond?'

'The approximate time, then?'

'More than three hours before I examined her at the scene. Probably less than fifteen. And now you're going to ask me about secondary injuries, and you could have found them listed in the report if you'd bothered to read it instead of turning straight to the conclusion. There were not many. A couple of broken fingernails, but that could have happened post-mortem. She didn't put up much of a fight. However, she was not sexually assaulted. The usual forensic tests are being carried out. If any of the killer's DNA was recovered we'll let you know, but I wouldn't hold your breath.'

'I'd like to bring her partner out to Bristol to make the identification.'

'Bring who you like. I'll be on the golf course.'

*   *   *

'These days,' Diamond said to Ashley Corcoran on the drive back from Bristol after viewing the body, 'we have a family liaison officer to help you through a tragedy like this.'

'I'm all right.'

'It's the children I'm thinking of. They'll have to be told now we're certain it was their mother.'

'Sure.'

The casual attitude was not unusual. In the first few hours and days, Diamond knew from experience, the practicalities take over and you believe you can get through without anyone's

27

support. That stage passes.

'If I were you, I'd ask their grandmother to be present.'

'Sorted. They're staying with her now.'

So the man had done something right. Those two small girls were much on Peter Diamond's mind. Steph's hysterectomy had meant his own marriage had been childless, but that had never stopped him empathising with other people's kids. 'We'll do our best to keep our distance. But the story is going to break this afternoon. I'll have to call a press conference.'

Corcoran turned to look at Diamond, the overconfidence replaced by creases of concern. 'You don't want me there?'

'No. What I'm saying is make sure the girls are told before they see it on TV—or their friends do.'

'I'll do that.'

'The press will be a pain in the arse in the first days. Take a firm line, refuse any offers to tell your story and they'll get the idea.'

'I've got sod all to say to anyone.'

'Good. Hold fast to that.' He let a second or two pass before adding, 'But if you have anything helpful to tell me, I'd like it now.'

'I've told you all I can.'

That old cliché wasn't stopping Diamond. 'We do a reconstruction of her last twenty-four hours. You're certain, are you, that she didn't make contact?'

'Not with me,' he said, 'and not with Marietta, the child-minder.'

'I have to ask this, Ashley. Do you have any suspicion that Delia was seeing anyone else?'

28

He looked away, out of the car window. 'Oh, come on.' But there was something in the tone that undermined the words.

'Was she like that, one for the men?'

Corcoran scraped his fingers through his hair and gripped the ponytail. The answer was a long time coming. 'Guys liked her. She was something. She really was. She laughed a lot. But we trusted each other, right?'

Diamond gave a nod to that 'right', but he wasn't sure if Ashley Corcoran's trust had been well founded.

'And you're quite certain, are you, that there wasn't any dispute with the girls' father about custody?'

'Danny? He's a jerk. He's never shown any interest. If he surfaces now and wants them back, he can go to hell.'

'I'd take a more cautious line if I were you. As the father, he has more rights than you.'

*   *   *

Back at Manvers Street police station, the investigation machine powered into motion. Extra civilian staff were brought in to deal with statements. A press conference was scheduled. Halliwell was sent to Tosi's, the Italian restaurant where Delia had worked, to see how much they knew of her missing days. Ingeborg continued to try and trace Danny Geaves.

Georgina, the ACC, liked to think of herself as a hands-on executive. Diamond liked the high-ups to keep their hands off. 'Leave it to me, ma'am,' he said when she looked in for the second time

29

that day. 'Have I ever let you down?'

'We've had our moments, Peter. I put you on to this one, remember? Amanda sings with me. What's the motive here? Have you thought about that?'

'I will when I get a moment,' he said.

'The woman was strangled first and then suspended from the swing to make it look like a hanging,' Georgina said. 'That's not the behaviour of a professional crook. Any villain worthy of the name would know forensics can tell the difference. I think we're dealing with a first-time murderer who panicked when faced with a dead body. He didn't think it through.'

'I'll bear that in mind, ma'am. And now if I can get on ...'

'An amateur, in other words. But the motive is the problem. I don't understand the motive.'

'Neither do I, yet.'

'It doesn't seem like panic,' she said without realising she'd just contradicted herself. 'It wasn't manual strangulation. He used a ligature. And it's pretty cool to transport the body to the park and string it up, however naïve it was.'

'It beats leaving it in his car.'

'What do you mean?'

He shrugged. 'Neutral ground. Nothing to connect him.'

'Good point.' She weighed it before speaking again. 'Perhaps he *is* a professional. This is shaping up as a beast of a case.'

'Thanks, ma'am.'

She gave a sideways smile. 'But I have every confidence.' And that was her exit line.

He crossed the room to where Ingeborg was

using a computer. 'Any progress?'

She shook her head. 'This Danny seems to have gone to ground, guv. We've asked at all his usual haunts. No one knows him well enough to have heard of his plans. He isn't a loner exactly, but he gives nothing away.'

'There's no talk of a girlfriend?'

'Not in Freshford anyway. He does a lot of walking, serious walking, with a backpack.'

'I've seen you with a backpack and I wouldn't call you a serious walker.'

She rolled her eyes. 'Mine is a fashion accessory.'

'Does he work for a living?'

'No one seems to know.'

'See if he's on the social.'

Keith Halliwell, when he returned from Tosi's, had more to report. 'Delia did her waitressing as usual on Tuesday, the night she went missing, guv.'

'Did she now? But according to Dr Sealy she was killed Wednesday night or early Thursday morning, so where was she?'

'That's a mystery. I spoke to the owner, Signor Tosi himself. He said she was the best waitress he'd ever had, dependable, a lively personality and popular with the customers. He's very emotional about the murder. Even wept a little while we were talking about it.'

'What time did she leave after work?'

'He thinks about eleven.'

'Thinks?'

'He'd already gone. His wife wasn't well, so he left the restaurant early and his head waiter Luigi closed the place.'

'Did you speak to this Luigi?'

'I'm going back later. He's on at five.'

'I'll come with you.'

Before that, he spoke to the entire murder squad, seated around the incident room. 'The press are waiting downstairs and I'm going straight to them after this. What I won't be telling them at this stage is that the victim was fun-loving, as they say, and not getting much fun from her partner. Ashley is so wrapped up in his work he doesn't even notice when she isn't home. She has a child-minder for her two kids, and they don't fret when she's away. Why? Because she's done it before. She's that kind of mother. She needs space, according to Ashley. We have no clue where this space was, and if it involved another man. We're damn sure it involved someone else on the night she was strangled.' He spread his hands. 'Of course it won't take the press boys long to work this out for themselves, but I want to start with the shock of the young working mum strangled at night and left hanging in the park. We'll issue her photo and hope to get some feedback from the public. She was a waitress, so we're sure to hear from people who remember her, who could have spotted her with a man in the hours leading up to her death. We may even get lucky and hear from someone who saw her with her killer. The phone lines are ready. It's a crucial time and we're up for it, right?'

*   *   *

The phone on his desk was beeping when he returned to his office. He gave his surname, as always.

A woman said, 'Hi, Peter.'

He couldn't place the voice, but she seemed to know him and she wasn't going to help by saying her name.

'Er, hi.'

'So how was the cake?'

'What?'

'They did give it to you?'

'Ah.' The response was verging on 'arrgh' now he realised who was on the line. After the rousing speech to his squad he was in no mood for trivial chat with his secret admirer.

'It was meant for you.' She paused, and her tone changed. 'The blighters. If they had it themselves, I'm going to raise hell.' She was ready to go to war with the desk team downstairs.

He had to deal with this. 'Oh—the cake?' All experience told him to say the minimum, but he'd been trained in good manners since he was a kid. After clearing your plate you say thanks. He'd eaten the damned cake and forgotten it. Where was his gratitude? 'Am I speaking to the lady who made it? Very tasty. The cake, I mean.'

She laughed.

He didn't. He wasn't trying to be amusing.

'It's all right,' she said. 'I'm not fishing for compliments. I know I'm not the greatest cook.'

The good manners took over again. 'Everyone said it was the best. I shared it round.'

'You should have taken it home.'

'I did—what was left of it.'

'Let's not talk about the wretched cake,' she said. 'You're not daft. You know who I am.'

'Do I?'

'The woman you didn't meet at the Saracen's last night. Did my letter put you off?'

'It's nothing to do with your letter, nothing personal,' he said. 'That's the point. It can't be personal because I don't know you. And you certainly don't know me, or you wouldn't bother.'

She wasn't giving up yet. 'I told you quite a bit about myself in the letter.'

'Yes, ma'am, and now I know you make a fine chocolate cake, but it doesn't mean we'd enjoy a drink together.'

'Why not? We haven't tried.'

He was getting annoyed. 'Because I don't do that stuff.'

'What stuff?'

'Going out with women I haven't met.'

'But how do I get to meet you? I'd really like to.'

'Sorry, ma'am, but it's not going to happen. Goodbye.' He hung up.

Confused emotions churned inside. He felt mean, heavy-handed, unchivalrous. She'd gone out of her way to be friendly and he'd slapped her down. But she had no right to demand a meeting. He was entitled to say no, wasn't he?

He went straight out. There was serious work to be done. The little voice inside him said Diamond you're a coward, walking away from the phone in case she tries again.

4

Tosi's was in George Street, up the hill from the police station. Halliwell suggested they walked there, but Diamond was panting like a bulldog before they reached the top of Milsom Street and he asked Halliwell to slow down. 'You've made your point, Keith.'

'What point is that?'

'You don't normally go as fast as this, do you? Man in my condition can't keep up.'

'Hadn't crossed my mind, guv.'

'I was fit once.' He had to stop altogether on the corner. 'There was a time when I played rugby for the Met every Saturday and trained two nights a week. Soon as I gave it up I put on the weight.'

'I wouldn't say that,' Halliwell said, trying to be charitable.

'Look at me.'

There was no way of telling whether Diamond wanted to prolong the self-criticism, or was just too puffed to move on.

Halliwell tried again. 'You're a man of substance, guv. People don't mess with anyone your size. Look at the way the press swallowed everything you gave them this afternoon.'

He eyed Halliwell, uncertain how serious he was. 'Let's see what they print tomorrow. Then we'll know how much they took in.' He started walking again.

It was a tiny basement restaurant under a travel agent's. They were met at the foot of the stairs by Signor Tosi himself, a man whose immense bulk

35

restored some of Diamond's self-esteem. 'I catch Luigi,' Tosi said, as if his head waiter were a contagious disease. He waddled inside and shouted Luigi's name and something in Italian about the *carabinieri*.

A man in a white shirt and bow tie came from the back.

'I translate, eh?' Signor Tosi offered.

'I figure we'll get by,' Luigi said in a smooth mid-Atlantic accent. He was tall and slim, with brown eyes that gave you undivided attention. 'This is about poor Delia, I guess.'

'*Torto, torto,*' his boss said. 'Delia *Williamson.*'

'Can you get rid of this clown?' Diamond said to Halliwell.

Halliwell grasped Tosi's arm and led him to the kitchen at the back of the restaurant.

'What was he on about?' Diamond asked the waiter.

Luigi gave a wide smile. 'He's the boss. Thinks he has a divine right to know what I tell you.'

'You don't have any problem with the language, that's for sure.'

'Too much time watching movies.'

'OK. While we've got the boss out of the way let's talk about the set-up here. How many staff does he employ?'

'Three only. Carlo, Delia and me. Carlo is the cook.'

'You're the head waiter?'

He laughed. 'I could live with that if it meant extra pay.'

'Were all three of you on duty the night Delia went missing?'

'Yes.'

'How did she get along with you?'

'No problem. She was great, a good worker, always willing to help if I was under pressure.'

'You get busy in here, then?'

He shrugged. 'People like Italian.'

'When are you open. Evenings only?'

'Six to midnight, depending how busy we are.'

'On the evening we're talking about, the Tuesday, I gather Signor Tosi went home early and left you in charge.'

Luigi frowned, troubled that some of the blame might be coming his way. 'He told you that?'

'It's true, isn't it? You locked up?'

'Sure.'

'So who was here at the end of the evening?'

Luigi curled his lip, not liking this line of questioning one bit. 'She was, and so was I.'

'The cook had left?'

'Twenty minutes before she did.'

'What sort of evening had it been?'

'What do you mean?'

'Customers.'

'I get you.' The shift away from him personally came as obvious relief . 'A quiet night. Party of four. Two couples. One man dining alone.'

'Regulars?'

'Yes, the four have a regular booking. Retired people. And one of the couples comes often. The others were new to me.'

'Do you happen to remember who Delia was serving?'

'That couple I just told you about. And the single man.'

'Who you hadn't seen before? What was he like?'

37

'I didn't speak to him. A businessman maybe, visiting the city. Suit and tie. Twenty-five, twenty-six.'

'Why do you say he was visiting?'

'Guy on his own. You get to recognise them. They're stuck overnight in some hotel, so they look for a place to eat out. Most guys don't eat alone if they live just up the street.'

'Would he have booked?'

'No, but I have his name, if that's what you're asking. When I heard you were coming, I looked through the credit-card slips for that evening. He was Mr D. Monnington.'

It was a long time since Diamond had carried a notebook. He helped himself to a paper napkin from the nearest table and scribbled the name. 'Did you notice if he was trying to chat her up?'

'Hard to tell. Delia always talked to customers, 'specially if they were alone. I saw her at his table towards the end of the evening, after the coffee was served.'

'What—just talking?'

'I thought she was working for her tip, that's all. We do if we think there's a chance.'

'She was no more friendly than you'd have expected?'

'I didn't hear what was being said.'

'And Mr Monnington left when?'

'Towards the end. Say about ten minutes before we closed.'

'Ten to midnight?'

He looked towards the kitchen, to make sure the manager couldn't hear. 'Actually, it was earlier. We had no more customers, so I closed at eleven.'

'Tell me some more about Delia. Did she talk to you about her life at all?'

'Not much. She once said she had kids. She lived with someone in the music business.'

'Was she acting normally on that last evening?'

'I thought so.'

'Was anyone waiting for her when she finished work?'

'She didn't say.'

'What was she wearing?'

'Same as usual. Jeans and a top. I can't remember what colour. Trainers.'

'She'd worn those things while she was working?'

'No. We have lockers for our working clothes. We change into our own things when we leave.'

'Changing rooms?'

'One, the size of a cupboard.'

'Unisex?'

'One person at a time. You'd have a job getting two in there.'

'In a minute you can show me. Who changed first?'

'Delia did. When she came out I said goodnight and that was the last I saw of her. I changed into my day clothes and locked up and left.'

'What, a few minutes after Delia? Didn't you catch up with her?'

'She goes a different way.'

'I was going to ask about you,' Diamond said. 'Do you live alone?'

Luigi blinked nervously now the focus was back on him. 'Yes.'

'So do I,' Diamond said. 'It's not a crime. Where's home, then?'

'I have a flat in Twerton.'

'I know Twerton. Which street?'

'Innox Road.'

'D'you walk it?'

'Bike.'

'Pushbike?'

'Yes.'

'Good man. No petrol fumes. Where do you keep the bike?'

'Under the stairs you just came down.'

'Do you have a car as well?'

He hesitated. It was obvious what the question was really about. Delia's killer had probably used transport. He said, 'An old Honda, but I don't use it for coming into work.'

Carlo the cook was next up for questioning. His English wasn't so fluent as Luigi's, but he was better than Signor Tosi. In his kitchen, he continued peeling and chopping vegetables with a rapid movement that spoke of long experience. The knife was razor-sharp. Carlo had a mild, disarming manner. Short and bald, with a black moustache, he gave his answers in a subdued voice. No, he hadn't emerged from the kitchen at all on Tuesday evening, so he couldn't speak about the diners. Delia had seemed the same as usual. He liked her. She never hustled him when he was trying to get the orders out.

'Did she talk to you about her life?'

'That night?'

'Any night.'

'She liked Bath, she say. Plenty good ladies' shops. Azzuro, Annabel Harrison, Kimberly. All her money go on nice Italian clothes. I have a joke with her that she serve Italian so she can buy

Italian.'

'Did she mention her two daughters?'

'To me? No. Luigi tell me she have daughters.'

'How about you, Carlo? Are you married?'

'Am I married?' He stopped chopping and drew the knife across the front of his throat, rolling his eyes. 'Three times. Five kids. Four back in Napoli with wives one and two, must have cash every month. One baby son here. And wife number three.'

'Here in the city?'

'No chance. I keep her away from those dress shops. Combe Down.'

'Do you drive?'

'Can't afford. I take the bus.'

Diamond asked to see the locker room. It was through the kitchen and Tosi the owner took this as his chance to grab the limelight again. He wanted it known that his facilities met the hygiene regulations and insisted on showing the staff toilet and washroom as well. Luigi's description of the locker room was right. It was little more than a cupboard with three metal lockers and barely space to change your clothes. When Diamond had established which locker was Delia's, he asked Halliwell to go in and force the lock.

'No, no,' Tosi said in alarm. 'No damage please. I have extra key.'

He went away to fetch it.

Halliwell leaned against the locker door and it opened. 'Not much of a lock,' he said.

The faint smell of scent carried to them, as if Delia herself was protesting that her privacy was being invaded again. Diamond took Halliwell's place in the small space. He found a hanger with

41

two white blouses and a black skirt. On the shelf above were two bars of KitKat, a box of tissues, a mirror, a lipstick and a comb.

Tosi returned with the key. 'So I waste my time, eh? Open after all?'

Ignoring him, Diamond stooped to pick up a pair of low-heeled black shoes. Under them was a book of matches. 'Was she a smoker?'

'No smoking, no.'

'Are you sure?'

'Nobody here smokes,' Luigi said.

So why did she want matches? Diamond returned the shoes to the locker, picked up the matches and folded back the flap. None had been used. They were black, with white tips, from the Hilton Hotel, Bath. Someone had written the number 317 under the flap. He slipped them into his pocket.

On the way out, he stopped to look at Luigi's bike, chained to a post in the space under the stairs. 'I should get one of these,' he said to Halliwell without meaning it. 'Give me six months and I'd be as slim as that waiter.'

'It's the job that keeps him in shape,' Halliwell said.

'What are you saying—that I should get off my butt more often?'

'I was talking about the waiter, guv.'

Towards the bottom of Milsom Street, outside Waterstone's bookshop, Diamond stopped walking again, causing Halliwell real concern about his health. The short distance they'd covered had been all downhill. 'We'll go in here,' the big man said.

'Are you after a book, guv?' Halliwell said,

playing along with him.

'They have a coffee shop up here,' he said, surprising Halliwell by climbing the stairs two at a time. At the top he was still breathing normally. 'I was counting on Tosi offering us one. He missed an opportunity of cosying up to us there. Not so much as a complimentary peppermint on the way out.' He looked over the display of pastries. 'We'll go halves on one of those almond croissants, right?'

Halliwell, who never took snacks, didn't like to disappoint him.

At a table by the window they shared their findings. Luigi the waiter had to be a prime suspect. He'd been the only man in the restaurant at the end of the evening, the last known person to have seen Delia alive. Never mind his insistence that he'd used a bike that evening. He owned a car and he could have parked it nearby and offered her a lift and driven her to his home for a night of passion.

'Two nights,' Diamond said, recalling that she wasn't found until Thursday. 'That's a lot of passion.'

'Maybe he was keeping her there against her will,' Halliwell said. 'Most Italian guys think they're God's gift to women.'

'And finally killed her when it didn't work out the way he wanted?'

As for the others in the restaurant, Diamond said, he didn't rate them as suspects. He couldn't see the pot-bellied Signor Tosi suspending a body from a swing. It would require considerable strength. Neither could he picture Carlo as the killer. The way the little cook had talked of having

43

three wives—rather than two ex-wives—suggested he collected women rather than disposing of them.

'There's the lone diner as well,' Halliwell said.

'Mr D. Monnington. Decent of Luigi to go to all the trouble of getting the name for us,' Diamond said with irony.

'You think he's keen to swing it on someone else?'

'That was my reading.'

'Monnington's top of my list,' Halliwell said. 'I can see it happening: the businessman stuck in a hotel, looking for amusement. Goes for a meal, picks up a waitress, invites her back. Likes her enough to spend the next day with her. Something goes wrong between them and he gets in a strop, strangles her and hopes to fake the suicide and get away with it.'

'Put like that, it's possible. Have him checked out when we get back, Keith.'

'How do you mean? See if he's got form?'

'And check the hotels.' Diamond muttered something under his breath as another thought struck him. 'But would a stranger to the town know where to string up the body?'

'Maybe they took an evening walk in the park and he saw the swings and took his opportunity.'

'With a length of plastic cord someone had conveniently left?' Diamond said, sitting back and shaking his head. 'I don't think this was dreamed up at the scene, Keith. The killer planned it.'

'And you're backing Luigi?'

'I'm saying he's got to be taken seriously, along with the missing father of her children, Danny. And of course Ashley, the laid-back musician.' He

44

looked across at the rest of the almond croissant sitting on Halliwell's plate. 'Aren't you going to eat your half?'

Out in the street again, he put his hand in his pocket and felt the hard edge of the book of matches. 'Let's cut through Shires Yard. I wouldn't mind visiting the Hilton.'

The curious thing about working in a city is that you don't get to see the hotels that visitors regard as a major part of the experience. Diamond wasn't all that familiar with the Hilton. Built as the Beaumont Hotel in 1973, a low point in Bath's architectural history, its blocklike exterior, with yellow stone cladding pretending to be the real local stone, led locals to describe it as a giant hunk of cheese.

To be fair, the management had done much to upgrade the interior. And Jenny the receptionist proved to be a star. 'Does this count as helping you with your inquiries?' she asked Diamond after he'd shown her his warrant card.

'You'll really help my inquiries if you can solve this puzzle,' he said, handing her the book of matches. 'It's one of yours, right?'

'Yes, they're complimentary in the bar. What's the puzzle?'

He asked her to open it.

'Is it a trick?' she said, as she unfastened it. Then she saw the number and smiled. 'A room number?'

'That's what I was thinking,' he said. 'Do you have a 317?'

'We do indeed.'

'And would your computer tell us who has been staying in there over the last few days? It could be

45

important,' he added.

She got them a printout.

There were five names. The fourth was Dalton Monnington.

Diamond exchanged a look with Halliwell.

'Would you have this one's address?'

Jenny used the keyboard. Dalton Monnington was from Wimbledon. He'd stayed one night at the hotel and paid with a voucher from a travel agent.

'You wouldn't happen to remember him?' Diamond said, and this was the moment when she proved herself a star.

She must have dealt with scores of guests, but she had perfect recall of this one. 'Quiet, black hair and brown eyes, mid-twenties, average height, dark grey suit, white shirt and striped tie. He carried a biggish case, the kind reps have for their samples, and a sports bag for his clothes.'

'You spoke to him?'

'Twice about the parking. And later he asked for a city map and I gave him one.'

'You didn't register him?'

'No, that was someone else.'

'He stayed Tuesday night, right?'

'Yes.'

'And went out to eat? Well, we know he did. Would you remember what time he came in?'

'No, I knocked off early. And you don't see all the comings and goings from here, especially if guests don't want to be seen.'

He showed her the picture of Delia. 'Have you seen this woman at all?'

She glanced at it, then shook her head. 'Sorry.'

'You don't have to be sorry, Jenny,' he said,

46

picking up the photo and the matches. 'You cracked the puzzle.'

5

DC Paul Gilbert, the latest member of the murder squad, had transferred from headquarters a month ago. He was still in awe of Peter Diamond.

'Tell him,' Keith Halliwell said.

'Should I? It's only a suggestion.'

'Save it for the briefing, then. Let him say his piece and then bring it up.'

And now the opportunity was imminent. It was Saturday morning and Diamond was holding forth to the team, dramatising the crime to get total attention. 'He strangles her. We don't know where. Possibly in a hotel or his home, wherever that is. Then he has to dispose of the body. He could dump it in the woods, bury it, dismember it. He does none of these things. He transports it to a public park and hangs it on a swing where everyone will see it. What kind of nutcase is this?'

He seemed to be waiting for an answer. The older hands said nothing.

DC Gilbert glanced towards Halliwell, but there was a shake of the head. This was not the moment.

It was Ingeborg who piped up with, 'A publicity seeker?'

'You mean with a stunt like that he's sure to make the papers. You're the expert.'

'If he'd buried her, like you just said, nobody would hear about it.'

47

There was some amusement at this, but not from Diamond.

'All right, let's say he wants the world to know about his crime. What's it about—his ego? Am I going to have to bring in one of these profilers?' The way he said the last word showed what he thought of the science of offender profiling.

Halliwell said, 'There's got to be some reason for taking a risk like that, stringing her up in the park.'

From the back of the room DI John Leaman said, 'He was trying to pass it off as suicide.'

'We've been over that,' Halliwell said. 'Any fool knows a hanging leaves a different mark.'

'Hold on,' Leaman said. 'Who are we dealing with here? Not you or me. Anyone in this room would think it a dumb idea, but this is a guy who just killed someone and is stuck with a body. He's in deep trouble. He's not trained in forensics. He's not thinking straight. All he wants is to get rid of that body without being found out. Rigging up a suicide could have seemed like a brilliant plan.'

'You're saying he did this in the heat of the moment?'

'Well, if killing someone isn't a hot moment, I don't know what is.'

More amusement all round.

Leaman didn't smile, however. He was the most serious-minded member of the team.

Diamond said, 'Fair point, John. You're trying to see it from the killer's point of view and so am I. If he could pass it off as a suicide, all his problems would disappear. The fake suicide theory stays on the table.'

Three days into the investigation, he was willing

to consider anything. Now that the story had broken in the papers, he'd hoped for a better response, sightings of Delia Williamson with her killer. Of the twenty-two calls they'd taken, more than half could be dismissed straight away and the others were no help. Nobody had seen her on the night of the murder. A few women of her description had been seen in various towns up and down the country the day before she was killed and there were three callers who thought they'd spotted her in Bath. No one had seen her with anyone else.

'What about the former boyfriend, Danny Geaves?' he said. 'He must have read the papers. Why hasn't he surfaced?'

Ingeborg took this as criticism. 'I've run every kind of check I can think of, guv. He hasn't drawn his benefit for over a week.'

'He's got something to hide,' Halliwell said.

'Or he's dead,' Leaman said.

Diamond struck a more positive note. 'We've got three named suspects, apart from Geaves. That's a start.'

There was a pause. He looked round the room. This time he seemed to be inviting contributions.

Paul Gilbert flushed all over his young face and asked, 'Would DNA help?'

The focus shifted to Diamond. 'What did you say?'

'DNA, sir.'

'It would if we had some.'

Ingeborg almost cut Diamond off in her eagerness to help her new colleague. 'Up to now forensics haven't found any, or they would have told us. This wasn't a sex crime. And if Delia

49

fought her attacker she didn't scratch him. There was no skin under her fingernails.'

Paul Gilbert should have stopped there, but after waiting so long he wanted some credit for contributing. 'It doesn't have to be a skin sample,' he said. 'Just a touch can leave a contact.'

'Are you lecturing me on DNA?' Diamond said, and everyone waited for the explosion. Instead he leaned forward and lowered his voice. 'I'll tell you something in confidence, constable. Upstairs on the top floor'—his eyes turned upwards, as if he was speaking of something religious—'up there they have our personal records, yours and mine and everyone else's. We're all on computer. The high-ups like Georgina spend a lot of time looking at those records. And there's a special file labelled "professional training". It goes without saying that any of us with ambition should keep up to date by going on those courses they run at Peel Centre and Bramshill. Anyone notice last month's on forensic science? I was asked to go. The ACC thought it would do me good. My name is now on that all-important file, and beside it you'll see the letters DNA.' He gave young Gilbert a penetrating stare, and then a slow smile. 'Did Not Attend.'

The rest of the team enjoyed it. Given time, Paul Gilbert would appreciate it, too. Working for Peter Diamond was no picnic, but every so often you got a helping of sauce.

*   *   *

The trip to Wimbledon was a day out for someone, definitely a perk. Diamond bagged it for

50

himself, with John Leaman in support as his driver, note-taker and sympathetic ear. They reached the M25 when the traffic was building.

'What's all this for?' Diamond asked.

'Football,' Leaman said. 'It's Saturday remember?'

'All right for some.'

Secretly he was relieved to go slowly. Fast driving was no pleasure for him. His stomach was behaving like a sack of frogs. He produced some extra strong mints and insisted Leaman had one. 'Reward for the driver.'

Leaman wondered if Diamond was telling him he had bad breath, but decided the boss wasn't so subtle as that.

The address they had was a turning off Worple Road. The CID at Wimbledon had checked Dalton Monnington's routine and he was due home at lunchtime.

'What his line of work?' Leaman asked.

'Hot tubs.'

'What—jacuzzis?'

'He's the West Country sales rep for a company called Give it a Whirl. Ho ho ho. Probably seemed a good idea at the time.'

'I wonder if he'll offer us a cut price.'

'Dream on.'

'I wouldn't mind having my own jacuzzi.'

Diamond turned to see if Leaman was serious. 'Have you ever sat in one? Give me a six-foot bath I can lie in. And I like my water still.'

'It's not the same as having a bath, guv. You take your girlfriend with you and drink champagne.'

'Is that what you get up to of an evening?'

'I haven't got one yet, guv.'

'Girlfriend or hot tub?'

Leaman didn't have to answer. They'd found the street. Monnington's house was a suburban semi like all the others, with a Honda on the drive in front of the garage. They cruised past two more and found a space to park.

A woman in an apron opened the front door. Before they could wave an ID she said, 'Hold on a mo. I've got a stir-fry and two boys on the go.' She left them standing there and dashed back to the kitchen at the rear.

'Sounds like cannibalism,' Diamond said.

'How long is a mo?' Leaman said.

Diamond spread his hands as if boasting about the one that got away.

'Do we go in?'

'Better not.'

She was soon back, wiping her hands on a tea towel.

Diamond showed his warrant card. 'We picked the wrong time, obviously, but we came to see someone else. Dalton Monnington lives here, doesn't he?'

'What's he been up to now?' she asked.

'It's just questions. He may have witnessed something.'

'Well, you'd better come in. He's due any minute.' She showed them into a front room with toys spread across the carpet. 'Kids,' she said, picking up bits of a plastic train set and throwing them into a cardboard carton. 'There's nowhere you can bring a visitor.'

'Are you Mrs Monnington?'

'Mrs? Some chance. Angie Collier, Dalt's

52

partner. Look, I've got to go up to the boys. They're supposed to be tidying their room, but it sounds like a water fight. You don't mind if I leave you to it?'

Left alone, they tossed a few more toys in the box and looked at the photos on the cupboard behind the sofa. Angie with a baby in her arms and a young man, presumably Dalton Monnington, with his arm round her shoulders. Another in a gilt frame, one of those studio shots against a blue background, the two adults with the boys in front. Monnington had the black hair and brown eyes they'd heard about from Jenny at the hotel. Diamond decided he looked the part of the proud father, then asked himself how much you can really tell from a photo.

'I wasn't expecting him to be a family man,' Leaman said. 'Doesn't chime in with what happened in Bath.'

'We don't know what happened in Bath,' Diamond said on his way across the room to the window. 'We may find out shortly.'

A Ford Mondeo had drawn up behind the Honda on the driveway. Out of it stepped the man in the photo, wearing a striped shirt. He pressed his hands against the back of his neck and stretched and yawned as if to remove the tensions of work. He was home and his stir-fry would be waiting. He wasn't to know two detectives were standing in his front room.

He entered the house and shouted, 'Hi, guys.'

'Hi, Daddy,' came in unison from above. Angie was heard running downstairs. It wasn't possible to pick up her hurried exchange of words with her partner.

Then he opened the front room door, well in control, the sales manner keeping any anxiety well hidden. 'Dalton Monnington. You wanted to speak to me?'

Diamond did the introductions and said, 'It's in connection with the death of a woman in Bath a few days ago. Delia Williamson.'

Monnington's first reaction was to turn and close the door behind him. Then he said, 'The death of . . . ?'

'A waitress from Tosi's restaurant. You were in Bath on Tuesday, right?'

'Er, Tuesday. I think so.'

'Can't you remember?'

'OK. Tuesday. I was there on business, visiting clients.'

'People wanting to install hot tubs?'

'Correct.' He hesitated, as if to ask himself how much more these policemen knew. 'I had three appointments in the area.'

'And you stayed overnight. Why was that?'

'They tend to be evening appointments, after my clients have finished work. I go to their homes, you see. It can finish quite late. The last appointment was at eight. I wasn't away until gone nine. I don't enjoy night driving, so I put up at a local hotel.'

'And went out for a meal at Tosi's?'

'Off-hand, I couldn't tell you the name.'

'George Street.'

'If that's what you're telling me, then it must be true.' He was being deliberately vague, making time to get his thoughts in order.

'Delia served you.'

'Did she? I wouldn't know the name of the

54

waitress.'

'She was the only one in the place.'

'Then you must be right. She's dead, you say? That's awful.' He shook his head.

'It's in the papers,' Diamond said. 'Haven't you looked at them?'

'Now that you mention it I heard something on the car radio. I didn't make the connection.'

'Then you know she was strangled and left hanging on a swing in a park.'

'Er, yes.'

'What time did you leave Tosi's, Mr Monnington?'

'Don't know. Not too late. Around eleven, I think.'

'And then?'

'Back to the hotel. I was staying at—'

'The Hilton. Room 317.'

Concern creased his face. They had too much detail for his comfort.

Diamond said, 'After you left the restaurant, did you see Delia Williamson again?'

'See her? Why should I? I'm in a relationship already.' As if to underline the point his small sons upstairs started chanting, 'Daddy, where are you?'

'Did you make an arrangement to meet her?'

'No.'

The denial was just too quick.

'I'll give you a chance to answer that question again,' Diamond said. 'She had in her possession a book of matches from the Hilton with your room number written inside it.'

'That?' He swallowed hard. 'It's not what it seems.'

'What is it, then?'

He glanced towards the door as if he feared his partner was behind it. He lowered his voice. 'You know how it is, being alone in a strange town?'

'Speak up.'

'I'm saying it's no fun being stuck in a hotel when you're used to company. The waitress was friendly, looking after me well in the restaurant, just doing her job, I suppose.' His glance flicked from Diamond to Leaman and back again, seeking some clue that he was getting his point across. 'I'm a bit of an optimist. I thought she fancied me. I wasn't seriously trying to pull her, like you said. I just played a long shot, so to speak. I'm a smoker, and I happened to have the matches in my pocket. At the end of the evening I scribbled my room number on the inside and left the matches with the tip.'

'Thinking she might look you up later?'

He looked sheepish. 'Not really. I was being playful. In real terms there was no chance at all that she'd follow it up, but I guess it might have amused her.'

'A spot of harmless fun?'

He seized on that. 'That's it. Harmless fun.'

'You'll have to do better than that, Mr Monnington. We found the matches in her locker.'

'Maybe she was a smoker.'

'Don't push me. This is a murder inquiry. Someone met her after she finished work and later strangled her.'

He blinked. 'You don't think I'm responsible?'

'What did you do after leaving the restaurant?'

'Made my way back to the hotel.'

'Directly?'

56

'I called at a pub for some cigarettes, but that didn't take five minutes. I went straight to the Hilton after that.'

'Getting there at what time?'

He shrugged. 'Between eleven and eleven thirty.'

'Did you speak to any of the staff?'

'No. I went straight to my room.'

'Then what?'

He gave a half laugh. He was trying to make light of it and not succeeding. 'I got ready for bed.'

'Did you go out again that night?'

'Of course not. Look, I don't like what's behind these questions.'

'Did anyone visit you in your room?'

'No.'

'She didn't phone?'

'The waitress? No.'

'Is there any way you can prove you were in the hotel? Did you make any calls yourself?'

'It was after midnight. You don't start phoning people in the small hours.'

'You didn't ask for room service?'

'I took a shower and got into bed.'

'Next morning did you have breakfast in the hotel?'

'I don't bother with breakfast. I left early.'

'After checking out?'

An impatient sigh. 'They had a voucher from my firm's travel agent. If I have any extras they have my card details, so I didn't need to.'

'You got in your car and drove away without speaking to a soul?'

'You're making me sound like a guilty man.'

'Agreed, Mr Monnington. It's a pity, because

57

we've only got your word for it that you spent the night in the Hilton. May we look inside your car?'

'What's that going to tell you?'

'We believe the victim was driven to the park where she was found.'

'Fuck off, will you?' His salesman's facade had crashed.

Diamond reached for the door. 'We'll take a look at your car.'

Outside, Angie was waiting. She may have heard it all. If so, she wasn't giving much away. 'Are you finished? Your meal's ready, Dalt.'

'Shove it in the oven.'

'Charming. You're not going out, are you?'

He ignored her and led the detectives out to the black Mondeo. Diamond asked him to unlock it. 'Nice condition. When was it cleaned?'

'Yesterday.'

'So recently?'

'I'm meeting clients all the time. Appearances matter.'

Leaman had the door open. 'Valeted inside as well as out.'

Diamond unfastened the boot and looked inside. 'The full works, by the look of it.' He leaned over for a closer inspection. A vacuuming doesn't always remove everything. That young DC Gilbert was right. A single hair, a piece of fingernail, an eyelash even, could prove that Delia Williamson's body had been lying here. But he couldn't see anything obvious. He said to Leaman, 'Got your phone? I'd like a crime scene expert to go over this.'

From the doorway, Angie called out, 'Don't they need a warrant, or something?'

'Yes, where's your warrant?' Monnington asked Diamond while Leaman was using the mobile.

'Why? Aren't you going to cooperate?'

'This car is my livelihood.'

'Because if you get awkward, we can look at the tread on your tyres and check your emissions. Why don't you leave this to us? Go and eat.'

This salesman wasn't equal to Diamond's hard sell. With a shrug and a shake of the head he left them to it.

Wimbledon CID said they would arrange for a crime scene investigator to come out within the hour. She was faster than that, under twenty minutes. She looked about seventeen, but had the confidence of someone twice that age. She put on her white zipper overall—causing some curtains to twitch across the street—and went over the interior of the car and the boot minutely, using adhesive strips to lift fibres and particles and then a hand vacuum for anything she might have missed.

*   *   *

'Would you still buy one of his hot tubs?' Diamond asked Leaman on the drive home.

'Possibly not, guv, but we didn't see him at his best.'

'At his best! He was bricking it from start to finish.'

'He didn't want Angie finding out too much.'

'Angie—or you and me?'

'Any of us, I guess.'

Diamond said nothing while they made a turn at a roundabout. London drivers took no prisoners. He took it up again with: 'Would you say it was one big lie, about returning to the hotel and spending the night there?'

'He went back to the hotel without a doubt.'

'Why do you say that?'

'He'd left his room number, hadn't he? He'd have been waiting to see if she called.'

'Good point.' There was logic in what Leaman was saying. He could be a pain, but he was one of the brightest on the squad. 'Did she visit his room or did he go out to meet her? That's the question. Did you notice any CCTV at the Hilton?'

'They must have it.'

'Get it checked, John.'

'I'm not a betting man,' Leaman said when they reached the motorway, 'but there's something odd about that guy. I've got a gut feeling.'

'*You've* got a gut feeling? I've had a gut feeling ever since you started the car,' Diamond said. 'Do me a favour and drive a little slower, will you?'

6

Back in Bath he got in his own car and made his regular shopping trip to Sainsbury's. These days he relied mainly on tinned food, pasta and eggs. He was capable of more adventurous cooking, but it wasn't high in his priorities. Wasn't everyone supposed to have oily fish two or three times a week? Well, he consumed his quota of tinned pilchards, several times over. The fact that everyone was also supposed to have fresh salad didn't impress him. Salad was too fiddly. He had better things to do than washing lettuce and cutting up beetroot.

He also shopped for Raffles, his cat. More tins. When the Whiskas ran out, Raffles was willing to stretch a point and subsist on pilchards. Between them they must have sent a thousand empty tins for recycling. 'We're saving the world, you and me, puss.'

This evening he picked the cashier he called Fast Edie and was soon through her queue, pushing his trolley of bags to the exit. Traffic permitting, he'd be home for Channel Four News.

Then the usual challenge: where had he left the car? This was one of Sainsbury's most elegant sites in Britain, at the converted Green Park station, a Victorian building with bold architectural features that tended to distract when you arrived. He clicked his tongue, thought hard, and headed in the right direction. Loaded the boot, returned the trolley to the bay, got into the car, started up, made sure his way was clear and reversed.

Something was wrong. He felt some resistance, as if he'd left the handbrake on. A glance at the control panel told him he hadn't. He checked in both mirrors and continued reversing and now there was a definite lumpy feeling to the movement. A flat tyre?

'That's all I need.'

Then a man rapped on the window.

He wound it down.

'Can't you see what you're doing, you berk?' the man said. 'You're going over your shopping.'

He got out and had a look at a sorry mess. He'd reversed over two Sainsbury's carriers. The first must have contained at least a dozen eggs and some milk. Egg yolk was dripping from his tyre into a puddle of milk, egg and what looked like jam or pickled beetroot. The second was still wedged under the wheel. Little, if anything, could be salvaged.

He said to the man, 'It isn't my shopping.'

'It's nobody's now,' the man said. 'It's history.'

He said by way of an excuse, 'You can't see from inside the car. It wasn't there when I got in. I would have noticed.'

A few more people came over to look. 'That's them expensive free-range eggs,' one woman said, bending for a closer inspection. 'Extra-large free-range eggs. I can see the packet.'

'Semi-skimmed milk,' another woman said. 'Scottish shortbread. What a waste.'

'Who does it belong to?' Diamond asked loudly enough to be heard by everyone. 'It's not my stuff.' He crouched and tried without success to free the second bag. If he could move the car forward a few inches he might save some of the contents. He stepped back inside.

One of the women said, 'He's going to drive off.'

'Hit and run,' said someone else. 'That's someone's shopping you've squashed. Bastard.' She started hammering on the back window.

Diamond eased the car forward and got out. All the excitement had attracted quite a gathering, and the mood was not sympathetic. Not to him, anyway. He felt under the car and retrieved the second carrier bag. It dripped strange liquid over his shoe.

'I can smell garlic,' the woman who'd called him

62

a bastard said. 'That's their best pesto sauce.'

Her righteous tone riled him. He looked in the bag. 'You're wrong,' he said. 'It's minestrone soup.' He wouldn't have spoken if she hadn't been so quick to condemn. 'See?' He lifted out a squashed carton. This is bizarre, he thought, a senior policeman arguing over a squashed packet of soup.

'They put garlic in their minestrone,' the woman said, looking round for support. 'I told you I could smell garlic. What are you going to do about it?'

'Someone bought this stuff,' he said. 'They should be back.'

'A nice surprise they've got coming,' she said. 'You'd better speak to the management. Look at the mess you've made. That's a traffic hazard. You'll get cars skidding in it.'

On this she was right. The mess had to be mopped up. He asked if anyone would mind waiting there in case the owner of the shopping came back while he was getting help from the shop. His main critic didn't volunteer, but a man with a child in his arms said he didn't mind waiting.

Five minutes later Diamond returned with a Sainsbury's employee with mop and bucket. The crowd had dispersed except for the man and child. Diamond thanked them and scanned the car park to see if anyone was searching for their missing shopping. He didn't like to leave without offering to pay for the crushed items.

Just as he was thinking about leaving his phone number in the shop, he spotted a woman in the next aisle but one, turning her head as if she'd forgotten where her car was.

63

He went over. 'Excuse me, but you're not by any chance looking for two bags of shopping?'

'Do you know where they are?' she said. 'I feel such an idiot. I put them down, and I can't find them.'

At least she didn't look the sort to make a scene. She stared at him with anxious, nervous blue eyes, her blonde tinted hair in disarray where she'd been rubbing her head. She was probably in her mid-forties, a few years younger than he was, dressed simply in a pale blue top and jeans.

He cleared his throat. 'I, em, I'm afraid your shopping came to grief, ma'am. I ran over it in my car. Didn't see it when I was reversing.'

She said, 'Oh.'

'I'm really sorry.'

But she was going to be reasonable. She shrugged and said, 'Never mind. It's obviously an accident. My fault for leaving it in a stupid place.'

'It's over there where the man is mopping up. I don't think there's anything left,' he said. 'Listen, why don't we fill your trolley again and let me pay?'

'You can't do that,' she said. 'It wasn't your fault.'

'But it was. I should have noticed. A driver is responsible for the damage he does.'

'It's all right,' she said. 'I'm blaming myself, not you.'

'That's generous, but not quite right. I'll sleep easier tonight if I've taken my share of the blame. At least let me help with the bill.'

She smiled. 'You're a true gent, but—'

'It will ease my conscience.'

She gave another shrug and her lips curved

again and she started walking towards the shop with Diamond at her side. 'You're probably wondering why this happened, why I abandoned my shopping.'

'I'm curious.'

'I was on my way to my car and I saw a child, a young girl of eight or nine, with a puppy on a lead. One of those gorgeous little dogs they use in the Andrex commercials.'

'Golden Labrador.'

'Right, very appealing. But the collar must have been loose because it pulled away from her and slipped its head free. It was off straight away and the child burst into tears. I saw this and put down my bags and set off in pursuit. A puppy running free in a busy car park isn't going to last long. I wish I could say I caught it.'

'You mean this has a sad ending?'

'No, someone else picked up the pup. At least I was able to say whose it was and return it to the little girl. I met the mother and we tightened the collar a notch and all was well again. Happy ending.'

'Depends what you mean by happy. In the meantime I'd destroyed your shopping.'

She gave the sort of smile that forgives without a word being spoken.

'It wasn't a pretty sight,' he added.

He collected a trolley and they started shopping. She said she couldn't remember what she'd bought.

'Don't you have a list?'

'In my head usually,' she said. 'All this has played havoc with my concentration.'

He named the free-range eggs and the

minestrone and told her about the dispute with the woman who could smell garlic. She laughed and said she hadn't realised what a rough time he'd had. They walked the aisles trying to refresh her memory. A few items went into the trolley, but not enough to fill two bags. He suspected she was keeping the bill down.

At the checkout he gave his credit card to the cashier.

'You said help with the bill, not pay it all.'

'It's OK.' He had already keyed in his pin number.

On the way out she said with more seriousness, 'It isn't OK. I'm sorry, but I'm uncomfortable with this.'

'Don't be. I drove over two of your bags. This is only one.'

'At least let me buy you a drink.'

'Now? I'll be driving home and so will you, I expect.'

'Later, then.'

He was unprepared. He didn't know how to respond.

She said, 'My treat.'

'Tonight, you mean?'

'Say about eight thirty. Are you local?'

'Not far.' This had thrown him. He'd turned down her offer of a drink more sharply than he intended. She was insistent that she wanted to square things. She couldn't have been more reasonable about losing her shopping. To walk away now would sour a pleasant encounter. 'All right. You're on.'

'How about meeting here?'

'The scene of the crime.'

7

In his own house with all its memories he was less comfortable about what he had agreed. He hadn't gone out for a drink with a woman in years, except for police colleagues when there was some work topic to be discussed. If he was going to take the plunge he'd have preferred not to be pulled in. 'You won't believe this, Raffles,' he said as he opened a tin and forked tuna flakes onto the cat's plate. 'I'm going for a drink with a woman and I don't even know her name.'

It wasn't in his make-up to break a date with a lady, so he showered and thought about what to wear. He decided his daytime suit wasn't right for this adventure. So what did he have in the wardrobe that was more relaxed and didn't look as if it came out of a charity shop? Leather jackets had never gone out of fashion and they were safe from moths. He took his off the hanger for the first time in a couple of years and decided it would fit the occasion even if it didn't fit the body. He wouldn't button it up. Under it he'd wear a check shirt, jeans and trainers. He looked in the mirror to see if he needed another shave. Stubble was sexy these days, wasn't it? Man, oh man, you're acting like a sixteen-year-old, he told himself.

He drove back to the car park where all this had been set in motion and chose a slot at the opposite end from where he'd been before. Early as always, he sat listening to a football commentary without caring who the teams were. At eight thirty he got out and looked across the roofs of the parked cars to see who was about. Nobody he recognised. He locked up and strolled towards the spot where he'd driven over the bags. Sainsbury's staff had done a good job of clearing up. Just a few bits of eggshell were lodged in a crack in the tarmac. It wasn't all that long since he'd worked as a trolleyman and dogsbody himself in London, at that low point after he'd resigned from the force. He knew what it was like to be called to a mess with his mop and bucket.

He stood there, whistling quietly.

Ten minutes passed and he was getting reconciled to her not coming. Reconciled? Relieved, really. Sensible woman, she must have decided she'd acted on impulse. Just as he had.

Then a horn sounded behind him and he saw her at the wheel of a silver sports car. 'I'll find a space and join you,' she called out.

He pointed to one in the row behind. She raised a thumb.

'Nice little run-around,' he said when she got out.

'It gets me where I want to be,' she said. She, too, had decided on a change of clothes, a blue and yellow jacket patterned with chrysanthemums and worn with a terracotta top and white linen slacks. She'd put up her blonde hair with two combs. A musky scent was part of the makeover.

'We could have that drink right here in the Brasserie,' he suggested to keep it simple. The Brasserie was part of the old Green Park station complex. It had once been the booking hall and wasn't a bad place for a drink.

'Uh-uh,' she said, wagging her finger and smiling. 'My treat, remember?'

'Got somewhere else in mind?'

'I phoned ahead. It's not far.'

Phoned ahead? That sounded ominous.

'You look worried,' she said. 'Are you thinking it might rain?'

'Hadn't even crossed my mind. I'm Peter Diamond, by the way.'

'Paloma Kean. And before you ask, the nearest my parents got to Spain was the paso doble at the local Mecca ballroom. They simply liked the sound of Paloma.'

'So do I. Good taste.'

'I didn't think so when I was going through school. I was known as Plum.'

'Did you mind?'

'I got used to it. There are worse names.'

She stepped out across James Street with him at her side trying to guess where they were heading. No bar he knew in Bath insisted on advance bookings.

'We agreed just a drink,' he reminded her a little way up Charles Street.

'Why—have you eaten?'

'No, but I will later.'

In Saw Close they passed the theatre and she stopped next door, at Strada, an Italian restaurant newer and smarter than Tosi's.

'You're not bringing me here?' he said in concern.

'Why not? They'll serve us a drink. I often come here.'

To Diamond, this was unfamiliar territory. For years, it had been Popjoy's, known for its fine cuisine and high prices. You couldn't see any of the interior from the street. It had been a private house that had once belonged to Beau Nash, the man who made Bath fashionable in the eighteenth century. They were admitted by a waiter who greeted Paloma as Mrs Kean and showed them to a reserved table in the Georgian sitting room.

She was handed the wine list, and she asked what he would like.

'Do they stock a low-alcohol lager?'

'Come on,' she said. 'Live dangerously. They do a good range of wines.'

'No, I mean it.'

'Worried about the drive home?'

'I'd better come clean with you. I'm in the police. The sure way to put a damper on the evening.'

'I can't think why,' she said without even blinking. 'You won't find my name in your files.'

If she wanted some banter, he was up for it. 'Is that because you're good, or good at getting away with it?'

'I leave you to guess.' She ordered champagne for herself.

'Now I know why they call you Plum.'

Another waiter approached with the menu.

Diamond started to say, 'I really didn't—'

Paloma made a slight downward movement with her hand. 'It's my choice.'

He stopped protesting, ordered a mushroom risotto, and then said, 'I owned up to my job.'

'And?'

'I get the impression you also have a career.'

'In the absence of a sugar daddy? Yes, I'm one of the self-employed. Any guesses?'

Difficult. He didn't want to cause offence. She had a good income if she was used to eating out.

70

'Something artistic?'

'Only marginally.'

'Theatrical?'

'Vaguely.'

'You write plays.'

She laughed. 'I'm not creative at all. I have a business supplying illustrated material for the media, pictures of past fashion basically. If someone is writing a piece about Edwardian ball gowns, for example, they look on the internet and find I have hundreds of contemporary pictures they can choose from.'

'You collected these?'

'It's been a lifelong passion. Plum the schoolgirl was filling scrapbooks when she was eleven years old. When I got older I bought from dealers. Now I have the biggest collection in the country, probably in the world. Magazines, newspapers, pattern books. Someone asks for examples and I scan them and send them back in a very short time. The internet has transformed the way it's done.'

'And this is mainly as a service to journalists?'

She shook her head. 'There are all kinds of requests. Film and television costume departments are always wanting ideas. There are classics being filmed all the time. They know they can rely on me for something the rival company hasn't already used.'

'What's your business called?'

'Once in Vogue.'

'Cool,' he said, borrowing from Ingeborg. 'Do you supply the costumes as well?'

She winced at the idea. 'Couldn't possibly. Just the pictures.'

'You must have an efficient filing system.'

'I'm well organised. If you really are interested, I could demonstrate. Do you have a computer at home?'

'Rarely used. It belonged to Steph, my late wife.'

The mention of Steph didn't throw her at all. 'Well, if you want to look me up, if you ever want a picture of a Victorian policeman, or a Bow Street runner, click on *onceinvogue.com*.'

'I will.'

'But you must give me a challenge. Surprise me with a really unusual request.'

There was just the hint of playfulness.

'I'll try and think of something. Speaking of surprises, you certainly ambushed me with all this,' he said.

'Their desserts are good.'

'Thanks, but I'll pass on the dessert.'

'Don't run away with the idea that I come here every night,' she said. 'I do most of my eating out of packets, same as you, I expect.'

'Tins, in my case.'

'Baked beans?'

He grinned. 'You've got me sussed.' But he wished he hadn't said it. He wasn't the helpless man and he didn't want to give that impression.

'Was your late wife a cook?'

'She was good at it. We both went out to work so I did my share with the saucepans.'

'On the baked bean nights?'

'Actually I can manage a few other dishes. Cooking is less appealing when you live alone.'

'Tell me about it.'

'Were you married?'

'Until he traded me in for the new model,' she said. 'Once my self-esteem recovered, it was a huge relief to be shot of him.'

'Kids?'

'A son, grown up now. Jeremy's got one of those jobs that didn't exist until someone thought of it—personal trainer, persuading rich people to use their treadmills. It's paying well at the moment, but I don't know if you could call it a career. And you? Do you have any family?'

He shook his head, not choosing to go into the detail of Steph's gynaecological problems. 'There's just Raffles the cat, who allows me to share the same address.'

'A cat. What sort?'

'More than one sort, you could say. A tabby, a handsome tabby.'

'Who considers you his slave?'

He grinned. 'Have you got one? Sounds to me as if you know all about them.'

'No longer. I had a black and white called Fritz, a wicked old character who lived to seventeen, and I miss him dreadfully, but it's too soon to replace him. The birds can visit the garden in safety now.'

'You have a garden? In the city?'

'On the outskirts. I live in Lyncombe. We still think of it as our village, even though it was swallowed up by the city council about two hundred years ago. And you? Are you a Bathonian?'

'I pay the council tax,' he said. 'I live in Weston. Don't know if I can call myself a Bathonian.'

'If you're defending us all from villains, I'm sure you can. You're the first policeman I've met on a social basis. That's the best way to meet one, I

73

suppose. Better than being stopped for speeding.'

He told her he didn't work in traffic.

'More of a back-room boy?'

'Back-seat boy.' He wasn't going to volunteer that he was CID.

After the coffee, she said, 'I've enjoyed this, Peter.'

'You took the words out of my mouth.'

She signalled for the bill. 'I must get back now and do an hour or so on the internet. My clients expect a quick response.'

He was relieved. She was drawing a line under this evening. She'd saved them both the awkwardness of the invitation home for another coffee or a drink, or whatever. He certainly wasn't ready for whatever. She wasn't pressing for a closer relationship and neither was he.

They walked back to Green Park and talked about films they'd seen. As if by mutual consent they'd done enough exchanging personal data. When they reached her car she opened her bag and took out a business card. 'As I was saying, you can look me up if you're interested in the agency.'

'Thanks. I'm not so well organised as you,' he said. 'Don't carry a card.'

'Now I feel pushy.'

He shook his head. 'I know when people are pushy, and you're not.'

She got into her car. 'Where's yours?'

He pointed across the car park.

She said, 'Watch out when you reverse.'

He came out with a line that made him cringe as soon as he'd said it. 'After tonight no carrier bag is safe.'

She smiled and drove off.

8

One thing is worse than an alarm clock going off when you are sleeping, and that's a phone. Diamond didn't know where he was. He reached out to the sound and knocked over his glass of water.

Now he knew. He'd been dreaming. This wasn't Paloma's bedroom. This was home.

'Jesus,' he said when he got the thing to his ear.

This seemed to confuse the caller. After a long pause came a tentative, 'Sir?'

'I don't expect calls in the middle of the night.'

'Is that Mr Diamond?'

'What do you want?'

'I've got the Assistant Chief Constable for you, sir.'

'On a plate?'

'On the other line.'

'What time is it?'

'Six fifteen just gone, sir.'

'Nearly lunchtime,' he said with sarcasm that was wasted on the switchboard operator.

'I'm about to connect you.'

'Do I have a choice?'

Georgina greeted him as brightly as if she was suggesting coffee and crumpets in the Pump Room. 'Peter, are you up and about?'

He could feel a tide of cold water advancing across the sheet he was lying on. 'I will be shortly.'

'You're not an early riser, then? Listen, something has happened overnight. Another hanging, a man this time.'

He was jolted fully awake. 'Where?'

'This is it, Peter. It couldn't be more public. He's over the Bristol Road near the railway station. Motorists are calling in to report it.'

He couldn't picture this. 'Over the road?'

'Hanging from the viaduct.'

'What viaduct?'

'By the station. You know where the railway crosses the river and the road, that thing that looks like a castle wall, with battlements? Uniform have closed the entire southern approach to the city and they want to cut him down. It's going to cause horrendous traffic problems, but of course it could be tied in with this case of yours. Get down there, will you, and deal with it?'

Some people start the day with a fried breakfast, he thought. I get a hanged man.

Disturbing images crowded his brain. The black, turreted viaduct where trains thundered across. The corpse twisting above the road. Traffic queues. SOCOs. That sarky pathologist. All to be faced. His thigh was getting damp. He rolled out of bed and felt splintered glass under his bare foot. Not a good beginning.

*   *   *

When Isambard Kingdom Brunel brought the Great Western Railway to Bath in 1840 he had a sharp sense of what the city fathers would tolerate. Starting from the Bristol end he cut a direct route through streets of working-class housing but steered south and east of the Georgian glories of the city. The track had to cross the main road and the River Avon and he

76

did it in style with a handsome viaduct dressed to look as if it was a section of the city wall, grand in concept, with twin turrets, ornamental shields and a crenellated top outlined against the green of Lyncombe Hill. Never mind that the fortifications faced inwards as if the city had to be protected against itself. Never mind that the south side was as plain as a prison. The facade visible from across the river was what mattered. Bathonians compared it to the classic front of a Cambridge college. You would never suspect it was a railway until you saw an inter-city express crossing the battlements.

No one was thinking of Brunel's achievement when Diamond arrived. Such was the traffic chaos that he had to leave his car across the river and walk over the Churchill Bridge. The fire brigade were at the scene—a good thought on someone's part because it would take more than a household ladder to recover the body. They had positioned a cherry picker under the bridge.

The corpse was dressed in black jeans and a tank top. Worn trainers that must have been white when bought. Dark, close-cropped hair from what could be made out from below.

'Do you want a closer look at him?' the fire officer asked after Diamond made himself known.

He'd had more tempting invitations in his time. 'Has anyone been up already?'

'We were told to wait for you.'

'And I didn't let you down. Has the pathologist arrived? I left a message for him.'

'Not yet.'

'He's the man to go up. He shouldn't be long. How do you propose to recover the body?'

77

'We'll work from the top. Hoist him up.'

Diamond looked up at the body again. From where he was the ligature looked like plastic again. The top end was attached to one of the battlements. 'How do I get up there—without getting into that thing, I mean?'

'You'll need to go up to the station and come back along the track. The cherry picker is quicker.'

The phrase conjured up summer afternoons in Kent orchards.

'I appreciate that,' Diamond said, but appreciation didn't mean assent. This wasn't his kind of cherry-picking. He looked at his watch. 'The doctor shouldn't be long.' A pious hope. He remembered having to wait for Dr Sealy the morning Delia Williamson was found.

He walked across to where a uniformed police inspector was talking into his mobile. Someone at the other end was going spare by the sound of things. It was after seven and the traffic was backed right to the top of Widcombe Hill in one direction and Wellsway in the other. 'Can I use your phone?'

'What?'

He pointed to the phone.

'I'm speaking to traffic control.'

'Stuff them. Nothing is moving until I make this call.'

It was handed to him.

He had to call headquarters first to get Sealy's mobile number. Then he got through. The pathologist was going nowhere, sitting in his car in the queue on the Lower Bristol Road.

'We'll get a motorcycle escort for him,' the

78

inspector said. 'Good idea of yours.'

'I thought it was obvious.'

Sealy eventually arrived with his outrider. 'God help us—am I stuck with you again?' he said to Diamond.

All he could think of as a riposte was: 'Hope you've got a head for heights. You'll need more than your milk crate for this one.'

'I'll cope.' And, annoyingly, Sealy did, stepping into the cherry picker as if it was a taxi and rising with arms folded. Up there, he turned the corpse to face him and made his inspection. He was talking into his recorder for at least fifteen minutes. Above, on the rampart, four firemen got ready to lift the body upwards.

When Sealy had been lowered, he said, 'What do you want to know apart from the obvious?'

'What's obvious?' Diamond asked.

'This isn't like the woman in the park. This is a proper hanging. Fractured vertebrae. It was a long drop.'

'Unrelated, then?'

'Pathologically speaking, yes. I'll tell you more when I've done the PM. Make sure they handle him with care, would you?'

'What age would he be?'

'Thirty to forty. Nobody looks at their best when they're dangling on the end of a cord. Why don't you take a look?'

'They want him off the bridge so the traffic can move.'

'The places people choose,' Sealy said. 'What was he after? Maximum disruption? He achieved that all right.'

After Sealy had gone, Diamond took the short

walk to the railway station and emerged along the platform and down the slope to the gravel beside the lines. It didn't take long. Ahead the firemen were approaching with the corpse in a body bag on a stretcher.

'I'll take a look,' he said.

One of them unzipped the top end. A short length of the noose was still tied with a slip knot round the neck.

He recognised the victim.

No question. He'd been circulating pictures of the same face for days. This was the missing man, Danny Geaves, the one-time partner of Delia Williamson.

His first reaction was guilt. They'd failed to find Danny in time. This could have been prevented. Then he told himself they'd made every reasonable effort to find the man. The police are not guardian angels. They are limited by resources and manpower.

He zipped the bag, walked on and checked the parapet. He'd get the SOCOs up here to search everything, but this had the look of a suicide. Danny had slung the cord twice round one of the battlements and secured it with a good knot. It was still in place. It was easy to picture him fastening the noose round his neck, sitting between the battlements and choosing his moment to drop.

9

'You can relax,' he told Ingeborg when he looked in at the incident room. 'Your search is over. The hanged man is Danny.'

'Topped himself because of what he'd done?'

'What do you think?'

She tapped a pencil against her chin. 'So Danny is the killer.'

'Was.'

'Murdered Delia and then killed himself?'

'So it appears.'

'What drove him to it—jealousy, I bet. He couldn't have her, so neither could anyone else. You guys are so possessive.'

'Hang on, Ingeborg,' he said. 'Before you slag off the whole of my sex, the story we had from Ashley Corcoran was that Danny had given up on Delia and the children. He took no interest. That doesn't sound like jealousy.'

'Why would he have killed her, then?'

'Maybe his life wasn't worth living any more, and he blamed her for all his troubles.'

'So if it's not jealousy, it's the blame game. That doesn't say much for the whole of your sex.'

'Give it a break, Ingeborg,' he said. 'I've been on the go since six this morning. Bloody phone ringing and a wet bed into the bargain.'

She said no more. Even an enquiring mind like hers didn't want to know about Diamond's wet bed.

From across the room Halliwell said, 'So what do we do, guv? Dismantle this lot?'

81

'We wait for the post-mortem report. Meanwhile you and DC Gilbert had better get into his lodgings in Freshford and see if he left any clues. A suicide note is too much to hope for.'

He went through to his office and shut the door. His thoughts had turned away from Geaves and Delia Williamson to the children they had left behind. Deprived of both parents in horrific circumstances, those two small girls couldn't have faced a worse shock. He hoped they would find inner strength. He picked up the phone and called their grandmother, Amanda Williamson.

Her voice was nervous. She'd heard on the local radio that a body had been found. 'I didn't like to think who it might be. They haven't named him, have they?'

'It's not officially confirmed, but I think you should be prepared to hear that he's the girls' father, Daniel Geaves,' he said, trying to break it gently.

There was a pause, and then she said, 'Dreadful.'

'It is, ma'am.'

'You're certain of this?'

'I've seen the body myself.'

'Is he ... did he kill my daughter?'

'That's what we have to find out. There will be an inquest. We should all know more after that. I'm calling you now because you may want to think about the children, what they should be told, and whether you want to take them away for a few days. The press are going to want pictures if they can get them.'

'Pictures of the girls?'

'It's what they call a human-interest story. It

82

will soon blow over. If they aren't there to be photographed when the story breaks, no one will pester them in a few days.'

'I understand. I'll see what can be done.'

She sounded a good woman, calm in a crisis, controlling her own emotions while she was responsible for the children.

Looking at the phone he'd just cradled he tried to understand why Geaves had chosen to hang himself in such a public place. Almost all suicidal hangings are carried out in familiar surroundings, the home, or garage or workplace. This one had been done covertly, at night, but the location couldn't have been more public. Perhaps, Diamond mused, the man had felt some remorse for the way he'd strung up his ex-wife in the park. Perhaps he'd condemned himself as he'd condemned her, to be a public spectacle after death. Skewed thinking, but then it needs a skewed mind to top yourself.

For Diamond personally this was a grinding anticlimax. Until this morning, he'd had an intriguing murder case with suspects and lines of inquiry. The killer had snatched it away from him. There was only paperwork in prospect now, and plenty of that.

First he'd go downstairs for a late breakfast.

*   *   *

In the corridor he saw Georgina coming. At this minute he didn't want to be told he was looking peaky, or peakier, so he opened the first door on his right and found himself face to face with a large poster of a dog with teeth bared. To his left

83

was a desk and behind it was seated the sergeant in charge of dogs, head cocked, eyes shining.

'Sorry, wrong door.'

'No problem, sir.'

The good manners were being tested again. 'But now I'm here I've been meaning to ask you something.'

'Yes?'

Something canine, if he could think of it. He dredged deep. 'Bloodhounds. Whatever happened to bloodhounds?'

The sergeant frowned. 'We don't use them, sir. They're not well suited to the work.'

'Why's that?'

'They pick up a scent faster than anything, but they tire easily.'

'Good sniffers but poor athletes?'

'In a nutshell, yes. And their temperament isn't good. They're timid by nature. When you're pursuing a suspect you don't want a dog that won't follow through. A German shepherd does the job better.'

'That explains it, then,' he said. 'Thanks.'

He opened the door and looked along the corridor. Georgina was not in sight. Deciding it was safe, he stepped out.

As if it were fated, Georgina came out of the room opposite. 'Peter, there you are.' She stared at him. 'Are you all right? You look as if someone just walked over your grave.'

'My temperament,' he said. 'Timid by nature.'

'I'd never noticed.'

He was going to add that he was a good sniffer even so, but it would have been lost on Georgina. She'd think he was snorting coke.

'If you're really all right, can we talk about the hanging?'

She was up with the morning's developments. She just wanted his take on them. In her office upstairs he settled into a leather armchair and confirmed that it looked as if Geaves had killed himself.

'Is there any doubt?' Georgina said.

'We haven't had Dr Sealy's report yet, but at the scene he called it a proper hanging.'

'That's straight talking from a pathologist. By that he meant there weren't any signs the man had been strangled first, as Delia Williamson was?'

He nodded. 'It's all about the marks on the neck.'

'So Geaves killed his ex-wife and then took his own life. Why—because he despised himself for what he'd done?'

'Possibly.'

'Or because he didn't want to face the hue and cry? You were on to him.'

'I wouldn't put it as strongly as that, ma'am.'

'You were actively searching for him. He'd disappeared from his lodging in Freshford and no one had seen him for days.'

'I can't argue with that.'

Georgina drummed her fingers on the desk. She wanted closure on this case and she wasn't getting much help from the man in charge. At some stage she would have to face her fellow chorister, Amanda. 'Get a grip, Peter. You must have a view of what happened.'

'I'm puzzled about the choice of location.'

'The viaduct? What's wrong with that? I thought a long drop was the best way to do it. The jerk on the rope must have broken his neck immediately. People who do it by stepping off a chair condemn themselves to slow strangulation.'

'You're missing my point, ma'am. This was so public. Why didn't he hang himself in private as most suicides do?'

She drew in a sharp, impatient breath. 'Well, the place where he strung Delia up was public. He treated himself the way he'd treated her.'

'Out of conscience?'

'Presumably. We don't know what was going on in his mind.'

'That's the problem,' he said.

'There was no note?'

'Not at the scene. I'm having his place searched.'

'Good. You might find evidence linking him to the murder.'

'That would be a bonus.'

'Don't think of it like that,' Georgina said in a tone of reproof, actually wagging her finger. 'Just because the killer and his victim are both dead it doesn't mean we treat the investigation lightly. We must make every effort to prove he murdered the woman.'

'I intend to,' he said.

'Have you got the motive?'

'Motive?'

'The reason he killed her.'

'Not yet.'

'I suggest you work on that as a priority instead of waiting for evidence to fall into your lap.'

'Right you are, ma'am,' he said, and he stood up as if to prove he wasn't waiting for anything. If he stayed here any longer being treated like a schoolkid he would say something mutinous.

She flapped her hand and he left the room.

*   *   *

The late breakfast was so late it became lunch. Afterwards he called Keith Halliwell, by now inside the Freshford house Geaves had lived in. 'What's it like?'

'Tidy, guv. Horribly tidy. No sign of recent occupation. The stuff in the fridge is past its sell-by.'

'Nothing so helpful as a suicide note?'

'No letters at all except junk mail. No bank statements, passport, credit cards, address book. I get the impression he took everything important with him when he left.'

'Not intending to come back?'

'There are clothes in the bedroom, but he wouldn't need a suit if he was planning to top himself.'

'Wouldn't need a passport, so far as I know. Have you talked to the neighbours?'

'They never got much out of him. The one thing that's certain is that he hasn't been living here the last few days.'

'Do you think he had a bolt hole somewhere else?'

'Looks that way, guv. We did find one thing—a weird photo that had slipped down the back of a chest of drawers, but I wouldn't read too much into it. Could have been left by some previous tenant.'

'Weird in what way?'

'You can't see much. It's badly focused or taken

87

in very poor light. Some kind of hairy creature with eyes and teeth, but like nothing I've ever seen. Might be a still from a horror movie.'

'Bring it in. I'll take a look at it. You'd better come back here, then.'

'See you shortly.'

'Probably not,' Diamond said. He'd been on the go since the crack of dawn and he was knocking off early.

10

The disappointment was huge. Truly challenging crimes are rare. You might get four or five in a career. Sure, there were questions to be answered, but they were just for the record. All the impetus had gone. He'd fallen prey to wishful thinking.

Back to reality. He stuffed his week's washing into the machine and switched on. Ten minutes into the cycle he realised there was something amiss with reality. His thoughts weren't fully on the job and he hadn't put in any soap powder. He'd made this mistake before. Adding the tablets now was no use. They'd still be sitting in the dispenser when the wash finished. And if he opened the door—as he had a couple of times— he got water all over his kitchen floor. He'd just have to wait until this soapless wash was through.

He left it running and went to his overladen bookshelves in the front room, where the biographies of Scotland Yard's finest, men like Fred Cherrill and Bob Fabian, kept company with his eighty-three-volume set of *Notable British*

Trials, the most valuable possession he had. Reading about old murders could be therapeutic when he was hard pressed on his own investigations, reminding him that sometimes good sleuthing brought a result.

Some of those shelves dipped dangerously in the middle. He kept telling himself he would thin the books out, but he hated throwing them away. There was a whole row of Agatha Christies that Steph had collected. He hoped to find someone who would appreciate them.

He picked a book that had him absorbed until the wash was ready for its second try. The case was an old one, dating back to 1864, and so intriguing that he almost forgot the tablets again. And when he reached one footnote, he recalled a recent conversation, and smiled. His thoughts had turned to someone else who would be interested.

Later, he went to the computer that he still thought of as Steph's, because she'd made the most use of it, contacting her friends and finding out the details of films she wanted to see.

The machine started all right, but wasn't receiving e-mail, which meant he couldn't send it either. He tried various options on the keyboard and then a message appeared suggesting he phoned his server. They must have given him up for dead, or decided he was a deserter. He dialled the number and found himself listening to syrupy music until his ear ached. A voice broke in occasionally to tell him he was in a queue. And paying for it, he thought.

Finally he got through to a living individual.

'You don't seem to have used it lately,' the woman on the line said.

'But you're getting my money each month,' he told her. 'It's on direct debit.'

'No problem,' she said.

'What do you mean, "No problem"? I'm telling you there is a problem.'

'Sir, if you wait a few minutes,' she told him, 'you'll receive whatever has come in since you last opened your mail. There's quite a lot of it.'

'All junk, or spam, or whatever you call it,' he said. 'Don't bother.'

'I have to send it to reactivate the service.'

'All I want is to send an e-mail myself.'

When the avalanche arrived and the little counter logged up something over six hundred messages, he could tell at a glance that he'd not deprived himself of much. Ignoring the invitations to improve his sex life unimaginably, he clicked *create mail* and typed in Paloma's address, copying it from the card she'd handed him. Surprise me with a really unusual request, she'd said.

He kept the message terse.

How about a Muller cut-down?

Didn't even add his name at the end. She'd see it was from Diamond when she downloaded.

This had to qualify as an unusual fashion item. Franz Müller, he'd learned from the book, had been the first train murderer in Britain. He was a young German tailor. One foggy evening in July, 1864, he'd stepped into a railway compartment and sat opposite an old man wearing a gold watch and chain. The temptation was too great. Müller battered the old man senseless with his own walking stick, relieved him of the watch and his gold-rimmed glasses and pushed him out. The victim was found on the line between Hackney

Wick and Bow. He died soon after. But Müller made a critical error when leaving the train. He mistook the old man's black top hat for his own and left his own hat behind with the victim's stick and bag.

Within twenty minutes a reply came from Paloma.

Is that Müller or Miller?

She hasn't heard of it, he thought. She'd also added a PS.

This might be easier if we use a chatline. Are you on one?

Good suggestion, he thought. Steph once used a chatroom to reach her friends. He went back to the desktop, found the icon and opened the page. Now what was her password? He typed in *Raffles* and it worked. Proud of his new-found computer skills, he put in Paloma's address and was ready to go.

Muller is correct. Should have an umlaut, but my machine won't do one.

These days, a hair sample from the killer's hat would have provided DNA evidence. In 1864, proof of identity was more difficult. Fortunately for the police, the young tailor had remodelled his own hat, cutting it down an inch and a half and sewing it together again. Neatly stitched, of course. But it was not the work of a hatter, who would have used glue. Franz Müller's altered hat became crucial to the hunt for the killer. His cut-down topper caught the interest of the newspapers. And started a fashion.

Paloma answered. *There will now be a short*

91

delay.

He smiled and looked at the time. After twelve minutes came back the response.

It's a style of top hat shortened, circa 1865. Am I right?

She'd done her research by now and probably knew the grim story behind it.

Perfectly. Your reputation is safe. This isn't a fashion question, but how about a Muller Light?

I'd enjoy that. Where and when?

He smiled. She'd fallen into his trap.

A Muller Light was an idea from the railway company to tempt people back onto trains after all the bad publicity. It was a peep-hole cut between compartments so that passengers would feel safer. It had the reverse effect and put them off.

She wrote back. *I'm a fashion person, not a railway expert. My last message stands. Why not come here about seven tomorrow and I'll get some in?*

This time it was his turn to delay. He'd started this. Perhaps subconsciously he'd been pitching for a date, and this hadn't been about Franz Müller's hat but Peter Diamond's suppressed desires. He stared at her message for another minute before writing: *Just checked my diary. I'd be delighted to come*

He hesitated. Now what? A full stop, or a 'but' ... ? Go for it, he told himself, and pressed the full stop key.

11

Two reports were on his desk next morning. The first, from the Wimbledon scene of crime people, had an immense amount of detail about hairs and fibres found in Dalton Monnington's car, but nothing to connect the travelling salesman with Delia Williamson. He slapped it on the heap of papers waiting to be filed. Monnington was old news.

Dr Sealy's report was just as predictable. A Post-it note was attached to the front. 'Knowing you prefer it simple,' the sarcastic little doctor had written, 'the deceased died at the scene, of spinal damage caused by sudden suspension. It was like a judicial hanging except that the drop was longer, so the jerk of the rope was more than enough to dislocate the neck and cause instant death. There were no contrary indications.'

Not liking the assumption that he was ignorant, Diamond glanced through the detailed findings, but the pathological jargon only irritated him more. It was as if Sealy had dressed it up to demonstrate his superiority. *The cervical spine was disrupted at the atlanto-occipital joint, rather than the more usual mid-cervical portion.* Cleverclogs.

He showed the note to Halliwell.

'That's it, then, guv?'

'You'd better stand down the team,' he said. 'The pressure to find the killer is off.'

'But we still have to report to the coroner, don't we?'

'You and I do that.'

93

'It won't be easy,' Halliwell said. 'We know sod all about Geaves.'

'We know he was a callous bastard who walked out on his partner and two little daughters and didn't bother seeing them again.'

'According to Corcoran.'

'Well, yes. It's all second-hand stuff. We know he ended up in Freshford and had the reputation of a loner. Liked to do the crossword in the pub and speak to no one.'

'Anyone who appears in a pub can't be all bad.'

'I wouldn't put money on that.'

Halliwell dropped a small photo on the desk. 'This is what I was telling you about. The creature.'

'Found in his room?' He picked it up. He could just about make out the shape. There was no colour to speak of. It could have been a black and white print. Small gleaming eyes, caught perhaps by the camera flash. Large ears, pricked. Some kind of snout. 'Horrible. What is it?'

'Don't ask me, guv.'

'A bat?'

'Now that's a good thought.'

'I do have them sometimes. Maybe he's a bat expert. There's a fancy name for it, I'm sure.'

'Batman?'

He aimed an imaginary pistol at Halliwell's head. 'Did you try running a full trace on him?'

'He hasn't got form if that's what you were thinking.'

'No, I'm thinking we can find more stuff about his background, where they were living and what job he did. It's all on record somewhere. Run a check on the man. Meantime I'll go and see the girls' grandma, Amanda Williamson. She's the best hope.'

Not so. When he tried Amanda Williamson's home number, her recorded voice announced, 'I'm sorry but I'm not taking calls this week or next. You can leave a message after the tone.' Shot yourself in the foot, Diamond, he thought.

Maybe she gave her temporary address to Corcoran. He called him and got another recording. Whoever invented the answerphone should be made to listen to recorded messages for eternity.

He believed in seeing people face to face. He drove to Walcot Street and was about to press Corcoran's doorbell when he became aware of a young woman at his side, small, dark and oriental. She could only be Marietta, the Filipino child-minder. Her arms were full of shopping, and as she struggled for a door key a French loaf slipped out of its paper wrapper.

Diamond held on at the second attempt, inches from the ground. Not bad for the world's worst catcher, he told himself. But in handing the loaf back he knocked it against his other elbow and snapped it.

'Sorry.'

She seemed to forgive him without speaking.

He felt for his ID and showed it. 'I came to see Mr Corcoran, but maybe you can help. I need to speak to Mrs Williamson—Amanda. I know she has the children and she's gone to a different address.'

Marietta shook her head. 'I'm sorry, sir, this is not possible.'

'Little girls? Sharon? Sophie?'

She shook her head.

He put out his hand for the door key. 'Let me do that.'

'Sorry, sir. This is not possible. I cannot allow this.'

'I must speak with Mr Corcoran,' he said.

'No,' she said. 'You go away, please, sir.'

'Police,' he said, taking her hand and guiding it into the lock.

She sighed as the door swung inwards.

The moment he stepped in he understood why he wasn't welcome. Ashley Corcoran was on his back on the Afghan rug. He was naked and so was the large blonde riding him like a three-day eventer.

12

He didn't check the time, but he guessed it was about ten fifteen in the morning. He hadn't imagined this kind of thing going on in Bath when other people were sitting at their desks or doing the shopping. And his arrival didn't affect the performance. The bouncing blonde came to a resounding climax. Literally resounding. She repeated 'yes' seven times, as positive an endorsement as any lover could wish for.

After the last 'yes', Diamond looked away and discovered Marietta had disappeared with her shopping.

The blonde disconnected and stood up. She was built like a ship's figurehead. She spotted Diamond and padded across the wood floor, slapping the fronts of her thighs. 'It really gets you here,' she said. 'You wouldn't have a ciggy, by any chance?'

From the floor, Corcoran called out, 'Who's that? Who are you talking to?'

'One of your muso friends, I guess,' the blonde said.

Corcoran sat up. At the sight of Diamond, he put his hand over his crotch. 'Who let you in?'

'Does it matter?' Diamond said, doing his best to emulate the blonde's self-possession. 'I tried phoning first.'

'What do you want this time?'

'To find Amanda.'

The blonde put her hands on her hips. 'And who the fuck is Amanda?'

'I take it she's got Sharon and Sophie with her,' Diamond said, trying to confine the conversation to Corcoran and himself.

'A threesome?' the blonde said in an outraged voice.

'They're little girls,' Diamond said in an aside to calm her down.

'That's disgusting.'

'Her grandchildren.'

'I've heard enough,' she said. 'I'm off. Do you mind? You're standing on my bra.'

She was right about that. He moved his foot. Her clothes were in a heap just inside the door. It seemed she'd stripped the moment she'd arrived. Whether she was here on a professional visit or out of friendship he didn't ask. Whichever it was, Ashley Corcoran hadn't wasted much time grieving for his former lover.

Diamond took a few steps towards him,

allowing the blonde to get dressed out of his line of vision. 'She must have told you where she was going.'

'The noticeboard above the kettle.'

He crossed to the kitchen and found the address scribbled on the back of an envelope pinned to the board. Amanda had gone to friends in Bradford on Avon.

*　　　*　　　*

Back in his car, driving out of town, he thought about the effect this scene had had on him. He hadn't seen a naked woman for a long time, let alone having sex on the floor. Strange that the experience hadn't turned him on. Was he past all that? He'd gone three years without sex. Hadn't felt deprived. Hadn't fancied anyone. The celibate life wasn't of his choosing. Steph's murder had put everything into a different perspective. Was his abstinence out of loyalty to Steph? Partly. There was also the thought that no other woman could compare with her.

Steph wouldn't have insisted he remained a lonely widower. One evening they'd had the conversation most couples have at some stage in their marriage: what if one of us dies suddenly? They'd agreed it would be selfish and unloving to deny the surviving partner another relationship. 'But only after a decent interval,' she'd joked. 'I wouldn't want you chatting up my sister at the funeral.' He'd promised her solemnly that he wouldn't trouble Angela, ever. Then Steph had said she couldn't make any promises if some gorgeous bobby representing the Police

Federation was sent to offer condolences. 'I often wondered what "condolences" meant,' he'd said, and they'd laughed and poured another glass of wine, and sudden death had seemed remote.

So there it was. Three years of the monastic life had left him indifferent to a spectacle that would have turned most guys into rampant studs. The blonde had been on the large side, true, but she was pretty, young, firm-bodied and happy to be seen. He faced the depressing prospect that his sex drive had run down like an old battery, not from overuse, but neglect. Did it matter, considering his situation? Yes, it did. He didn't care to admit he was past it.

*   *   *

The address he'd got for Amanda Williamson turned out to be one of the seventeenth-century weavers' cottages high up the steep hillside overlooking Bradford, higher even than the spire of the parish church. A woman too young to be Amanda answered his knock and was threatening to send him away until he showed his ID and said he thought Mrs Williamson would be willing to talk to him.

Amanda came out and they shared a bench in the tiny front garden. She was over sixty, dressed informally for someone her age, in a loose top and black jeans. 'The girls are inside watching *National Velvet*,' she said in a voice that could have presented *Woman's Hour* in 1950. 'I brought some DVDs with me. That film is over sixty years old, but they don't seem to mind.'

'Liz Taylor at eleven.'

'You saw it?'

'Not when it first came out.'

She smiled faintly. 'What did you want to ask me?'

'Would you mind if I tape our conversation? I'm supposed to type it up later.'

'Do I have to wear a mike, or something?'

'No,' he said, showing her the small pocket recorder he'd brought. 'Just ignore this. Would you mind telling me about Daniel Geaves. I've heard from Ashley Corcoran, but—'

She cut him off. 'What does Ashley know? He never met Danny.'

'That's why I'd like your impression of him.'

She drew in a sharp breath. 'That's going to be difficult when I think of what he did to Delia.'

'Try, please. I didn't meet him—in life, that is.'

'I can find a photo if you want. Give me a moment. I know where to put my hands on it.' She returned indoors.

He clicked off the recorder.

He was happy to wait. A picture of Geaves would be a real help. He watched car windscreens catching the sunlight as the traffic crossed the town bridge way below.

'It was taken at some nightclub. Not very good of Delia, bless her,' she said when she came back and handed him the picture, 'but that's him to a T. Hardly ever smiled, even for a photo.'

No question, Danny Geaves had a sour-faced look. He was at a table beside Delia, self-absorbed. She had leaned in towards him for the photo, but he appeared oblivious of her, elbows on the table, his hands tucked under his chin.

'Can I keep it?'

'By all means.'

'This is helpful. We haven't found anyone else who knew him.' He pressed *record*.

'That I can understand. He wasn't the sort to have many friends.' She directed her gaze across the town towards the blurred grey line of Westbury Down. 'I wouldn't say he was unfriendly. Just a quiet man, harmless, I thought at the time. Delia liked him well enough at the beginning, and they seemed suited to each other. She was more outgoing and made up for his shyness, or whatever it was. But he had qualities she lacked. He was steady. That's an old-fashioned virtue in a man, but my headstrong daughter needed someone to be a calming influence. She was excitable, you know, apt to do spur-of-the-moment things. Danny was . . . methodical.'

She made the word sound menacing. A picture crept into Diamond's mind of the methodical Danny tying his strangled lover to the swing in the park.

'To be fair, he did most of the parenting,' Amanda went on. 'He made sure those girls were up in time and fed and ready for school. I've seen him combing their hair while my daughter, bless her, was sleeping on, or pampering herself in the bathroom.'

'Was there any resentment?'

'On Danny's part? I never noticed any.'

'Arguments?'

'No more than normal. She'd have told me if he was unkind to her, or violent.'

'So what went wrong? Why did they split up?'

In a reflex gesture she pressed two fingers to her lips and then withdrew them and exhaled. An

101

ex-smoker feeling some tension, Diamond decided.

He waited.

When the answer came it was no help.'Who can tell what goes wrong in a relationship except the people involved? I made a point of not interfering.'

'She didn't confide in you?'

'We'd speak, mother and daughter, but not about him. It's not as if he was hitting her, or something.'

'You're certain of that?'

'She'd have told me.'

'There's such a thing as mental cruelty.'

'She dumped him for another man, didn't she? That's what did for her in the end.'

'Just like that?'

'She went through a bad patch, needed lifting emotionally, and Danny didn't see it, or was too busy to notice. He was doing all the caring for the girls, and she'—Amanda sighed—'she had time to look around. She met Ashley, and then the writing was on the wall so far as their relationship was concerned.'

'Ashley had a more glamorous lifestyle?'

'The grass is always greener.'

'Danny took it hard, did he?'

'Difficult to tell. As I said, he was so much quieter than Delia. You couldn't tell what he was thinking. I can see it must have hurt him more than any of us realised.'

'There was no outburst at the time?'

'I wasn't with them, so I don't know for certain, but from what I knew of Danny he wasn't capable of an outburst over anything. All his upsets were internalised. Seeing what happened, I can imagine that the hurt went deep. He must have brooded on it until it became an obsession. You can criticise people like Delia for letting their emotions run riot, but the quiet ones are the dangerous ones.'

'He seems to have cut himself off from the family after the parting.'

'Yes. I used to ask about him and she never had any news.'

'Even if he was angry with Delia, you'd think he'd want to stay in touch with his children.'

'Which is what I said to her more than once. She would just shrug and say he was welcome to spend time with them if he asked.'

'So this wasn't a case of a father denied access?'

'Absolutely not.'

Diamond watched a crow glide in the breeze above the weathercock on the spire of Holy Trinity. 'Did you ever meet any of Danny's family?'

Amanda shook her head. 'It's not as if there was a wedding. That's when you meet the other parents, isn't it?'

'Did she speak about his background ever?'

'I think he was from East Anglia originally. He went to college and got a good qualification. I couldn't tell you if it was a degree, but it was in zoology or something similar. He knew all about animals and birds.'

'Was that his job—working with animals?'

'Not directly, anyway. He spent a lot of time at home, on the computer, which was why he was always there for the children. But if you went for a walk with him he was very knowledgeable about the countryside.'

'Was he interested in bats?'

'What, flying bats?'

What else did she think he was asking about—cricket bats?

'He was, now you mention it. He'd go for a late-night stroll and Delia would tell me he was looking for bats.'

Diamond wished Halliwell had been there to hear this.

Amanda went on, 'They give me the creeps and I'm sure Delia didn't like them. He was self-employed, he did tell me that. It didn't bring in a fortune, but they lived within their means, and Delia was earning as well.'

'As a waitress?'

'Yes. In those days she wasn't at Tosi's. She worked at several places, hotels mostly.'

'The Hilton?' he said, sensing a possible link.

'I don't think so.'

'Getting back to Danny and his quiet ways, did you ever get the impression that he might be depressed, or even suicidal?'

'Never. He was quiet, yes, but never depressed while I knew him.'

'Mentally stable, then?'

'I would say so.'

He was silent again for a while, thinking over what she'd told him. 'It seems to me that your daughter picked two men quite similar in some ways. They both did more than their share in looking after the children, getting them up, off to school and so on.'

'"More than their share"?'she said. 'You'd better get up with the times, Mr Diamond, if you

104

don't mind me saying so. That generation of men share the household duties and take it as normal.'

'Not all of them,' he said. 'Another thing both her boyfriends had in common was that their work took up so much time that Delia felt neglected. She was a friendly, outgoing young woman.'

'Anybody's,' Amanda said. 'You can speak frankly. I knew my own daughter. It's in the genes. I was no saint when I was her age.'

'And she didn't realise how deeply Danny was hurting.'

She took in a sharp, angry breath. 'Being hurt is one thing. It didn't entitle him to kill her.'

'Nothing justified that.'

His firm response encouraged her. 'And the fact that he killed himself later doesn't make him any less evil.'

'I understand you, ma'am,' he said, 'but I'm trying to keep an open mind until I'm one hundred per cent certain Danny was the killer.'

She turned to look at him, frowning. 'Is there any doubt?'

'My job is to make certain.'

'Why else would he have killed himself?'

'That's what I have to explore. Sadly it happens often, a deeply disturbed man killing his partner and sometimes their children as well and then topping himself. It's such a familiar pattern that it's easy to assume this is what happened here. I can't do that. I have to try and find evidence.'

'You can't know what was in Danny's mind,' she said.

'He could have spoken to someone, or written it down in a diary or a suicide note. Nothing has turned up yet, but I have to investigate.'

'And if you find nothing?'

'Then we report to the coroner and the court decides.'

The door behind him made a sound and a child's face appeared round it at the level of the handle. 'Gran, we're bored. Can we see *The Invincibles*?' She was dark, with large blue eyes.

Amanda was on her feet. 'In a minute, dear.'

The face was gone.

'I was about to go, anyway,' Diamond said. 'You've helped a lot.'

'That's the six-year-old, Sophie,' Amanda said, and there was a note of pride. 'I expect her big sister pushed her forward. Could you see her mother in her features?'

He wasn't going to remind her that his only sight of Delia was after she'd been dead a few hours. 'I think she takes after you.'

'What—outspoken?'

'No. Up with the times.'

On the drive back to Bath he weighed what he had heard about Danny Geaves: caring, quiet, supportive, a far cry from Corcoran's version of the jerk who'd never shown any interest. But then you couldn't expect Corcoran to give a glowing testimonial to the ex-lover. On the other hand, it was disputed by no one that Danny had ceased to take an interest in his daughters after Delia left him. That suggested callousness rather than caring. Perhaps the truth lay somewhere between.

13

That evening he drove up the steep rise of Lyncombe Hill to where Paloma lived. He'd always thought of Lyncombe Vale as aloof from Bath, once promoted as a spa in rivalry to the city amenities, with a public house and pleasure garden grandiosely called King James's Palace. A local legend persisted that King James II went into hiding in Lyncombe after abdicating in 1688, but the royal connection didn't bear examination. Even so, in the jargon of estate agents, Lyncombe was still a sought-after residential area.

He saw at once that Paloma had a house better described as dreamed-of than sought-after, a three-storey building with a fine Georgian front and a cobbled drive in a large circle around well-kept lawns. Paloma's silver Porsche was in front of the house and so was a blue Nissan Pathfinder. With a sudden dip in confidence he wondered if this evening would turn out to be a dinner party. She'd surprised him once before.

After ringing the doorbell he had a moment of near panic when he heard her say, 'That'll be Peter. I'll get it.' Visions of other guests in suits and long dresses. He'd gone for the casual look: short sleeves and light-coloured trousers.

There wasn't time to cut and run. She was opening the door.

She did look dressy, in a black creation trimmed with pink chiffon. But her smile made him feel she'd dressed for him alone.

He handed her a bottle of red wine, a good one,

they'd said at the off-licence. 'Just in case you're not into light American beer,' he said.

'Come in and meet Jerry,' she said and added in a whisper, 'He's on his way out.'

So that was who she'd been talking to. Jerry was the son, he remembered. The personal trainer. He was standing in the room to the right, dark, with designer stubble. He was in faded jeans and a T-shirt. He had blue eyes like his mother and the same set of dimples when he smiled.

Diamond said, 'How are you?' and Jerry said, 'Hi,' and gripped his hand with a force that spoke of the hours in the gym.

Paloma said, 'Jerry dropped in some shopping for me. He's on his way to hospital.'

What can you say to that? Nothing. But you might be thinking that fit people who pushed themselves physically and got injuries shouldn't be using the National Health Service.

'He's a volunteer,' Paloma added, and Diamond took back the thought and felt mean.

'Driving patients around?'

'Nothing so useful as that,' Jerry said. 'It's low-key stuff, mine. Mostly I go round with my book trolley, and sometimes I get lucky and I'm on tea and biscuits.'

Paloma chimed in, 'Jerry, you make it sound as if you drink the tea yourself.'

'I do in slack moments. It's allowed. Are you local?' he asked Diamond.

'Weston.'

'That's local. I've drunk at the Old Crown.'

'Peter is in the local police,' Paloma said to her son. 'At Manvers Street.'

Jerry gave one of the standard responses every

off-duty copper is used to hearing. 'We'd better watch out then.'

'No need,' Diamond said and trotted out the standard reassurance. 'Like everyone else, we try and leave the job behind at the end of the day. I like a drink at the Old Crown, too.'

'Hey, I'm obviously missing something,' Paloma said. 'I must try this pub.'

'You'd love it, Mother,' Jerry said. 'Quaint old building. Terrace garden looking out across the Locksbrook valley. A pleasure in store, perhaps.' He grinned at Diamond, man to man, and then looked at his watch. 'I'd better shoot if I'm going to get round all the wards.'

Jerry wished them a good evening and left.

'You must be proud of him,' Diamond said to Paloma. 'At his age my life consisted of rugby, girls and beer.'

'I don't know about the rugby,' she said, 'but I think the girls and the beer feature in his life. Still, he's a good son. He's always looked out for me.'

'That's his four-by-four, then?' Diamond said, hearing the deep thrumming of the engine. 'Personal training must pay all right.'

'Jerry's well qualified. Sports science at Loughborough. I couldn't see where it was leading at the time, but when he got his degree it was perfect timing because everyone was suddenly into fitness. Do you think it will last? I sometimes wonder what he'll do if everyone turns to meditation, or gardening.'

'He'll adapt.'

'Yes, but to what?'

'Teaching higher thoughts while using the treadmill.'

She laughed.

'Or how to mow the lawn without bringing on a coronary.'

'You wouldn't be mocking my son's career?'

'Making light of your concern. His generation don't know what the next trend is, but they take it on. I admire them. And Jerry must be OK if he gives up his time to a good cause.'

'It's quite a commitment,' she said, nodding. 'He visits most of the hospitals in the area. The books are collected mainly by young people in his church, all in nice condition. The books, I mean.' She laughed. 'Well, I guess the young people must be in good condition, too.'

'He is, obviously.'

'Yes, I suspect some of the female patients look forward to seeing him with his trolley.'

'If he needs more books I might be able to find some.' He'd just remembered Steph's Agatha Christies at home. She would have wanted them used for a good cause.

'That would be great. It's run like a library, but they lose a fair number. It's properly managed, though, from a depot on some trading estate. Now what about you?' she said. 'Are you happy in your work?'

'Me, I'm stuck in a rut.'

'But you like being in the police, don't you?'

'It's what I do. I try and make a fist of it. Yours is the ideal job, turning your hobby into a thriving business.'

She looked pleased. 'Want to see where it happens?'

'I'd love to.'

She led him across the hall and up a wide

staircase. The wall to their right was lined with photos of Edwardian beauties in fine clothes, but he was watching the swing of Paloma's hips as she ascended. Maybe she took lessons from her son, because she moved well and had a good figure.

At the top was a room that must have been two large bedrooms knocked into one and they were lined with shelves. Books, filing boxes and bound magazines filled the space from floor to ceiling with an impression that everything had its place. Many were old, yet there was no smell, no sign of dust. At one end facing a window was a huge antique desk, its surface clear.

'That's what I use when I'm opening books, looking for items,' she said. 'The office bit is through here.' She opened a door between the shelves and showed him a room set up with computer, printer and scanner, photocopier, filing cabinets and phone.

'What's this?' he asked, looking at a square screen with some kind of winding gear at its base.

'My microfilm viewer. I have a run of the *Illustrated London News* up to 1940 and various journals too big to store next door. About a thousand reels.'

'I'm reeling, too.'

'There's another room with scrapbooks, but I'm not taking you in there. I'm ashamed of it. They come in all sizes and they're the devil to keep tidy.'

'You obviously like order,' he said thinking of the tip that was his own work space at home.

'Without it, I'd disappear under a million newspaper cuttings.'

'So this is where you tracked down the Müller

cut-down. It didn't take you long.'

'It was in one of my fashion encyclopedias. It's funny. Top hats were supposed to be the mark of a well-dressed man, yet they have quite a sinister reputation.'

'As worn by undertakers?'

'True, but I'm talking about what happened to the people who made them. They treated the felt with salts of mercury, so they were breathing in poisonous fumes. They'd get the shakes and twitch. That's how the phrase 'mad as a hatter' is supposed to have originated.'

'I thought that was *Alice in Wonderland*.'

'No it goes back a good thirty years before Lewis Carroll.'

'I've learned something new, then.'

'Shall we go downstairs? I've got a quiche warming up. I thought it might go nicely with the beer.'

The living quarters were on a scale he'd not often seen. The kitchen was like a Zanussi showroom, big enough for a double-door fridge to slot in among fitted units and not be noticed until Paloma took out a bowl of salad. Two trays were ready on the work surface in the centre.

'As it's a nice evening I thought we'd eat on the terrace.'

'Seems a good idea,' he said, as if he was well used to eating on terraces.

'As I warned you in Strada the other night, I don't have much time for cooking.'

'Heating up the quiche is more than I do,' he said.

'You warm up those baked beans you told me about, don't you?'

'The beans, yes,'

'So don't undersell yourself, Peter Diamond. I have no doubt you have talents you keep well hidden.'

They took the trays through a sitting room bigger than some hotel foyers and set them outside on a wrought-iron table under a green and white striped canopy. The garden, all trimmed lawns and well-stocked borders, stretched away to a grove of beech trees. No other house was in sight.

She took champagne from an icebox and asked him to open it.

'Funny kind of beer.'

'You don't have to drink it.' She produced a can of Miller Lite from the same box.

'I can't let a lady drink champagne alone.' He popped the cork and poured two glasses and handed her one. He lifted his own. 'To my gracious hostess.'

She said, 'You have a nice way with a woman.'

He laughed. 'Then I must have learned something in more than fifty years.'

'Did you go to a co-ed school?'

'Actually, no. I grew up with a sister. That makes a difference. And I was married twelve years. Steph took me on and I won't say she turned the frog into Prince Charming, but I'm not the yob I once was. What else? My boss is a woman of a totally different sort. I treat her as a challenge. And the best detective I ever had in my team was called Julie.'

'No stranger to the fair sex, then. Must be useful in your work.'

'You mean understanding the criminal mind?'

She smiled. 'Not all women are baddies, are they?'

'No, but I have to be on my guard.'

'Against feminine wiles?'

'I try not to get sidetracked.'

She raised an eyebrow. 'You're speaking of your work in the police?'

'Yes.'

'And when you've left the job behind, as you put it to Jerry, are you just as cautious?'

'I wouldn't be here if I was.'

'That's true.' She lifted her glass again. 'Here's to leaving the job behind.'

'As often as possible.' He lifted his and touched hers. When they'd drunk some he topped up her glass.

'Give yourself some.'

He smiled. 'What's left is yours. I brought the car with me.'

'And it wouldn't do for a policeman to get over the limit. So you don't actually leave the job behind.'

'Anyone in charge of a car should watch his intake.'

'Now you're talking like a policeman. No, that's unfair.' She gave a light slap to the back of her hand. 'I'd do precisely the same, except if I'm going for a few drinks with someone I travel by taxi.'

After they'd finished the quiche, she brought a selection of sorbets. 'You mentioned your wife again,' she said when she'd served them, 'but you haven't said much about her.'

'Steph died three years ago,' he said without elaborating.

'And you told me you have no children? By choice?'

'She miscarried several times.'

She looked at him for a moment in silence. 'That must have been dreadful for you both.'

'More so for Steph,' he said, remembering, and he started to speak more freely. 'Each time she went for four or five months and then at one routine appointment the medical professionals listened for the heartbeat or did a scan and the heart wasn't beating.'

This time she didn't speak at all. Her hand went to her mouth.

He hadn't talked of these painful memories with anyone before. Here in this peaceful garden with this calm, interested woman, it was all right. It was more than that. It was a help to him. 'They gave her a tablet to induce labour and sent her home to wait. That's the worst time, the two days before we went back to hospital and our dead baby was born.'

'Were they kind to her?'

'Immensely. And after the delivery they make sure you're kept busy with all the arrangements, the form-filling about the post-mortem and funeral. Good psychology, I suppose.'

'But the grief catches up with you?'

'Mm.' He exhaled quite sharply. 'Sorry, I don't know how I got started on this.'

'It was me,' she said. 'I asked.' She looked across the lawn without focusing on anything. 'My experiences couldn't be more different. Jerry was born precisely nine months after I married Gordon, the man I told you about, who dumped me later. I was a failure as a mother. Some women

115

have this powerful maternal instinct. I'd hoped when I had the baby that the mothering, nurturing thing would magically take me over, but it didn't. I was uncomfortable even holding the child. I didn't want another.' She sighed.

Blackbirds in the garden were outdoing each other in joyous song that was a counterpoint to the confidences being exchanged.

Paloma went on, 'But then we slipped up, as they say. I opted for a termination. When you hear something like that—after your experiences —it must make you angry.'

'No,' he said. 'We all have to cope with what life throws at us.'

She turned to face him and her blue eyes held his for a moment. 'In the choice versus life debate, I'd have thought you'd be pro-life.'

He shrugged. 'In my job you see so much that's gone wrong in families, unwanted, abused kids, that you can't take such a firm line. I can think of situations when my values tell me abortion is morally right. But as a routine procedure, I'm not so comfortable with it.'

'I can understand why.'

Later, when the sun and the champagne had almost sunk from view, he asked how she managed the house and garden and she said she had a treasure called Rita who was in every morning and Carl the gardener came in twice a week. Diamond praised the state of the lawns and said he thought of his own as a wild flower meadow. She took him seriously and asked if he was an environmentalist and he laughed and said he was sorry to disillusion her, but no. He'd have a show garden himself, but he lacked one vital

116

element. 'What's that?' she asked.

'Carl the gardener.'

She smiled. 'Before it gets properly dark I want to show you the secret garden. Do you know about night-scented stocks? It's full of them. Gorgeous. Come on, Pete.' She took him by the hand. It was a while since anyone had called him Pete or held his hand. 'Look, the fairy lights are coming on,' she said. 'They show us the way.'

She didn't let go of his hand as she led him across the lawn towards the solar-powered lamps marking the path round one of the borders. The clouds were inky-black tinged with the last suggestions of red and this wasn't the best light for looking at a secret garden, but he sensed this wasn't the real object. Paloma had finished the champagne without help from him and was happy, if not merry, if not plastered. Soon it would be make-up-your-mind time. He started mentally rehearsing what to say.

As it turned out, the secret garden had a door set into a brick wall, and the door was locked, so Diamond didn't get to see inside. What followed was down to his heightened anticipation and her inebriation and would embarrass them both for days to come.

Paloma rattled the door and said, 'Oh, fuck.'

Diamond made the little speech he'd been struggling to put into words: 'I really like you, Paloma. It's just a bit sudden for me.'

She said, 'That's not what I meant.'

He said, 'Nor me.'

Appalled with himself, not knowing how to follow that, and with his dignity in free fall, he leaned towards her and kissed her, but the kiss

117

was clumsy and desperate and didn't improve matters one bit.

In under ten minutes he was driving home, going over what he'd said and should have said, like a schoolkid who has messed up his first date.

14

Over the next week he plunged himself into his work. He and Halliwell tried to put together enough evidence to show beyond doubt that Danny Geaves had murdered Delia and then hanged himself. The one indisputable fact—that both the principals in the case were dead—made it an unappealing exercise, but it had to be gone through. The forensic reports had come in, and added little to what was already known. Nothing so helpful as a DNA sample had been found to link Geaves to the crime scene in the park.

'If we knew where he spent the last week of his life we might find something,' Diamond said.

'A suicide note that tells all?' Halliwell said. 'You're an optimist, guv.'

'I was thinking of some trace of Delia. She was away from home on the Tuesday night and found dead on Thursday. If we could show she spent those two nights with Geaves, we'd be home and dry.'

'Are you thinking they got together? Deep down, guv, I believe you're a romantic.'

His thoughts strayed back to the secret garden. 'Some chance.'

'I thought they'd parted for good.'

'People change. She wasn't getting much attention from Ashley Corcoran. Maybe she heard from Danny and decided to see if there was still a spark in their relationship.' He sketched the scenario. 'She agrees to meet Danny thinking it might work out, but the magic isn't there. On their second evening together she tells him she isn't going back with him. He loses it and strangles her.'

'I can believe that.'

'Then there's the unromantic theory,' Diamond said. 'He was planning to kill her from the start. Old wounds. He'd never forgiven her for leaving him the first time.'

'What—and he has sex with her before he strangles her? That's sick.'

'He *was* sick. He was suicidal.'

'Sometimes,' Halliwell said from the depth of his experience, 'it's no bad thing to admit you're not one hundred per cent sure.'

Diamond wasn't having such defeatist talk. 'Sometimes you have to make more of an effort. There's going to be an inquest and the coroner will expect more than guesswork. We need to find Danny's bolt hole. We appealed for help in tracking Delia's movements. What have we done about Danny? Asked around in Freshford. That's not enough. What if he was seen in Trowbridge, or Westbury, or Bath, even?'

'Are you thinking of going on TV again?'

He shook his head. 'We wouldn't get air-time. Everyone else thinks the case is done and dusted.'

'Especially the boss.'

'Especially her, yes. You and I are supposed to paper over the cracks and tiptoe away.'

Halliwell gave him a speculative look. 'And we're not happy with that . . . are we?'

'You know me, Keith. I have to find out what really happened, even if it turns out exactly as Georgina thinks.'

'So what's the next step?'

'We make an appeal in the local papers: did anyone see Danny Geaves in the week leading up to his death?'

'Smart move. Have we got a picture? I mean of when he was alive?'

'I was given one by Amanda. We issue a press release saying we're keen to trace his movements in the week before his death.'

'I'll see to it.'

'No. We have a tame journalist in our ranks.'

'Ingeborg?'

'She knows how to make the front page.'

'I wouldn't mind seeing her on page three,' Halliwell said.

'I'd keep that to myself if I were you.'

*   *   *

The *Bath Chronicle* ran the piece next day on an inside page. The Danny Geaves story couldn't compete with a sighting of Jane Austen's ghost promenading along the Gravel Walk. But there was still a result. Two *Chronicle* readers called the police, positive they had spotted Danny in the village of Bathford in the days before his death.

The first was a woman who had seen a man of Danny's description loitering, as she put it, near the school. She'd taken note of him because she was a parent and felt it was up to parents to be vigilant. The man hadn't approached any children or she would have reported him, but he looked in need of a shave (a sure sign of decadence in Bathford), and was 'unkempt', apparently unlike any of the parents meeting their children. Her description of the man's clothes matched those found on the body at the viaduct.

The second sighting was more promising still. Two days running a postman had noticed someone looking like Danny walking along Farleigh Rise, the road to Monkton Farleigh. Postmen are usually reliable witnesses. They know the locals. Anyone else stands out. This postman described the man as looking 'up to no good'. When the post van stopped across the road the stranger had gone behind some bushes as if trying to avoid being spoken to. There was nothing there except scrub and trees, the postman said. It looked suspicious, but people sometimes go behind bushes for calls of nature, so he hadn't followed. He'd decided simply to take note. When he'd seen the picture in the *Chronicle* he'd recognised the man for certain.

Armed with a stack of copies of the picture of Danny Geaves, Diamond drove out with Halliwell and a minibus loaded with uniformed officers. Bathford is built on a rise bounded by the confluence of Box Brook and the Avon to the north and Bathford Hill to the south. They parked above the village at the top end of Farleigh Rise and began a search on both sides for evidence of someone living rough. Flattened vegetation and the remains of a bonfire would be a good indicator.

Inside the first half-hour one of the search

party found the ashes of a bonfire close to a hut.

'We may have got lucky,' Diamond said.

'I don't think so, guv,' Halliwell said when they reached the place. 'The burnt area is too big. This is a forester's fire, used to burn unwanted timber.'

'So how long were you in the boy scouts?'

'There'd be signs of food in the embers.' Untroubled by the sarcasm, Halliwell spread the ashes with his foot. Then he tested the padlock on the door of the hut. 'It hasn't been tampered with.' He looked through the window at the side. 'I can see a crosscut saw.'

'All right. You made your point.'

The searchers fanned out again and moved on. After another hour Diamond left the party and returned to the minibus. He asked the driver if the tea was brewing.

'What tea, sir?'

'Are you telling me you don't carry an urn? I've got sixteen men and women gasping for a cuppa.'

'It wasn't mentioned, sir. I'm the driver, not—'

Diamond held up a menacing finger. 'What are you about to say? You're not the teaboy? I'm sorry, sunshine, but I just promoted you. You'd better motor back to Bath and get something organised. I wouldn't say no to some cheese and pickle sandwiches while you're at it.'

The searchers wouldn't be getting their tea for a while, but they deserved a break, so he returned to them and ordered one.

Someone asked if there was a toilet in Bathford.

'Five or six hundred at a guess,' Diamond said, 'but if you think I'm going to knock on someone's door and ask if sixteen coppers can use the bathroom, you're mistaken. What do we use?'

One of the sixteen said, 'Our initiative, sir.'

'I couldn't put it better myself. Well away from the bit we've been searching, right?'

It was a good thing he'd ordered the tea. Morale ebbed at a worrying rate after the search resumed. Several were complaining that this could go on for days without anything turning up. Then someone stepped in a wasps' nest and three people were stung. The first-aid kit was in the minibus somewhere on the road to Bath.

'Try rubbing it with a dock leaf,' Diamond said.

'That's for stinging nettles,' Halliwell said.

'You're not much support.'

'Where's the bloody driver when we need him?'

The eventual return of the minibus was greeted with ironic cheers.

'I'm worried, guv,' Halliwell said when everyone had tea. 'They were almost mutinous.'

'I was thinking the same.' He announced to them all that he was calling a halt, and got a cheer of his own. 'It'll be dark in another hour. We're back tomorrow morning.'

There were groans.

'Doing house-to-house.'

If there is one thing policemen like less than searching fields, it is knocking on doors.

*　　*　　*

DI John Leaman had been holding the CID fort while Diamond and Halliwell were out. He was well capable of directing operations. The main responsibility was to take any more calls that came in as a result of the piece in the *Chronicle*. The phone kept buzzing, but most calls that came through had nothing to do with Danny Geaves. Leaman started to suspect that the switchboard operator was routinely diverting every outside call to CID. In the middle of the afternoon someone with a voice that oozed elegance asked to speak to the 'senior officer'.

'At your service,' Leaman said.

'Forgive me, but are you the chief constable?'

'Chief constable? No, sir. You're through to CID.'

'You don't mind if I enquire what rank you hold?'

'Only detective inspector, I'm afraid.'

'Don't apologise,' said the caller. 'This couldn't be better. Detective Inspector . . . ?'

'Leaman.'

'Well, inspector, this could be your lucky day. My name is Charles Fetherington-Steel and I'm publicity director for the Theatre Royal. As you probably know, next week sees the opening of our main summer production, *An Inspector Calls*, the J. B. Priestley play that has been revived with such spectacular success.'

'I wouldn't know about that.'

'But you will shortly. That's my job, publicity. You see, we've had this rather special idea of inviting a real police inspector to the press night— with a partner of his choice, of course—and getting his impressions of the play. We'll take a couple of photos with some of the cast, and then the local paper will do a follow-up piece.'

'Before you go any further,' Leaman said, 'that's not my thing at all. You've been put through to the wrong person. Hold on while I get you reconnected.'

'But you're a real inspector and you sound ideal.'

'You're mistaken, sir. We don't do PR work in CID. You want our press office by the sound of things. Hold the line, please.' He pressed the button for the operator and said, 'Someone's got their switches in a twist. All the flaming outside calls are coming straight to us. Some luvvie from the Theatre Royal just got through. You'd better sort yourself out, and fast.'

The female voice that responded said, 'I don't think you know who you're addressing.'

'Tell me, then.'

'Dallymore.'

Georgina, the ACC. Leaman held the phone away from his mouth and said, 'Oh my sainted aunt.' Then he spoke into it again. 'Sorry, ma'am. Crossed line.'

'You made that very clear,' Georgina said. 'I'm through to CID, aren't I? You're DI Leaman, are you not?'

Nailed.

'Yes, ma'am.'

'I want to speak to your superior. Put Superintendent Diamond on.'

'Ma'am, the Theatre Royal is on an outside line.'

She said, 'I don't want the theatre. Where's Diamond?'

'He's out, ma'am, on a job.'

'Out where?'

'Bathford.'

'Does this have anything to do with a vanload of uniformed officers being driven away from here

125

this morning?'

'Quite possibly, ma'am.'

'So that's why I can't get hold of anyone. This is too much.'

Then Leaman heard another voice. The theatre man was back on the line. 'There you are. I seem to have been talking to myself for the past two minutes. Who is this?'

'ACC Dallymore.'

'How charming. Assisi as in St Francis of? Well, my dear, this could be your lucky day.'

Leaman gently replaced the receiver.

15

Bathford has about eight hundred houses. 'That's a mere fifty each,' Diamond told his team, assembled in the Crown car park at eight thirty next morning. He wanted to be positive from the start. 'No challenge at all. DI Halliwell will tell you the streets you are covering and issue you with a mugshot of Danny Geaves. You ask if they've seen him around the village over the past ten days. And—this is important—if they have, you find out if he was seen with anyone else. Report every sighting to me at the first opportunity.'

Wonderful the difference a night's sleep can make. They listened without a murmur, picked up their streetmaps and mugshots and moved off briskly as if house-to-house was as good as a pub crawl. And results started coming in almost at once. A stranger in a village stands no chance of staying undercover. Five sightings were reported in the first hour. Diamond spoke to each witness himself. By their accounts Geaves had been in the area for about a week to ten days, mostly on the southern outskirts in the area where the postman had seen him. One woman complained that two of her chickens had been taken, and not by a fox. ('How do you know a fox didn't take them?' 'Because I've never come across a fox with size-nine footprints.') No one could say where Geaves was spending the nights. And no one had seen him with Delia, or any other woman.

Diamond looked up the steep ascent of Bathford Hill. 'What's up there?'

'The church.'

'Past it, I mean.'

Halliwell had the map open. 'Farleigh Rise, where we were yesterday.'

'To the right.'

'Mountain Wood. There's a footpath.'

'And what's that tower thing at the top?'

'Browne's Folly, it says.'

Jutting above the foliage was this lone grey building with a flat Italianate roof and arched windows.

'I didn't notice it yesterday.'

'We were on the other side. Am I wrong, or have you just had an idea, boss?'

After the house-to-house was completed, and lunch eaten, Diamond led his little army up the hill. One of them had grown up in Bathford and was able to make the stiff climb more bearable for everyone by relating the history. A quarry owner called Wade Browne had built the tower in 1848. The official story was that he was a public-spirited man who gave employment to local workers in a time of depression. In the more cynical version he was a self-admirer who wanted a memorial as impressive as William Beckford's tower on Lansdown. Probably there was truth in both.

Twice Diamond called a halt to admire the scenery, as he put it. 'You can probably see the way my mind is working,' he said to Halliwell between gasps.

'Yes, but could he get inside the tower, guv?'

'A desperate man can get inside anything.'

On the ridge of the hill the going got easier. The tower was about fifty feet high and Browne's initials and the date 1848 were on a plaque over the door. Unfortunately the door was made of iron, and locked, and there was no sign of a forced entry. The only windows were at the top, out of reach of anyone except Spiderman.

The searchers stood at a distance and looked on while Diamond slowly circled the building. Good thing he couldn't hear what was being said about follies.

Halliwell went over and said in confidence, 'We marched them up to the top of the hill. What now, guv?'

'Ask that local lad to come over.'

The constable looked nervous, as if fearing something he'd said had been overheard by the detective superintendent.

'What's your name?' Diamond asked.

'PC Flint, sir.'

'And you grew up in Bathford?'

'Yes, sir.'

'You must have come up here a few times.'

'Years ago, I did, sir. I knew it as the pepperpot. That was the local name.'

'Did you ever see inside?'

'Being kids, we were curious, like. In those days the door was off its hinges.'

'And what's it like in there?'

'Nothing much to see. Stone steps going round the inside walls to the top. We climbed up them. The rail was broken in places. There was a wooden viewing platform up at the top once, built across two iron girders, but it had all rotted when I looked in. There were bits of it at the bottom. Old rubbish and all sorts.'

'Not a good place to hole up in?'

'Definitely not. Damp, cold and nowhere to lie down. Mind, they tidied it up since and repaired the roof, and the door, of course.'

'And made it secure. Who would have the key?'

'The Wildlife Trust people. It's all part of the nature reserve.'

'Where do we find them—in the village?'

'I think their office is in Bath.'

Diamond's options were running out. 'As a local man, Flint, if you were on the run and wanted a place to hole up, where would you go?'

Flint gave it some thought. 'An empty house, sir?'

'Where the neighbours would spot you soon enough. They haven't. I don't think he was in a house.'

There was a longer pause.

'The only other hidey-hole I can think of is the caves, sir.'

This was more promising. 'There are caves up here?'

'Underneath us. This is quarrying country. The hill is riddled with them. At one time it was all

129

linked up with Monkton Farleigh mine.'

'I know about Monkton Farleigh.' The vast subterranean stone workings there had been used in the war to store munitions and the place had since been opened as a tourist attraction, with rides on the underground tramway.

Flint added, 'The Browne's Folly quarries were just as well known in their day. There are entrances all along the Pepperpot Trail.'

'Come again.'

'The path along the ridge. We're on it.'

'Show me, then.'

PC Flint strode out, puffed up with his importance on the team.

'Don't stand there like a load of bollards,' Diamond yelled to the rest of them. 'We're on the Pepperpot Trail.'

The little path led south, towards Warleigh, and the views of the city testified to the height they had climbed.

'Caves up here?' Diamond said. 'I find that hard to credit.'

'You have to look out for them. Some of the entrances are overgrown,' Flint said. After just a few minutes of walking he stopped and said, 'Through there.'

Half hidden by a crop of nettles was a dark hollow that plunged deep into the hill.

'Is that it?' Diamond said. 'It's got a grille over it.'

'That's for protection, sir.'

'Protecting stupid people like us from getting inside.'

'Protecting the bats.'

'Bats?' The word impacted in Diamond's brain.

'They nest in there, don't they?' Flint said. 'Ten or twelve species, I was told. The grille is big enough for them to fly in and out. The trust does its best to stop them being disturbed.'

Diamond wasn't too concerned at this stage about the welfare of bats. He went closer and took a grip on the grille. It was very secure. 'Our man had a picture of a bat in his room. He must have known about these caves. There are other entrances, you said?'

'Four or five.'

'Let's look at the others.'

At first sight the next cave entrance was just as secure. But when Diamond shook the bars there was some movement. He pulled sharply and the whole thing came away from the rock. 'Someone had this out and replaced it,' he said, laying the grille on the ground.

He ducked and looked inside—except that looking wasn't any use. Couldn't see a thing. Just felt the chill. Then he was aware of something soft against his foot. *In a cave?* He gave a yelp and stepped away. Backed out into the daylight and asked with a transparent attempt at dignity if anyone had a lighter.

The only smoker in the party had a rare boost to his self-esteem.

With more caution, he tried a second time. The flame made the experience easier to endure. Nothing was moving on the floor, which was a relief. He was not overfond of things that lived in caves. He could see the soft object he had touched: a folded blanket. There were candles, some spent matches and a plastic bottle of water. There was an inflatable pillow.

131

He stepped outside and said to Halliwell, 'We may have found his sleeping quarters. Ask the men in white suits to do a job in there.'

While Halliwell was phoning for the crime scene investigators, Diamond prowled around outside. 'You lot make yourselves useful,' he told the team. 'There's got to be the remains of a fire around here.'

They soon discovered it, not twenty yards from the cavern entrance. Of even more interest, in the embers, along with chicken bones and orange rind, were some fragments of newspaper, and even though it was scorched almost black, they could see that it was the Saturday edition of the *Daily Mail*, the day before Danny Geaves's body was found suspended from the viaduct.

Diamond stayed kneeling and presently picked out a piece of cardboard about three inches by four. Just visible under the scorchmarks was an embossed design of a coat of arms.

'Now we know what happened to his passport,' he said. There were other printed papers too far gone to be recognisable, but forensic scientists can do amazing reconstructions.

'So—assuming this was Danny—he quits his comfortable cottage in Freshford to live in a cave. He takes his personal papers with him and makes a bonfire of them at some stage. He strangles Delia in Bath and rigs it up to look like a suicide. Three days later, he hangs himself. What's it all about, Keith?'

'Mental breakdown?'

'Possible. The balance of his mind was disturbed, as they used to say when a nutter was sent to Broadmoor. Has anyone mentioned

132

previous mental problems? Amanda didn't.'

'I can check.'

'Do that. Even if it's true, we still have another mystery. Where was Delia on the two nights before her death? She didn't come home. I can't believe she was sleeping in this horrible cave with Danny. It knocks my theory on the head.'

The CSI team arrived within the hour and were set to work in and around the cave. Diamond showed them the site of the bonfire. The senior man said, 'I notice your fingertips are black, sir.'

'And?'

'Would you, perhaps, have done some rooting in the fire already?'

Diamond gave him a look like a cat accused of chasing birds. 'Don't come onto me as if I contaminated the scene. If I hadn't done some rooting I wouldn't know there was a passport and I wouldn't have called you out.'

'No offence. I just need to know what we're dealing with.'

'Right. And I suppose it will take days before I hear from you.'

'If you want the job done properly.'

He left them to get on with it.

In a more upbeat mood, the search party descended the hill. The mission had been a success. In the van on the return to Manvers Street, Diamond discussed the day with Halliwell.

'I've been thinking about your theory.'

'Which theory was that, guv?'

'Nervous breakdown. It's too easy.'

'What's wrong with it?'

'There was planning involved. Cool, deliberate planning.'

'Madmen can plan stuff.'

'I know. I just want to dig around. I'd rather you didn't mention the nervous breakdown to Georgina.'

'Why is that?'

'She'll jump at it. She wants this whole thing sorted, so she can go to choir practice and tell her friend Amanda she's completed the job.'

'And you believe there's more to it?'

'I looked inside that cave. It wasn't a nice place to spend one night. We now know Geaves was sleeping rough for about a week, at the end of which he was found hanging. About a week, Keith. That takes it back to before Delia was murdered, so he didn't go into hiding as a result of the murder. Why did he quit his comfortable house in Freshford to act like a fugitive in Bathford? I think he was afraid. Terrified.'

16

The mid-week tea dance was in progress at the Melksham assembly hall. Sixteen couples quickstepped to a Victor Silvester arrangement of 'Ain't She Sweet', watched by an appreciative audience seated at card tables. The average age must have been close to seventy and the majority were women. The arrival of Peter Diamond, not much over fifty and not bad-looking either, created a certain amount of interest.

Which was a pity because he'd come to look for a man.

Jim Middleton was a retired forensic

134

pathologist and this other blue-rinsed and sequinned world he inhabited had been unsuspected by Diamond until this afternoon. Wanting advice from one of the few scientists he respected, the big policeman had called at Middleton's house on spec, tried the doorbell and got no answer. The neighbour had told him where to find old twinkletoes on a Saturday afternoon.

And Jim looked the part, managing a nifty lockstep as he steered a substantial lady past Diamond without a flicker of recognition. The dance was claiming all Jim's concentration. In a dove-grey suit, white shirt and red bow with matching socks he was another creature altogether from the gum-booted, anoraked figure familiar at crime scenes. His movement was quick and inventive. When it seemed he and his partner would be trapped in one corner by other dancers he executed a double reverse spin and nipped through a small space.

The music reached its final bars. The dancers smiled and thanked each other. Observing the old-fashioned gallantry of the ballroom, Jim began to escort his partner to one of the tables on the far side. Diamond pursued them round the edge of the floor. He'd not got more than halfway when the MC announced that the next dance would be a ladies' invitation waltz. The words didn't register with Diamond. The first he knew of it was when his path was blocked by a little silver-haired woman in a purple dress and granny glasses who said, 'My dance, please.'

He started to say he wasn't there to dance and she said, 'Ladies' invitation.' Then the music started up again. The little lady said, 'Can't hear

135

you, mister. I'm eighty per cent deaf. But the rest of me is in perfect order.' With that, she gripped his left hand, put her right on his upper arm, and reversed, tugging him into action. He'd never mastered dancing, but it didn't matter because his partner knew the steps and was so close that her sinewy thighs made sure he moved the right legs. She said, 'Relax. You'll be all right with me. I'm Annie, by the way, and I'm eighty-two. I end up with all the handsome men and the other girls can't understand how I manage it.'

Those ingrained good manners of his took over. 'I'm Peter.'

'Walter?' she said. 'Old-fashioned name. Walt suits you better.'

He would be Walt for the rest of the dance.

'I'll give you a tip, Walt,' she said when he was trying to pivot like the other dancers. 'Rubbers don't work too well.'

He didn't like to think what she was talking about.

She said, 'Leather soles next time.'

This had happened so fast that he had some sympathy with the ladies who couldn't understand how Annie got her man each time. He'd barely set foot in the place and here he was doing the one-two-three as if it was his chief joy in life. Jim Middleton glided by so close that their shoulders almost touched. This wasn't the moment to talk.

He lost the tempo.

'Don't look down, Walt,' Annie said. 'That's a sure way to go wrong. Just follow me. Walk. Side and Close. Better.'

Here he was, the hard man of Manvers Street nick, getting a dancing lesson from an eighty-two-year-old. What a good thing Halliwell, Ingeborg and the rest of them couldn't see this. He wouldn't be telling them about it.

'We call it floorcraft,' Annie said after he'd backed into another couple and almost caused an accident. 'You have to be aware of other dancers, you know. Feet together and start again.'

He had to keep starting again. It seemed to him that the waltz lasted twice as long as the quickstep he'd watched, and it was one of those tunes that repeated, giving no clue as to when it would end. No use asking Annie if she'd had enough. She was humming the tune.

The last bars were a mercy, like the bell at the end of a one-sided boxing match. Annie finished with a flourish, a twirl worthy of old Vienna, followed by a dip and a curtsy with a saucy lift of the skirt. Diamond nodded, smiled, thanked her and went after Jim again, who this time was heading for a table at the far end.

He caught up with him and said, 'Dr Middleton, I presume.'

Jim turned and squinted at him. 'We know each other, don't we? Can't place you right now.'

Diamond introduced himself.

'Stone the crows,' Jim said. 'It's two years since I retired and I've wiped most of that from my memory. You're the fellow whose wife was shot. A tragic case.'

'That sums me up nicely.'

'I don't mean it personally. And you're still in the police?'

'Keeps me occupied.'

'Rather you than me. Well, it's good to see you here. Welcome to the tea dance. Bit of a change from chasing villains, but you need to be speedy here to get the best partners.'

'Oh, I'm not here for the dancing.'

Jim smiled at that and leaned forward for a confidential word. 'Good man, honest like me. It's a great place to meet birds. They're well in the majority.' He put a hand on Diamond's shoulder and spoke out of the corner of his mouth. 'By the way, I don't talk about my old job here. They think I was something in the secret service. Do me a favour and play along if anyone asks.'

With that, the music started again and Jim was on his feet. 'Foxtrot. My speciality. They queue up to foxtrot with me. Why don't you give one of them a treat? See you later—if one of us doesn't get lucky.'

The pattern was set for the next half-hour. Such were the demands that Jim couldn't have stopped for a serious conversation if he'd wanted. He didn't miss a dance.

Diamond became a wallflower, retreating to the dark area under the balcony trying to think what excuse to make if they had another ladies' invitation. He was in two minds whether to stay. He couldn't see how he'd get another chance with Jim Middleton.

Then he heard the clatter of crockery from an inner room and it dawned on him that a tea dance must involve tea at some stage. There would be an interval and he might after all get a few more words with Jim. Some spare tables were pushed together and loaded with cups and saucers. Cakes and scones began to appear. The people who weren't dancing started moving towards the tables, taking positions. They weren't so obvious about it as to form a queue, but they were making sure that when one did form they wouldn't be at the end.

Jim was doing something called a square tango that seemed to require a tighter clinch than any of the dances up to now. He'd found the lady with the deepest cleavage and was holding her as if it was his mission to hide the display from everyone else.

The teapots were brought from the kitchen and a queue formed quicker than a Boston two-step. The music continued with only Jim and his partner on the floor, swaying in a kind of trance.

Diamond felt his arm gripped. Deaf Annie was telling him to get in line because all the best cakes would be gone.

He thanked her and pointed his free hand towards the toilets.

She relaxed her hold. 'You go, and I'll keep your place.'

He headed across the room and with nice timing the music stopped and Jim started walking in the same direction. They met at the door of the gents. 'You look as if your need is greater than mine,' Jim said, holding it open.

'I'm fine,' Diamond said as he stepped inside. 'Just need some advice.'

'Have you pulled already?' Jim said. 'Go for it, matey.'

'Professional advice. Would you mind reading through a post-mortem report and telling me what you think?'

The chumminess drained away. 'No chance. I've put all that behind me.'

'Off the record, of course.'

139

Jim Middleton leaned back and for a moment Diamond thought the dancing had been all too much and he was about to fall over, but he was checking that the cubicles were not in use.

Diamond said, 'I wouldn't ask if it wasn't important.'

Jim said, 'If they find out I did dissections for a living I'll never get another partner.'

'Your cover blown. The James Bond of the ballroom unmasked.'

'Is that a threat? You wouldn't . . . would you?'

'Play along, Jim, and it won't come to that.'

Jim used his second line of defence. 'You want a second opinion? This is a dodgy area, my friend. If I throw doubt on someone else's findings I could end up in the courts. My profession has taken a lot of flak lately. Forensic pathology is getting a bad name. There have been some juicy cases, as you're well aware.'

'This is a Dr Sealy.'

'I remember Bertram Sealy,' Jim said. 'He's good at his job.' His rising tone on the last word suggested this was not the whole story.

'You may have seen the case in the paper. Woman found hanging in Sydney Gardens. It turned out she was strangled first.'

'I don't bother with the papers.'

'Three days later the woman's ex-lover hanged himself from the railway viaduct.'

'That's two deaths.'

'Yes, and Sealy dealt with both. He's good, you say?'

'Never heard anything adverse. What's the problem?'

'There's some circumstantial stuff I won't go

140

into now. There were other suspects. Then this suicide happened and everyone jumps to the conclusion that the man killed the woman and took his own life.'

'Familiar pattern,' Jim said. 'I had a couple of cases like it. You think it's too obvious, do you, the killer who can't live with what he's done?'

'I'm under pressure to write the report and put the whole thing to bed.'

'And you want me to second-guess Bertram Sealy's opinion?' He vibrated his lips. 'This is dynamite, Peter. Even the sniff of an error can finish a man's career.'

'We're not talking about a miscarriage of justice,' Diamond said. 'It hasn't gone to court. This is just me wanting to find out what happened.'

'But he's a professional colleague. There's a national shortage of pathologists, did you know that? Hundreds of autopsies and not enough of us to cope. There isn't much glamour in the job.'

'I'm not trying to undermine Dr Sealy.'

'But you wouldn't invite him round for a drink.'

'It's mutual. I'm just one of the plod to him.'

Jim managed a smile. 'I've heard it said that he turned to pathology because he doesn't have to talk to his patients.'

Diamond smiled too. 'Maybe I should act dead.'

'Not when there's a pathologist about.'

'But he'd enjoy stitching me up. Look, I'm not trying to get the man struck off. I just want the kinds of pointers I used to get from you. I wouldn't say where I got my information. I guarantee I wouldn't bring you into it.'

'You really believe there's something iffy in his reports?'

'I'm in no position to say. Let's put it the other way. If I could have his findings verified by someone I respect, then I'd go along with my boss and close the case.'

'You mean that?'

'I'm a man of my word.'

'And I'm missing my tea and cake,' Jim said. He sighed. 'You're a pain in the arse, Peter Diamond. Have you got these reports with you?'

'In the car.'

'Let's transfer them to mine, then. I'll look at them tonight.' A sudden gleam brightened his eyes. 'If anyone sees us they'll think you're one of my MI5 contacts.'

*   *   *

That night when he was trying to sleep his brain kept replaying the episode at Paloma's house. He'd been doing his best to wipe the memory, but here it was almost as vivid as the real thing, sharp and painful. There was no denying how ineptly he'd behaved. The stupid speech saying he wasn't ready for sex when it wasn't even being offered. The collision of a kiss that he could still feel on his mouth. His rapid exit.

Mortifying.

He'd give two weeks of his annual leave to run the scene again, with changes. No chance. Paloma would have decided he was a witless, gutless oaf.

And it had all started so well, her telling him he knew how to treat a woman. What a let-down.

The pity of it was that she was like no one he'd

met since Steph. The way she looked, spoke and moved appealed to him. She was bright and enthusiastic, successful, enterprising, a sympathetic listener, yet didn't take herself too seriously. She was willing to admit to things other women might try to conceal, like the husband who traded her in for the new model. And she'd given out signals that she quite liked being with him—or so he imagined. Women who felt comfortable with him were not plentiful. Most seemed to treat him as a 'man's man', a polite way of saying he was an ogre or a bore.

'Or a sad old fart,' he said aloud.

Self-pity wasn't the way to go. He reached for the light-switch and rolled out of bed. From the other end of the quilt Raffles raised his head briefly and lowered it again. The man was behaving erratically again. The time was all wrong for a feed.

Downstairs in the kitchen Diamond filled the kettle and tried to put his mind on other things. He looked at the *Guardian* crossword and decided this wasn't the time to make a start. Crosswords were Steph's thing, anyway. He'd thought of cancelling the paper. He didn't often open it these days.

He wondered if Paloma was a *Guardian* reader. The *Independent* was more her style, he decided. Bugger it, he thought. I'm down here because I want to stop thinking about the woman.

He poured the tea and stood looking out of the window at the moonlight on his small patch of lawn. Put your mind on something else, Diamond. Something simple and natural, like the wildlife out there.

143

Hedgehogs. From this window on one sleepless night he'd seen a family of them crawling among last year's leaves looking for slugs. He'd gone out with a torch and they hadn't run off.

His memories of hedgehogs were soon used up. Nature studies had never been a strong enthusiasm. Occasionally on the road at night he'd see foxes, badgers or deer, but he thought of them more as hazards to drivers than native mammals with their own right to existence. What else was there to distract him? His knowledge of nocturnal birds was limited to owls and nightingales and there weren't many of them in Lower Weston. So much for night creatures, then. He had little else to contemplate except flowers and so—with a sense that the fates would not give him a break— he was round to night-scented stocks.

Night-scented bloody stocks. There had to be a remedy for this or he wouldn't get any sleep at all.

The solution arrived with something of a jolt. He'd twice been treated to a meal by Paloma and not written a word to thank her. In his distracted state he'd neglected a common courtesy.

A letter now, a full week later, wasn't the way to go. What then? He really had to do something in the morning.

Flowers.

And with that decided, he returned to bed and had his best sleep for a week.

17

Orders from an assistant chief constable have to be obeyed. The incident room for the Delia Williamson murder had been stripped of computers and display boards and was restored to its former use as a briefing room. CID were back in their cramped quarters on the first floor. A new inquiry was under way into a ram raid in Combe Down in which two hundred state-of-the-art mobile phones had been taken. Stock lists were being studied, witness statements filed. Just about everyone was involved.

Some less than others.

When Diamond walked past her desk, Ingeborg said, 'Can you spare a minute, guv?'

'Come into my office then.'

'No. Could you pull up a chair?'

'I beg your pardon.' No one except Ingeborg had the face to speak to him like that.

'I'd like to show you something.'

At the back of the room Keith Halliwell got a laugh by saying, 'Know what I mean? Nudge, nudge. Say no more.'

Ignoring them, Diamond stood with arms folded looking over Ingeborg's shoulder at the computer screen. He spurned the invitation to sit beside her.

She pressed some keys. 'I thought I remembered something from a couple of years back, when I was stringing for the *News of the World*. So much has happened since then and I couldn't pinpoint what I wanted, so I started putting words into a search engine and up came this website that collects statistics of suicides. Isn't it fantastic?'

He gave it a glance. 'You can get this stuff from the Stationery Office.'

'But this has so much more. Look.' She highlighted a section of the screen. 'Name, age, method, location. Every case for every year this century. That's about twenty-five thousand suicides. I don't know who collects all this material, or why.'

'Or if it's accurate.'

'Lighten up, guv. I found what I was looking for, and I'm bloody sure I wouldn't have got it from the police computer.'

He didn't like detective constables telling him to lighten up. 'I haven't got all day. What have you found?'

'It may be just coincidence, but two years ago there was a double hanging here in Bath, wife and husband, separated by a couple of days. Their name was Twining, John and Christine Twining.' She found the names on the screen and highlighted them.

Diamond's annoyance evaporated at once. The flickering screen had all his attention.

Twining, Christine, 28, of Madras Villa, Hinton Charterhouse, Avon, on 26 July 2004, found hanging from a tree in Henrietta Park, Bath.

Twining, John Merson, 34, of Madras Villa, Hinton Charterhouse, Avon, on 28 July 2004, found hanging at Sham Castle, Claverton Down, Bath.

146

'What do you make of it?' Ingeborg asked.

He was making a whole new scenario out of it, yet trying to stay calm. Experience had taught him not to jump in with both feet. 'Double suicides happen.'

'Yes, but on our patch?'

'Sadly, yes.'

'Twice in two years?'

'Our case isn't quite the same, is it? Ours were unmarried and separated. Good spotting, even so,' he said, letting a little of his enthusiasm show. 'I must have read about this myself at the time. I can't think why it slipped my mind.'

'Two years ago your mind was on something else, guv.'

She didn't need to say what. For at least a year after Steph's murder he'd focused on that and nothing else: finding and charging the killer and seeing the judicial process through. 'Like you say, could be coincidence, but the fact that they both seem to have hanged themselves within a couple of days is odd.'

'And in the open, in public places.'

His pulse beat faster. He'd missed that. 'Good point. Have you looked this up in the newspaper files?'

'Not yet. I haven't had a chance.'

'Better do it.'

She turned and gave him the full beam of her wide blue eyes. 'If you remember, I'm supposed to be comparing witness statements for the ram raid.'

'Someone else can take that on. Anything you can dredge up on the Twinings. Find out who did the post-mortems and see if you can get hold of the reports. This is probably one huge red herring, but we can't ignore it.'

He strolled back into his office, trying to look as cool as he'd sounded while his thoughts galloped ahead. What was going on here? Two double suicides in two years on his patch? A copycat effect? He couldn't think why. The obvious assumption was that the two couples had something in common. Did they know each other? Had there been some kind of pact to take their own lives?

Impressionable people sometimes get drawn into oddball communities with a morbid sense of alienation from the world, like the Manson 'family' or the Jonestown community or the Waco crowd, falling under the influence of a dominant figure with a destructive urge. Things like that happened in California or Texas, places where screwy behaviour surprised no one. Was it conceivable that some cult such as this—with suicide as a laudable objective—was active in staid old Bath? He couldn't discount it. Even Bathonians were capable of weird behaviour.

*   *   *

Georgina stepped into his office soon after, wanting to know what progress he'd made on the ram raid. She looked as if she already knew the answer, so he decided to surprise her.

'Significant progress.'

He could have saved his breath.

'Because it's a shocking crime,' she went on. 'An incident like this alarms the public. Driving a vehicle into a shopfront is a violent act. Shops are vital to the local economy.'

'I know, ma'am,' he said. 'I use them myself ...
when I get the time.'

She wasn't listening. 'In a way it's an act of
rape.'

He raised his eyebrows at that. What a pig-
ignorant remark. If he'd come out with it she'd
have jumped on him from a great height, and
rightly. A ram raid was a ram raid and rape was
another class of crime, more selfish, more
cowardly and more despicable.

Georgina must have seen his expression
because she tried to justify what she'd said. 'In an
abstract sense, I mean. A rape of property. A
shopfront violated. I want these people arrested
and put away for a long time, Peter. Do you have
descriptions?'

'Not when I last checked. It happened at night.'

'Nothing on video?'

'No cameras.'

'Suspects?'

'More than enough.'

His phone buzzed.

'Pick it up,' Georgina said. 'It may be for me.'

The switchboard operator said, 'Personal for
you, sir.' And before he could deflect her he was
listening to Paloma.

'Peter, I hope you don't mind me calling you at
work, but this gorgeous basket of flowers just
arrived. How did you know I adore the scent of
freesias? And the message. So thoughtful. You
really didn't have to do this, but it's made my day.'

His own day was disintegrating. 'Actually,' he
said, 'I'm in a meeting.'

'Oh, trust me to pick the wrong moment!'

149

'Doesn't matter.'

'I'm so sorry.'

'Don't be.'

'Can I call back?'

'That would be nice.'

'This afternoon?'

'About two would be good.' He put down the phone. 'Sorry about that.'

Georgina couldn't have heard every word, but she would have a fair idea that the caller was female. She said, 'I hope you're giving this top priority.'

'What?'

She emitted a rasping sigh. 'The ram raid.'

'They're working on it at this minute, ma'am.'

'You say "they" as if you're not personally involved.'

'It's all part of the ongoing work of the CID. I do have other things on my plate.'

'Like those two hangings? I thought you'd have written your report and forgotten about them by now. You're like a dog with a bone. What were you doing taking a vanload of policemen out to Bathford?'

'We got a result—found the cave where Danny Geaves was holed up.'

'And how does that assist us?'

'Well, it's, em—' he was flapping around like a drowning man and they both knew it '- a guide to his state of mind.'

'For heaven's sake, Peter, we know he was suicidal.'

He dug deep for some dignity. 'If you remember, ma'am, on the day he died you woke me at six in the morning to go and investigate. I

150

took it to mean the matter was important.'

'Only because we can't have bodies hanging from bridges.'

'I understand now. Spoiling the scenery?'

'There's no need for sarcasm, Peter. The Geaves case was last week. We've moved on. I expect you to take a personal interest in the ram-raid inquiry. Is that understood?'

*   *   *

Ingeborg burst in a few minutes after. The excitement was in her eyes, her stance, her voice. 'The Twinings, guv.'

'Twinings?' He was bruised by Georgina's attack. A dog with a bone. Was that how she thought of her top detective?

'The couple who hanged themselves.'

'I wish they had another name,' he said. 'Makes me think of tea.'

'Guv, this is serious.'

'So am I. You can tell me downstairs.'

In the canteen, Ingeborg was on hot bricks. She started on about the case while they were in line at the self-service.

He muttered, 'Wait till we get to the table.' The canteen ladies were his friends, but they dispensed as much gossip as food and he didn't want it getting back to Georgina that he was checking on yet another double suicide.

'I've dug out the *Bath Chronicle* reports and it's the same pattern,' Ingeborg finally managed to tell him. 'There was no suicide note. They didn't do it together. The woman went first, and then the man, two days later. And this is the really

151

interesting bit. In those two days, nobody saw John Twining. He wasn't at home or at work. He disappeared off the radar—just like Danny Geaves.'

'Have you looked at the autopsy reports?

'Not yet. I've asked for them.'

'Who did the autopsies? Not our friend Sealy?'

'No, it was another name.'

'Bring them in as soon as they arrive. What else do we know about this couple? Was there anything in the papers about the people they mixed with?'

'I don't think so.'

'I'd be interested to know what sort of life they led. Were they part of any community?'

'Religious, do you mean?'

'Religious, hippy, drug-dependent. Get the drift? Some fringe group, alienated from society, that might have put them up to this.'

'Were Delia and Danny part of some cult?'

'That's what I'm asking,' he said. 'It's got to be considered. There's a new dimension now, Inge, and it's darker than I thought.'

*   *   *

On his return to the office after lunch he found an envelope on his desk. His name was on it.

'This is all I need,' he said to Leaman, who happened to look in.

'What's up?'

'Georgina's writing. Could be the old heave-ho.'

He was wrong. He found two theatre tickets inside. Georgina had attached a note saying, *Hope you can use these. It's one of my choir nights, unfortunately.*

A peace offering, he decided, with a whole new perspective on his boss. She'd been well out of order earlier and no doubt regretted it now.

Leaman asked, 'Something nice after all?'

'How did you guess? Close the door as you go out.' A smart idea had popped into his head. He looked up Paloma's number and called her.

She answered at once.

'Sorry about this morning,' he said. 'I had the dragon sitting in my office.'

'The lady boss? I'm sorry. Shouldn't have called on spec like that. Just wanted to thank you for—'

'You did,' he said. 'Look, I know you like the cinema, so I guess that goes for the theatre as well. I've been given a couple of tickets for the Theatre Royal tomorrow night and I thought we might do another restaurant afterwards. My chance to treat you for a change.'

'I'd really enjoy that,' she said. 'What's on?'

'Can't say I know it,' he said, 'but it sounds appropriate. *An Inspector Calls.*'

18

Later the same afternoon, Diamond took a trip to Norton St Philip and it had nothing to do with the ram raid. He'd asked John Leaman to drive him, leaving Halliwell in charge. Georgina wouldn't be overjoyed to hear that her top man was elsewhere, but she'd know his deputy was capable of progressing the investigation.

'You know what this is about?' he said to Leaman.

'The couple who hanged themselves a couple of years back? Ingeborg filled me in, guv.'

'I would have asked Inge along, but she's digging out files for me and she knows what she's got and what she hasn't. You and I are going to meet Harold Twining, the older brother. He's a teacher on leave of absence at the moment, suffering from stress. So we treat him gently, right?'

For all his fault-finding, Leaman had a sympathetic side that sometimes showed. After some thought, he said, 'Brute of a job, teaching. I wouldn't like it, facing a roomful of bolshie kids.'

'If the teacher's any good, the kids aren't bolshie. You remember that from when you went to school, don't you?'

'When I was at school they clipped you round the head if you messed about. Teachers have got no sanctions now.'

'They used the cane in my day. You favour corporal punishment, do you?'

'They had other methods,' Leaman said.

'Like what? Slinging blackboard rubbers at the kids? Cold showers? Those were the bad old days, John.'

'Didn't do me any harm.'

'So you end up in the police, whacking villains with batons. The old, old story.'

Leaman realised he'd walked into that one. 'Hey, what about you, guv? You're part of it.'

'Me? Haven't you noticed? I'm the Mr Chips of Bath nick.'

Leaman smiled and said no more on the matter. Presently they left the A36 and turned right. 'I'm in your hands now,' Leaman said.

154

'Took that to heart, did you, about me being a gentle soul?'

'What I'm saying is that this is Norton St Philip coming up and I don't know where we're meeting Harold Twining.'

'Do you know the George?'

Leaman nodded. Everyone who has been to Norton knows the George Inn, a mighty and magnificent pub said to have been built by the monks of Hinton Charterhouse. Samuel Pepys, Oliver Cromwell and the Duke of Monmouth stayed there, although not at the same time or Pepys' Diary might have had an interesting entry.

'He's waiting for us in the main bar,' Diamond said.

'Off school with stress and he goes to the pub?'

'Not much stress there.'

'Unless like me you happen to be the driver.'

They parked and went in and found a cheerful character at the bar telling a joke to a barmaid. They let him reach the punchline, which was, 'Don't laugh. You're next.' Then he turned and said, 'These must be my visitors. What's your tipple, gentlemen?'

'Mine's a draught bitter,' Diamond said. 'A pint. His will be lemonade. And you're ... ?'

'Skint,' said Harold Twining, 'so you've copped the first round.' He chuckled at his own wit and Diamond remembered a history teacher from his grammar school who had the same annoying habit. 'I hope you're on expenses,' Twining went on. 'I'd love to treat you, but I know my limitations. If you press me, I'll have the bitter as well.'

At Twining's suggestion—and Twining was

155

making all the running, but it probably eased his stress—they took their drinks out to the garden at the back. The pastel softness of the Somerset scenery was worth it. A groundsman was using the mower on the village cricket green beside the church and the smell of cut grass wafted up to them.

'Good to be alive, looking out at this,' Diamond said to get the conversation under way. It was a distortion of his true state of mind. Having just put his hand in his pocket for the drinks he didn't feel it was good to be alive at all.

'Is it?' Twining said. 'I'm used to it. Lived here all my life.'

'Do you teach here as well?'

'In Norton?' He rolled his eyes. 'Too close to home. Maths and physics at Frome.'

'When you're fit.'

'Quite.'

'How long have you been off work?' All thoughts of giving this freeloader a stress-free time had gone.

For the first time since their arrival, Harold Twining's smile deserted him. 'I thought you were here to talk about my brother.'

'We are. I'm being friendly. Can't dive straight in.'

'It doesn't sound friendly when the first thing you mention is my problem. People don't understand psychosomatic illness. It isn't obvious, like mumps or asthma, but it's just as real. Some of those buggers at work believe I'm having a high old time of it.'

'There's no accounting for human nature,' Diamond said and turned to Leaman. 'Did it cross your mind that Mr Twining was skiving off, John?'

'I take people as I find them, guv.'

'There you are.' Diamond smiled at Twining. 'Let's talk about your brother, then. And his wife. Because I understand it was a double tragedy.'

'Dreadful,' Twining said. 'Afterwards you ask yourself if you could have helped in some way, but I had no inkling they were so unhappy.'

'Were they?' Diamond said. 'You'll have to give us some background. We don't know the full circumstances.'

'I doubt if anyone did. The coroner couldn't work it out. Mentally my brother John was a hundred per cent and so was Chrissie. They had no money problems. Each of them was earning more than I ever will. Alpha people. You asked on the phone if I could bring a picture and I dug one out.' He took a postcard-sized photo from his pocket and flicked it across the table in a way that seemed to express his contempt for the couple.

Diamond picked it up. It had been taken with flash at some party. A good-looking couple with drinks in front of them. John Twining had receding hair and a thick moustache; she was blonde, the hair scrunched back. They both looked comfortable being photographed. The smiles weren't at all forced.

'What did they do?'

'She was a buyer for Marks and Spencer, a high-powered job. And John was an architect. They had a beautiful property he designed for himself in Hinton Charterhouse, just down the road from here. Holidays in the Caribbean, a sports car each. No kids. No ties, not even a budgie to look after.'

157

'They seem happy with each other in the photo.'

'I never saw a sign that they weren't.'

'So what was said at the inquest? How was it explained?'

'I don't think it was. The coroner came out with some claptrap about successful, wealthy people suddenly realising that their lives were vacuous. His word. *Vacuous.* It's not in my vocabulary. I can tell you what a vacuum is because I'm a physicist. But a vacuous life is an unscientific term. He reckoned they must have made a pact to put an end to themselves. He said if they'd had children, or even a dependent relative, they might have felt their lives had more purpose. I'll be honest with you, I would have volunteered to be a dependent relative. No problem.'

Diamond didn't need convincing of that. 'They left no note?'

'Nothing was ever found.'

'Did they write wills?'

'Yes, that was taken care of, but not as a last-minute thing. They'd drawn them up four years before they died. Everything went to charity except what the government took. I didn't get a penny.'

'Were they religious?'

'John and Chrissie? The only thing they believed in was their bank account. They might have gone to the Christmas midnight service, but you do in a village. It's a social thing.'

'Is it possible that they wanted a child and couldn't have one?'

'Another misguided theory. She had a baby stopped a year after they married. They "slipped up", John told me. No question they could have started a family if they'd wanted.'

'So do you have a theory of your own?'

'I can tell you why my brother took his life. He was heartbroken after Chrissie hanged herself. It's obvious, isn't it? But what her problem was, I haven't the faintest. As I said, I always thought of her as sensible.'

'She wasn't in trouble at work?'

'No. The coroner read out a statement from Marks and Spencer. They valued her contribution. She was going to be difficult to replace. Stuff like that.'

'Did she have family—parents, siblings?'

'She was Australian.'

'Even Australians have parents.'

'What I mean is that they were half the world away. Nothing was said about them troubling her.'

'She hanged herself in Henrietta Park, I understand. That's the one at the back of Great Pulteney Street. Why would she choose there?'

'You mean why didn't she go to another park? Don't know. Because she knew of it, I suppose. She'd walk a lot in her lunch breaks, the only exercise she had time for. She was found hanging from a tree. They tried to inform John, but he'd gone missing. They got onto me, and I couldn't tell them anything. We weren't close. He was found up at Sham Castle two days later, as you probably know. My guess is that he knew what she'd done. Maybe she left him a note. He was so shocked that he simply walked around in a dazed state and finally decided he couldn't face life without her.'

'Was Sham Castle a place he knew well?'

159

'No idea. You know what it is, literally a sham. You're meant to see it from down in the city and think it's a real castle when all it is is a facade. As an architect he may have been making some sort of point.'

'What sort of point, Mr Twining?'

'About his life being empty.'

'Vacuous,' Leaman said.

Twining frowned and said, 'What did you say?'

'Never mind,' Diamond said with a glare at Leaman.

But Twining didn't take offence. He'd launched into yet another theory. 'Some time after it happened I heard the old story of why Sham Castle was put there.'

'As a *trompe l'oeil*?' Leaman said.

'Come again,' Diamond said. His sidekick might need a kick if he carried on like this.

'An eye-catcher, anyway.'

'That's only part of the story,' Harold Twining said. 'Ralph Allen, the quarry owner who provided the stone for Regency Bath, had it built on the skyline so he could see it from his town house. Everyone knows that much. But local tradition has it that he had the thing built for another reason—this was in the seventeen-hundreds, remember—to conceal a dead highwayman hung in chains on a gibbet. By law the corpse was left dangling there as a warning. Ralph Allen thought it was gross, but he couldn't change the law, so he did the next best thing and screened it off with his so-called castle.'

'Is that well known?' Diamond asked.

'Not to me until I heard about it from some Job's comforter. My brother may have known the story.'

'And decided to go up there out of some sense of history?'

'Or affinity with the highwayman?' Leaman said, and got another glare from his boss.

Twining shrugged. 'Your guess is as good as mine.'

Diamond didn't want to leave it there. 'Most people who take their own lives do it in private. I get the impression from all you've said that your brother and his wife kept to themselves.'

'True. If you want to be a success you don't have much time for other people unless you're making money out of them.'

'They didn't do drugs?'

'What's that got to do with it?' Harold Twining then proceeded to answer his own question. 'Oh, I see. You think they might have been out of their skulls when they did it? Well, it didn't show up in their blood. Nothing was found in the post-mortem or we'd have heard about it at the inquest.'

'Do you recall who the pathologist was?'

'No, except he seemed to know the coroner. It's an old-boy network, the coroner's court. Pathologists, expert witnesses. They go through the motions while the family sits there listening in horror.'

'How well did you know your sister-in-law?'

Harold Twining hesitated, as if playing the question over to himself. 'Tolerably well.'

'Then you'll probably know if she had friends of her own, apart from her husband.'

'I get you now,' he said. 'For a moment I thought you were suggesting I had a fling with her.

161

You want to know if she got in with the wrong crowd. No, like I told you, Chrissie was a career woman. She didn't have time to join a coven. I'm sure the old black magic is rampant in Bath, but that's another false trail. We Twinings are a dull old lot.'

There wasn't much more to be got from this obnoxious man. They didn't stand him another drink. Before leaving, Leaman said, 'By the way, you were telling a joke when we came in.'

'What was that? I've forgotten.'

'I think the punchline was, "Don't laugh. You're next." But what was the joke?'

'That one? It's the one about the Irish guy whose wife discovers him holding a pistol to his head. Get it?'

19

'For simplicity's sake, if a certain person should come in,' Diamond said, 'we're discussing the ram raid. Understood?'

It was Friday morning and he had called his senior detectives—Halliwell and Leaman—to his office. They knew who the 'certain person' was. They also knew the topic he was refusing to abandon.

'This double hanging.'

'The Twinings,' Halliwell said.

'You've been keeping up, then?'

'Can't say I know a lot.' But his tone said plenty. It told Diamond he was piqued at being sidelined on the ram raid while Leaman seemed to be taking over as number two on the team

'There isn't a lot. Married couple found in Bath two years ago. Made no big impact at the time. Ingeborg picked it up.'

'She's a bright kid.'

'I know, but I don't want to talk about Ingeborg. I want your thoughts on what appears to be going on. There's enough in common with the deaths of Williamson and Geaves to persuade me that the incidents are related.'

'Seems a possibility,' Halliwell said with a shrug.

'I'd put it stronger than that. In each case, the woman dies first, the man goes missing for a day or so and then his body is found. Each of these hangings was in the open, in a place people were sure to notice. Public parks, the railway viaduct and Sham Castle. Most people choosing to hang themselves do it at home or at work, not in a public place. No suicide notes were left. The ages of the victims were similar.'

'And it happened on our patch,' Leaman said.

Diamond gave him a sharp look, suspicious that he was being sarcastic. 'I thought that was self-evident.'

'But statistically significant,' Leaman said. 'If the Twinings had been found in South Shields, we wouldn't be sitting here talking about them.'

'True,' he said without gratitude. 'Let's get to why we're here. Do we agree that the post-mortem evidence on Delia Williamson points to murder?'

'Are you thinking the Twining woman may have gone the same way?' Halliwell said.

'If she did, it's less obvious.' He picked up a file.

'These are the autopsy reports on the Twinings. There's no suggestion that Christine Twining was strangled first, no ligature mark other than the inverted 'V' pattern you get with a hanging.'

'Who was the pathologist, guv?'

'A Dr Shinwari. Anyone know him? I don't.'

There was no response.

'His report comes across as careful and thorough. I can't believe he would have missed a double set of marks like those found on Delia Williamson.'

'So we take it that Christine Twining died by hanging?'

'That was Dr Shinwari's conclusion.'

'And the husband went the same way?'

'Yes. And Dr Shinwari did both autopsies.'

Halliwell said in a mystified tone, 'Where does this take us, guv? You're leaving me behind.'

Diamond raised his palms, appealing for patience. He would explain if they would listen. 'It's easy to assume Christine Twining hanged herself. That's what the coroner decided. But with hindsight—with the knowledge we have that Delia Williamson was murdered—we can make another hypothesis. We can ask ourselves the question you put a moment ago: was Christine Twining murdered, too?'

Now it was Leaman who was frowning. 'The cases aren't the same. You just said there weren't any secondary marks.'

Diamond sighed. He was being sniped at from both sides. 'Agreed. I'm not suggesting both women went the same way. We'll come to that. I'm saying it's worth investigating whether Christine's wasn't a voluntary hanging.'

164

Halliwell screwed up his face in distaste. 'The husband strung her up? Nasty.'

It was as if Diamond himself had offended by imagining such a gruesome act. But he wasn't going to retract. 'We believe Danny Geaves killed Delia, so why shouldn't John Twining have murdered Christine?'

'There's no evidence.'

'Oh, come on. We're working backwards here. I just listed all the circumstantial evidence linking the incidents.'

'Yes, but . . .' Leaman's protest ended in a sigh. Diamond wasn't doing enough to persuade his senior men.

'Look at it this way. Twining did the thing as it was intended, hanged his wife and later hanged himself. Danny Geaves botched it. He planned to do the same, only Delia put up a fight. Instead of hanging her he was forced to strangle her. Then he faked the hanging.'

'I'm not sure I follow you,' Halliwell said. 'You're suggesting both women were murdered and the men committed suicide?'

'That's right. But John Twining was more efficient and the murder was passed off as suicide.'

'It's a whopping great assumption, guv. Is there anything in the autopsy report to back it up?'

'There wouldn't be.'

Halliwell shifted in his chair, unwilling to concede. 'I was trained to understand murder in terms of motive, means and opportunity. What's the motive here? You spoke to John Twining's brother. Did he know of any problems between the couple?'

In his head Diamond played over the question and answer from that session in the George. He'd remarked that in the photo they'd seemed happy with one another. *'I never saw a sign that they weren't,'* was the reply.

'Not really,' he was forced to admit, 'but he couldn't understand why they were suicidal.'

'They hadn't separated, or anything?'

'No. That's a clear difference from Geaves and his partner. Delia had found a new man and it's understandable if Danny harboured a grudge.'

'I don't want to be awkward,' Halliwell said, 'but I think you've got to find a motive before you cast John Twining as a wife-murderer.'

Diamond was silent, forced to recognise the truth of what Halliwell was saying. There was more work to be done.

Then Leaman said, 'Even if your theory is right, why should Danny Geaves want to try the same thing two years later?'

'That's the next big question,' Diamond said. 'All right, fellows. You've given me plenty to think on.'

After they'd closed the door, he brooded on the matter. Halliwell and Leaman were good detectives and he hadn't persuaded them. They were reluctant even to speculate.

He picked up the phone. 'How do I get hold of a certain pathologist, Dr Manzoor Shinwari, who did the autopsies on a couple of suicides two years back?'

He was asked to wait. They would call him back.

When the call came, it wasn't what he wanted to hear. Dr Shinwari had returned to Pakistan

166

eighteen months ago and there was no contact address.

20

One thing you could say for Peter Diamond: nothing would grind him down. Dr Shinwari might have left the country, but there was always Jim Middleton. Why hadn't Jim been in touch? He'd had ample time to read those reports.

His mobile number was on the back of an envelope.

'Damn you,' Jim said. 'I should have turned the bloody thing off. I'm in Starbucks, enjoying a quiet moment here.'

'Well, I'm not. I'm working,' Diamond said. 'Are you alone?'

'At this minute, yes, but one of my friends could arrive any time.'

'So we can talk. What did you think of those autopsy reports?'

'Look, this is hardly the place.'

'Do you want speak from the toilet?'

'I draw the line at that.'

'I wouldn't worry, anyway. I've overheard some amazing conversations in coffee shops. What have you got to tell me?'

Jim must have sensed that the man was unstoppable. He started to open up. 'I have to say there isn't much to quibble over. He seems to have done a workmanlike job in both cases. Not everyone provides the kind of detail Bertram Sealy gives you.'

This wasn't what Diamond had hoped to hear. 'You agree with his conclusions, then?'

'Can't fault him.' Jim paused, probably to look round and see who might be listening, then lowered his voice. 'There's no question the woman was murdered, strangled first and strung up later. And the man was hanged from the railway bridge, just as Sealy suggests.'

'You say there isn't much to quibble over. Is there anything?'

There was another hesitation. 'Almost every autopsy has its points of interest.'

'And you found some?'

'You gave me both reports to read, so I had the advantage of an overview. Sealy dealt with each case in isolation. Quite properly.'

This was all too cagey for Diamond. 'I gave you both reports for a reason, Jim. I want that overview.'

'I know. And what I say to you, Peter, is that any pathologist worthy of the name treats each autopsy as a separate event, and that's what Sealy has done. It's not a good principle to go into the dissection room with ideas of what you might expect to find.'

'Point taken. What have you got for me?'

'In no way is this a criticism of a colleague.'

'You've made that very clear. You're simply suggesting lines of inquiry.'

Jim sounded happier with that. 'Right. You're the SIO and your job is different from his. He presents you with his findings and you weigh them with all the other evidence you have. You're dealing with both incidents, aren't you?'

'I was until I got told to wrap up the case.'

'You saw both bodies in situ?'

Now Diamond hesitated, reminded of his own refusal to climb into the cherry picker at the viaduct. He could at least claim he'd been at the scene and viewed the suspended body from below. 'I did.'

'Did you get close up?'

'Close enough. At the second incident they cut the man down and I saw him on a stretcher.'

'The cord was still in place?'

'Yes, they cut it and left it knotted round the neck, if that's what you're asking.'

'Notice anything special about that second corpse?'

He tried picturing it in his mind, unzipping the body bag. His overriding concern at the time had been to identify the body as Danny Geaves. 'I give up. What should I have spotted?'

'Did you look at the knot?'

'The knot?'

'That's what I said.'

'I'm trying to remember. You'd better help me.'

'He used a slip knot. That's of interest because it wasn't a slip knot in the first incident. The woman was suspended from a loop with a fixed knot. You got the characteristic mark on the neck rising to a peak at the knot. That was why it was apparent that she'd been strangled previously with a ligature.'

'Two sets of marks.'

'Exactly. Hold on. I think someone is coming to this table.'

Diamond found himself listening to a commentary on movements in the coffee shop.

'No, they're going past. They've seen me using

169

the mobile. Wait, they're coming back, I think. It's all right, they just wanted to borrow a chair. Do you know what I mean by a slip knot? It's a running noose, as distinct from a fixed one. When a slip knot is used, and the cord takes the weight of the body, the noose tightens. The ligature mark is different. It runs right round the neck. Follow me?'

'Because there's no slack?'

'Correct.'

'Why would he use a different knot the second time?'

'This is where the pathologist shuts up and lets the detective take over. Our job isn't to answer questions like that. We report what we find. Bertram Sealy has done that.'

Diamond closed his eyes, concentrating hard. He knew Jim Middleton was hinting at something without wanting to compromise a professional colleague. 'Can we look at this another way? If he'd used a slip knot when he suspended the woman from the swing, it could have covered the mark of the strangling, and we wouldn't have known she was murdered.'

'That's if the rope was tight all the way round the neck and covered the original ligature mark.'

'So how can we be sure the second death was a genuine hanging?'

'The vertebrae were broken in the mid-cervical section of the spine. That's what you expect from a hanging involving a drop. A judicial hanging will produce the same result.'

'So the point of interest, as you put it, is the knot. Was there any need for a slip knot?'

'Whatever knot he used, the outcome would

have been the same.'

'A quick death?'

'Very.'

'I'll need to think about this some more.'

'That's up to you. And sod you, Peter Diamond. My coffee's gone cold.'

And the shop had probably emptied, too.

*　　　*　　　*

Halliwell came in after lunch looking as if he'd won the lottery. There was a breakthrough on the ram raid. An informant had fingered a pair of villains called Romney and Jacob who were well advanced on plans for a second raid.

'Is this reliable, Keith?'

'It sounds kosher to me.'

'Who's the grass?'

'A new guy, name of Gary Jackman. He's got a record for doing up stolen vehicles. Moved into the area last Christmas. He figures that if he puts new plates on a four-by-four that's going to be driven into a shopfront there's a fair chance something will go wrong.'

'Such as the front plate falling off?'

'Right, and if we don't get him, the villains will, for messing up.'

'Who did they use last time?'

'Nobody. They nicked the vehicle the same night from outside the technical college. This time they want to limit the uncertainty so they knocked off a Range Rover last weekend and asked Jackman to give it a new identity. He's not happy.'

'Yes, but what does he want from us?'

'A blind eye to his activities.'

171

'What, for ever more? That's ridiculous. We can trade leniency, but not carte blanche.'

'We'll make that clear, then.'

'See that he goes on the register. Every meeting and transaction. Who's handling him for us?'

'Our new boy. Paul Gilbert.'

'Gilbert made the contact?' This was worrying, the most junior member of CID.

'Yes.'

'Good lad. What's the plan?'

'Ours or theirs?'

'Both.'

'They want the Range Rover ready for Sunday night, according to Jackman. We don't yet know which shop they're targeting.'

'Nothing is simple in this game.'

'If we find out, we'll have a reception committee waiting. We'll bug the vehicle anyway and have a high presence on Sunday.'

'What about Romney and Jacob? Do they have form?'

'Not as ram raiders. Jacob may have done some stuff as a juvenile, petty theft mostly, but it's possible it was someone else of the same name. They're not out of their teens yet. This is new territory for them.'

'Sounds like it. Rank amateurs.'

'Do you want Georgina in the loop?'

Diamond thought for a moment and grinned. 'Not yet. Let's surprise her. Sunday night I reckon she puts her feet up and watches the *Antiques Roadshow*. We'll put on a roadshow of our own.'

21

This time he took a taxi up to Lyncombe. Paloma was ready and looking like one of the nominees on Oscars night, her cleavage framed by a white pashmina. Diamond told her she looked stunning, and meant it. He was glad he'd put on a suit and tie, but now wished the tie wasn't just the Met Rugby Club stripes.

He was holding a cardboard box marked Heinz. 'This is not what it may appear,' he told her. 'These are for Jerry's hospital trolley.' He'd remembered to bring Steph's Agatha Christie collection.

'That's so generous. If you leave them in the hall he'll pick them up next time he comes by.'

In the taxi she gave his hand a squeeze. 'This is a lovely idea.' The embarrassment of their last evening together wasn't showing at all.

'I can't claim any credit,' he said. 'The tickets were passed on to me by my boss.'

'The dragon?'

'Georgina, yes.'

'She doesn't breathe fire all the time, then?'

'Once in a blue moon she surprises me with something like this. Maybe there's a payback that I'll learn about later.'

Sooner, as it turned out.

At the theatre they bought a programme and chocolates and went to the bar for a drink and heard the announcement telling people the performance would begin in ten minutes. When they presented their tickets the usher asked them

173

to step to one side. A tall, thin man appeared from nowhere and said, 'Ah, you must be the real inspector.'

Diamond raised an eyebrow.

The man said, 'It's no mystery. We know from the ticket number. I'm Charles Fetherington-Steel, publicity director. You are Inspector—'

'Detective Superintendent actually. Diamond is my name. And this is Mrs Paloma Kean.'

'I was promised an inspector,' Fetherington-Steel said as if he'd got second best. 'Never mind. The main thing is that you're from the police. I'm sorry to be such a pain, but the photographer wants his shots before the performance starts. You know what the press are like. If you'd kindly step this way, we'll get it over with, and then you can take your seats.'

'Nobody told me about a photograph,' Diamond said.

'Oh, I'm sure I told Miss Assisi. We definitely need some shots. It was made very clear.'

'I don't know a Miss Assisi.'

'If I were you, I'd make a point of getting to know her,' Fetherington-Steel said. 'She makes the decisions at the police station. Ah, here he is, camera at the ready. It's quite painless, officer. Relax and give him a smile.'

Diamond stiffened and gave him a scowl. 'Sorry about this,' he said to Paloma. 'I'm not sure what it's about, but I think I've been set up.'

'Let me fix your tie. It's coming loose.' As she stepped close she said in an undertone, 'A smile doesn't cost anything, Pete.'

If she had not been there, they wouldn't have seen him for dust. He didn't want another

174

blighted evening, so he stood beside a pillar and submitted to the camera, even managing a twisted grin.

'Much better. All done,' Fetherington-Steel said, beckoning to the usher. 'There's champagne for you both in the interval. The patrons' room.'

Their seats were the best in the house, in the centre of the front row of the lower circle. No time to talk. The curtain went up at once, as if the entire production had been waiting for them. Pity the poor players because Diamond took in very little of what was happening on stage. His mind was on what had just happened and might yet happen.

*   *   *

'Isn't it gripping?' Paloma said when the interval lights came up. 'I'm hooked. Is he behaving like a real inspector?'

'Shall we skip the champagne with the patrons and have our own later?' he said. 'If we move out in the other direction we can give the tall man the slip.'

'You're wicked.'

They went downstairs and bought drinks in the crush bar and took in some fresh air by one of the exit doors. 'What was that all about when we arrived?' he said.

'The photography? It's just a publicity stunt, I imagine,' Paloma said. 'They want to get something in the *Chronicle* about a real inspector calling. No harm in it, is there?'

'Someone at the nick should have warned me.'

'That would have spoilt their fun.'

She was right. He remembered showing the tickets to Leaman. The bastard hadn't let on. They were all in on it, no doubt.

'I'm trying to think who Miss Assisi is,' he said. 'I can't place her. She's the one he spoke to.'

'I'd leave it if I were you. Think what you're going to say about the play.'

He swallowed hard. 'What do you mean?'

'They've got your picture. They'll want a decent quote to go under it.'

'The newspaper?'

'There's sure to be a reporter waiting for you when we come out and I don't think we should turn our backs on them. Don't upset the press. You never know when you might need them.'

Wise words, but now he had a moment of panic. 'I haven't been giving a lot of thought to the play.'

'It's still unfolding, isn't it? This inspector is investigating a poor girl's suicide, or so it appears, and nearly all the characters seemed to contribute in some way. You might want to say that real crimes have to pin the blame on one individual, but here the guilt is spread more widely.'

'That sounds good. Could you write it down?'

'Better if you put it in your own words. Mind, I have a feeling that the whole play could swing around in the second half.'

'I'm not sure if I'm up to this.'

'You are. Think of your workmates in the police opening their papers and finding you carried it off like a professional critic. A couple of sentences will do it. You'll have the last laugh.'

He watched the second half as if his career depended on it, paying close attention to Inspector Goole and his domineering presence.

176

There were procedural details that grated, but of course the play was written more than sixty years ago and referred back to a much earlier period, before the first world war. Who knows whether detectives worked alone or in pairs in those days? Anyway, as the tension built and the inspector's questioning increasingly took a moral tone it became clear that Paloma's 'or so it appears' was a crucial insight. Everything was not as it appeared. This inspector was acting more like a judge than a policeman.

The last line of the play confirmed that something very weird had been going on. The Bath police theatre critic wasn't sure how to take it, or if it could be explained, or needed to be. Probably not. The story was satisfying in a bigger sense.

'Clever,' he said to Paloma over the applause.

'Terrific,' she said. 'Have you thought of what to say?'

'I'm trying.'

'That inspector's an enigma.'

'I can use that.'

As they came down the steps to the foyer, Fetherington-Steel was at the side, waving. He had a young woman beside him, notebook at the ready. As soon as the introductions were over and she was about to start on her questions, Diamond said, 'I'll have to be brief because we have a table booked at Woods, but you don't need much, do you? A fascinating play, brilliantly done. Inspector Goole wouldn't last long in the modern police, but then he isn't modern and he isn't a policeman. He's an inspector in a different sense.'

'What?' the reporter said. 'Inspecting the

corruption of a society that puts profit and self-interest at the top of its priorities?'

'You took the words out of my mouth. He's a wily old fox, but if he was in my squad, I'd keep him in the back room. Will that do?'

'Couldn't be better,' she said. 'I'll just get your name and make sure I spell it right.'

*   *   *

In Woods, Paloma said, 'You socked it to them. You were great.'

'I forgot to mention the enigma bit.'

'You didn't need to. You said it in your own words.'

They ordered and the champagne was brought to the table and uncorked.

'To the drama critic,' Paloma said.

'For one night only.' They sipped, and he said, 'It's odd. Just now I'm investigating suicides in my real job. I go about it rather differently, though. A lot of background stuff, pathologists' reports and so on.'

'I expect you talk to the families like he did.'

'Not exactly like he did, but yes. It's part of the job. And the relatives aren't always as you expect them to be. That's one good thing about my life. I meet all sorts.'

'I didn't think suicides needed investigating.'

'We have to make sure they weren't homicides.'

'Oh.'

'Sorry. Not the best topic for an evening out.'

'I don't mind that,' she said. 'I'm not squeamish. Police work interests me. I watch a lot of police series on television. It's more exciting

178

than historic costumes, though I do get excited when I find some illustrations I didn't know existed.'

'Where do you find them?'

'In auctions sometimes. And second-hand bookshops. The ones I like are the really disorganised smelly old shops with cartons filled with stuff they haven't even bothered to unpack and put a price on. We don't have any left like that in Bath.'

'No treasures, then?'

'Hardly ever. But let's not talk about work. Are you going to spend the night with me?'

He wasn't sure how he reacted except that his answer was slow in coming. He hoped he hadn't gone slack-jawed or turned white. She'd surprised him totally. The possibility of sex was somewhere in his mind, but after the debacle in her garden he'd not been able to imagine how it would happen. Certainly he hadn't expected it as a question over dinner. Finally all he could manage was, 'Wow.'

She smiled. 'Can I take that as a yes?'

'A strong yes.'

'That's all right, then. We can enjoy our meal without all the stress of wondering what will happen after we leave the restaurant. Now let's talk about something else. What's the tie you're wearing? It looks as if it represents something.'

You had to be mentally agile to keep up with Paloma. He told her about his rugby playing until the starters were served. They talked sport for a while, and over the main course covered holidays abroad (she'd travelled widely) and motoring in Britain. They chose to miss the dessert. He settled the bill and the waiter phoned for their taxi.

During the drive back, Paloma leaned towards him and nestled her head against his shoulder. 'Did you bring your toothbrush?'

'I wasn't that confident,' he said.

She laughed. 'I bought you one in Boots this morning.'

In the house when the door was closed, she reached for him and they kissed, tentatively at first, and then as if they meant it.

She picked up a remote control and there was music and they held each other like dancers, swaying rather than taking steps. They kissed again, several times. Then she made coffee and poured liqueurs, hers a crème de menthe, his a brandy.

'A suggestion,' she told him. 'We're not all that young and let's face it, we're not the perfect shape, either of us. Showering together might not be the turn-on we'd like it to be. I'm going upstairs presently. My bedroom is the last door on the left. There's a shower for you in the room opposite if you want. Let's meet in my bed with the light turned really low.'

'You've twisted my arm,' he said.

22

There was no 'How was it for you?' The joy they both experienced was obvious. After the setbacks in their dating, it was a mercy that the sex went so well. For Diamond, nerves could have spoilt the occasion after three years of self-imposed celibacy. Paloma appeared to sense what was in his mind and coaxed him through with tact, affection and even a little humour. Afterwards they said nothing, held hands, murmured a little and slept.

He woke to the sound of a phone.

Assuming—as you do—that he was in his own bed, his first thought was that Georgina was on the line again and another hanging had been discovered. But when he reached for the phone it wasn't there. The sound was coming from behind him and he realised where he was. Surely Bath nick hadn't tracked him here?

Paloma didn't seem to have heard. Or maybe she hoped the caller would give up. Finally she said, 'This early?' and reached for it.

Diamond lay still, unsure what to do, half expecting the call was for him.

But she was listening with an intensity that told him this was someone whose voice she recognised at once. Difficult. You don't listen to other people's private calls. To have got out of bed and left the room didn't seem appropriate either.

Going by the concern in Paloma's voice, it didn't matter who was overhearing her. Someone was in trouble. 'What's up?' she was saying. 'There's something wrong. I can hear it in your voice.'

After a pause she said, 'What—stolen, darling? Where was it?'

The 'darling' confirmed that the call couldn't be for him. But he didn't relax. He sensed that this darling wasn't a woman friend.

'Have you reported it?' she went on. 'You've got to report it.'

Now she was talking like a parent and he guessed she was speaking to her son, the fitness trainer.

'Yes, of course, darling. You can't manage without. Come and collect it. If I want one I can rent it . . . . Yes . . . Oh, what a pain. Why do people do this kind of thing? . . . Yes, as soon as you like. I'm here.' She put down the phone.

'Your son?' Diamond said.

'Jerry, yes. Someone stole his car from Broad Street last night. Isn't it appalling? He's going to have to borrow mine. He can't do his job without transport. He has to visit his clients in their homes.'

'Do you want me to leave?'

'Not at all. You're better placed to advise him than I am.'

He said, 'I meant that you might not want Jerry to know I spent the night with you.'

She laughed. 'I'm not ashamed. Let him know his mother isn't past all that.'

So two lovers who could have been basking in the warmth of their intimacy were transformed into counsellors for a crime victim. They rose, showered and got ready. In the bathroom Diamond found not only the promised new toothbrush but a disposable razor and shaving cream.

By the time Jerry arrived they were finishing breakfast—a light one of cereal, toast and coffee. Everyone tried to be cool.

'You guys have met, of course,' Paloma said.

'Bad luck about the car,' Diamond said.

Jerry's eyes had widened for one moment at the sight of Diamond at the breakfast table, but he responded warmly enough. 'Thanks. I guess it's a risk you run, parking on a city street at night—with a decent motor, anyway.'

Diamond had never measured his success by the cars he owned, but he could sympathise with a young man who'd worked hard for his status symbol and still made time to do hospital work. 'I noticed it on the drive when I was here before. A blue Nissan four-by-four, right?'

'The Pathfinder. My pride and joy. Cost me thirty grand, with some generous help from mother, bless her.' He sighed. 'What a waste. I haven't had it five minutes.'

'What time did it go missing?'

'Late evening. I was eating with friends. I came back round about midnight.'

'You reported it?'

'Right away. Your people said it could be kids joyriding and it might be found abandoned somewhere.'

'That's a possibility. Did you call the station again this morning?'

'Yep. They've heard nothing.' He ran a distracted hand through his hair and gripped the back of his neck. 'What if it isn't kids? People steal cars and sell them on, don't they?'

'That could happen, too,' Diamond said, thinking something else. This wasn't the moment to mention that four-by-fours are the chosen vehicles for ram raids. 'Do you know the chassis number?'

'Got a note of it somewhere.'

'Look it up and let us know. Car thefts are handled by someone else at the nick, but when I get in I'll see if there's anything I can find out.

Sometimes you get reports of bad driving on the motorway and that can be joyriders.'

Paloma said, 'It's a damned shame it gets called joyriding. Sounds like something glamorous when in reality it's a shabby little crime and bloody dangerous as well.'

Jerry drank some coffee and said he'd better leave. Paloma handed him her car keys. In the hallway, he called out, 'Are these Agatha Christies for me?'

'No,' Diamond called back. 'They're for people in hospital.'

'Appreciate it.'

The door slammed.

'He does, too. He's very committed to this voluntary work,' Paloma said to Diamond when they were alone again. 'You never know what's going to happen, do you?'

'Could have been worse,' he said. 'He had the good sense not to call you last night.'

She smiled. 'We'd have really felt jinxed, wouldn't we? Thanks for being patient with him. In a strange way I think this may do Jerry some good, having something go wrong. We all need challenges.'

'What do you mean?'

'It's me being overconcerned, I expect. I wish he'd get a proper job, a career, I mean.'

'What's a proper job? The civil service? They get laid off in thousands by each new government. Jerry went through college for what he's doing. And he must have worked damned hard to get clients and keep them. If I'm any judge, he's got life worked out. And all those evenings at the hospital show he has a social conscience.'

'He has that all right. Church every Sunday, which is more than I manage.'

'So will he disapprove of me being here?'

'Don't worry. I've disappointed him plenty of times and we're still talking.' She put her hand to her mouth and gave a nervous laugh. 'Oh, dear, that sounds as if I've had a string of lovers and I didn't mean that. I disappoint Jerry in other ways like spending too much on clothes. He gives me the occasional text to think about. "Consider the lilies of the field . . ." et cetera. It's a hoot, isn't it, getting told how to behave by your son?'

' 'Specially if you carry on in your own sweet way.'

'Exactly.'

He looked at the time. 'I'd better report in. They haven't been able to reach me since yesterday.'

'Don't you carry a mobile?'

'Me?' He just laughed.

'What's funny about that?'

'I'm out of the age of the dinosaurs.'

'But you're a senior policeman.'

'Yeah. Superintendent Flintstone.'

'You ought to overcome that. They're really useful. Essential almost.'

'I can't disagree with you after all that's happened, but they strike me as the end of civilisation as I know it, all those idiots walking along the street with their hands to their ears broadcasting to all and sundry.'

'Peter, that's not the point. Mobiles have their advantages.'

'I haven't discovered any yet.'

'Like being in contact.'

185

'I don't always want to be in contact. Last night I didn't want to be in contact. When your phone went this morning I was bricking it in case my colleagues had traced me to your house.'

'They hadn't.'

He nodded and smiled. 'That's why I don't use a mobile.'

'You don't see it, do you?' she said with amusement. 'When someone calls you on a mobile they don't know where you are. If you want to stay over with me another time—as I hope you will— you can make calls and take calls and they'll assume you're speaking from home. For a man with a complicated private life it's the indispensable aid.'

The man with a complicated private life cradled his chin as if deep in thought. 'There's a flaw somewhere, but you're very persuasive. And I had better go into work. They'll be cockahoop to find out how I got on at the theatre.'

'I could tell them,' Paloma said. 'You're almost as good a drama critic as you are in bed.'

'I'm not sure how to take that.'

'It's a compliment. When can I see you again?'

'One day next week?'

'Early next week—yes?'

23

Against all his expectation, no one asked how his theatre visit had gone. Frustrating. He'd have told them loftily to buy the evening edition of the *Chronicle*. All he got was the usual 'Morning, guv'.

186

Better apply himself to the main job. On the pad on his desk he'd written *KNOTS?* as a reminder of what he'd heard from Jim Middleton. But he didn't need reminding. The slip knot employed by Danny Geaves to hang himself was a puzzle. All the evidence suggested that Danny strangled his ex-partner Delia before stringing her up on the swing to give the appearance of a hanging. He'd used a conventional noose for her. So why use a different knot to hang himself?

Danny's curious behaviour couldn't be considered in isolation. The Twining couple had employed a noose. Ingeborg was right about the Twinings. There were enough points in common to make it a racing certainty that there was a link with the deaths of Delia and Danny.

'The obvious explanation for the deaths of the Twinings is a suicide pact,' he said to Halliwell and Leaman, freshly updated on the mystery of the slip knot. 'They became convinced that they must die. Let's leave aside the reason for the moment. The Twinings did it as planned, or nearly so. They hanged themselves in the conventional way except that the man delayed his suicide by a couple of days.'

'Just like Danny,' Leaman said.

'But there's a difference.'

'Danny murdered her,' Halliwell said.

'Apparently, yes, but I had something else in mind.'

'They were no longer a couple,' Leaman said. 'She'd found a new partner, so they wouldn't have made a pact.'

'You've got it. Now try this for size. Danny—like the Twinings—has this death wish and for some reason believes Delia should go with him. She agrees to meet him without realising what is being planned. She resists and he strangles her. Quick change of plan. It was supposed to be a hanging, so he fakes it. Three days later—just like John Twining—he hangs himself.'

'Using a slip knot,' Halliwell said. 'Why use a different knot?'

'He should have used the slip knot on Delia,' Leaman said. 'Then we might not have found out she was strangled.'

Diamond was thinking back to the morning he'd led the party up that steep climb in Bathford. 'When we found the cave where he was sleeping rough there were fragments of a newspaper in the ashes of that fire.'

'The *Mail*,' Halliwell said.

'For the day before he died.'

Neither of them had twigged.

Diamond said, 'I gave a press conference the day before that and the nationals all carried the story. That issue of the *Mail* told Danny we were treating Delia's death as murder.'

'Are you thinking he read the report and decided to top himself, guv?'

'Come off it, Keith. I'm more subtle than that, aren't I? Danny was a man with a mission, to stage a double suicide, just as Twining did. He already planned to top himself. What really upset him was reading in the paper that we'd worked out that Delia was murdered.'

'He'd messed up,' Leaman said.

'Precisely. And why had he messed up? Because the original ligature mark, the strangling mark, showed on her neck. If he'd used a slip knot to suspend the body from the swing he would very likely have got away with it. So what was his thinking at this point? He was about to hang himself anyway, so why not confuse everyone by using a slip knot? Then we might assume he, too, was killed in the same way as Delia, strangled first and then suspended from the viaduct to make it look like a hanging.'

'What would that achieve?' Halliwell said. 'I thought this was all about making it look like suicide.'

Leaman said, 'You've lost me, guv.'

'Too subtle,' Halliwell said with a faint grin.

'Fair enough,' Diamond said. He'd begun doubting himself even as he outlined the theory. 'But there *is* an explanation. Got to be. OK, let's deal with what we do know. Danny strangled Delia and there's some kind of link with the Twining couple. We must put more effort into finding that link. Did they all belong to some weird sect? Did they meet?'

'The Twinings didn't have many friends,' Leaman said. 'The brother said they were too busy with their careers. What was it? If you want to be a success in life you don't have much to do with other people unless you're making money out of them.'

'That brother's a cynic,' Diamond said. 'John Twining was an architect, so he must have had clients. And his wife Christine had a top job with M&S. She would have met plenty of people through her job.'

'Not the likes of Danny and Delia,' Halliwell said. 'He was on the social and she was bringing up two kids.'

'I went to see Delia's mother, Amanda,' Diamond said. 'She seemed to think Danny worked from home on the computer and got some kind of income. He was interested in wildlife, bats in particular.'

'A world away from the Twinings,' Leaman said.

Diamond sighed. 'Yes, and Amanda told me he didn't have many friends.'

'The landlord at Freshford said the same. Danny was a loner.'

'There must be a link and it's the key to everything,' Diamond insisted. 'We're going to have to dig back two or three years to when the Twinings were alive and Danny and Delia lived together. That's the critical time. I'll talk to Amanda again. I doubt if we'll get much more out of Harold Twining, but Amanda must remember something.'

With that decided, he turned to the plan to intercept the ram raid on Sunday night. The swoop was still on. The two robbers, Romney and Jacob, were picking up the converted Land Rover from Jackman on Sunday morning. It would be fitted with a bug and monitored right up to the moment of the raid.

'Do we know the shop?' he asked.

'You want it on a plate, guv,' Halliwell said. 'No, they're keeping that to themselves.'

'But you reckon we can pursue the Land Rover without giving ourselves away?'

'That's the object. And we'll have response cars out on the streets in force.'

'Good. This man Jackman, the snitch. What have you promised him?'

'Like we said, leniency.'

'That can mean anything from a blind eye to a word in the judge's ear. He does up stolen vehicles as an occupation, right?'

'Yes, and we figure he could be useful in the future.'

'Only up to a point. When the word gets around that he's linked to a number of failed raids, the bad boys will drop him. They may drop him literally.'

'C'est la vie.'

'You said DC Gilbert is the handler?'

'Paul Gilbert, yes. He made the first contact in some pub Jackman uses.'

'Gilbert is still very new in the job. Is he aware of the risk?'

'Seems to be.'

'I'll have a word with him myself. Can you send him in?'

*   *   *

Gilbert did look worryingly young. Quite how he'd gained Jackman's confidence in a pub, Diamond couldn't fathom. Until he spoke. Then he came across with a streetwise manner that explained a lot.

'Yes, guv,' he said, 'I met Gary Jackman in the cellar bar of the Porter. Do you know it? No, I guess you wouldn't. It's for twenty-somethings like me. George Street. Live music most nights and the comedy club Sundays. One of my drinking mates knows Gary and told me he was dodgy but great company and we got talking and it moved on from there. A couple more weeks and a lot of lager and he was ready to do the biz.'

191

'He knows you're in CID?'

'Bit of a shock when I told him, but he soon saw the possibilities.'

'He does up hot cars, is that right?'

'Basically, yes. The front is a repair shop out at Winsley and some of the business is legit. He's good, and the word gets round.'

'This ram raid on Sunday. You're convinced it's going to happen?'

'Gary's certain of it.'

'So why is he shopping these guys?'

'They're going to cock up. They're too ambitious.'

'Let's hope he's right.' Diamond switched to the real point of this briefing while trying to sound as cool as his young colleague. 'Look, I happen to know of a car that went missing last night, a blue Nissan Pathfinder, almost new. I reckon it might just find its way into Jackman's repair shop. You could tip him off that it wouldn't be wise to work on it. The smart move would be to let us know as soon as he hears of it.'

'Is there a link?'

'No. It's something else I'm taking an interest in.'

Gilbert nodded. ' 'Nuff said, boss.'

24

'If you were planning this raid,' Diamond said, 'what time would you go for?'

Keith Halliwell hesitated, wary of hypothetical questions from his boss. 'The early hours, I reckon.'

'Say two to three?'

'Probably.'

'And when would you pick up the vehicle?'

'Is that important?'

'Just that I'm getting edgy. What is it now—eleven twenty?—and there's been no word.'

'They don't need the Range Rover until late, gov. They could pick it up ten minutes before they go.'

'That would cut it fine.'

'Eleven, then.'

They were sitting in the canteen at Manvers Street, but not because supper was available. At this late hour the staff were no longer on duty. If anyone wanted a hot pie they would be disappointed. Drinks were on tap, but only from an old machine that made the coffee taste of chocolate and the tea of dishwater. The advantage of being downstairs was that their transport was conveniently close. And it was better than sitting in an office.

At some point in the night the team on watch at Winsley—where the informer Jackman had his repair yard—would radio in, and Operation Fleece, as Halliwell had named it, would take off. The stolen Range Rover with its new colour and new plates—and its homing device—would be tracked by four vehicles at strategic points across the city.

DC Gilbert had been honoured with the Winsley surveillance, using an unmarked car fitted with radio communications. There was no sense in having everyone out there. Better to let Gilbert and his driver report on the pick-up and have the

193

other teams close in as the bugged car moved towards the shop.

'Fancy a game of snooker?' Halliwell said.

'No.'

'It helps to pass the time.'

'I think I'll look into the CAD room again, call up young Gilbert and make sure he's awake.'

'He'd better be. I'll come with you.' Nothing more was said, but there was a clear understanding that this was Halliwell's op. He didn't want Diamond muscling in and taking the glory.

The Computer-Aided Dispatch room was the communications base, in use round the clock. Unknown to Halliwell, Diamond had been in there already to see how the bugged vehicle would be tracked.

He asked an operator to contact DC Gilbert.

The response from Winsley was immediate. 'Sierra One.'

Halliwell grabbed the microphone. 'SIO speaking. What's the scene, Sierra One?'

'Same as before, sir. Clear view of the four-by-four standing in the lane outside the yard. No one is about. Not yet, anyway.'

'And where are you?'

'Also in the lane, five vehicles back and in shadow.'

'You'll give nothing away when they come? You don't need to keep them in sight once they've picked up the vehicle.'

'You told me, guv. We've been over it.'

'Several times. I know,' Halliwell said. 'Stay with it, Sierra One. Over and out.' He spread his hands as he turned back to Diamond. 'It's like baking a cake. You have to give it time.'

The mention of cake made him think of his secret admirer. He was trying to forget her. 'It's bread,' he said.

'What's that, guv?'

'When you make bread you give it time to rise.'

Back in the canteen, Halliwell tried another diversionary tactic. 'I may have thought of a possible connection between the Twining couple and Danny and Delia. When did Delia get the job as a waitress?'

Diamond perked up. There was only so much you could say about an impending ram raid. 'At Tosi's, do you mean? Do you know, I don't think we found out. What's the point here?'

'Could she have been working there when the Twinings were alive? They were the kind of people who'd use restaurants.'

'It's possible, I guess. But even if it's true, you don't discuss suicide pacts with the woman who serves your meal.'

'Right.' Halliwell nodded. 'It wouldn't do much for the appetite.'

Diamond pondered for a while. Halliwell might have hit on something. 'Her mother told me she was working as a waitress for some time, certainly when she was living with Danny. She was in other places before she worked at Tosi's.'

'Worth checking?'

'Another job for Ingeborg. Why isn't she part of this op?'

'Special dispensation,' Halliwell said. 'A date.'

The old blood pressure threatened, and Diamond made himself count to ten and see if it still mattered—a method his doctor had recommended.

It didn't matter.

*   *   *

The alert finally came from Winsley at twenty past midnight. 'Two suspects in a white van,' Gilbert radioed in. 'Can't see the registration. One got out and went straight to the stolen vehicle. The van has driven off.'

'Not the Range Rover?'

'Not yet. Wait—he's moving out. We'll go with him.'

'Not too close.'

'Trust me.'

'I'm trusting you to keep your distance.'

Diamond asked Halliwell if the bug was active, and it was. No reason to rush until they had a sense of where the ram vehicle was heading. They walked to their car and got in and made radio contact with the other teams. Everyone was awake. They tuned to Gilbert's radio wavelength.

'Heading west towards the city,' Gilbert reported. 'I can see the tail-lights of the van up ahead. They're in no hurry.'

The van would be the getaway vehicle—for the getaway that wouldn't be allowed to happen.

'Crossing the river now and heading up to the aqueduct.'

Diamond knew the route well enough, but he had a map out and was following the progress by torchlight. Seeing it on paper and being reminded of the distances was reassuring. The ram-raiders were moving in his direction and he wanted to make sure they were properly received. Three armed response vehicles in addition to his own were ready to swoop.

'Would you believe it? They've stopped at the traffic lights,' Gilbert said. 'We've pulled in to the side and dowsed our lights. These are law-abiding villains. OK, we're all on the move again. Doing a dog-leg and up over Brassknocker by the look of it.'

'Appropriate,' Diamond said to Halliwell. 'That's where the highwaymen used to operate, the top of Brassknocker Hill.'

'Until they were collared and hanged in chains. Not much changes.'

Did that sound a tad too smug? Diamond asked himself.

These modern villains were using the more secluded route to Bath, much favoured by the locals, avoiding the busy A36 that looped round the city following the curve of the river. A winding climb over Claverton Down brought you to a long descent down Widcombe Hill. The railway station and the city centre lay ahead.

'Approaching the T-junction at Claverton Down Road,' Gilbert reported. He was good at this. Eager to impress, no doubt, but so were all the others and not many of them communicated so well.

'What's your money on?' Diamond asked. 'Another phone shop or something more ambitious?'

'They're after small stuff, that's for sure,' Halliwell said. 'A jeweller's, maybe.'

'Turning right,' Gilbert's voice told them. 'Still observing speed limits.'

'Maybe the judge will take that into account,'

Halliwell murmured.

'Passing the university campus. The road is straight here. I'm having to stay well back.'

'Doesn't matter,' Halliwell told him. 'The bug is working nicely. We can follow the route by radio if needed.'

The white van and the Range Rover took another short cut, down Prior Park Road, avoiding Widcombe Hill. Local knowledge.

'Crunch time coming shortly,' Diamond said. 'Why don't you radio the others and tell them to have their engines running?'

'I can do that, but let's see which way they come in.'

'It's obvious, isn't it? Under the viaduct and over Churchill Bridge.'

'But then what?'

'Fair enough. We'll see.' He hated chasing around in cars, and waiting to chase around was worse.

Paul Gilbert radioed that he was closing up on the Range Rover now. Then the unexpected happened. 'Bloody hell. They're not going into the centre. They're heading up Wells Road.'

'What's up there?' Halliwell said.

This was the south-west route *out* of Bath. Diamond knew it well. He'd lived on Wellsway for a time and done the drive every day. The suspects were dodging the trap. 'Doesn't matter what's up there. We're down here and we've got to move. Did you hear that, driver?'

He'd taken charge. Halliwell would have to make his protest later. He put out an instruction to the others to head the same way.

'It's mostly small shops,' he said, answering

Halliwell's question as they accelerated to the end of Manvers Street and swung right in front of the railway station. 'I can't think of anything I'd want to rob.'

'Do you think they spotted Gilbert tailing them?'

'Must have.' He was tight-lipped.

'So do we want to chase them?'

'We have to.' He leaned forward to speak to the driver. 'You've got a winker on your roof. Use it.'

They passed through a red traffic light, crossed Churchill Bridge and rounded the elongated island that stands under the railway. A left turn and they were racing up Wells Road.

'Report your position, Sierra One.'

'Just passing Bear Flat,' Gilbert answered.

'Leaving the shops behind?'

'Pretty well.'

'Are they both in sight still?'

'Yes. Turning left on Milton. Shall I follow?'

Milton was one of several avenues named after poets. The developers had grand aspirations. When built around 1900, the area was known as Poets' Corner. These days Shakespeare, Kipling, Milton and Longfellow were better known for bumper-to-bumper parking.

'Yes. We reckon they spotted you anyway. Keep them in sight. Don't do anything until the back-up arrives. We're coming up Holloway, only three minutes behind you.'

'Guv, they've stopped,' Gilbert said. 'Right in the middle of the road.'

'Both vehicles?'

'What do I do—nick them?'

'No. See what happens.'

199

'It's very narrow where they are. Parked cars either side. Door's opening. The guy's got out. He's left the Range Rover blocking the street and he's running to the van. There's no way I can get past. Oh Christ, they're getting away.'

Diamond studied the map and told the driver, 'There's a street called Chaucer that crosses all the others. They'll use that and double down Kipling or one of the others. If we pick the right one we can head them off.'

'Which one, sir?'

Shakespeare, Kipling or Longfellow? He'd never had time for fancy writers.

'Kipling.'

He radioed to the others to block the remaining avenues as soon as they arrived.

Gilbert came on again, saying the van had disappeared fast and he couldn't see which turn it had taken on Chaucer Avenue. 'I'm stuck behind the Range Rover. There's no way I can get round it. Oh my God—it's on fire! He's torched it.'

This was turning into a nightmare. Diamond radioed for the fire service.

The car swung at speed into Kipling Avenue. They could see at once that they'd boobed. Nothing else was moving. There were just parked cars stretching to infinity.

Halliwell said, 'Personally, I would have gone for Shakespeare.'

'Sod off, Keith.'

There was still an outside chance that one of the other vehicles would intercept the van. But did it happen? This wasn't Diamond's night.

They waited ten minutes and drove round to Milton Avenue and watched the firemen dowse the flames. The Range Rover was exposed as a black, steaming wreck. The adjacent cars would be write-offs. 'The end of Operation Fleece,' he said.

It wasn't quite.

While they were returning down Wellsway there was an all-units alert. 'Break-in reported in Westgate Street. A four-by-four drove into the shopfront of Brackendale's the jeweller's. Repeat, Brackendale's in Westgate Street. Two suspects have left the scene in another vehicle. No description yet.'

'Suckered,' Diamond said.

25

A select group assembled in Diamond's office at eleven next morning. With little more than four hours' sleep behind them, they were a sorry bunch.

'The good news is that Georgina is out all morning,' Diamond told them. 'A meeting at headquarters. The bad news is that she heard about the raid already. Wants me to phone her this afternoon with an explanation.'

'Does she know about ...' Keith Halliwell shrank from speaking the words. They had a different resonance now.

'Operation Fleece? I think not. But she will. There's no concealing it from her.'

Young DC Gilbert said, 'At least we were doing something.'

'Get real, son. We were shafted.'

'Hung out to dry,' Halliwell said.

Diamond turned to look out of the window as if he wanted to be anywhere but here. 'In all my years of service I can't remember an op that was such a disaster. I take my share of the blame, of course.'

'All of us fell for it,' Halliwell said.

'Yes, and Georgina will nail us to the wall. Are we agreed on what actually happened last night?'

Halliwell was desperate to get in first. 'We were led to believe these guys were teenagers.'

'They are,' Gilbert said, some colour rising in his gaunt face.

'Amateurs, then. Kids starting out, wet behind the ears.'

'I only had Jackman's word. He misjudged them.'

Diamond intervened. 'Wait a bit, you two. There's an assumption here that ... What do they call themselves?'

'Jacob and Romney.'

' ... that Jacob and Romney are the villains. Forget that. They were minor players. Their job was to set up the decoy, which they did. The Range Rover was never intended to be used for a ram raid. It was to draw us off limits while the real heist went ahead in Westgate Street. We fell for an elaborate con. My first question is: was Jackman a party to it, or was he conned as well?'

'Trust me, he's up and up,' Gilbert said. 'He was dead nervous. I could see it.'

'Nervous of what?' Halliwell said. 'He could have been nervous we would rumble him.'

'Either way, he was taking big risks,' Diamond said. He turned to Gilbert. 'You know what you're going to do? Follow up with this guy. Get heavy with him. Find out who he was dealing with. Did he meet the big boys? Who was paying him? How was it bankrolled? They won't use him again. They won't protect him, so he's easy meat.'

'I'll get onto it,' Gilbert said, starting to rise, hoping he could walk out of the door.

Diamond pointed his finger to keep him in the hot seat.

'Should we nick the two lads?' John Leaman said. He could afford to make suggestions. He'd played no part in the planning, and he was only in attendance through seniority.

'They'll have hightailed it by now.' Everything about Halliwell, his voice, body language, face, showed how hard he'd taken this.

'Put out an all-units. One of them is supposed to have form, isn't he?'

'That may have been a false lead,' Leaman said. 'Jacob is a fairly common name.'

'Get a description from Jackman, then. If you find these two, you're halfway to nailing the top men.'

'What do we have from the Range Rover?' Diamond asked. 'Prints? DNA?'

'The fire got too much of a grip.'

'All right. What do we have from Westgate Street? Any witnesses?'

Halliwell spread his hands. 'You know what the city centre is like on a Sunday night.'

'They must have left traces of some sort.'

'The crime scene guys haven't found much. These people knew their business. Gloves, masks, head covers of some kind.'

'What was the car?' Diamond said, and for one uncomfortable moment he remembered he was supposed to be on the trail of a stolen blue Nissan Pathfinder.

'Toyota Landcruiser,' Halliwell said. 'Taken the same evening from the Manvers Street car park.'

For a moment he breathed easy. It didn't last. 'Right next to the nick? God help us, am I going to have to break that to Georgina?'

'She may heard from someone else, guv. The owner is Pippa Peel-Bailey.'

The name meant nothing. 'Should I have heard of her?'

'The daughter of Councillor Peel-Bailey, who is on the Police Authority.'

He took it all in and then said, 'Oh goody. That saves me a phone call.'

The tension eased. There were smiles. He decided to leave it there, making clear only that Keith Halliwell remained in charge of the ram-raid investigation. But after the others had left the room, Halliwell lingered. It was obvious he had something else to get off his chest. He closed the door first.

'Appreciate your support, guv,' he said. 'I screwed up big time.'

'We all did,' Diamond said. 'I feel bad, too.'

'Something I didn't mention.' Halliwell felt for his tie and loosened it. He let out a nervous breath.

'Go on.'

'I'm a countryman.'

The small hairs rose on the back of Diamond's neck. The word 'countryman' has its own dread coinage in the police. Operation Countryman back in 1980 lifted the lid on police corruption in London. The supergrass whose evidence triggered the inquiry claimed that the entire Robbery Squad was bent: one third took money, one third favours and one third looked the other way.

Halliwell must have cottoned on to his boss's reaction, because he added at once, 'When I say I'm a countryman, I mean I was raised on a farm. I was a farmer's boy.'

For one anxious second Diamond wondered if his deputy was about to cry on his shoulder.

'Should have known,' Halliwell said. 'Just didn't think.'

'Didn't think what? You're not making sense, Keith.'

'The words *ram raid*. I took it for what it is— ramming a shopfront.'

'And . . . ?'

'A ram is also a male sheep.'

'So?'

'I only thought of it during the meeting when you made that remark about what they called themselves. Bit embarrassing, so I didn't mention it in front of the others. Jacob and Romney are breeds of sheep.'

* * *

Ingeborg brought in a packet and put it on his desk.

'What's this, then?'

His name was on the label in large letters.

She shrugged. 'Don't know, guv.'

At least it wasn't large enough to be another cake.

'It's already been opened. You must know what's in there.'

205

'That's security. They checked it and sent me up with it.'

'As long as no one's sending *me* up.' He unwrapped the loose end. 'It doesn't weigh much.'

It was a brand-new mobile phone. 'Someone's feeling generous,' he said in a throwaway tone, knowing for certain who had sent it. 'I guess I'll have to find out how to use the thing.'

'Can I see?' Ingeborg fingered the controls. 'It's ready to go. Someone has charged it up already and put in an SIM card.'

'Is that good?'

'It makes life easier.'

'You mean there's no escape?'

'Do you want a quick lesson?'

She went through it with him. His fingers were like bananas trying to use the keys.

'It's a fab little phone,' Ingeborg said. 'See, it's got a vibrating function.'

His face was a study in mystification.

'When you're in a meeting and a call comes in, it doesn't have to ring. You feel the movement in your pocket.'

'And have a coronary.'

Ingeborg didn't comment. She was scrolling up and down. 'Hello, there's a name already in your phone book.'

*   *   *

His priority remained the murder of Delia Williamson. Ram raids are regrettable, but a lost life can't be recovered. Leaving Halliwell to deal with the aftermath of last night, he drove out to Bradford on Avon.

Amanda Williamson was at the door of the weaver's cottage on the hill when Diamond appeared along Tory, as the little path was known. She had empty eyes and a tired stance. Anyone would after days of caring for two newly orphaned children. She told him she was about to go down into the town for some shopping. Her two granddaughters were inside in the care of her friend Meg, the young woman Diamond had met briefly on his last visit.

He offered to go with her and she must have known it wasn't from the goodness of his heart, but she didn't seem dismayed, especially when he said he was better than a pack-mule at carrying bags. 'It looks a stiff climb,' he said. 'I bet you feel it, coming up.'

'Don't I just.'

He asked how the girls were adjusting and heard that they seemed to be internalising the grief. They weren't saying much. It was no bad thing that they were living in a place new to them, and Amanda was glad she'd taken his advice and dodged the press.

She asked how he was doing and he surprised himself by confiding that he'd met someone and been on a date for the first time since his wife had died.

'Good for you,' she said, then added, 'It *was* good, I take it?'

He gave a shy smile.

'Good for her, too, then. Will you see her again?'

'It's kind of understood.'

'Lovely. There's too much grief in the world. I like to hear about anyone who makes another person happy. I've had my moments, too, and that's what they've been—moments—but no worse for that.' She giggled a little at some private memory. 'And how are you doing professionally?'

She wanted to know how the investigation was going. Too late, it clicked with him that this was what she'd meant the first time.

'Not enough progress in that department,' he said. 'More questions than answers.'

'And you have some for me?'

'Do you mind?'

'Go on.'

'I'd like to know more about your daughter and Danny. I didn't ask you about their beliefs.'

Her gaze moved swiftly to him, checking his meaning, and then ahead to the spire of Holy Trinity. 'Like religious beliefs?'

'It's one theory among many. People sometimes get too wrapped up in certain stuff that isn't good for their sanity.'

'The black arts?'

'Or some such. Cults.'

She gave it thought as they picked their way down the steps known as the Rope Walk. 'I think I would have known if Delia had got into anything like that,' she said finally. 'She was never morbid. Too excitable, if truth be told.'

'And Danny?'

'He was more guarded certainly, a bit strange, even, thinking of the bats, but I wouldn't say it was unhealthy. The natural world was what he'd studied for years. He cared about living things. I remember an incident once. We were driving along one of those lanes near Holt and a small bird flew out of the hedge and hit the car. He

208

stopped and got out and went back to make sure it wasn't suffering, as he said. I think he put it out of its misery. I didn't watch. How many of us would do that?'

They completed the descent to the centre of the small town. Her thoughts had turned to shopping. 'I need something from the butcher's and I always get my greengroceries in the Shambles. Is my pack-mule capable of carrying five pounds of potatoes?'

'Sure is steep,' he said. 'Why don't we water the old beast?'

They picked the Dandy Lion in Market Street, a comfortable, shadowy, low-beamed place that hadn't decided whether it was coffee shop, pub or restaurant. She had tea and he ordered a strong black coffee.

'Don't ask,' he said.

'I don't need to. The whole of last night is written on your face,' she said. 'I could probably get by with three pounds of potatoes.'

'I'll be fine. I suppose your daughter never worked here?'

'All her waiting jobs were in Bath.'

'Remember which restaurants?'

'The first was a pizza place that's long since gone. Then she was in the coffee shop in Rossiter's.'

His voice warmed as a good memory came back. 'Upstairs, padded armchairs, king-size scones, the newspapers. I used to go there with Steph. That went, too, more's the pity. How strange. I may have met Delia, then.'

'Quite possibly.' She didn't seem to think there was anything remarkable. 'Then I think she started at Tosi's. She had quite a long time there. She enjoyed it.'

'She was able to go to work in the evenings because Danny was home looking after the girls?'

'Yes. And sometimes I think she went on dates. I'm her mother, so I can say that. My Delia was easily tempted.'

'And Danny was rather dull?'

She confirmed it with a soft, stricken sigh. 'They weren't married, as you know, but her relationship with Danny was steadier than a lot of marriages I've heard of. True, he wasn't every woman's ideal of a dashing young man, but he cared for her. He showed his love in practical ways, like looking after the children. It would be quite wrong to assume he murdered her.'

'Why do you say that? The break-up may have upset him more than anyone realised.'

'He wasn't like that, vengeful or jealous. To have harboured anger for years and then attack her—that's not the Danny I knew.'

'You suggest your daughter may have been dating other men,' he said, aware how hurtful this could be, yet needing to probe more. 'Can you name any of them?'

She smiled faintly. 'If Delia were here, I doubt if she could answer that.'

'But ultimately she moved in with Ashley. Don't you think Danny would have hated that?'

'I expect so.'

'And let it fester for a time?'

'For over two years? Danny? I don't see it.'

'He couldn't compete with Ashley.'

'Mr Diamond, just because Ashley had a more successful career it doesn't make him a

210

better man.'

'I'm saying this must have caused deep hurt to Danny.'

'No doubt about that.'

'Not enough to drive him to murder?'

She shook her head.

'People change,' he said. 'He lived alone after they split up. Dark thoughts can get to you when you don't have someone to help keep things in proportion. Don't I know it.'

In her calm manner, she dismantled his theory. 'In the time since it happened, I've thought a lot about Danny. You policemen know the facts of the case far better than I, and you're saying he murdered her and I ought to hate him. Try as I have, I can't see him killing her. He didn't have a violent impulse in him. Something isn't right, Mr Diamond. You're doing your best, I know, and I'm going mainly on what I saw. Please believe me. Danny isn't the man who killed my Delia.'

26

On fine mornings like this one, Giuseppe Tosi liked to imagine he was back in sunny Padua. In reality George Street, Bath, didn't much resemble Via Angelina, but when Tosi leaned on the railing at the top of the basement stairs with the warmth on his face he had no difficulty picturing blue shutters on the windows across the street and tiling the roofs in terracotta. Humming 'O Sole Mio', he beamed at everyone passing as if they were friends and neighbours. This was how he failed to recognise the policeman who had called before.

It was excusable. This time Diamond had Ingeborg in tow, and any full-blooded male from Padua was going to have eyes only for a woman as stunning as she.

Diamond greeted Tosi by name and got an, 'Uh?' in response.

'Remember me?' Diamond prompted. 'Detective Superintendent Diamond?' To Ingeborg he said, 'He's the owner, and he has less English than any of them.' To Tosi, he said, '*Carabinieri.*'

Tosi said, '*Mamma mia.*'

'There's a waiter called Luigi who speaks English,' Diamond said to Ingeborg.

Tosi heard the name. 'You come take Luigi?' He beckoned with his hand and led the way downstairs.

They followed. Before going inside, Diamond pointed out the bike resting against the wall under the stairs. 'Good, Luigi's in work.'

This was early in the restaurant day. No cloths were on the tables. Tosi pushed a vacuum cleaner to one side to let them through. Luigi, in T-shirt and jeans, came from the back and recognised Diamond and gave Ingeborg the up-and-down with those large brown eyes. 'More questions?'

'A few things we didn't cover last time. Do you mind?'

'No problem.' *COOL IT* was written on Luigi's shirt. He wasn't even making eye contact. Not with Diamond, anyway.

'So how long has this restaurant been going?'

Luigi shrugged and asked Tosi in Italian and

then translated the response. 'He says six years last September.'

'And when did *you* start?'

There was hesitation and Diamond recalled that Luigi disliked personal questions. 'I don't know. About four years ago, I guess.'

'And the cook, Carlo?'

'You'll have to ask him. He was here before me.'

'So all three of you were working here for at least four years. When did Delia start?'

He folded his arms. 'Are you still investigating Delia? I read in the paper that her boyfriend did it and hanged himself.'

An attempt to divert that didn't work with Diamond. 'Answer the question, please. When did she start?'

'What is the problem with Delia?'

Diamond waited, saying nothing.

Luigi rolled his eyes and then gave Ingeborg a long-suffering look. 'Two and a half years, maybe three. Do you want me to ask the boss? He may have it on paper somewhere.'

'I'll take your word for it. Another question. What happens about reservations in this place? Is there a book?'

'We went over this,' Luigi said. 'The night Delia died, we had only nine people in all evening.'

'I'm not asking about that night.'

'Sure, there's a book.' He went over to the bar, a small counter framed in plastic vine leaves. It doubled as the reservations desk.

Tosi said something in agitated Italian and Luigi replied and there was much shrugging and hand gesturing before the book was handed to

Diamond.

He turned to the front. 'This only starts in September. Where are the earlier books?'

More consultation. Then Luigi said, 'He chucked them.'

'Threw them out? Are you sure?'

'He just told me.'

Ingeborg, silent up to now, said, 'That's right, guv. I know enough to follow what was said.'

Luigi flashed her a big, approving smile. 'It's only reservations. It's not like he threw away the accounts.'

'But the accounts wouldn't show the names of customers, would they?' Diamond said.

'Nothing gets past you.'

Diamond bit back a rebuke. There was another way to go. Taking out the photo he had been given by Harold Twining, he asked, 'Recognise this couple?'

Luigi, so adept at ducking, said straight away, 'Who are they?'

'Never mind. Have they eaten here? It would have been some while back, say two or three years ago.'

'A long time.' He sidestepped the question by passing the photo to Tosi.

A nice moment followed. Tosi's big bulk started to wobble. He made a crowing sound and extended his hand and stretched all the fingers wide as if catching the memory. 'My friends. Good friends.'

'They came here?' Diamond said.

'Plenty times,' Tosi said, turning to Luigi for an animated exchange.

'What are they saying?' Diamond asked

214

Ingeborg.

'He seems to be telling Luigi he's bound to remember these people because they always gave good tips. But Luigi is saying they must have been before his time.'

Tosi gave up on his waiter and shouted towards the kitchen. 'Carlo, Carlo.'

'This should be interesting,' Diamond said.

Carlo surfaced, wiping his hands on a cloth. Tosi gave him an earful of Italian and handed him the photo. Carlo was slow to react. He peered at the picture for some seconds. Then his mouth curved and he made a sound like a steam train leaving the station. Finally he said, '*Si.*'

'Is he faking it just to please the boss?' Diamond asked Ingeborg.

Luigi must have overheard what was meant to be a quiet aside, because he grinned and nodded at Diamond.

'I'm sure about Signor Tosi,' Ingeborg said. 'He's positive he's seen them before.'

'Who are they?' Luigi said for the second time.

'Doesn't matter, does it?' Diamond said. 'You obviously haven't met them.'

Then Tosi clicked his fingers and said, '*Cristina.*' He grabbed the photo from Carlo and said with an air of triumph, '*Cristina.*'

'Pretty close,' Diamond said.

'*Cristina e Giovanni.*'

'Not so close.'

Ingeborg said, 'Closer than you think, guv. *Giovanni* is John in Italian.'

*   *   *

215

On the walk back to the nick he told Ingeborg, 'Tosi remembered them. I'd bet my house on that. They came to the restaurant often enough for him to know their first names.'

'The first real link we have,' she said.

' "Link" is putting it strongly.'

'OK, let's say their paths may have crossed.'

'More like it. The Twinings were customers and Delia could have been their waitress.'

'Which was when?'

'They died two years ago, didn't they?'

'Two to three years ago, then?'

'Maybe before then, if Luigi had no memory of them.'

'But can we believe Luigi?'

Diamond nodded. 'Shifty character, isn't he? The first time we interviewed him, I had him down as a suspect. He was on duty the night Delia was murdered, the last one to see her alive. The others had gone home. There were just the two of them. He said he locked up the restaurant and they went their different ways.'

'If he came on to Delia and was cold-shouldered he could have turned nasty. He's used to getting his way with women.'

'How do you know that?'

'Trust me, guv. I can tell.'

'You think he strangled her and rigged it up as a hanging?'

'It does sound a bit far-fetched, put like that,' she said. 'Particularly as he'd need to move her and he only has the bike.'

'He has a Honda at home in Twerton. I asked him.'

'Do you still rate him?'

216

'What interests me more,' Diamond said, 'is what we were talking about—this blank spot about the Twinings.'

'When you pressed him, he said he started at Tosi's four years ago. He must have met the Twinings if they were regulars.'

'That was my thought, too.'

'He's not the sort to have a blank spot, guv. He's sharper than broken glass.'

'You don't like him?'

'I wouldn't believe a word he told me.'

They reached the bottom of Milsom Street before Diamond spoke again. 'My problem with Luigi is that there's more to this case than a man trying it on and getting the frost. We're pretty certain there's a link with the Twinings.'

'Which he's in denial about,' Ingeborg said. 'Could it be that he murdered Christine Twining and strung her up the same way and nobody at the time suspected it was murder?'

'And the husband hanged himself because he couldn't bear to live without her?'

'No, guv. Luigi killed the husband as well.'

'Why?'

'To cover up the first crime.'

He said with disbelief, 'And it wasn't picked up at autopsy?'

Ingeborg seized on that. Her journalistic training was in play. Her words came in a burst. 'The same pathologist carried out both autopsies.'

'So?'

'I sent for the reports, if you remember.'

'And I was impressed by them. Unlike our friend Dr Sealy, he set out his findings in a way I could follow.'

'Shinwari,' she said as the name came back to her. 'Dr Manzoor Shinwari.'

'Correct, and he isn't available to speak to us. He returned to Pakistan and the Medical Council have lost contact with him.'

Her eyes were saucer-wide. 'Why? Was there a scandal?'

'None that I heard of.'

'Maybe he got out in time. There were all these high-profile cases involving mistakes by pathologists. What if Dr Shinwari saw the writing on the wall and did a runner?'

'You're speculating, Inge.'

'I'm going to check.'

'You'll find that difficult. The medical profession is notorious for looking after its own.'

'We've got copies of the autopsy reports. Can we get a second opinion?'

'Like I said, they stick together. This isn't a second opinion on someone's medical condition. This is asking one doctor to pick holes in another's work.' As he spoke, he was thinking of Jim Middleton, the ballroom king, the obvious man to ask. The prospect of approaching Jim once again didn't appeal.

'Suppose Dr Shinwari got it wrong,' Ingeborg pressed him. 'Suppose both Twinings were murdered. We could be dealing with a serial killer. We can't take the risk, guv.'

27

Police headquarters was twenty miles off, at Portishead, ridiculously inconvenient whenever Diamond was summoned there, ideally placed whenever Georgina attended and was gone for the day. But she could still use a phone and did this afternoon after Diamond forgot to call about Operation Fleece. She gave his ear a blasting for ten minutes, after which he decided she'd had her say. It was a fine judgement when to cut Georgina off. He reckoned at four fifteen in the afternoon she would be thinking about the tailbacks on the approach to Bristol and not wanting to dial the CID room a second time.

She would have no luck if she did, because he was making another call. He reached Jim Middleton at home, and knew from the tone of voice that Jim's home was Jim's castle. The retired pathologist had pulled up the drawbridge and was ready on the battlements with boiling oil. Appealing to his better nature wasn't going to work this time.

Diamond went for the weakest point. He said this was going to sound like a bad joke, but someone had lodged an official complaint about the Melksham tea dances. It seemed they were against the law, or at least against a by-law governing the use of the Melksham assembly hall, a carry-over from Victorian times, when public dances were thought to encourage immorality and maybe did. All was not yet lost, however. Fortunately he knew one of the Wiltshire magistrates and she had the power to issue a special licence making the dances into private functions.

Jim was relieved to hear this. He was quite disarmed. Diamond said there was no need for Jim to do anything or speak to anyone about the threat. But as a quid pro quo, would he give an opinion on two more autopsy reports? Jim swore at him and called him a conman, but there was just enough in the story to cause him doubt. He was hooked.

Diamond arranged to have them delivered to Jim within the hour.

After that, an early getaway beckoned. The big man emerged from his office into the open-plan area.

'Are you leaving, guv?' Paul Gilbert said. The lad had so much to learn.

'What if I am?'

'No problem. It can wait till tomorrow.'

This time it was Diamond who was hooked. 'What can wait?'

'Probably nothing. A burnt-out vehicle up at the racecourse. Kids, I expect.'

'Who is this from?'

'Uniform checked it out this afternoon. Call from someone out walking his dog. It's all right, there was no corpse inside. I just thought you might be interested because we know the ram-raiders burn cars, and this was a four-by-four.'

'Do we know the make?'

'Nissan Pathfinder.' Gilbert had a sudden thought. 'Isn't that the make you were interested in?'

Interested? It was sod's law that this would be

Paloma's son's car. 'Registration?'

'The plates were removed.'

'I might as well take a look at it. Not far off my route.'

He drove up to Lansdown with the evening traffic and soon spotted the burnt-out wreck in the first car park you can see from the road. He swung off and drew in alongside. When there is no race meeting the only people who park up there are those wanting a walk.

The Pathfinder was gutted. No doubt they'd used some kind of accelerant. He didn't want to mess his hands wiping away soot, but he could just make out that the original colour had been blue, like Jerry's. He walked around the wreck thinking how he would handle this.

*　　　*　　　*

Paloma came to the door in a white bathrobe. 'You!' she said. 'Well, at least it isn't the Jehovah's Witnesses.'

'It's obviously not a good time,' he said. 'I should have phoned ahead, but I was on the road.'

'I was showering after a long day in the office, that's all,' she said. 'No, in point of fact I was out of the shower and cutting my toenails if that makes you feel any better. Come in, Peter, it's good to see you any time.'

He hesitated. 'This is semi-official.'

'And I'm semi-dressed. Do I have to stand on my doorstep?'

He stepped inside and she closed the door. In her large sitting room she said, 'Now tell me what's up.'

He told her about the burnt car on Lansdown. 'We don't know for sure that this was Jerry's.'

'But it's the same make and colour?' She had her hand to her throat. 'He's going to be inconsolable. He was so proud of that thing.'

'Obviously we haven't informed him. It was only found this afternoon. When we check the chassis number, if it's still visible, we'll know.'

'He's with clients all afternoon and doing the rounds of the wards with the library trolley this evening. Do you think I should call him, or leave it till tomorrow?'

'If it were me, I'd like to know the worst as soon as possible.'

The worry was creasing her face. 'I wish I could think of some way of softening the blow.'

'If his insurance company is any good, he'll get a replacement. They usually cover theft and fire.'

'That's a thought.' She released a nervous breath. 'I'll break it to him now. Do you mind if I phone from the next room? Mothers say the silliest things to sons.'

'Can I get a drink ready?'

'What a good idea. A whopping great vodka and tonic. The cupboard in the corner.'

Left alone, with the drinks poured—his own more tonic than vodka—he looked at the art on the walls. No cheap reproductions, these. Abstract, large, in muted colours, they may not have been his choice, but they testified to the success of Once in Vogue. If he'd dabbled in shares he would have been asking if her company was open to investment.

She returned and said, 'Whew! That was tough. Give me a hug.'

He didn't just hug her, he kissed her as well.

'Now where's that drink?' she said.

He handed it to her. 'How did he take it?'

'Pretty badly, poor old lad. It wasn't his first car, but the first he'd really treated like a pet. He said he'll drive up to Lansdown after he's finished at the hospital.'

'He'd do better tomorrow in some daylight.'

'Try telling him. That was his baby.' She'd emptied her glass. 'I need more vodka in this, I think.'

He took the bottle across to her. She'd sat on the sofa. 'Is this your favourite tipple?'

'In times of stress. I was all of a tremble, seeing you *and* getting that unwelcome bit of news.'

'A double shock?'

She gave an embarrassed laugh. 'I didn't mean ...' She put the glass on the floor. 'Oh, come over here and shag me to bits.'

She'd opened her bathrobe and was naked under it. She lay on the sofa in total confidence.

The speed of the invitation might have troubled many a man. It didn't hamper Diamond. He did pretty much as asked.

*   *   *

They showered and Paloma found a bathrobe for him. Down in the kitchen she cooked a pasta dish with cream and chopped bacon and spinach. Fast food, but not from a packet. An Italian red wine came with it.

'You'll stay the night, won't you?' she said.

'That wasn't what I had in mind when I called.'

'You simply planned to tell me about the

223

wretched car and leave?'

'It's a mean man who takes advantage of a lady in distress.'

She said, 'It was me who took advantage. I'm like that, I'm afraid. Don't miss an opportunity.'

'Likewise.'

'Peter Diamond,' she said. 'You may be a red-hot detective, but you don't know the half of it where I'm concerned. You can't have any idea how much I wanted you.'

He smiled. 'Detective work doesn't apply here. You made your intention pretty clear.'

Now she was shaking her head and he could see she wanted to make a serious point. Her face had turned pale and she was twisting her fingers into knots. He wondered if he'd upset her. He wasn't much of a hand at flirting.

'Confession time,' she said, and her voice shook a little. 'I've been wanting to own up to this ever since that first evening. The bag of shopping you drove over at Sainsbury's. I planted it there. It was a set-up. I wanted an excuse to meet you. Isn't that appalling?'

He didn't fully understand. 'The child and the lost puppy? You made that up?'

'I know. I'm shameless.'

He thought back to the incident. 'Do you mean you saw me drive up in my car and decided you fancied me and planted your bag where I'd reverse over it?'

'No, it's worse than that.'

'How?'

'I was lying in wait.'

'But we hadn't met . . . had we?'

'No.' She sat back in her chair and studied her

224

fingernails, avoiding eye contact. 'Peter, I'm the woman who was pestering you. I wrote you a letter, and sent you the cake and spoke to you on the phone. You're right. We hadn't met, but not for want of trying.'

He was letting it sink in. 'I must be so dim. I didn't connect you with that letter at all.'

'It's scary, isn't it?' she said. 'I was stalking you.'

'I wouldn't call it stalking.'

'I would. How else did I know you do your shopping in Sainsbury's on Saturday evenings?'

'Scary' wasn't the word for what had happened, but it made him uncomfortable. Up to now he'd thought he had some influence on how they'd met. He'd just found out how little it was.

'You've gone awfully pale,' she said.

'Never could take a surprise.'

'I wanted you to know the truth of it.'

'Yes, and I appreciate that,' he said. He wouldn't let it damage the relationship, but in some ways he was wishing she hadn't told him.

*   *   *

They were watching a DVD of *The Third Man*, Paloma's head on his shoulder, when the doorbell chimed.

'That'll be Jerry,' she said. 'I thought he might show up.'

Jerry had the unlucky knack of showing up at inconvenient moments.

'Peter's with me,' Paloma said, as she ushered him in.

Jerry said, 'Hi, Peter.' But his mind was on other things. 'I've just come from Lansdown. I'm certain it's my car.'

'My poor darling,' Paloma said, putting an arm around him. 'Why did they have to set light to it? If they must steal a car, can't they content themselves with driving it around and leaving it somewhere?'

'They want to remove all traces of themselves,' Diamond said. 'Even the dimmest of joyriders have heard of DNA. We'll have forensics look at it, anyway. Something may have survived the fire.'

'Catching them won't be much consolation,' Jerry said.

'You'll be wanting to use the Porsche for some while longer,' Paloma said.

'Thanks, Mum, but no. It's yours again. I've rented something bigger. The space is the problem. I'm on the move so much that I use the car as an office. I'll call for a taxi in a minute and you can have your Porsche.'

'Where do you live?' Diamond said. 'I can drive you home.'

'What—and ruin your evening? You're not even dressed. A taxi will do fine. But I could do with a bite to eat. Is there anything in the fridge, Mum?'

'I expect so,' Paloma said. 'Have a look.'

When Jerry had left the room, Paloma gave Diamond a knowing smile and said, 'Comfort food.'

'Where does he live? I can easily run him back.'

'No,' she said. 'That's kind, but we can afford the taxi. Besides, I can see he's a bit embarrassed. Nothing personal, but he doesn't really approve of what I get up to.'

'Is that the church bit?'

'Probably. They're all pro-marriage and anti-

226

naughties from what I can gather. Wouldn't suit me at all.'

'Nor me,' he said. 'Where's the fun in that?'

'I'm told banging a tambourine is the height of ecstasy,' Paloma said.

'I'd be out of a job if it was.'

Jerry came back into the room spooning chocolate-chip ice cream from a tub. 'Taxi's on its way,' he said. 'I'm a bit low on bread, Mother, so I've helped myself to a loaf. And some slices from that chicken.'

'Take the whole bird if you want,' she said. 'I don't think I'm going to need it.'

'You don't know that,' he said. 'Peter might wake up feeling hungry.'

28

'Is this a takeover?' Diamond asked.

The pathologist Jim Middleton was sitting with eyes closed, gently revolving in Diamond's own chair and humming a tune as if his mind was on some intricate dance step. This at nine twenty the next morning.

'Nowhere else to park myself, squire,' Jim said, returning to the here and now. 'Where have you been? I came in specially. They tried calling you at home, but you must have left.'

'They wouldn't have caught me at home.'

'Don't you have a mobile?'

'I don't use it in the car.'

'I thought you people were working round the clock.'

'We squeeze in an hour of sleep every three or four days. What have you got for me?'

'Not what I expected,' Jim said. 'Not what you expected, I dare say.' He reached for a scuffed brown briefcase and removed the folders containing the autopsy reports on John and Christine Twining. 'Tell me about the fellow who wrote this stuff.'

'Dr Shinwari? There isn't much. He was attached to various hospitals in this area as a pathologist. He carried out hundreds, if not thousands, of autopsies. Eighteen months ago he resigned and returned to Pakistan.'

'He's definitely left the Health Service, has he? I want to be sure of this before I say any more.' Jim, as ever, behaving as if he was treading on glass.

'No question,' Diamond said. 'He's left, decamped, quit the stage, flown the coop, hoisted the Blue Peter. No forwarding address. No contact numbers.'

'Did you read these?'

'I could follow some of it. At least they're in simpler language than our friend Dr Sealy's reports.'

'The language is the problem.'

'What are you on about, Jim?'

'Is he a fluent speaker of English?'

'How would I know? I've never met him. What problem?'

Jim's eyes gleamed as they did when he executed a perfect chassé on the dance floor. He opened one of the reports. 'There's a section here. "Post Mortem appearance: face pale, lips, tongue and mucous membrane bluish. Petechial

228

haemorrhages under the conjunctivae. Early putrefactive discoloration on the lower abdominal wall."'

'You've lost me already,' Diamond said.

'Follow the words I've marked in pencil.' He handed the report to Diamond, and then turned to the second folder. 'You've got John Twining. This is Christine. "Post Mortem appearance: face pale, lips, tongue and mucous membrane bluish." And so it goes on, the wording precisely the same. That's just one example. It goes on for pages.'

'Well, if the method of death was the same, wouldn't the appearance be the same?'

'Peter, you don't repeat yourself word for word. And no two autopsies present precisely the same symptoms. Look at the other section I marked. "The line of the ligature followed the line of the jaw, then passed obliquely upwards behind the ears, where it was commonly lost." Exactly the same wording in both reports. But what does he mean by "commonly lost"? It makes no sense to me as a pathologist. Do you understand it?'

'Read it to me again.'

'It's just the phrase "where it was commonly lost".'

'Don't know. Typing error?'

'I think he didn't understand it himself. He's used a crib.'

'What—copied from something?'

'And I'm damned sure where he got it from.' Jim took from his case a black book that had the look of a much-thumbed Bible. He'd put markers between the pages. 'This is Glaister's *Medical Jurisprudence*, the standard work when I was going through college. Chapter 6: Asphyxia, sub-section

229

4: Hanging. See if this sounds familiar. "The line of the ligature must be carefully examined. In suicidal suspension, it usually follows the line of the lower jaw, then passes obliquely upwards behind the ears, where it is commonly lost." Glaister is talking about the generality of suicides by hanging. In its proper context the word makes sense.'

Diamond studied the textbook and then the two reports. 'You're thinking Dr Shinwari didn't know what he was writing about?'

'That's clear. The way he borrows the word "commonly" is the giveaway. He may have known how to dissect a corpse, but not enough English to report his findings.'

'So he copied out of the textbook?'

'I wouldn't mind betting that if you checked other reports you'd find Glaister being quoted verbatim.'

'To cover up Dr Shinwari's poor English?'

'That's the obvious inference, isn't it? Either that, or he was lazy and just copied out the same stuff each time.'

'Poor English seems more likely.'

'Whatever it was, he was going to get caught some time. My guess is that a coroner was on to him, which is why he quit the country. To avoid a scandal.'

'But I was told he was one of their busiest pathologists. Wouldn't he have been rumbled before this?'

'Peter, you have a touching faith in the system. Believe me, you can get by for a long time in the Health Service before any failings are picked up by management.'

'I'm surprised some lawyer didn't notice.'

'Dr Shinwari wouldn't often appear in court. He isn't a forensic pathologist. I would have known him if he was. He does routine autopsies.'

'Suicides are routine?'

'If the coroner decides so. If he has any suspicion about the death, he'll call up someone from the Home Office list, not a jobbing pathologist like Shinwari.'

Diamond said in disbelief, 'The Twinings were thought to be routine suicides?'

'Hanging is, as a general rule. Firearm deaths and overdoses are more open to doubt. So is jumping off a building. If you want to do away with someone and pass it off as suicide, you're unlikely to choose hanging.'

This was crucial to the suspicions Diamond had been forming. He needed expert help here. 'Haven't you ever come across a case of murder by hanging? Or murder dressed up as a hanging?'

'Personally, no,' Jim said. 'It's extremely rare. Off-hand, I can think of only two cases in recent times. There's Roberto Calvi, that Italian banker found on the end of a rope under Blackfriars Bridge. There were suspicions that he was murdered first. You had the double ligature mark around the neck. Keith Simpson, the pathologist, decided the two marks were caused by the movement of the rope when the body was shifting in the water and subject to the tide. He went for suicide. But there have been at least three inquiries since, and it's still an open question. Incidentally, one of the suspicious points was that the rope was fastened with a slip knot.'

'Really? Like Danny Geaves.'

'Yes. And the other suicidal hanging that some people say was suspicious was that of Rudolf Hess, the old Nazi in Spandau Prison. Once again, it was the mark that created doubt. It ran horizontally, rather than in the inverted 'V' that is typical. Several experts have concluded that Hess was strangled. But these are very unusual cases.'

'Coming back to the Twinings, these reports are useless, then?'

Jim smiled. 'He's got the dates right. And the places.'

'Big deal.'

'It's a pity there aren't any photos. If these had been forensic autopsies, you'd have more to work with. This far on in time, an exhumation wouldn't tell you much.'

'Wouldn't tell us anything. The Twinings were cremated. Thanks, anyway, Jim. You're a star.'

The prospect of stardom didn't appeal to Jim. 'I don't want publicity. It's off the record, everything I've said. If this man comes before the Medical Council, I don't wish to testify.'

'He won't. He's scarpered.'

'As long as that's clear. And you will see about that licence?'

'Licence?'

'For the tea dances.'

Just in time, Diamond remembered. He winked and tapped the side of his nose with his finger. 'Consider it done, old friend.'

*   *   *

For some minutes after Jim Middleton had left, Diamond pondered what he had learned. Dr

232

Shinwari's borrowings from Glaister meant that the autopsy reports were worthless, but it didn't alter the fact that a couple had been found hanging two years ago in circumstances remarkably similar to Delia and Danny, in public places, the woman first, and then the man a day or so after. There had to be a link. His priority was to find what those four people had in common.

Keith Halliwell put his head around the door, usually the cue for a coffee. Not this morning.

'Guv. We've been looking all over for you. That pathologist was here.'

'Seen him. He's left now.'

'You were in here all the time?'

He exaggerated slightly. They didn't need to know he'd turned up late for work, or where he'd spent the night. 'When I walked through the office you weren't about.'

'I know. I was chasing all over the building.'

'What's the panic, Keith?'

'There's been another hanging.'

29

'Where?'

'You know the big stone gates at Victoria Park? She's suspended from one of the arches.'

'*She?*'

On the short drive to the scene he was silent. Try as he did to suppress the memory of three years ago, driving to Royal Victoria Park to view his beloved Steph, he could not stop the thoughts crowding in. He told himself repeatedly that he

233

was over the shock, but an event such as this still had the power to ambush his confidence. He folded his arms so that Halliwell wouldn't see his hands trembling.

Put your mind on the bloody job, he told himself. You're a professional.

The professional analysis was this. He was faced with one more dead body in the series, no question. The location, a public place, fitted the pattern. Some macabre point was being made each time. The victims had to be exposed to public view, however briefly, before they were discovered and taken down.

The gateway to the Royal Victoria Park consists of two arches on either side of the road that are not arch-shaped at all, but perpendicular. Said to be 'triumphal' and in the Greek Revival style, they were built in 1830 to a design by Edward Davis. To Peter Diamond's eye they had the look of something made from a child's building blocks. He'd never liked them.

A patrol car with roof light flashing was parked across the road to prevent traffic from entering the park, and diversion signs were in place. Tapes had been drawn across to keep the inevitable gawpers well back. A crime scene photographer was getting pictures.

The dead woman was hanging on white plastic cord from the centre crosspiece of the right-hand arch. Framed by the massive pillars she appeared child-like in size. She was clothed in a pink sweater and white jeans and was without shoes. Because of the twist of the head, forced outwards by the cord, her dark, almost black, hair, covered most of her face.

'And you are . . . ?'

Diamond found himself addressed by a man in a white paper suit.

'Diamond, CID. Who are you?'

'Diamond.' He was writing the name on a clipboard. 'Rank?'

'Didn't you hear? I asked you a question.'

'Gledhill, scene manager.'

'Pleased to meet you. I'm a detective superintendent.'

Gledhill wrote it. 'The SIO, I take it?'

'You can take it, yes. And you're a civilian?'

'A professional crime scene investigator.'

'Not one of us, then.'

'Does that make any difference to you, superintendent?'

'Just getting it clear in my mind.' These jobs were often contracted out. Privatisation had become a feature of crime investigation. There were companies equipped to do all the forensic jobs, and presumably Georgina or someone from the nick had called in Gledhill's lot at an early stage. 'So what can you tell me?'

'About the body?'

'I wasn't asking how you spent your holidays.'

Gledhill didn't know it, but this irritability had a lot to do with Diamond's guilt about getting here late.

'The call came in at six twenty this morning. She was spotted by the driver of a milk-float. A response car got here at six forty or thereabouts and I may as well tell you they contaminated the scene trying to see if she was still alive, which she plainly was not. We were contacted at seven twenty-five and our arrival was logged at eight ten, more than an hour ago. I assumed CID would be here before this.'

It was like a reprimand and it struck home. Diamond counterpunched. 'You can assume what you like, Sunny Jim. What have you done in all this time? Why isn't the corpse screened off? She's entitled to some respect.'

'Our equipment isn't geared to this sort of situation. You'd need screens three metres tall.'

'Rig up some plastic sheeting. Tie a rope between that lamp-post and the tree. You do have plastic sheeting?'

'I believe so, but by the time we get it in place—'

'It will be needed. Has anyone told you this is number five in a series of suspicious hangings in this area? Obviously not. You're going to be here some time. Has the pathologist been called?'

Gledhill nodded. 'He's on his way. And the forensic physician came by and certified death before you arrived.'

'Who did you get?'

'The pathologist? Dr Sealy.'

'You've made my day. Is there anything to tell us the identity of the body?'

'Too soon. There was nothing in her pockets. No note.'

'You've searched the area for a bag, I expect?'

'Without success. We thought her shoes might be recovered, but we haven't found them.'

Diamond relented a little. Gledhill and his team had not been entirely inactive. 'Do you have a paper suit my size? I'd like a close look.'

Kitted out, and with Halliwell in support, he approached using the access path Gledhill showed him. That body looked pathetically frail.

236

The photographer had left a folding set of steps. Before mounting them Diamond examined the hands and feet. The toenails were painted and undamaged, the soles clean. She hadn't walked here without shoes.

The woman was suspended about a metre clear of the ground on the white cord or cable the thickness of a pencil, like the sort used for clotheslines—similar to the cord found on the other bodies he'd seen. He looked up to where it was lashed to the stone crossbeam using the eye of a bowline knot. Then he mounted the steps and examined the ligature. He didn't care to look at the face at this stage.

The cord was tight around the neck, making a deep indentation. There would be no giveaway secondary mark.

'What do you know?' he said to himself. 'It's another slip knot.'

30

'Where are the media?' he asked Gledhill.

'Who do you mean—the *Chronicle*?'

'Radio, TV, press. They should be here by now.'

'That's up to them. Press relations aren't my concern.'

Diamond turned to his ever-reliable second-in-command. 'Keith, this has got to have publicity. We need to know the identity of this woman as soon as possible. Make some calls.'

Gledhill stopped being indifferent. 'Is that necessary? I don't want television crews tramping all over the scene. They'll find us soon enough.'

'Did you look at the left hand?'

'Of the deceased? Not specially.'

'There's the mark of a ring there.'

'A wedding ring?'

Diamond gave him a how-would-I-know look. 'It's just the mark, but it's the third finger of the left hand. The chance is high that she was married. If this follows the pattern of the other hangings, the husband is due to die next, and soon. As of now I don't have a clue who he is.'

Gledhill leaned closer, as if he hadn't heard right. 'Do you think somebody is murdering couples?'

'I'd put it more strongly. I'd use the word "executing".'

'But why?'

'If I knew that, we wouldn't be here.'

The crime scene people improvised some screening as Diamond had suggested, using plastic sheeting draped over lengths of cord.

Bertram Sealy arrived and said with a stupid grin to Diamond that they couldn't go on meeting like this. The usual banter between pathologists and police didn't sit well, not when Sealy was making the quips.

'Where's the gorgeous Ingeborg this morning?' Sealy went on. 'I could do with her support on the steps.'

'Get a life, Doctor.'

Gledhill produced another paper suit and Sealy went to work without assistance, speaking into his tape-recorder.

Halliwell was through to the BBC news room in Bristol.

'Tell them I'm briefing the press as soon as they get here and it's a big story,' Diamond said. 'The same to ITN and the papers.'

He stepped outside the plastic sheeting and was pleased to find that most of the onlookers had gone. He tried picturing what had happened, the killer arriving with his victim, by car almost certainly. If the MO was the same as before, she was dead already. The object was to arrange a fake hanging. Anyone would think she died on the end of a rope. Not so. She was on show, dangling there, because this was how the killer wanted it to appear.

In the small hours of the morning this part of the city, set back from Marlborough Lane, well north of the main artery, the Upper Bristol Road, would have been quiet. The killer had thought this through. He'd backed his vehicle right up to the arch on the broad pavement without fear of being seen. Even if the occasional car passed, he wasn't conspicuous and the tyres hadn't left a mark on the stone surface. He'd slung the end of his plastic washing-line over the crossbeam and made it secure. Did he stand on the roof of his vehicle to do it? If that were the case, did he have a van, or a four-by-four or a saloon? A man in the business of rigging up gallows would surely have worked out the most convenient transport.

Then came the more risky part of removing the corpse from the interior and tying the cord round the neck. He'd judged how high the noose had to be. He must have. It was calculated so that the body would swing. He'd positioned her on the roof, or the boot, or the bonnet, and then driven away and left her suspended.

239

This all required planning. It was likely he'd done a dummy run to assess the task. But why go to all that trouble? Why take the risk of discovery? Most murderers go to great lengths to conceal their victims. They don't seek to display them.

Pondering these questions, Diamond returned inside the enclosure. Dr Sealy had stepped down—unaided—and was ready to report the preliminary findings.

'A woman under forty, I'd say, but not much under. Slimly built, about five six in height. No shoes, otherwise dressed casually. Manicured hands and feet. Nothing in the state of the nails to indicate a struggle. The undersides of the feet are clean, suggesting she was transported here. No obvious wounds.'

'Did you take the temperature?' Diamond asked.

'Nasally, yes. And before you ask, the temperature doesn't tell us much. There are too many variables. My first impression is that she was dead before she was brought here. I'm assuming she was brought here. If this were suicide we'd have a chair or something at the scene, something she'd stepped off. It's true that the pillars have a base with a ledge of sorts, but too low down to have supported the feet. The noose is interesting, tight round the neck and tied with a slip knot.'

'Which we saw up at the viaduct,' Diamond said.

'Yes,' Sealy said in the surprised tone of a schoolmaster getting the right answer out of the class idiot, 'but I'm trying to consider this incident in isolation. As I say, a slip knot, so tight that it would probably have throttled her if she had been

240

alive. Before she was suspended, I mean. Quite what it conceals, if anything, I won't know until after autopsy.'

'You'll do that today?'

'That's my firm intention.'

'I'd like more photos of the face, for recognition. Can we draw the hair aside?'

'If the man with the clipboard allows.'

Gledhill nodded, and Diamond called for the photographer.

The victim's eyes were closed, the mouth open a little, but not sagging. There's a question of taste about showing the faces of murder victims in the press and on television. Some picture editors are reluctant to challenge old taboos. It was essential that this woman was recognised as soon as possible. If the ligature was cropped from the picture there was nothing repulsive in her appearance.

The photographer took about twenty shots with the hair drawn back from the face. 'Good-looking woman . . . considering,' he said.

'Is that digital?' Diamond asked. 'Can we go on line with it immediately?'

'As soon as you like. Do you want some with the eyes open?'

'No.' He'd seen what Delia Williamson's eyes were like after being strangled. It wouldn't assist recognition. 'The press will be here shortly.'

'You can pick out the shot you want. Scan through them now.'

They were not offensive. The best were taken at an angle, eliminating the skewed effect of the head against the cord. He chose two, full-face and half-profile.

Halliwell informed him that the first reporter had arrived. 'Are you going to link this to the other hangings, guv?'

'That's the plan. Do you have a problem with it?'

'They'll go to town on it. A serial killer at large.'

He shrugged. 'It's true, isn't it?'

'I was wondering if you need to clear it with headquarters, the ACC, or someone.'

'I'm running this inquiry, Keith. Georgina wanted it shelved. She's more interested in protecting shop windows.'

'Yes, but I thought I'd mention it.'

'And you have. Where's the best place to meet the press? Across the road by the other arch?'

Halliwell was right. Georgina would go ballistic when she saw on television that a serial hangman was at work in Bath and she hadn't been informed. Press relations are a minefield for the police. Elaborate procedures are laid down. Every statement is supposed to be rubber-stamped.

Diamond didn't give a toss. Another life was at stake and there wasn't time for consultation. He wanted headlines tonight.

Bertram Sealy approached him again. 'So who wants a front seat at the autopsy?'

31

The entire murder squad stayed late that evening in hope that someone would call and say they recognised the dead woman. The *Bath Chronicle* was on the streets by mid-afternoon and, as

Diamond had predicted, the hanging in the park was the headline story. The regional TV news would go out at six.

About four thirty, when nothing had come in except calls from attention seekers, Leaman said, 'Could mean she isn't local. The killer could have brought the body in from miles away.'

'Thanks for that, John,' Diamond said. 'I can always rely on you to cheer us up.'

'The others were local,' Ingeborg said.

'But is there a local connection?' Leaman said. 'We haven't found one yet.'

'Keep going,' Diamond said. 'I'm hurting.'

'Anyway, the nationals will carry the picture tomorrow,' Ingeborg said. 'It's big news.'

Leaman said, 'So if we don't hear anything in the next hour, do we all go home and wait for tomorrow's papers?'

Next time, cleverclogs, Diamond thought, you can sit in on the autopsy instead of Keith Halliwell, who always does it. Some blood and guts might take the smile off your face.

His personal phone buzzed, but it was only Georgina's PA. The ACC wanted to see him as a matter of urgency.

He said, 'That's all I need. Would you inform the ACC I've got a matter of urgency down here?'

'I think she knows all about that, Mr Diamond.'

'I'm for the high jump, am I?'

'The pole vault, I would say.'

'Better show my face, then?'

'I strongly advise it.'

He told Leaman where he was going. 'But I'm not doing fifteen rounds with Georgina. Give me ten minutes, max, and then call her office and say

243

it's all happening and you need me, right? Don't let me down.'

On the way upstairs he rehearsed his explanation. He would say—and it was true—that time was running out. He needed to identify the latest victim and his only chance had been to break the story without delay. He would add—and it was less true—that he'd fully intended to report what was happening at the first opportunity.

Georgina didn't give him the chance. She'd rehearsed her piece, too, and came at him with all guns blazing. He'd heard most of it after previous insubordinations, so he fixed his gaze on the wall behind her and thought about other things. Finally the tirade stopped. Georgina said, 'Have you been listening? Have you heard one word of what I was saying?'

'Yes, ma'am.'

'You have this bumptious look on your face as if your mind is on higher things. Why don't you look me in the eye when I'm talking to you? What is it you find so riveting on the wall behind me?'

'The picture of Her Majesty the Queen, ma'am.'

The phone went. It needed to be Leaman.

She snatched it up. 'What is it?'

He waited.

Georgina eyed him like a caged lioness. 'You'd better return to your team. They seem to think there's been a development.'

*   *   *

The only development was that DC Gilbert had arrived with a tray of tea.

244

'I can do with that,' Diamond said.

'No chance of cake, guv?' Leaman said.

'What?'

'We were thinking the ACC might have baked you another chocolate cake.'

'*Another?* That wasn't from upstairs. Get real, John.'

'Did you ever find out who sent it?'

'Not Georgina.'

'She's a cracking good cook, whoever she is.'

Ingeborg said, 'Leave it, John.' She'd seen the danger signals.

Leaman had touched a raw nerve. Paloma's cake wasn't the delicious memory for Diamond that it was for everyone else. Maybe he should have been flattered that she had gone to so much trouble to get him interested, but it unsettled him instead. He'd been happier thinking he'd made the main moves in their coming together. It shouldn't matter. He still fancied her like mad. She was witty and intelligent and she seemed to think he was good in bed, which any man likes to be told. Go with the flow, he told himself. At your age you don't expect to have women running after you.

A call from the mortuary jerked him back to the world of work. Keith Halliwell was reporting on the autopsy. 'Dr Sealy reckons she was strangled with a ligature, the same as Delia Williamson. It wasn't so obvious this time, and the slip knot masked it, but the signs are there, he says.'

'She was dead when she was strung up? The same MO?'

'He's sure of it.'

'Did she put up a fight?'

'There were no indications. Maybe he got her drunk, or drugged. The blood tests will take a while.'

'Anything else I should know about?'

'She was sexually experienced, but you'd expect that at her age.'

'Which was what?'

'Round about forty. She'd had a pregnancy at some stage. She also had an appendix scar.'

'Good man. How's your stomach?'

'Fine.' He added with a hint that 'fine' didn't mean he did this duty willingly, 'This wasn't my first time.'

Diamond was unrepentant. 'See you shortly, then.'

'There was one other thing,' Halliwell said. 'It was rather peculiar. Dr Sealy noticed some particles that fell out of her hair. He said they were grains of sugar.'

'What—household sugar?'

'Yes. He was so sure of it that he tasted one.'

'Rather him than me. Why would she have sugar in her hair? Some kind of shampoo?'

'He doesn't think so. Sugar would dissolve, wouldn't it?

His theory is that there may have been some spilt in the vehicle used to move the body and her head came into contact with it.'

'So we're looking for a Tate and Lyle driver?'

'My feeling is that we could waste time on this, guv.'

'You're probably right. This is going to be a long evening anyway.'

The phones took over. Local television had just screened the picture of the dead woman and given the police number. The first few calls were duds. One of the hazards of releasing a picture is that you hear from people who want to be helpful and aren't. They convince themselves it's someone they saw yesterday, or once knew.

Then Ingeborg waved to Diamond from across the room. She'd taken details from a woman in Midford. 'I think you should speak to this one, guv.'

He took the phone. 'Would you mind repeating what you just told my colleague?'

The caller had the local accent and the slow delivery that sometimes goes with it. 'Well, it's about the poor soul who was found hanging in Bath, isn't it? They just showed her picture on the television and I'm certain I know her. I've seen her often. She's got a big house called Brookview Lodge, off the Midford Road, north of the village. She rides her horse around the lanes. That's where I've seen her. Always nicely dressed in her riding things.'

'Would you know her name?'

'That's it, my dear. I don't. I've never spoken to her. But I don't make mistakes about faces. She's the poor lady they showed on the television, I promise you.'

'Is she married?'

'I wouldn't know about that. She always rides out alone. The horse is chestnut, with a black mane. He's big and handsome.'

Another woman phoned in not long after. She, too, believed the victim was the horsewoman seen around Midford almost every day.

Diamond called across to Ingeborg. 'Get someone else to take over. You and I are going to

247

check on a possible sighting.'

*　　　*　　　*

Brookview Lodge took its name from Midford Brook, a misnomer for something more like a full-blown river that channels water into the Avon from its southern source in the Mendip hills. They approached by way of a narrow road through the north-facing Midford Woods where oak, beech and larch grow and nightingales were heard in recent memory. As the Ka descended, the tall-banked lane opened to a panorama of the Limpley Stoke Valley. Ingeborg spotted the sign for the lodge and swung right. A winding drive brought them to a handsome gabled building in well-weathered local stone. They drove onto a paved area at the front. A horse neighed from the outbuildings.

'Poor thing could be hungry,' Ingeborg said. 'Shall I check?'

'Later. We're not the RSPCA. Let's see if anyone's in.'

He got out and tried the doorbell. Lifted the letter-flap and saw mail inside. Tried the bell again. Walked round the side of the building. The flowerbeds were well maintained. At the rear was a large oval swimming pool. Recliners and small tables were set on the tiled surround, but there wasn't a sense of anyone in residence today.

He turned towards the conservatory extension that seemed to be used as an anteroom to the pool. Inside were towels on a clothes rack, more garden furniture, a rowing machine, a treadmill and a whirlpool.

The door was unlocked. 'I bet the inner door is locked,' he said as they went in.

He was right.

'And I bet there's an alarm system,' Ingeborg said.

'Let's find out.' He picked up a sandbox used to support a sunshade. It was good and heavy. He swung it at the door. The door stayed firm, but the alarm went off. 'You're right.'

He tried again.

Ingeborg said, 'Guv, should we be doing this?'

At the third attempt the box ripped through the bolt mechanism.

He stepped inside, through a living room and across a large entrance hall. 'Find the control panel and switch that bloody thing off.'

The place had the feel of somewhere that hadn't seen anyone for most of the week. He felt inside the wire basket containing the mail.

The names on the envelopes told him what he'd feared. More than one person lived here. Martin and Jocelyn Steel. The man had letters from the Law Society and other legal organisations. Probably a solicitor.

Ingeborg silenced the alarm and came from the back of the house to join him. He showed her the letters.

'A man as well? That's not what we wanted to find, guv.'

'What's through there?'

'The kitchen, I think.'

They went through. The smell was not nice. Ingeborg found two trout on the work surface wrapped in tinfoil. They reeked. 'Their supper, I suppose. Look, there are potatoes waiting to boil in the saucepan.'

'It doesn't suggest to me that Jocelyn Steel was planning to hang herself.'

A door from the laundry room connected to the double garage. Two cars were in there, the 'his' and 'hers' it seemed, a silver Porsche Cayenne Turbo and a red Mini Cooper.

He checked the answerphone. Nine messages, the first on Sunday morning. Four from the same person, who called herself Mummy. By the fourth, she was getting frantic and said so. 'Are you all right? I keep trying. You didn't say you were going away or anything. Darling, please call me, however late you get in.'

Diamond sighed. 'Someone had better break it to Mummy.' He would do it himself. He didn't wish every unpleasant duty on his subordinates.

Of the other calls, one was from someone called Agnes, who sounded like Jocelyn's friend and addressed her as Joss. Two were from Dawn, a younger-sounding voice with the soft West Country accent. At the second try she said she was bothered about Prince and she wouldn't mind getting him out and riding him.

'The horse,' Ingeborg said.

'There was I thinking Prince Harry.'

The other calls were from South-West Gas, to arrange a service of the central heating; and the library, because a book Mr Steel had ordered had come in.

He used the phone to arrange with Leaman for a forensic team to come out. 'I'm ninety-nine per cent sure we've found the right place. Is Keith back from the autopsy yet?'

'He just got in.'

'Tell him he's needed here.'

'Do you want me as well, guv?' Leaman asked.

'No. Someone has to keep taking the calls.' To Ingeborg he said, 'Let's go upstairs.'

She said, 'I thought you'd never ask.'

'Ingeborg.'

'Guv?'

'I do the jokes.'

The Steels shared a bedroom and it was clearly important in their lives, with a kingsize bed fitted into a wall unit with an array of soft toys, books, CDs and ornaments. A plasma TV and sound system were on the opposite wall. The white quilt on the bed was doubled back. There were wine glasses on the bedside tables, each with a tidemark of red wine.

'Doesn't look to me as if they were fighting,' Diamond said.

'Guv.'

Ingeborg had found a framed wedding photo. Beyond doubt the bride was the woman found hanging in Royal Victoria Park.

32

The doorbell chimed.

'Too soon to be Halliwell or forensics,' Diamond said. From the bedroom window all he could see on the front drive was Ingeborg's Ka. 'See who it is.'

He picked up the wedding picture and studied the groom, a tall, slim figure in a morning suit. It was helpful that Martin Steel was holding the grey topper, not wearing it. He hadn't much hair on top, a distinct point of recognition, and there were silver streaks in the sideburns. Some years older than his bride, by the look of him. The thought crossed Diamond's mind that this might even be Jocelyn's father, but he dismissed it just as quickly; the place for that picture wasn't in the bedroom.

'Guv, would you mind coming down?'

'On my way.' First he removed the photo from its frame and slipped it into his pocket.

Standing in the hall with Ingeborg was a girl of school age, probably not more than fourteen. She was in T-shirt and jeans. A stud in her nose and coloured stripes in her hair.

'This is Dawn, the stable girl. She looks after the horse twice a day.'

'Good for her.' He smiled at the girl. 'Better for the horse.'

There wasn't a flicker of amusement.

'She saw my car and called to see who we are.'

'Sensible,' he said, thinking a word of praise was no bad thing. He hoped this wasn't one of those sullen teenagers. 'Well, young lady, I expect Ingeborg has told you we're detectives. You work for Mr and Mrs Steel, then? Have you seen them lately?'

'Saturday,' Dawn said. 'Mrs Steel, not him. Her name is Joss, but I call her Mrs Steel.' She had that youthful habit of ending statements on a rising note, making them sound like questions. Fair enough. She was communicating, giving the answers and volunteering information as well. Kids aren't all bad.

'Saturday? That's three days ago.'

252

'He's all right, except he hates being locked up all day.'

Diamond wondered for a moment if he'd got this case all wrong. Then the penny dropped. 'You're talking about the horse?'

She nodded. 'Three days is too much. He needs to get out.'

'Between you and me, Dawn, we're interested in the people.'

'Why—has something happened to them?'

'We're trying to find out. They haven't been seen by anybody for a couple of days.'

'Yeah, it's weird. She always tells me if they go away. Then I get to ride Prince. He needs riding every day. She hasn't taken him out on the roads since Saturday. I can tell by the state of his hooves.'

'Does anyone call at the house? A cleaner, perhaps?'

'Lady in a van. Tidy House Services. It isn't always the same lady. They come Thursday.'

'Anyone else?'

'The gardener, Ted. He does Wednesday.'

'Is he local?'

'Just up the lane, cottage with the gnome in the front fishing in the pond.'

'Ted who?'

'Hawkins. Something like that.'

'No one else? No strangers—apart from us? This is important, Dawn. You may be our only witness.'

She pulled a face at that. 'You've got to be joking. I'm not a witness. I'm mucking out and grooming and feeding, aren't I? I don't stand about looking to see who calls.'

253

'You're certain you saw no one?'

'I told you.'

'Fair enough. There are no other regular visitors than you and the gardener, then?'

She hesitated and fiddled with her hair. 'Don't know if I should be telling you this. Sometimes when I come Fridays there's a posh car outside. Belongs to this bloke in his twenties. Quite a hunk, he is. He leaves about five.'

'You don't know who he is?'

'I've never spoken to him.'

'A friend of Mrs Steel's, would you say?'

She gave a coy smile.

'But he only comes Fridays?' Diamond said.

'That's when I see'd him.'

'So he won't have called yet this week. He's not from the village?'

'I'd know if he was, wouldn't I?'

'Can you describe him?'

She sighed and drew her arms across her chest, worried that she might have put her job at risk, and Diamond knew he wasn't going to get much of a description. 'There's nothing special.'

'What colour's his hair?'

'Dunno.'

'If you've seen him, you must know.'

'It's too short to tell.'

'A skinhead?'

'Almost.'

'Is he big, would you say?'

'Not really, except for his shoulders. Look, I don't know if I was meant to see him.'

'What's the car like?'

'I told you, posh. I don't know nothing about cars.'

'Not a sports car?'

'No.'

'Colour?'

'Silver.'

'Was he here last Friday?'

'He was leaving as I come up the drive.'

'So those are the callers,' he summed up. 'The cleaners, the gardener and the young guy in the silver car? They each have their special days, but you come twice a day all week?'

'I don't mind. He's awesome.'

'Who? Ah, you're on about that horse again? And quite right, too. You'd better keep coming and see that he gets his exercise. You can get back to him now. Is there a paddock he can run around?'

Dawn didn't think much of Diamond's ideas on horse management. 'I wouldn't let him out after being stabled so long. He'd get all excited. He could damage hisself.'

'What's to be done with him, then? It won't get dark for another hour and a half. Take him for a ride.'

'Cool.' But still she hesitated. 'Do you think she'll mind? Mrs Steel, I mean.'

'Take it from me,' he said. 'She won't mind.'

*　　　*　　　*

The forensic team arrived with Halliwell not far behind them. They came in a customised white van with *Safeguard and Search* written on the side.

'Another civilian outfit,' Diamond said to Ingeborg. 'Everything is being privatised. One of these days you and I will have a little advert in the

255

Yellow Pages. Mark my words.'

But it soon emerged that the Safeguard and Search people were ex-police officers who knew their job. He gave them the background and they brought out their equipment and started checking for traces of recent visitors, starting with himself and Ingeborg. Shoes and fingers. He owned up to breaking in. The senior man said there were no indications of another break-in, so it had to be assumed that the abductor had a key, or was admitted by one of the victims.

'In which case, he may have been known to them,' Diamond said.

'That can't be discounted.'

One early discovery was a noticeboard with some contact numbers and addresses, among them one poignantly listed as Mum. Joss Steel's mother lived only ten minutes away, in a retirement home at Monkton Combe. People were occupied with their jobs in Brookview Lodge. Diamond could safely leave them for a short while.

*   *   *

Later, in the room overlooking the pool, the murder squad touched base. After looking around for somewhere to sit, Diamond touched his own base on a gym machine looking like a futuristic throne. 'Is this thing safe, would you say? It's not going to launch me into outer space?'

Ingeborg said, 'It's for exercising the abs. You're in no danger.'

She and Halliwell, both lightweights, sat on chairs from the poolside.

Diamond said, 'These are the facts. There's no sign anywhere of a struggle. It's obvious they weren't held here for any time. That half-prepared meal in the kitchen shows they were interrupted late afternoon, early evening. The stable girl saw Jocelyn Steel on Saturday and the phone messages start Sunday, so we can assume this happened late Saturday. The killer calls and someone admits him.'

'Someone known to them,' Halliwell said.

'Unless he points a firearm. They did as they were told.'

'They could have gone willingly if they trusted him,' Ingeborg said. 'He may not have needed a weapon.'

'I doubt that. They were preparing a meal. They stop everything and go off with him. I sense some compulsion here.'

'You're assuming both of them were present,' Halliwell said. 'He could have taken them separately.'

'How do you mean?'

'Well, if the man—what's his name?'

'Martin Steel.'

'If he was doing something outside, say, in the garden. It's Saturday. He's at home, catching up on jobs. He gets taken first, tied up presumably, and taken to the getaway vehicle. Then our killer walks into the house and attends to the woman.'

Ingeborg said, 'What do you mean—rapes her?'

Diamond shook his head. 'There's no evidence any of these were sex crimes.'

'What I meant,' Halliwell said, 'is that he takes her to his vehicle—car, van or whatever—and drives off with the pair of them trussed up.'

'That would make it easier for our suspect to cope,' Diamond said. 'Could he have planned it like that, knowing the man would be outside?'

'Doubtful.'

'If the motive isn't sex,' Ingeborg said, 'why is he doing this? There's no profit in kidnapping unless you demand a ransom, and he doesn't. He just murders them. It's like some perverted power game.'

'It's no game,' Diamond said.

'He's taking big risks,' Halliwell said. 'Does he want to get caught? Deep down, I mean.'

Diamond rolled his eyes. He'd never had much truck with psychology. 'There's a pattern to all this, I'll give you that. It has to be done in a certain way that involves hanging them up, even if they're dead already. They must be left hanging— and in a place where people can see them.'

'Sick.'

'We agree on that, but where does it take us, Keith? What's behind this?'

Halliwell dug deep for an explanation. He pursed his lips and half closed his eyes. Then a look of revulsion passed across his face. 'No, that's too horrible.'

'Go on,' Ingeborg said.

'I was thinking if it wasn't one killer at all. If there was some secret society and the way to join it is to murder a couple and hang them up like that.'

'That's a bit extreme,' Ingeborg said.

'So is hanging people,' Diamond said. 'We're in extreme territory here. I'm listening to any suggestions.'

Ingeborg said, 'Let me get this straight. Keith is

saying it isn't one killer. It's three. Every time a couple is murdered it's someone else earning his pass to this secret society. Come off it, guys. There aren't that many crazy, evil killers in the whole of Britain, let alone Bath.'

'It only takes one dominant figure,' Halliwell said. 'He sets the agenda and influences his disciples. How about Charles Manson, that Californian hippie who had the so-called family and sent them out in squads to kill? His people were women as well as men. It's happened before and it could happen here.'

'That's not what you were saying just now,' Ingeborg said. 'You were talking about initiation rites.' She liked precision, did Ingeborg.

Halliwell wriggled a little under her scrutiny. 'No two cases are the same. The point is that suggestible people can be brainwashed into doing horrible things.'

Diamond said, 'If you're right, forensics are wasting their time trying to compare DNA and fingerprints. They'll get a different set at each scene.'

'What do *you* think, guv?' Ingeborg asked, unimpressed by Halliwell.

'On balance, I favour a single killer. I've thought a lot about cults. When it seemed we were faced with suicides this was a possibility, else how can you explain people doing away with themselves in near-identical ways? But we're dealing with murder now. Joss Steel didn't tie a noose around her neck and kick a chair from under her. She was put there.'

'With sugar in her hair,' Halliwell added.

'Let's not get sidetracked,' Diamond said.

Ingeborg said, 'We're assuming the husband was abducted too—but is that definite?'

'That's the MO,' Halliwell said.

'What are you thinking?' Diamond asked her.

'The husband could have killed her.' For Halliwell's benefit, she said, 'Before you arrived we talked to Dawn, the stable girl. There's a guy who visits on Fridays. He leaves as she's arriving, round about five. He's been here for the afternoon. It's obvious what Dawn thinks.'

'That he's the lover?'

'He's in his twenties, nice car, good-looking. What if the husband got wind of it?'

'Killed her for two-timing him?'

'Exactly.'

Diamond said, 'He'd bury her in the paddock. He wouldn't hang her in the park.'

She saw the logic in that, sighed and conceded with a faint smile. When a wife takes a lover, the husband doesn't want the whole world to know.

'We've got to assume Martin Steel is under imminent threat of death,' Diamond said. 'Here's the action plan: to get everything possible on this couple. Their recent movements, contacts, phone calls, e-mails, credit statements. I need at least three good people here going through their personal stuff. Keith, you talk to the gardener, Ted Hawkins, house in the village with the gnome fishing in the pond. Inge, get onto that cleaning service, Tidy House. See what they know.'

'What about lover boy?'

'Hold on, we're getting ahead of ourselves.'

'The mystery caller, then.'

'I'm going to call him Man Friday. We need to identify him first. He's top of your list of questions. Between the cleaners and the gardener we ought to find out more.'

'You don't mind them knowing?'

'What—that she may have been testing the mattress on Friday afternoons? She's dead, Keith. We're not protecting her reputation.'

'And if they don't know anything about it?'

'We turn up a contact number. Get weaving.'

Alone in the exercise room, he used the wall-phone to call the nick and get the reinforcements he needed. Leaman was managing well with those calls from the public, or so he claimed, as he would, being John Leaman. The phone lines were red-hot, but when pressed he had to admit that nothing more of importance had come in. Yes, Leaman said, it was no trouble to send three DCs.

Diamond replaced the phone. He looked around at the apparatus—the rowing-machine and the weights, and reflected on the time the couple must have spent toning their bodies—for what? He got up, and felt the flop of his beer gut over his waistband. Maybe he'd see how the abdominal exerciser worked.

*   *   *

More sore than refreshed, he went back into the main part of the house to check on Safeguard and Search. They were getting more sets of fingerprints than they wanted. He told them about the cleaners and Man Friday and they said it would be helpful to get their prints for comparison. 'You wish,' he said.

But he'd had an idea while he was trying out the exercise machine. Was it possible that Man Friday

261

was a personal trainer? Smart car, broad shoulders. Friday afternoon at a rich woman's house, a place equipped with an array of exercise machines. How many personal trainers plied their trade in Bath? he wondered. He knew a way to get inside information.

He took out his new mobile and called the only number stored in it.

33

A thought nagged at him while he drove to Paloma's. Ten minutes ago it had seemed obvious to get in touch. Her son Jerry was in the personal-training business, so here was a reason to seek help from friends. The closer he got, the less appealing it seemed. You don't let your work impinge on your private life. How embarrassing if Jocelyn Steel's Man Friday was none other than Jerry. Even worse if the training turned out to have been more intimate than personal.

Too much of a coincidence? He hoped so. There had to be other personal trainers in the city. Maybe Man Friday wasn't a fitness expert at all. Please God, he gave piano lessons, or did tarot readings.

'You did the right thing, letting me know you were coming,' Paloma said when she opened the door. She'd put on make-up and what looked to him like a party dress.

'It's a business call.'

'Yes, buttercup, you made that clear, but I can make myself presentable for a business call, the same as a social one.'

'And you have. You look terrific.'

'You can give me a business-like kiss if you want.'

'Is there such a thing?' He stepped into the hall and held her and their lips pressed and every other thought was blocked out.

But Paloma reminded him why he was here. 'You want some help from Jerry, you said. I called him and he's on his way over. A drink while you wait?'

'Better not.'

'It's not about that poor woman who was found in the park, is it? I saw her face on the television.'

'Afraid so,' he said, and told her about the exercise room in Jocelyn Steel's house and his theory that she had a trainer. 'I'm clutching at straws here, but Jerry knows more about this kind of thing than I do. He may have a few ideas I can follow up.'

'I'm sure he'll give any advice he can. It's a horrible case, by the sound of it.'

'They're all horrible for someone.'

'Doesn't one as bad as this give you nightmares?'

'Once in a while, but I've been doing it a long time. What keeps me awake is trying to work out where I've gone wrong. In this one there's a vicious twist. The husband is going to be killed unless I find the psycho who's got him.'

'That's awful pressure, Peter. I know I couldn't handle it.'

'You treat it as what it is—a job. Think too much and you're stuffed.'

Jerry let himself in, called out to them from the

263

hall and finally put his head round the door. 'You need a receptionist, Mum.'

He was in a silver tracksuit today. A useful lead-in. Diamond asked if the colour went with his new motor.

'The car's not mine, unfortunately,' Jerry said. 'It's rented. And it's black.'

One awkward suspicion removed. 'Good of you to come.'

'You want to pick my brains, Mum said. Not sure I have any, but you're welcome to try.'

Diamond gave him some background. Jerry hadn't heard about the latest murder. He wasn't the sort to listen to his car radio. He'd have Coldplay going at top volume.

'It's only an idea,' Diamond said, 'but she had a regular visitor—a young man—and I thought he might be a personal trainer. It struck me that you're likely to know of any others who do the job locally.'

'I wouldn't say I know them all.' Jerry thought a moment. 'Three spring to mind.' He stopped as if he regretted saying so much. 'I wouldn't want you to knock on their doors and say I sent you.'

'That's not in the plan. Three, you say.'

'What you can do is look on the noticeboard in any gym. That's how we get our clients.'

Paloma said, 'Peter doesn't have time for that. A man's life is in danger.'

'From a trainer?'

'I didn't say that,' Diamond said. 'I'm hoping to find a witness.'

'OK.' With reluctance, he said, 'Wayne McRae, Kev Cummings and Harry Lang are the local guys. I don't have their addresses.'

'No problem.'

'Wayne lives in the city. The other two may be from outside.'

'Fine. Would you know what they drive?'

'I've seen Wayne in a green Honda Civic. Couldn't tell you about the others.'

'How would they have got into this line of work? I don't suppose everyone goes through college like you did.'

He reddened. 'You've been checking up on me?'

Paloma said, 'Jerry, of course he hasn't. I told him. I'm proud of you. I bet these others aren't so well qualified.'

'Who knows? Anyone can set up as a trainer. You can hang around fitness centres chatting people up. There's a back-door route into most jobs. It's how good you are that matters.'

Diamond asked, 'Do most of your clients have weight-lifting equipment in their homes?'

'Depends. Some of the rich ones do.'

'This wouldn't be so unusual then: a rowing machine, treadmill and a machine for strengthening—what do you call them?—the abs?'

'Abdominal muscles. If you've got a big place and money to spend, why not? I know of four or five people with their own gear.'

Diamond hesitated. 'This is, em, difficult. Close your ears, Paloma. The clients tend to be rich women, conscious of their figures, right?'

'Some of them.'

'The trainers are young, fit guys like yourself?'

Jerry smiled, folded his arms and nodded. 'You're asking if it leads to anything? The first thing everyone wants to know.'

'It's not a personal question. I'm interested in these other guys. Does any of them have a reputation?'

'I wouldn't know,' he said, chuckling at the notion. 'I don't even talk about stuff like that.'

He'd resisted the chance to dish the dirt on the others and Diamond respected him for that, even though it could have aided the investigation. McRae, Cummings and Lang would be traced and checked as a priority.

There wasn't any more to be got from Jerry. The names were useful. He shrugged and left the room when Diamond thanked him.

Paloma reached for Diamond and hugged him. 'I know you'll stop this killer. I'm confident you will.'

'The thing is, can I stop him in time?'

She whispered, 'Be careful. I want you safe. You wouldn't believe how much I want you.'

He had to loosen her grip to get away. He drove back to Manvers Street thinking he was in a pig of a job.

34

He was with Georgina now, in her Manvers Street eyrie. One of those times when he needed her backing. His lamentable record—in her eyes—of neglected duties, flip remarks and open insubordination had to be put aside for the greater good, the snaring of a serial killer. It was a matter of persuading her. He'd listed the five hangings and told her he was convinced that the sixth was imminent.

'How can you possibly know?' she said, folding her arms across that awesome silver-buttoned bosom.

'It's a pattern, isn't it? This killer attacks couples. The woman dies first and then there's a short interval before the man is murdered. We're in that interval now.'

'How long have we got, according to you?'

'It could be tonight or tomorrow night and we know it will be somewhere in the city, which is why I'm asking for a blanket police presence. Vehicle checks, obbos, the lot.'

'That's easily said, Peter. We don't have the manpower for this. I can't just open another box of bobbies. Headquarters are already complaining about the overtime worked on the ram raids.'

The ram raids were a blind alley he refused to go down. 'This man will die unless we act.'

'Just having officers on the streets is a fishing trip, and you know it. Haven't you and your people got a suspect by now?'

'We're closing in.'

'You've had long enough.'

That remark was below the belt considering she'd insisted he stood down the incident room and put all his resources into the ram raids. Still, this wasn't the moment to remind her. 'Jocelyn Steel's murder has given us several new leads. We could have an arrest any time, but it's still vital to have this back-up.'

'What's the killer's motive?'

'If I knew that, ma'am, we'd have him by now.'

'A connection between the victims?'

'Nice idea.' He was trying so hard not to sound

sarcastic. 'Nothing yet.'

Georgina sighed. 'With a man's life on the line, I don't have much option, do I? I'll clear it with headquarters, but I look to you to make it unnecessary.'

*   *   *

Keith Halliwell was still out at Midford when Diamond phoned him.

'Have you caught up with the gardener?'

'Saw him in his cottage, yes. He's not in the frame, guv. Aged about eighty and worried he might lose his job.'

'Any use as a witness?'

'He's all right mentally. He's known the couple about four years. They don't mix much with the villagers, he said, but they treat him well. He knew Jocelyn Steel better than her husband, who seems to work long hours. She was always even-tempered, he said. Liked her riding and swimming. The pool and the exercise room were built after the Steels bought the house. She would swim and lounge by the pool with a book. Didn't have many visitors.'

'Did you ask about Man Friday?'

'He didn't know or wasn't saying.'

'Out of loyalty?'

'Hard to tell. He's a canny old bugger.'

'Had he heard of Agnes, the friend who left the phone message?'

'No. He's strictly an out-of-doors man. Brings his own coffee in a flask and drinks it by himself.'

'Not much help, then. What are you doing right now?'

268

'Looking through their filing cabinets. They're hoarders, which could be useful. Every invoice is filed away. They did a lot of buying on the internet. Clive is already out here going through their e-mails.'

Clive was the mainstay of the Avon & Somerset Hi-Tech Crime Unit and it was an open secret he earned more overtime than anyone else at the nick. Every case had its computer element these days.

'Ask him if there's a list of addresses.'

'Of people they e-mail? There has to be. But they won't be postal addresses, if that's what you were expecting.'

'Keith, I may be a computer illiterate, but I do know that much. Have you got a pen handy? Get Clive to check for these names in particular: Wayne McRae, Kevin Cummings, Harry Lang. They're three of the local personal trainers. What's Ingeborg up to?'

'Doing what you asked her—trying to reach the cleaning ladies.'

'Are the crime scene people still with you?'

'Yep. It's all go.'

'But no progress.'

'These things take time, guv.'

'That's a luxury we don't have.'

He ended the call and sifted through the photos of Jocelyn Steel's body when it was still suspended from Victoria Gate. By now the killer would have chosen a 'gallows' for Martin Steel, somewhere public and yet convenient for his purpose. Was there a clue in the locations he'd used already? The Twinings had been hung from a tree in Henrietta Park and the facade of Sham Castle.

Delia Williamson from the swing in Sydney Gardens and her partner, Geaves, from the viaduct over the Lower Bristol Road. Now Jocelyn Steel in Victoria Park. What had been picked for her husband?

The map in the incident room had large-headed pins marking the five crime scenes. Psychological profilers made entire careers out of sticking pins in maps. Was there anything in it? He was dubious. Most of their results could have been found by anyone with common sense, in his opinion. They'd study this little lot and tell you the killer was someone with local knowledge, someone who knew a bit about knots and worked by night. A boy scout with bags under his eyes.

Or just another crazy.

If the profiling lark was only common sense, there was a pressing need to apply some of his own. There was a pattern here. This killer believed in ladies first, and each of them left in a park. How significant was that? He was reluctant to read much into it. If you were looking for outdoor places to hang corpses you'd find parks convenient and quiet at night.

The male victims had ended up in the more spectacular settings. Sham Castle was a definite landmark, high above the city. John Twining's body must have been visible from many viewpoints. And Geaves, dangling from the railway viaduct, had caused traffic chaos. Was that any guide to where the next victim would be found? What would you choose to make a real impact?

He thought about the major tourist attractions: the Roman Baths, the Abbey, the Pump Room, the Royal Crescent, the Circus, Pulteney Bridge and Camden and Lansdown Crescents. Every one of them had its potential for a killer wanting to create an effect. Imagine a body suspended above the Great Bath, or against the west front of the Abbey, or from one of the chandeliers in the Pump Room. Bath's horror show could run and run.

Trying to predict the location was not a practical option.

His phone went again and Ingeborg was on the line. 'I tracked down the woman who runs Tidy House, guv, and she put me onto Jean Buchan, who cleaned the house last Thursday and has been before. She's bright and reliable, I'd say.'

'As a cleaner—or a witness?'

'Both, probably. She described Jocelyn Steel as friendly and a bit lonely, she thought, but not so depressed she'd want to kill herself. She'd make coffee for them and be happy to chat for half an hour or so out of the time she was paying to have the house cleaned. Said she looked forward to Thursday mornings because it was a chance to chat with another woman.'

'What about?'

'Mainly what was in the papers or on television.'

'Nothing about our victim's personal life?'

'I was coming to that. She had a woman friend she'd phone sometimes.'

'Agnes, who left the message on the answerphone.'

'I suppose so.'

'Did the cleaner listen in?'

'Not really, but there was a lot of laughing and

271

a kind of animation in the way she was talking that Jean Buchan took to mean they were discussing men. It's something you instinctively recognise if you're a woman.'

'Nothing more definite?'

'Afraid not.'

'We must find this Agnes. Are there stored numbers in the phone?'

'I'll check that next.'

'Good.'

'Before you go, guv, DI Halliwell is here. He wants a word.'

Keith came on and sounded more buoyant than he had for some time. 'Those names you gave me, guv.'

'The personal trainers? Yes?'

'They weren't in the computer.'

'But . . . ?'

'But what?'

'You're holding something back, you bastard.'

'If one of them works for a firm called Home Workouts we could be on to him. There's a bunch of invoices in the filing cabinet. Bloomfield Road, Bath. Little logo of a woman doing a side stretch. And there's a phone number.'

35

It was after ten next morning before anyone at Home Workouts picked up the phone. The woman was on the defensive as soon as Diamond said he was from the police. 'Has there been a complaint? We pride ourselves on being very professional. We only employ trainers with a proven record.'

'No complaint,' he said. 'It's just someone we're trying to trace.' He gave her the names.

'We don't offer massage.'

'I didn't mention massage.'

'Or anything else that goes under the name of massage. We do get enquiries and you can take it from me that nothing of the sort is offered or considered. It's strictly fitness training. We're registered with the Institute of Personal Trainers.'

'Can we rewind?' he said.

'I beg your pardon?'

'The names I just gave you.'

'I was coming to that. Even if one of these was on our books and broke the rules I wouldn't give you particulars without speaking to them first. They have a right to know.'

'For pity's sake,' he said. 'This isn't about sex for sale. If anyone's in trouble, you are, for withholding information. That's a criminal offence. What's your name?'

The line went silent.

Diamond said, 'I told you my name at the beginning. What's yours?'

She caved in, at least on the point that mattered. 'Only one of those names you mentioned is known to us.'

'And who is that?'

'Harry Lang. He's been with us about a year. He came with excellent references.'

'And does he by any chance give personal training to Mrs Jocelyn Steel of Brookview Lodge, Midford?'

There was a gasp. 'That's the woman who was

273

on the television. She was found hanging in Victoria Park.'

'And was she one of your customers?'

'Clients.' Even in the face of tragedy the little formalities needed to be observed. 'I didn't make the connection.'

'That was obvious. All I need from you are Harry Lang's contact details.'

*   *   *

Not wanting to alert Lang, Diamond didn't phone. He drove out to the trainer's home address, a council flat in Ballance Street, off Julian Road, above the Royal Crescent and just a few hundred yards from where Jocelyn Steel's body was found. The block is notorious for being an eyesore built in the 1970s to replace a so-called eighteenth-century slum. Its location on the slope of Lansdown means that its lemon-coloured slabs and sham mansards dominate an otherwise idyllic view. There is a theory that when the planners saw Ballance Street they were so appalled at their own creation that they called time on a dreadful period of architecture, not just in Bath, but across the country.

Keith Halliwell was already there. This wasn't a one-man job. Halliwell had parked by the church in Burlington Street to avoid being seen too close to the suspect's flat.

He was rubbing his hands. 'Watch out, Man Friday, we're coming to get you. Nice work, guv.'

'Save it, Keith. What's the set-up here?'

'Corridor access. He's got the ground-floor flat with the broken slats.'

'Have you checked the rear?'

'Not yet. But I've asked for back-up. Do we know he's at home?'

'He's off-duty. I know that much.'

'Does he have form?'

'Nothing on file. Could be using a false name. He's been with the agency about a year and doing this so-called personal training with Joss Steel since he started. Good references and no complaints from any of his lady customers.'

A police car moved fast up Julian Road, beacon and siren going.

'Typical. Tell the whole bloody world,' Diamond said.

But it swept straight past, on its way to another incident. A second, silent car appeared soon after and parked beside Halliwell's. Two young officers in uniform got out. Diamond pointed out the flat and told them to stand guard at the back. 'Watch him. He's fit and if he comes your way it's because he's frightened.'

He and Halliwell walked through the communal entrance and found Harry Lang's door. Some had names on them. Lang's didn't.

Halliwell knocked and pressed his ear to the door.

'Any joy?'

He shook his head.

'Stand aside.' Diamond kicked the door in.

Inside, the TV was going and a mug of steaming coffee was on a table in front. The flat was a two-up, two-down and the back door stood open. Diamond pointed to the stairs and Halliwell went up. Diamond ran through the back door to the tiled patio behind. Over the gate he could see

275

the chequered caps of his back-up team. They weren't moving. Obviously they hadn't seen him yet.

He dashed back inside. The man had to be upstairs. Halliwell would need support.

But Halliwell was on his way down. 'He's not here, guv.'

'He must be.'

They checked cupboards and the backs of furniture. In a box-like place like this there wasn't much cover at all.

'Is there a loft?'

'No.'

'The hot coffee proves someone was here.'

'The invisible man.'

Diamond went outside and checked with the two bobbies. They said he definitely hadn't escaped through the back gate. He looked up at the flat roof. In theory it would have been possible to scramble up there by way of the bedroom, but the windows appeared to be closed.

Then he noticed how low the dividing walls were between the patios. He looked into next door's back yard. No one was crouching there, but it would have been a simple matter to step over. Diamond did exactly that and tried the neighbour's back door. It wasn't locked.

Inside, an old lady was sitting in an armchair staring at him. He pushed open the door.

'It's all right, ma'am. I'm a police officer.'

'It's not all right at all,' she said. 'It's disgraceful, invading people's homes. The other one didn't even speak.'

'Someone else was here?'

'He came running straight through the house

without a by-your-leave and out of my front door. Enough to give me a heart attack.'

He had his explanation now. Harry Lang had got clean away and was on the run. 'What was he wearing?'

'A black jumper and blue denim trousers. A young man.'

'What was his hair like?'

'There wasn't much of it. Heavily cropped. It's the fashion, isn't it? But I'll tell you one thing about him.'

'What's that?'

'He looked rather familiar.'

'He would. He's from next door.'

'Do you know—I think you could be right.'

He turned and ran to her back gate and told the two bobbies to get round the front and in pursuit. He didn't have much faith in a result.

Back on Lang's side of the wall he told Halliwell.

'He'll be in his car and away, guv,' Halliwell said. 'Do we know what motor he drives? We could put out an all-units.'

'Silver saloon, according to the stable-lass.'

'Big deal. Didn't she recognise the make?'

'She isn't interested in cars.'

They spent the next ten minutes trying to get through to the dragon at Home Workouts. She told Diamond curtly that transport was not provided by the firm and she had no idea what make of car Lang used.

'OK, get rooting through his stuff,' Diamond told Halliwell. 'Registration certificate, insurance details.'

'We don't have a warrant, guv.'

'Come on, man. This is a murder suspect on the run.'

The paperwork took some finding. It was in the wardrobe upstairs, in a briefcase. Harry Lang owned a silver Subaru Legacy.

'Not bad for a council-house tenant. You and I are keeping this scumbag and he has a better car than either of us. What's the reg?'

Halliwell used his mobile to pass on the details. An all-units alert would go out. There was still a chance Lang would be stopped, even if he'd made it to the motorway.

'What else do we have in that briefcase?' Diamond said.

'Payslips from Home Workouts. A tax return, yet to be filled in. Birth certificate. Henry Spellman Lang was born in Lewisham, 1978, so he's—what?—twenty-eight, twenty-nine. And some letters and photos.'

'Photos of what? Let's see.'

They were amateurish snapshots of middle-aged women in leotards. One seemed to be blowing a kiss. 'Satisfied punter?' Halliwell said.

'Client. We have our standards.'

Diamond glanced through the letters. Someone using a rounded feminine hand thanked Harry for his 'much-needed visit' and wrote that she'd been on cloud nine ever since. She couldn't wait for next Tuesday. After signing off 'With much love, Kitty' she'd added a couple of kisses. Whatever that suggested, it wasn't evidence of serial murders. Two other letters were in a language neither detective recognised. It seemed Harry had linguistic talents on top of his other charms.

At the back of the file was a shot of a man in

278

shorts and singlet standing with arms folded beside an electronic scoreboard showing 9.85. Some high point of Harry's gymnastic career, maybe. He looked pleased with himself. Diamond slipped the photo into his back pocket.

They searched the flat for a few minutes more. 'We'll get a warrant and take this place apart,' Diamond told Halliwell, meaning, in effect, that it was up to Halliwell to draw up the application and approach a magistrate.

'On what grounds, guv?'

'A serious arrestable offence, suspicion of.'

'Will that wash?'

'It's a series of murders, Keith. What's more arrestable than that?'

'What else is there to find?'

'Prints, DNA—stuff you and I are not going to pick up. We believe there's material evidence on the premises that will link the suspect to the victims. Will that do?'

'I guess.'

'Sometimes I wonder if your mother knows you're out.'

They started the drive back to the nick in silence. Diamond was sorry for that last remark. Halliwell was his closest colleague, the one man he could always depend on. When they were held up by the traffic in Northgate Street, he said, 'That thing I said just now. It was out of order. I take it back.'

'No sweat, guv.'

'You're on your second marriage, aren't you?'

'Er, yes.' Halliwell kept his eyes steadily on the car ahead. Good thing they weren't moving, or he might have jerked the steering. The talk with

Diamond hardly ever took a personal turn.

'If you don't mind me asking, is she much different from your first wife?'

'Totally, thank God.'

'And has she changed you at all?'

'I haven't thought. I suppose she must have.'

Diamond hadn't planned this. The moment presented itself and the set-up was as right as he could want, talking at the windscreen, rather than eye to eye. Confiding in an old friend was not just a possibility, it would be a huge relief. 'Keith, this is between you and me. I've been seeing a woman.'

Halliwell said with formal politeness, 'Congratulations, guv.'

Diamond talked over him. It was cards on the table time. 'She's lovely. A bit younger than me, not much. Paloma is nothing like Steph, but it wouldn't be right to compare them. She's a businesswoman, self-made, successful. Her marriage didn't work out. The man found someone else.'

'So she's divorced?'

'Years ago. There's a grown-up son. Matter of fact, he was the owner of that Nissan four-by-four that was nicked the other night and torched up at Lansdown. I broke the news to him.'

'If you get on all right with the son, that's good,' Halliwell said as it became clear to him that some advice was being sought. 'That can be difficult, taking on family as well, if you're serious, I mean. I've got two stepchildren. It was no picnic at first.'

'Easier when they're grown-up with their own lives to lead.'

'Is she talking about marriage, guv?'

'Whoa—not yet, but I guess it will come up. We've slept together.'

'And are you as keen as she is?'

'You know me better than most, Keith. I'm resistant to change, but I can't say I enjoy the single life.'

'Ideally, you'd like to re-run your marriage to Steph?'

'Dead right, and that's not fair to any woman. If I move in with Paloma I'm going to have to break with the past.' He cleared his throat. 'Well, now you know what's bugging me. It doesn't excuse me for snapping at you just now.'

The traffic was moving again.

'If it's any help, I'm well happy at home,' Halliwell said, shifting the gearstick. 'That's how I put up with all the shit at work.'

*　　*　　*

The desk sergeant beckoned as they entered the nick. With a surge of optimism, Diamond went over. 'Have we got him?'

'Got who, sir?'

'Lang—the man on the run.'

'I haven't heard anything.'

'So why call me over?'

'You've got a visitor upstairs. A Mrs Agnes Tidmarsh, friend of the dead woman. She came in twenty minutes ago and offered to help.'

281

36

'First-time caller, as they say on those radio phone-ins,' Agnes Tidmarsh said, 'so my knees are knocking, but I heard you on the television and thought it was my duty to come in.' She had tinted red hair back-brushed into a kind of aureole and eyes so dark that the iris and pupil merged into one. Her pale face was heart-shaped, dominated by the cheekbones and ending in a pointed chin. She was in black, a cobwebby blouse and calf-length skirt with a fringed hem. Difficult to tell if it was mourning for her friend or fashionable gothic. The only jewellery was a hefty silver cross pendant on a black leather tie.

Diamond said, 'All I know about you is your voice from the answerphone. Are you local?'

'If Midsomer Norton is local.'

'Local enough.'

Young DC Gilbert, sitting in on this interview, said, 'Isn't that the village with the stream running through the high street?'

'Yes,' she said, giving him an appreciative smile, 'it used to flood regularly until they dug a drainage tunnel.'

Diamond let Gilbert know with a look that small talk wasn't required. To Agnes Tidmarsh he said, 'You came in out of duty, you said?'

'Or friendship.' A shiver ran through her. 'I still can't believe this. We were friends since university. I was her chief bridesmaid.'

'Which university?'

'Oxford. Joss read modern languages at St

Hilda's. She was very good.'

'And you?'

'Criminology.' She reacted with a disarming smile when he raised his eyebrows. 'Which I was hopeless at. I'm afraid I overindulged in the social life. I left without taking my degree—or getting a husband, for that matter. But I'm not here to talk about myself. Is Marty still missing?'

This required a quick mental adjustment. Marty was Martin Steel, the husband.

'He is. We'll come to him. You were telling me about Jocelyn. What did she do after Oxford?'

'Went straight to Luxembourg as an interpreter in the European Court of Justice. Real pressure, but very fulfilling. After about five years she was moved to London and did government work. That was when she met Marty. He was a solicitor with a top London law firm. They married quite soon and lived in Holland Park. Gave lovely dinner parties. I met some terrifyingly clever people there and would have felt completely inadequate, but Joss was marvellous. Made a point of drawing me into the conversations and giving me confidence. She was a brilliant hostess and a dear friend.'

'So they didn't come down here until later?'

'Only on visits. The West Country had been Joss's first home. Her parents lived at Monkton Combe. Her mother still does, but in an old people's home. Sweet little lady. How she'll stand up to this I've no idea.'

'She's taken it bravely.'

She glanced at him, then at Paul Gilbert. 'She's been told?'

'I saw her this afternoon,' Diamond said,

wanting to move on.

'Did you? That was difficult, I'm sure. I couldn't have faced that. But now she knows, I'll visit her tomorrow. I know where she is.'

'When did they buy the house at Midford?'

'Four years ago, at least. Marty changed his job. There was a falling-out with some of his colleagues. Not his fault. He's brilliant with clients and they were jealous of his success. Two or three of them ganged up on him and were taking the work that was rightly his, so he resigned and bought into this partnership in Bristol. By then Joss's mother was living alone down here and they saw it as an opportunity to move closer, and keep an eye on the old lady.'

'Joss retired at that point?'

'Yes, she became the country gentlewoman, as she used to say. She'd learned to ride when she was growing up and the prospect of owning her own horse and riding each day excited her. But I think—well, I know for a fact—she didn't realise how isolated she would feel. We'd meet sometimes for a heart-to-heart and I could tell she was restless. Marty worked long hours, weekends sometimes, setting up this new legal practice. Joss was bright and gifted, very friendly, but didn't enjoy her own company.'

'Depressed?'

'That's putting it too strongly. Frustrated. What she really wanted was to start a family, but it doesn't always happen when you want it. The sad part is that a couple of years before they moved down here she had a termination. She was in that high-pressure government job and it wasn't the right time. Neither of them was ready for a family then. She kept it quiet from everyone, including her mother.'

'And when the right time came along, the stork didn't?'

She gave a little shrug as if to say that life was like that.

'Did she ever discuss the fitness regime?'

'Well, of course. I saw that gym with all the machines, and the swimming pool and the hot tub. She had her own trainer, you know. I used to tease her about him.'

'In what way?'

She blushed and shook her head. 'Girlie talk. Unrepeatable.'

'About what they got up to?'

'What they *might* have got up to, but didn't. I could only joke about it because we both knew she was ...' She paused for the right word. 'I was going to say undersexed, but I don't mean that. Well-behaved is more like it. Having a fling with anyone else was out of the question.'

Diamond listened to her evaluation of her friend with an increasing sense that there was some jealousy behind it.

'This personal trainer. Did you ever meet him?'

'No. I knew he was there Friday afternoons, so I stayed away.'

'Did she talk about him?'

'Only when I poked my big nose in. I'd ask if he was good-looking and she'd make out she hardly noticed. I can believe that was true, knowing Joss. She did tell me his name once.'

'Harry?'

Her eyes widened. 'That's right.' A smile. 'And she made a point of telling me he came from a respectable firm who only employed qualified trainers.'

'I was told the same thing.' For a moment he let his thoughts stray to the hunt for Harry Lang on the roads outside Bath. This case might be over soon, and the present interview rendered unnecessary. But it had to be got through. 'Can we talk about the husband Martin? You call him Marty?'

A touch of pink coloured her cheeks. 'Everyone does.'

'We believe he's being held by the person who murdered Joss. We need to find him, and fast.'

Her teeth closed over her lower lip. 'Have you heard something new?'

He shook his head. 'The person who's holding him won't get in touch. We're not dealing with anyone who wants to negotiate.'

'How do you know?'

'It's the way he does things. Is Marty strong?'

'You're asking if he would try to escape?'

'Not really. The way these crimes are planned doesn't leave much opportunity. Is he mentally tough?'

She exhaled sharply, forced to think about Marty's situation. 'He's no coward, I'm sure of that. He's used to coping with stress in the job.' Almost as an afterthought she said, 'It isn't as if I know him all that well. We meet at parties sometimes, but that's not the best situation to judge anyone.'

'What kind of legal work does he specialise in? Criminal law?'

She nodded and drew in an audible breath. 'Are you thinking this is some crook with a grudge, looking for revenge?'

'We cover every angle. Did he or Joss ever mention cases he was involved with?'

'Not to me. She hardly ever talked about his work, except to complain he was doing long hours and getting in late.'

He picked up on that at once. 'She never suspected him of being with other women?'

She swayed back at the suggestion. 'Good Lord, no. I don't think it crossed her mind, and I'd be surprised. Their marriage was rock solid.' She was frowning, fingering the wisps of hair on her neck. 'You don't know anything to the contrary, do you?'

'Just asking.'

'Another angle?'

'Possibly. When did you see them last?'

'Joss, about a week ago. She was fine. Slightly bored, as usual, but far from suicidal. We spoke on the phone since and I had no reason to think she was in any kind of trouble.'

'And Marty?'

'Haven't seen him in weeks. Months. I think the last time was on her birthday in February. A party of us went to the theatre together.' She sighed. 'A nice memory to hold onto.'

He sat back and folded his arms. 'That isn't quite true, is it, Miss Tidmarsh?'

Now her face turned almost the colour of her hair. 'What?'

'It's been obvious from the moment you came in that you're closer to Marty than you ever were to Joss. You're desperately worried about him. With good reason. I'm worried, too, but for different reasons.'

She stared for a moment and then lowered her face into her hands and sobbed.

'You and he are lovers, right?'

DC Gilbert turned to look at Diamond in amazement. He hadn't detected any of the signals.

'There's a box of Kleenex on the filing cabinet next door,' Diamond told Gilbert.

'That's Ingeborg's.'

'She isn't here.'

Quite possibly Agnes Tidmarsh was trying—between sobs—to decide how much she would reveal about her relationship with Martin Steel. Diamond was willing to wait.

Finally she looked up and said, 'I feel such a heartless bitch. My best friend, and now she's dead.'

'Don't give me that heavy stuff,' he said. 'I'm not impressed. You've been stringing us along. I'm not judging your morals. I just want some truth from you.'

'You've got it now.'

'Some of it. I don't suppose Joss knew you were sleeping with her husband. Did she?'

She gripped the cross at her breast. 'Please God, she didn't.'

'When did it start?'

'Soon after they came to live down here. They had no sex life at all after the abortion. She was on a huge guilt trip. Marty tried to be understanding. He's the kindest of men. He started to tell me about the problem with their marriage one time when I called and she was out riding, but she came back early so I suggested we met for a drink—Marty and me, I mean.' She sighed. 'You know the rest.'

288

'The late evenings were spent with you?'

'And weekends sometimes.'

'So when did you see him last?'

'Friday afternoon at my cottage. He left me about seven.'

'Did he say anything about the upcoming weekend? Were he and Joss planning to meet anyone?'

'If they were he didn't mention it. I got the impression it was just the usual routine.'

'Was he anxious? Under pressure?'

'Not that I noticed.'

'Did he ever speak of anyone else threatening him or Joss?'

'Never.'

'How much does he confide in you? Do you talk about your lives?'

'A lot.' She dabbed her face with a tissue. 'It isn't just the sex. We go back a long way. He understands me better than anyone.'

'Did either of them ever speak of belonging to a secret organisation?'

'The Law Society?'

'I don't think that qualifies.'

'The Rotary?'

'Probably not,' he said, straight-faced, but avoiding Paul Gilbert's eyes. He moved on without explaining why he'd explored that avenue. 'Did Marty ever speak about suicide?'

She shook her head. 'He's very positive, even though his marriage was going wrong.'

'There have been other cases of people being found hanged in Bath. Did you ever discuss them?'

'We had better things to do with our time.'

A faint smile played on Gilbert's lips. This young man was getting above himself.

There was an interruption. John Leaman put his head round the door and signalled to Diamond that something new had come up.

'Is there anything else you want to tell us?' Diamond asked Agnes Tidmarsh. The interview had run its course. 'In that case, the constable will help you make a written statement. Thanks for coming in.'

He went out to Leaman. 'Have we caught Lang?'

'No, but we're getting warmer, guv. We've found his car.'

37

'Where?'

'The Avenue at Combe Down.'

'Really?' The significance escaped Leaman, so Diamond added, 'Only a stone's throw from Midford.'

This was an underestimate. It would have taken a relay of stone throwers to span the three-quarters of a mile across Horsecombe Vale, but the two places were close enough for comment.

'Let's go. You can do the driving.'

'Me?' Leaman said.

'Why not? The phone calls must have tailed off by now.'

'I wouldn't bet on it.'

'Delegate, man. The first principle of management.'

Leaman looked for the office dogsbody, Paul Gilbert, but he was busy on Agnes Tidmarsh's statement. One of the civilian staff offered to oversee the taking of calls. 'The boss sounds hearty,' she said.

'He's expecting a result,' Leaman said.

'The ram raids?'

'I should live so long.'

Combe Down was once a quarrymen's outpost of eleven cottages to the south of the city. When Bath stone was in heavy demand for the great Georgian phase of building, the place grew into a mining village. Only after the mining industry declined in the nineteenth century were the south-facing slopes developed for suburban living, ideal, potential buyers were told, for sun-seekers and convalescents. In the second world war the Admiralty decamped from London and set up a vast establishment on the Fox Hill side. Now Combe Down is indistinguishable from Bath's urban sprawl except that it has a hidden hazard. Its glory and its undoing is below ground, the gorgeous cream-coloured oolitic limestone that can be sawn or squared up with relative ease regardless of the alignment of the joints. Fine buildings across Britain—Buckingham Palace and Brighton's Royal Pavilion among them—are mainly of stone mined in huge quantities from the workings there. The downside is that the 45-acre honeycomb underground created a huge problem of subsidence. Subterranean roof collapses happened too often for comfort. Something had to be done. Various schemes for infilling and reinforcement were debated for years. To complicate the problem, the mine-owners could not be held responsible; the workings were abandoned half a century before. In law, the landowners above ground owned what was—or was not—beneath them. Trying to negotiate with hundreds of house-owners was a planner's nightmare. Finally in the twenty-first century government funds were secured for a stabilisation project and a programme of infilling with 'foam concrete' was started. Over a hundred miners, most of them Welshmen, had been at work for some years using timber and steel platforms. They were likely to be employed for some time yet.

The unique character of the place was on Diamond's mind as Leaman drove them up the steep, narrow rise of Prior Park Road. What if Harry Lang had found a way into one of those disused mines and was holding Martin Steel down there? The job of finding them would be daunting and dangerous. Nobody knows the full extent of the workings. Attempts to map them are foiled by roof collapses and the waste rock dumped by the original miners. You can get a certain way if you are willing to take risks and squeeze through narrow openings, but it is a job for cavers, not policemen. For a fugitive it offers the chance of hiding up for a long time.

He hadn't forgotten that Danny Geaves had holed up in the mine above Bathford at the Browne's Folly quarry, a few miles east of here. Had Geaves unwittingly given his killer the idea of using these quarries?

You have to be positive in this job, Diamond told himself, or you go bananas. Maybe Lang was still above ground.

He was getting to know this area south of Bath

better than he'd ever done. A sign to Lyncombe came up and he realised they were passing close to Paloma's place. He looked forward to telling Paloma how Jerry's help had been crucial to the inquiry, leading them directly to Lang. Better nick Lang first, though.

They linked up with Ralph Allen Drive where the gatehouse signified that this was once the carriage road to Prior Park, the quarry-owner's Palladian villa. Not only was it graced with pillars, long since gone, but a tramway ran beside it to bring freshly mined stone from the quarries down to the river.

Half a mile on, they reached the Avenue and spotted the police car next to Harry Lang's silver Subaru Legacy.

Diamond was muttering as he got out. If the officers who'd found the car thought they were due for a pat on the back they were mistaken.

'Why haven't you got tapes round this?'

'We weren't told, sir.'

'Weren't told? What have you got between your ears? You know the driver is a suspected killer. It may have been used to transport corpses. Get it done now. Have you checked for witnesses?'

'Interesting question. In point of fact we don't know how long the car's been here,' the same officer said.

Lippy. Diamond could imagine this jobsworth holding forth in the Manvers Street canteen. 'That isn't what I asked.'

The second constable had the sense to say, 'No witnesses as yet, sir.'

'So when you've secured the car, start knocking on doors. Soon as you find some curtain-twitcher who saw the driver, call me over.'

'We're supposed to be on patrol,' motormouth said.

'My heart bleeds.'

The two glanced at each other, no doubt wondering how this would play with their supervisor.

Diamond at a crime scene was a formidable presence. He gave them a look that ended the exchange. They went to their car to collect those tapes.

To Leaman, he said, 'Try the boot. If it's locked, force it.'

Leaman was bold enough to say, 'Guv, don't you think we should let forensics have first crack?'

'Get with it, John.'

'Just playing it by the book.'

'And what does the book say if Martin Steel is in there coughing his last?'

Leaman tried the boot, found it locked and set to work with a crowbar while Diamond called for back-up, the full works, not forgetting hard hats, flashlights and the local cave-rescue team.

The doorstepping got under way while Leaman mangled the boot-lid of the car. Subaru make sturdy locks but brute force eventually triumphed. The lid sprang up. There was nobody inside. Just a holdall with some gym kit.

Across the street one of the uniformed officers shouted, 'Over here, sir.'

Diamond went over.

A man in a singlet and shorts was at his front door and—praise be—keen to pass on information. 'Like I just said, I saw him drive up getting on for an hour ago. Short hair, jeans, black top. He seemed in a hurry. Went that way.' He pointed his thumb up the street.

'Have you seen him before?'

'No, mate. He's not from round here.'

'The car?'

'Bit flash for here.'

'In a hurry, you say. Was he running?'

'If he wasn't, he was walking at a good rate.'

'Was he carrying anything?'

'Nothing I noticed.'

'What's the road to the left?'

'Williamstowe. Doesn't lead nowhere.'

'Are there mines under this part?'

'Is the Pope a Catholic? The man two doors up lost half his garden the year before last. Straight down the hole. It's a disgrace. His kiddie could have been playing there.'

'Where's the nearest entrance?'

'Try stamping your foot, mate.'

'Proper entrance.'

'Behind the pub, top of Firs Field. Same way the bloke went.'

They went to check. The landlord of the Hadley Arms confirmed that there was an entrance in his yard. 'I can open it if you want and show you where the steps are, but you won't go anywhere. It's blocked now.'

He sent them to the 'works' in the middle of Firs Field—a well-secured site surrounded by ten-foot-high metal fencing where nobody was working today. A notice warned of the dangers. Diamond walked round the perimeter.

'Unless he's a bloody pole vaulter he didn't get in this way.'

The man they'd first questioned had followed

them. 'He wouldn't need to. There are shafts I could show you that even the council don't know about. The place is riddled with them. Some have been filled in, but plenty aren't.'

'Where?'

'I know of two in people's gardens. They were for air, or light. There's just a grille over them.'

'Show me.'

Diamond sounded resolute, but his optimism was being tested. If Lang had gone underground it could take a small army of searchers to ferret him out.

He followed his guide back to the main street. A second police car had arrived and Leaman was updating the newcomers, but they weren't cavers by the look of them.

The shaft was in the garden of an old lady who sounded as if she didn't know which century it was. A runaway killer could have walked through the house and wished her the time of day without her noticing. The garden had gone wild.

'He hasn't been here,' Diamond said, seeing the brambles arching over the grille. They hadn't been disturbed in years.

They moved on to the next, in a better-kept garden. The owners were out. There was a gate at the side you could step over. The people had made quite a feature of their shaft by giving it a stone surround and siting the grille at knee height. Trays of seeds were arranged across the top.

'I don't think so. Is that all?'

He was taken to another entrance more like a cave, smaller than the first he'd seen. A sheet of corrugated iron was supposed to keep intruders out, but it was no longer anchored. A slim person could have squeezed past it, and when Diamond tugged at it he made room even for his far-from-slim body. 'We'll look in here,' he said.

Three more vehicles had arrived in the Avenue, one belonging to the Mendip cave-rescue team. They'd brought enough hard hats and overalls for the police as well as themselves. Diamond briefed them on the operation and they briefed him and his officers on safety procedures. Roof collapse was a real possibility. Natural fractures in the limestone meant that the slightest disturbance could cause a rock fall.

He had to give an assurance that none of his men were armed and that he doubted if the suspect had a gun.

They levered back the iron barrier and went in, three cavers and nine policemen.

'How big is this mine?' he asked while they were going down some steps.

'Twenty-five acres or more. Firs is the biggest and it links up with Coxe's,' the senior caver said, 'but it's not so much the size, it's the complexity. It's a warren. They worked any number of faces.'

Flashlights were in use from the start, picking out the way ahead. The roof at the bottom of the steps was some ten feet high and supported by massive pillars left by the miners as they cut their way deep into the bedrock. To left and right the lights exposed tunnels of variable depth.

'Shouldn't we send someone into these?' Diamond said.

'If you do, I won't answer for their safety.'

He doubted if anyone's safety was guaranteed, but he didn't say so. In this situation he had to defer to the experts. The caver who'd just spoken seemed to know what was on Diamond's mind. He stopped by an odd-shaped pillar much narrower at the base than the top. 'You find this near the entrances. It's called pillar robbing. After the mines were abandoned, the locals would come in and hack off slabs of stone for their own use. Some pillars got shaved down to spindles.'

They moved on and crossed an intersection where you could see the tramlines of the old transport system for moving the blocks to the surface.

'Before we go on,' Diamond said, 'I wouldn't mind looking at what we're walking over, in case of footprints.' The floor was thick with dust.

'Good thinking,' the caver said. 'Let's have some more light here.'

Nothing obvious was revealed. Diamond didn't admit to his inner misgiving that nobody had been down here in years. 'Maybe he was ultra careful.'

'Could be,' the caver said. 'Want to go on?'

'Of course.'

They entered a narrow passage where they were forced to stoop. It soon opened into a bigger area where a rusty hand-cranked crane had been abandoned, still attached to the face with steel cables. Saw lines were visible in a bed of stone that for some reason had not been cut right out. A huge heap of rubble lay to their left, partly blocking their route. They crunched over it.

There was a choice of tunnels ahead. Each decision was like the toss of a coin with the chance of making the wrong call. Diamond flicked his flashlight from one to the next and tried to sound confident.

'That way.'

The earlier sense of awe at the surroundings was waning and some of the party were starting to talk. He stopped and asked for silence.

What he got was better than silence. Somewhere ahead came the definite sound of a movement that could have been somebody kicking a small piece of stone. They all heard it. The party moved on at a faster rate.

The senior caver said to Diamond, 'I wouldn't get too excited. Bits of stone are falling all the time.'

He didn't answer. He pressed on for another fifty yards or more and then stopped because he'd heard another sound, more drawn out and heavier.

'T Rex,' some wag said.

'Shut up.'

The caver said, 'It'll be traffic overhead. The roof is shallow here. We're right under the Bradford road.'

'Let's move on, then.' But he stopped a moment later, a Robinson Crusoe moment. His light had picked out a set of footprints in the dusty stretch ahead. They were not made by some miner a century ago. They had the zigzag pattern of modern trainers and they led into a side-tunnel.

Another vehicle drumrolled overhead as if dubbed in to emphasise the drama. Nothing needed to be said. Everyone appreciated the significance.

The tunnel looked no different from others the cavers had declared too dangerous to enter. Diamond didn't give them the chance to object. He dipped his head and went in first, shining the beam as far ahead as possible. His hard hat struck overhanging parts of the roof more than once. The way through had been roughly hewn, suggesting it was a trial cut, or a passage linking with another part of the mine. He could just about walk without going on his knees, but he didn't fancy stooping like this for long.

Suddenly he heard the scrape of stones only a short way ahead. He raised the torch beam and it caught the gleam of white trainers moving scarcely less than forty yards in front.

He shouted, 'Police! Stop where you are, face down on the floor.'

If he was heard, he wasn't heeded. The trainers moved on and disappeared.

He didn't understand how, unless there was a side-passage. He didn't think he could be outpaced that rapidly, although Lang was presumably a fit man. All he could do was press on and hope for another sighting. The flashlight showed nothing yet. More tunnel, but nothing else.

He shouted, 'Harry Lang?'

There was just an echo.

But the tunnel ended not far beyond the point where he'd sighted the man ahead. It opened out into a far larger space where stone had been mined extensively and there were massive pillars supporting the roof . He stepped out and straightened up and the others emerged as well and stood with him, taking in the new situation, a roof ten to fifteen feet high and a choice of directions.

It was a relief to stand upright, but with it came the depressing realisation that Lang could have gone any one of six ways. No footprints here. Any dust was confined to the edges of the working.

'I spotted him,' Diamond said. 'I definitely saw him.'

'This is Coxe's mine,' the senior caver said, as if it was the other side of the moon. 'We'll be somewhere under Fox Hill.'

'Is it large?'

'Large enough. I'd say the odds are stacked in his favour now, but it's your call.'

Whatever else you could say about Diamond, he wasn't a quitter. 'In that case, we split up. Three teams of four. A caver with each. Do we have enough lights? Meet back here in half an hour. The team that brings back Harry Lang gets free drinks at the pub.'

38

The tunnel Diamond had picked was one of the main arteries of the system, so at least it wasn't as back-breaking as the previous stretch. Harry Lang could well have chosen the same way believing it offered the best chance of putting distance between himself and his pursuers. They were moving at the best speed they could, a brisk walk. One hunted individual will generally travel faster than the pack, but there would surely come a point when they would corner him—if this was where he'd headed.

Maybe it was a promising sign, Diamond thought, that he could feel particles of grit in his mouth and nose. If Lang had come this way he must have disturbed some dust.

'Let's have another listen.'

The team stopped. There was definitely a sound, but it was from behind them, a distant voice from one of the other teams.

Diamond looked to his left. The caver now at his side wasn't the senior man.

'Do you know this mine?'

'Most of it.'

'How far does this tunnel run?'

'I'd say another quarter mile, no more.'

'Is there any way he can get out?'

'Not without climbing gear.'

One of the bobbies said, 'Plenty of places to hide, though.'

'Thanks a bunch—just what I wanted to hear,' Diamond said.

About half a minute on, they stopped again, this time because a piece of stone the size of a dinner plate crashed down in front of them and broke into pieces. The caver spread his arms to stop anyone going forward. He shone his flashlight on the section of roof the slab had come from. 'This is the problem. See the hairline cracks? There's more to come.'

'We can't stop now,' Diamond said.

'I'm saying this part is unstable.'

'Let's get past, then.'

'I don't advise it.'

'I wasn't asking for advice. What are hard hats for?'

He didn't check to see if they were following. This wasn't a boy scout trip. They were hot on the trail of a man who'd killed five people. You don't give up when you're that close. He pressed on, dipping the flashlight beam at intervals to check

302

for footprints.

Then there was a sound from up ahead. Unlike anything they'd heard up to now, it was certainly not the rumble of traffic. This was a cracking sound followed immediately by a five-second boom.

They barely had time to react before a cloud of dust surged along the tunnel towards them. The force pitched Diamond against the man behind and they both fell backwards. Fine sand whipped their faces and invaded their eyes and noses. The flashlight had fallen and gone out.

'What the hell was that?'

'Roof collapse,' the caver said. 'We're out of here.' He'd managed to get his light going and it was pointing the way they had come.

If Diamond had remained, he would have been alone. The team was already in flight. Even he wasn't that stubborn. He remembered the image that local man had conjured of half a garden disappearing down a huge crater. He got up and staggered after the others. They didn't stop until they reached the end of the tunnel at the place where everyone had agreed to meet.

'Didn't I warn you?' the caver said. He was red-eyed, but so were they all. 'We could have been buried alive.'

'Maybe someone is,' one of the officers said. 'He must have triggered the fall.'

'If it's a rescue situation, we won't have you lot buggering it up,' the caver said. 'The rest of my team will be here soon. They must have heard it. They're not that far away.'

Diamond said nothing. He was shaken. The young caver was right. Four lives had been put at risk and he was mainly responsible. Even the probable capture of a serial killer wasn't worth so much.

The two other groups weren't long in returning to the main area. It was agreed that the roof fall had almost certainly been caused by the suspect running through an unstable stretch of tunnel. The cavers were rescue experts and it was their duty to get the man out alive if at all possible. Diamond said the police, too, had an interest in saving the life of Harry Lang.

'The best help you can give,' the cavers' team leader said, 'is to get out and let us get on with our job.'

'You might need to shift some heavy stuff.'

'We'll deal with that.'

'He's a dangerous man.'

'If he's under a ton of rock he won't give any trouble. Go to the top and get them organised up there. We need picks and spades, a phone line, stretcher, paramedics and ambulance waiting. And more cavers to work from the other side of the fall.'

This was an expert speaking and Diamond knew he was right. A bunch of untrained policemen would be a hindrance. The priori-ties had changed.

'You don't have to go all the way back into Firs,' the team leader said. 'There's a way out which is quicker.'

They took it, a short walk, a steep climb up a ramp into the bliss of fresh air. Daylight, too, unreal after the darkness underground.

With mobiles working again, he put out the necessary calls. Soon ambulances would be waiting at two of the mine entrances and a second team of cavers lowered by rope through an airshaft. The theory was that Lang might be alive on the other side of the roof fall. This would be the only way to reach him.

Someone saw the state of them and offered the use of a shower. Kettles were boiled and tea provided. Crowds were gathering now. Most of Combe Down seemed to know that a wanted man was underground.

John Leaman drove up to the house where the police had freshened up. He wanted to be updated. Diamond said like a veteran caver, 'These things take time. Safety considerations.'

'I'll radio the CAD room. Do we need more help?'

'We'll cope. Get Lang's car transported for a full forensic check.'

'Already in hand, guv.'

More than half an hour had passed since Diamond and his dusty team had emerged from the mine. A scratchy phone line was in place underground. The original team of cavers had found the tunnel totally blocked by a fall about two hundred yards beyond the point Diamond had reached. The second team, working from the other side, had located the site of the collapse without yet finding Lang.

'Doesn't look good for him,' Leaman said.

'Doesn't look good for any of us if he's dead meat,' Diamond said. 'We know sod all about him.'

Another twenty minutes passed before a message came from underground. The original team had reached a man under the rubble. He was out cold, but they'd found a pulse. A doctor was in attendance.

Harry Lang was stretchered to the surface and driven to the Royal United Hospital to be put into intensive care. He hadn't recovered consciousness.

39

'Now I know how an expectant father feels,' Diamond said as a nurse came out and walked past without even making eye contact.

Leaman thought about that for a while. 'You want five?'

'What?'

'A break. Five minutes. I don't mind hanging on here.'

Diamond turned to face him. 'John.'

'Guv?'

'If I'd wanted five, I'd have taken it.'

'Oh, cheers.'

They'd been here twenty-five. In that time they'd checked Harry Lang's discarded clothes and found little of interest. At the time of the accident he wasn't carrying a wallet or a mobile. All that was found with him was a hand-torch. It was likely, Diamond suggested to Leaman, that during the chase Lang had thrown away anything that might link him to the crimes. The clothes would be checked at the forensics lab but if there was anything apart from limestone dust it would be remarkable.

Yet another trolley was pushed along the corridor. This wasn't the tea urn or medicines. It was library books. Diamond snapped his fingers and said, 'Hey.'

The man with the trolley looked round. 'Sorry, the books are for inpatients.' Then he did a double-take and said, 'Peter, what brings you here?'

For Leaman's benefit, Diamond said, 'Jerry Kean, John Leaman. I have news for you, Jerry. Remember those names you gave me—the personal trainers? One came up trumps.'

'Which one?'

'Lang. Harry Lang. I was going to speak to your mother, ask her to pass on my thanks. As a matter of fact, we're waiting to interview Mr Lang any minute now.'

'Here?'

'He's in intensive care.'

Jerry's eyes swivelled.

'Not what you're thinking,' Diamond said. 'We're not the heavy mob. He had an accident.'

'What happened?'

'Long story. We just hope he pulls through.'

'Poor guy,' Jerry said. 'I'll pray for him. By the way, I've got something for you.' He ducked and pulled out a book from the bottom shelf of the trolley. 'Here. *A Murder is Announced.*'

One of Steph's Agatha Christies.

'Unsuitable?' Diamond said.

'No. Open it and you'll see.'

A bookmark was inserted at the title page. There, Diamond saw, in his own writing, *To my one and only love, on her birthday, from Pete*. He felt a stab of self-reproach and his eyes moistened. So easy to be ambushed.

Jerry was saying, 'One of the patients noticed.

You wouldn't want it doing the rounds, would you?'

'Thanks.'

Jerry rummaged in the bottom shelf again and produced a black totebag. 'Put it in this. You don't want to be seen walking around with an Agatha Christie. Not in your job.'

He had a point.

Diamond thanked him and dropped the book in, noticing as he did that the word 'Hosannah' was written in gold lettering on the bag.

'A plug for my church,' Jerry said. 'If you want the matching T-shirt, just ask. Look, if you don't mind I've two more wards to get round.' He steered his trolley away and rejoined the flow along the corridor.

This was the busy time, visitors with flowers and grapes making their way to the wards. One of Diamond's neighbours gave a wave as she walked past.

'I get the feeling if we sit here long enough everyone we ever met will come by,' he said to Leaman.

'I don't follow that.'

'No, with your logical mind you wouldn't.'

'Was your friend serious about praying?'

'Since we're being precise, he's not so much a friend as the son of a friend. Is he serious? I believe he is.'

Leaman's mouth turned down in distaste. 'Pray for a serial killer?'

'We're all sinners, aren't we?'

'Are you a church-goer, guv?'

'I went to Sunday school a few times. I was trying to see it from his point of view. He's a believer. Praying is what they do.' He took the bookmark from the Agatha Christie. He'd noticed all the books in the trolley had one sticking out. It read: *Hosannah Free Church, Green Park Road, Bath, reaching out to one and all. Lord's Day Services at 8 a.m., 11 a.m. and 6.30 p.m. Join us and be joyful.*

He handed it to Leaman. 'Get the message?'

Leaman gave it a glance and handed it back. 'The joyful bit puts me off. But I'll say this for your friend. He's not just a Sunday Christian.'

'Yes, it humbles you, doesn't it?'

'What, other people going to church?'

'Doing their best to save sinners when toerags like me are hoping they'll save someone else, not us. His mother isn't quite so caught up in it, I'm glad to say.'

'Are you agnostic, guv?'

'Not really.'

'So what would you call yourself?'

'Fat and lazy.'

Having sorted out religion, they lapsed into another period of people-watching.

'Changing the subject,' Leaman said, 'while you were underground, Ingeborg called in from Midford wanting to speak to you.'

'She's still there?' Brookview Lodge seemed as remote as last week's news. 'What was she on about?'

'She wouldn't say. I sensed she'd found some little item and didn't want you hearing it second-hand.'

'That would be the journalist in Inge. They like their credits.'

'She's supposed to be one of us now.'

'Don't take it personally, John. She's a team player in every other way.'

A doctor came out of the ward, hesitated and looked round. Diamond was on his feet at once. 'Are you looking for us?'

'Are you from the police?'

'I am.' He identified himself. 'Is there any improvement?'

'He opened his eyes ten minutes ago.'

'Can we go in?'

The doctor shook his head. 'You'll get damn all out of him. Leave it an hour. He'll come back to us by degrees. There's a canteen for outpatients downstairs.'

'An hour—as long as that? Someone else's life is on the line, Doctor.'

Such statements don't carry much weight with doctors in intensive care units. 'Didn't you hear me? He's not coherent yet. What's he been up to—if it isn't a state secret?'

Diamond stepped closer and lowered his voice. 'He's a suspect in a murder case. It's vital we interview him at the first opportunity. He may know the whereabouts of a missing person every police force in the region is looking for.'

'You won't get two sensible words out of him. What was he doing down the mine?'

'On the run.'

'Well, he won't be running anywhere tonight. Both legs are broken below the knee. You're sure of your facts—his name, and so forth?'

'Harry Lang.'

The doctor looked thoughtful. 'This was definitely the man you were pursuing?'

'I saw him on the stretcher.' Diamond frowned.

310

'Is there a problem?'

'Just that Harry Lang sounds such a British name. When he came round a few minutes ago he was talking gibberish, as they do, only it wasn't English gibberish. I'm no linguist myself, but I'd say it was one of the Slavic languages.'

Down in the canteen they tried making sense of this latest twist. Leaman asked if it really mattered if the man was Polish or Ukrainian. 'He may have given himself an English-sounding name because his own was unpronounceable. It doesn't stop him being the main suspect.'

Diamond was shredding a Bath bun as if it contained a hidden message. He didn't respond.

Leaman went on rationalising. 'It fits in quite well with the personal-trainer thing. These guys from Eastern Europe love their sport. I bet the female clients are impressed by a foreign accent, too.'

'I saw the birth certificate. Harry Lang was born in Lewisham.'

Leaman flushed and sat back in his chair.

Some seconds passed before Diamond said, 'When he did a runner I assumed it was because he was our suspect. He was out of that house and through the neighbour's as soon as we turned up. He drives out to Combe Down and goes underground. It's the action of a guilty man—isn't it?'

'Is there any doubt?'

'I'm less confident than I was.'

'Why? His kit was in the car. It can't be anyone else.'

Diamond reached into his back pocket and took out the photo he'd found in Lang's flat, the 9.85

points pose. No question this was the man he'd seen stretchered into the ambulance.

'Is that him? Jocelyn Steel's trainer?' Leaman said.

'Yep.' He was still looking at the photo. 'Where we found this there were also a couple of letters in a foreign language. I didn't think anything of it at the time.' He glanced at the clock on the wall. 'Let's go upstairs.'

'We haven't been here twenty minutes, guv. You haven't eaten your bun.'

Diamond was on his feet and making for the exit.

Two nurses were in the intensive care unit when the detectives walked in. Diamond showed his ID and said he'd spoken to the doctor and now he needed a word with the patient—a justifiable economy with the facts.

Harry Lang had his eyes closed and was tubed and wired. His face had been cleaned up since he was on the stretcher. Instead of dust, bruising on his cheek and forehead bore witness to the rock fall.

'Harry.'

No reaction.

'Harry Lang.'

The lips moved and spoke something incomprehensible. Polish? It could have been anything.

'I'm a police officer. Police, do you understand?'

He did not. One of the nurses stepped forward and said, 'I don't know what the doctor said to you, but this is too soon. He's getting it together, but slowly. There's a canteen downstairs.'

'Has he said anything at all in English?'

She shook her head. 'He sounds like a foreigner to me.'

They left the unit. Instead of taking a seat outside, Diamond marched on through a set of swing doors and turned right into one of the general wards. Leaman, uncertain what this was about, followed. Diamond took one look along the ward, turned about and almost collided with his colleague.

'Not this one.'

He moved on. Halfway up the next ward with his trolley was Jerry Kean, helping someone choose a book. Two patients in dressing gowns were by the trolley leafing through novels.

'Jerry.'

The young man looked back over his shoulder and saw Diamond and Leaman. 'What's up?'

'You put me onto Harry Lang. Do you know him well?'

'Look, I'm doing my job here.'

'Understood. So am I, and I need help. What can you tell me about the man?'

Jerry gave the patients an apology and turned back to Diamond. 'Harry's been around a year or so. Works for an agency. I haven't heard anything bad about him.'

'But you've met him?'

'At the gym a few times. You asked if I know him well and I wouldn't say I do.'

'Spoken with him?'

'Like I said.'

He put the key question to Jerry. 'The accent. He's a foreigner, isn't he?'

Jerry scratched his head and frowned. 'His

313

English is pretty good, but yes, there's something about the accent.'

'He's never mentioned coming from anywhere else?'

'All we've talked about is football and cars.'

'He drives a nice car, a new Subaru.'

'There's nothing remarkable in that. It's about image. The clients don't expect you to turn up in some old banger.'

'Yes, but he lives in a council flat.'

'No mortgage. He can afford a good car.'

Diamond had heard enough. 'Thanks, Jerry.'

He went to the quiet end of the ward and used his new mobile to call Keith Halliwell. 'Did you get the search warrant?'

'Sorted. The scene of crime team are in Lang's flat already.'

'That birth certificate. They'll have that, presumably?'

'It'll be bagged up by now, guv.'

'Just my luck. Do you remember the details?'

'Not everything. Harry Spellman Lang, wasn't it? Born in Lewisham, 1978.'

'Did it look genuine to you?'

'It was a copy certified by the General Register Office.'

'But anyone can apply for one.'

'They'd need the name and details.'

'Which are in the index in the search room at the Family Records Centre. What I'm saying is if someone wanted to pass himself off as Harry Lang all he has to do is get the details and apply for a certificate. You could call yourself John Lennon and ask for a copy of the birth certificate.'

'What's this about, guv?'

'This character in intensive care is speaking in some foreign language. I don't think he was born in Lewisham. I'm wondering if the reason he did a runner is because he's an illegal.'

The call stopped there because a hand clutched Diamond's arm and forced the phone away from his ear. The ward sister had taken over. 'Can't you read?' she said. 'There are notices all over the hospital telling you not to use mobiles.'

'Sorry, Sister,' he said.

She was staring at the bag he was carrying. 'I hope you haven't been harassing the patients.'

'I'm a senior police officer.'

'I don't care if you're God. Out.'

40

'You could have warned me she was coming,' he said in the car.

Leaman said, 'She was too quick. You were standing right outside her office.'

'Well, you could have reminded me that phones are banned.'

'Yep.' Leaman, like Halliwell before him, had read the signs. The boss was stretched to breaking point. It wasn't wise to prolong the exchange.

They were driving down Entry Hill towards Bear Flat and for once the place they were going was on the same side of town. Home Workouts, Harry Lang's agency, operated from a private house. With luck, the dragon who ran it would be at home. After the run-in with the ward sister, Diamond was relishing a situation where he

315

wouldn't be in the wrong.

There were lights in the house in Kipling Avenue.

His ring was answered, but the chain remained on the door. 'If this is a business call, you'll have to come back tomorrow,' the mouth in the gap said. 'It's out of hours now.'

'We're the police,' he said, pushing his ID forward, 'and we work all hours. May we come in?'

'What's it about?'

'One of your people, Harry Lang.'

'That's business.'

'Madam, if you want a ride to the police station, say so. If you want the special treatment, shut the door in my face and I'll batter it down and collect you. If not, open up and we'll talk in the comfort of your own home.'

'Don't you threaten me,' the mouth said.

'Threaten? I've got your welfare in mind. In fact, I'll give you a safety warning. Stand well back.'

'I've done nothing illegal.'

'Then prove it by cooperating.'

They heard the chain being unfastened.

This one punches above her weight, Diamond thought when he saw her. She was no more than the height of his elbows, pencil slim and with pinched flesh that spoke of questionable nutrition. The only things of substance were the thick lenses in her glasses. He guessed she was in her fifties. The long blonde hair looked all wrong for the face.

The striplighting flickered, functioned and showed the front room. Filing cabinets, desk with computer, stationery cupboard. She flapped her hand at the chair in front of the desk and Diamond sat in it. Leaman would have to lean against one of the cabinets. As for the little lady, she appeared to grow as she positioned herself on the other side of the desk. Either she used a couple of cushions or the chair was mounted on a dais.

Her name, they learned, was Daphne De La Fleur and that was the only frivolous thing about her. 'Can we get to the point?'

They hadn't even started. Diamond threw her an easy one. 'I expect you enquire into the background of the trainers you take on?'

'Of course.'

'What does that involve? References, experience?'

'Certainly, but all that is confidential.'

'What do they have to supply? Proof of identity?'

'That's a standard requirement.'

'What—a passport?'

'Or a birth certificate.'

'A passport if they come from abroad?'

She folded her arms. 'I don't like the drift of this. What exactly are you investigating?'

'It's all right,' Diamond said. 'We're nothing to do with immigration. I spoke to you before and you know it's Harry Lang who interests us.'

An extra degree of disapproval crept in. 'That was you being heavy-handed on the phone, was it? I know of nothing to Harry's discredit. He's good at his job and popular with the clients. I'm sure he had nothing to do with that ghastly murder in the park.'

'Where's he from originally?'

'South London, I believe.'

'The accent isn't south London. It's East European.'

'Perhaps his parents were from there.'

'Quite likely. But if he was born and brought up in London he'd have a London accent.'

'I've seen his birth certificate.'

'So have I,' Diamond said. 'Did you check his passport as well?'

'As a British subject, he doesn't have to produce one.'

'You mean you ask no questions.' He put this as a statement and he could see she didn't like it. 'How many others get jobs here by producing freshly copied birth certificates?'

She took a noisy breath. 'If you're suggesting I knowingly employ illegal aliens, you're very much mistaken.'

'You're missing the point,' he said. 'I told you we're not immigration officers. We're investigating several murders. Harry Lang is under suspicion because he was one of the last to see Mrs Jocelyn Steel alive, last Friday afternoon. She was strangled some time between then and Sunday morning, when the body was discovered. We called to interview Lang today and he took off at a rate of knots, right through a neighbour's house and up the street to his car, ending up in an underground quarry at Combe Down. The roof fell in.'

'Oh, no.' She reached up and grasped her neck. 'Is he . . . ?'

'In intensive care and too far gone to question.'

'Poor man. That's dreadful.'

318

'We're here because you know him better than anyone.'

'I wouldn't say so,' she said, guarded again.

'You could be right. Some of his rich lady clients may have a more, em, intimate knowledge. Furnish me with the names and addresses and I'll send my officers round.'

The colour drained from her face. 'I can't allow that. These are valued clients. Respectable people.'

'And Lang is the main suspect in a murder case.' He ran his finger over the address cards in the rotary holder on her desk. 'What are your valued clients going to say when they find out?'

She reached for the Rolodex and returned it to her side of the desk.

'It's up to you,' he said without letting up. 'I want the reason why he ran. Is it because he's a serial killer, or because he's working here illegally under a false identity?'

She held his gaze for a moment and then the defiance oozed away. She looked down at her fingers and, of all things, laid the blame on the Community of Europe. 'It's so difficult keeping up with everything now. I'm not saying his birth certificate is wrong, but if it turned out he was from one of the new countries it wouldn't matter, would it?'

Leaman, logical as usual, said, 'It would to us. It would mean he had another reason for leaving in a hurry.'

Diamond had seen the loophole Miss De La Fleur had created and was willing to see how she used it. 'True. Do you have a suspicion, Miss De La Fleur?'

She sighed and adjusted her glasses. 'One of the clients told me she thought Harry was from Kosovo. I didn't know what to think. Those poor people suffered dreadfully in the war. I didn't question him about it because it was only hearsay. If that's a crime, I hold up my hand.'

'Kosovo?'

She enquired on a rising note of expectation, 'Is that part of the enlarged community?'

'I don't think so. Are there any other foreigners on your books?'

She said in a prim tone that gave away more than she intended, 'Not to my knowledge.'

He'd done enough skirting round the truth. He went into hard policeman mode. 'I want the details of each of your trainers—full names, addresses, contact numbers. The same for the people they visit.'

'Now?'

'A printout. Your schedule as well, listing all the home visits.'

'This will destroy my business,' she said.

'Come on,' he said. 'Musclemen on tap, for home visits? Any clients you lose you'll soon recoup with the extra publicity.'

An outraged sound came from the back of her throat, but she knew he wasn't playing. While she busied herself with the computer he took out his new phone and tried to get a number. He gave it a shake.

Leaman said, 'Try switching it on.'

'Nothing gets past you.' He made a call to Keith Halliwell. 'Are the crime scene people still at Lang's flat?'

'Finished, guv.'

320

'And?'

'Too early to know.'

'Did they pick up those letters?'

'Yes. Do you want them translated?'

'Do I want them translated? No, I'll use my pocket dictionary. Get with it, Keith. First I'd like to know what language they're in. Try Kosovan.'

'Albanian.'

'What?'

'Kosovan is not a language. Most Kosovans speak Albanian.'

'I was pulling your chain, professor. What else came to light?'

'They lifted masses of prints,' Halliwell said. 'That could be a problem. He has more callers than a cat on heat.'

'Any recorded messages on his phone?'

'There's no landline here. He must use a mobile.'

'We didn't find one on him.'

'And there wasn't one here.'

'In his car, maybe.'

'Sorry, but no. The car is with forensics. They bagged up everything and gave me a list.'

'Must have slung it. ' Diamond looked at the clock on the wall. 'OK. We're leaving any minute now. It's overtime for everyone on the team. Are they all about?'

'Apart from Ingeborg. She's on her way back. She kept trying to call you from Midford. Was your phone switched on?'

He felt a small stab of guilt from which he recovered at once. 'A mobile doesn't work underground, dumbo.'

41

'Let's face it, we're too late for Martin Steel,' John Leaman said to the rest of CID, now gathered in the incident room. 'Going by what happened to the others, he'll have been strangled already. He'll be strung up overnight in some public place for the first hapless berk who comes by to discover tomorrow morning. We've failed him.'

'John, that's a load of bull,' Halliwell said. 'The men aren't strangled first. Danny Geaves was hanged, and hanged at night. There's still a chance to save this guy.'

'Well, I could be wrong, but I know this much. The boss was down a mine all afternoon while I was above ground watching some kids kick a ball around. I'm a senior detective. I could have been better employed.'

Someone muttered in a passable imitation of Brando, 'I could have been a contender.'

Halliwell said, 'The boss caught up with Harry Lang.'

'Top result!' Leaman said with sarcasm.

'What's your problem with that?'

'Turns out he's an illegal immigrant and that's why he scarpered when we raided the flat.'

'So he's an illegal. He's still in the frame, isn't he?' Halliwell said. 'Jocelyn Steel's personal trainer and one of the last to see her alive. Has the boss given up on him?'

'He should.'

'Am I missing something here?'

'Did any of the other female victims have

322

personal trainers?' Paul Gilbert asked, trying to be constructive.

'Come on,' Leaman said in the jeering tone you would only use with a rookie. 'Delia Williamson had two kids and was working evenings as a waitress. She didn't need to find ways of exercising. And Christine Twining had a demanding job with Marks and Spencer. Her brother-in-law told us a lunchtime walk in the park was the only exercise she got.'

'I wouldn't count Lang out of it until we get some forensic results,' Halliwell said.

'You think there's more to him?' Gilbert said.

'A twenty-grand car, for starters. Where did he get that money when he's living in community housing?'

'Ask him when his head clears,' Leaman said. 'It doesn't help us. There isn't a profit motive in these killings.'

'What is the motive?' Gilbert asked.

'If we knew that, we'd be making an arrest,' Halliwell said.

'We're chasing a nutter,' Leaman said. 'We can forget about motive.'

Unseen by Leaman, Diamond had come in with Ingeborg at his side. 'What's your plan, John? Call in a shrink?'

'It might be no bad thing.'

Halliwell rolled his eyes and looked towards Diamond. 'Guv, I don't know how much you heard. The thinking seems to be that Martin Steel is as good as dead already and we ought to be second-guessing where to find his body.'

'Anyone who thinks like that had better leave now,' Diamond said.

323

No one moved. No one blinked.

'To business, then,' Diamond said. 'I saw Georgina earlier. Every park in the city is under surveillance tonight.'

Leaman said, 'Bridges?'

'What?'

'Danny Geaves was hanged from a bridge.'

'The plod are all over the city.'

'You know what'll happen? Tomorrow morning the cells will be full of rough sleepers and courting couples.'

Nobody smiled. Leaman had lost his audience.

'What about Lang?' Leaman said. 'Is he in the clear?'

Diamond sidestepped that one. 'He's no threat to anyone where he is now. But there is a development.' He turned to Ingeborg. 'Tell them what you just told me.'

It was obvious to all that team spirit had sunk to a low point. Not an easy situation for Ingeborg, noted for her desire to please the boss and achieve early promotion. Her good looks simply added to the feeling that she started with an advantage. And no one would forget that she had been an investigative journalist. From their faces her colleagues might have been watching Lucrezia Borgia at a wine-tasting.

'It may be nothing,' she said. 'The boss asked me to go through the filing cabinet in the Steels' house. I was looking at some of the invoices. The fitness room was added about eighteen months ago. They installed the exercise machines and had a jacuzzi fitted.'

'Who by?' Halliwell said.

'Give it a Whirl.'

'Jesus!'

'Nice work,' Leaman said.

Some of the team hadn't yet picked up the reference.

Ingeborg said, 'Give it a Whirl is Dalton Monnington's firm. Monnington—remember? The sales rep who dined at Tosi's restaurant and tried to make a date with Delia Williamson.'

Leaman was not yet convinced. 'But we went all the way to Wimbledon to interview him. The tests on his car were negative. The CCTV footage at the hotel didn't pick him up.'

'Doesn't mean he's in the clear,' Diamond said. 'He slipped out of the frame at a time when we were thinking Danny Geaves was Delia's killer.'

'He's linked to two out of our three incidents,' Halliwell said. 'Let's pull him in.'

'Is there any connection with the other couple, the Twinings?' Leaman asked.

'We don't know yet,' Ingeborg said. 'We haven't had time to check. The Twinings were in the money. No reason why they shouldn't have had a jacuzzi.'

'We can find out,' Diamond said. 'Remind me where they lived.'

'Hinton Charterhouse. John Twining was an architect and he designed it himself. All mod cons. It would be surprising if they didn't have a pool at the very least.'

'Check it out, Inge,' Diamond said.

'Now?'

'Get the present owners on the phone.'

She looked bemused. 'Do we know who they are?'

'Initiative test,' Diamond said and turned to

Halliwell. 'I want a check on Monnington's present whereabouts. Is he back home in Wimbledon or on the road? Get onto Wimbledon CID and ask them to visit the house.'

The incident room was recharged. The mood was up now. Phones were in use, files being retrieved. Dalton Monnington was hot again.

Ingeborg swiftly tracked down the current owners of Longsword Lodge, where the Twinings had lived. They told her that the property included a swimming pool, built when the Twinings had lived there, but no jacuzzi.

'Back to square one,' Leaman said.

'It doesn't mean there was no contact,' Ingeborg said. She was flushed with excitement and wasn't giving up. 'Monnington could have been to the place and tried to sell them one. A big, modern house is the sort he would target. If they chose not to buy he would still have met them.'

Paul Gilbert said, 'If they refused to buy, he'd have even more reason to kill them.'

'Buy one of my jacuzzis or else,' Leaman said with a curl of the lip. 'If that was the motive, there'd be dead couples all over the West Country.'

'Back off, John,' Diamond said. 'This is the best lead we've had. Ingeborg, go on the internet and see what you can discover about Give it a Whirl. We may need to contact someone tonight.' Like Ingeborg, he wasn't discouraged. Investigations don't often pan out so obviously. Her point was a good one. Monnington may well have met the Twinings as a would-be salesman.

A call came in from a Wimbledon police mobile

326

patrol. They were at Monnington's house and he wasn't at home. His partner Angie Collier had told them he'd left three days ago. The couple had argued because she'd smelt perfume on the pyjamas he'd given her to wash. She'd accused him of having affairs when he was supposed to be on business trips.

'Does she have any idea where he was heading?' Diamond asked.

'Hold on and I'll ask.' There was a pause and then: 'She says to hell for all she cares.'

'Great.' Diamond turned to his team. 'So it's not impossible that he's here with us in Aquae Sulis. Inge, how are you doing?'

She had found the Give it a Whirl phone number and was trying to get through.

'You won't get anyone. It's after office hours,' Diamond said. 'Try the Bath Hilton. These reps are creatures of habit.'

Leaman shook his head. 'He's not going to have Martin Steel locked in a hotel bedroom.'

'Yes, but he needs a base. Steel could be trussed up in the boot of his car.'

Ingeborg was through to the Hilton. They told her Monnington was a regular guest, but he wasn't in residence now and hadn't made a reservation.

'Nice try,' Leaman said, meaning she'd wasted her time.

'Do we have his mobile number?' Halliwell asked.

'Good suggestion . . . . No.'

'His partner will have it.'

The sergeant in the Wimbledon police car was not overjoyed at being asked to return to Angie Collier.

Ten more minutes passed.

Wimbledon came on the line again with the number. Before disconnecting, the sergeant asked with heavy sarcasm if there was any other service they could perform for their colleagues in Bath.

Diamond tapped in Monnington's number and put on the amplifier for everyone to listen.

'Hi,' a bright voice said to the whole of CID, 'who wants me?'

Definitely Monnington, but a more bobbish Monnington than they'd encountered the last time.

'Depends what you have to offer,' Diamond said. 'Where are you?'

'Bath, my friend. The city, not the soap and water.'

'Where exactly in Bath?'

'Tosi's restaurant, for an early supper.'

Creatures of habit. Diamond eyeballed the sceptic on his team.

42

Seven in the evening and Bath was empty. Only later, when the pubs spilled out and the clubbers appeared would it look like a real city. Halliwell drove his boss at speed through the streets and reached George Street before the response car they'd asked for. But the back-up wasn't needed. Monnington was no longer there. Tosi's had no customers when they arrived. On a table at the far end a half-finished bottle of red stood between two oval dinner plates.

The substantial owner, Giuseppe Tosi, explained in his less-than-substantial English, 'Mr Monnington? He go. Mobile, yes, brr, brr, and he go quick. See?' He indicated the table.

'Which way?' Diamond asked.

'*Scusi?*'

This would have tried a patient man and Diamond wasn't that. He stabbed his forefinger left, towards Gay Street, and held out his hands, Italian fashion.

Tosi nodded emphatically.

Diamond tried again. 'On foot?'

'Foot?'

Diamond lifted his leg and tapped the sole of his shoe.

Tosi took this as an Englishman's attempt to learn Italian. '*Si. Piede*. Like football, eh?'

'So he walked away?' Diamond said, wiggling his fingers.

'No, no.' Tosi could do sign language as well. He stretched his forefinger and thumb as wide as they would go. 'The *signora*, she have the *tacco a spillo.*'

'You've lost me.'

'Stiletto shoes, *capisce*? Walk? No way.'

'Are you saying there was a lady with him?'

Tosi frowned. 'Lady?'

In desperation Diamond remembered the waiter who spoke passable English. 'Is Luigi here?' Before getting a response he said to Halliwell, 'See if the waiter's out back.'

Luigi was brought from the kitchen and confirmed that Monnington had been in with a woman guest. The couple had left in a hurry after receiving the call on the mobile. They'd got into a taxi ten minutes ago.

'Did you see them go?' Diamond asked.

'Sure.'

'Which taxi firm?'

'Abbey Radio.'

Halliwell called Abbey and hung on while they put out a message. The driver confirmed from his cab that he'd picked up a couple in George Street and dropped them off at a private house on Widcombe Hill.

'What number?'

'He didn't get the number. They told him when they got there.'

'Oh, great.'

'Opposite a bus-stop about halfway up. A big house with stone griffins on the gateposts.'

'Stone what?'

'It's a mythical beast.'

'Never mind.' They got in and drove off.

'It'll be easier than looking for a house number,' Diamond said, trying to be positive, and he was right. The gate with the griffins came up on their right. Even better, a car he recognised as Monnington's black Mondeo was on the drive.

There were lights behind the curtains of the tall Victorian villa. Halliwell radioed their position and said they were going in. The back-up team was being informed, they were told.

A delay in answering made the two policemen uneasy. Then the door was opened by a dark-haired woman in a low-cut black dress with spaghetti straps.

Diamond held up his ID and asked to see Dalton Monnington.

She looked apprehensive, but invited them in.

330

In the large, luxurious living room, Monnington, shoeless and in shirtsleeves, with tie loosened, was lounging on a sofa watching a DVD of some Johnny Depp film. He reached for the remote and touched the mute button.

'Kill it,' Diamond said. 'I want your total concentration.'

Monnington switched off and then made his protest. 'You're hounding me. It's a bloody imposition.'

'We questioned you once in your own home. That's no imposition,' Diamond said.

'This is someone else's home.'

'And you disappeared to it double-quick when I called you at the restaurant. We could have spoken there.'

'I'm entitled to a private life.'

'Or two, or three?' Diamond said.

'What do you mean by that?'

'Car keys, please.'

'What?'

'We need to search your car.'

'Again? What is it with you? You've been over my car. There's nothing in there but brochures.' He sighed and put his hand in his pocket.

Diamond passed the keys to Halliwell and indicated with a tilt of the head that the search had high priority.

'And get your shoes on,' he told Monnington. 'We're taking you in for questioning.'

*   *   *

Monnington's woman friend watched in mute amazement as her date was escorted to the police

331

car that had just arrived on her drive. Diamond remained with her, leaving the two uniformed officers to take the suspect in. There was a job to do, and it required the lady's cooperation. She was Charlotte Brown, she said nervously when asked, known to everyone as Lottie. She'd met Dalton Monnington only last month when he'd asked to sit at her table at a busy time in the Retro Café in York Street. They'd clicked at once. This was their second evening together—or should have been.

'I hardly know him at all,' she said, and then realised how this could be taken and added, 'It's not what it sounds like. I don't sit in cafés looking for men.'

'You can relax, Lottie,' Diamond said. 'He's the suspect, not you. We don't know for sure, but between you and me, you may have had a lucky escape. Where was he staying?'

She reddened. 'Isn't that obvious?'

Halliwell returned from outside, eyes gleaming. 'You'd better come and look at this, guv.'

'Hang on a bit. When did he arrive?' Diamond asked Lottie Brown. 'Today?'

'This afternoon, about four thirty. He called me this morning and said he was visiting Bath and I offered to, em, put him up.' She was a serial blusher.

'So did he have an overnight bag?'

More embarrassment. 'It's upstairs.'

'Mind if I look?'

'I suppose.'

Halliwell was practically jumping up and down in his eagerness to tell Diamond what he'd found. On the way upstairs he said in a low tone, 'I think we've nailed him.'

332

Monnington's leather holdall was on a chair in Lottie Brown's bedroom. Inside Diamond found a laptop among the clothes. He handed it to Halliwell. 'I want our whizz-kid Clive to look at this.'

Lottie was getting uneasy. 'Don't you need a search warrant, or something?'

'No, my dear. It's your house and you invited us in. You're not going to make our job more difficult, are you? Is that the door to the en-suite?' He opened it and looked in. 'He's made use of it already, I see.' A battery-powered razor was on the shelf over the hand basin. 'Unless this is yours?'

'No, that's Dalton's.'

'And the washbag?' He passed it to Halliwell.

'That's his, too. I don't think you should help yourself to his things.'

'He won't need them here tonight. Let's go downstairs again.'

In the living room, he asked if anything about Monnington had struck her as strange.

She was still unwilling to concede much. 'I suppose I was surprised when we had to leave the restaurant in such a hurry.'

'Did he say why?'

'It was something to do with the phone call. Someone was being a nuisance, he said, and we'd better not stay.'

'That was me,' Diamond said. 'The ultimate pain in the butt. Before he got the call was he acting normally?'

'I thought so. He was being nice.' Her look suggested that present company could take lessons from Monnington.

'Did he talk about himself at all? His work?'

'He told me all about that the first time. He's a sales rep and he comes through Bath every month. What do they call those things? Jacuzzis. He said he could get me one at a knockdown price if I wanted, but he wasn't pushing or anything.'

'To sum up, then, there was nothing to cause you any concern in what he was saying?'

She shook her head. 'What's he supposed to have done?'

*   *   *

Out on the drive, Halliwell opened the boot of the Mondeo with the air of a conjurer producing the rabbit. 'How about that?'

Diamond was prepared for something special, but nothing so special as this. His heart thumped against his ribcage.

'The same, isn't it?' Halliwell asked.

After a long hesitation he found words. 'Looks like it to me.'

'What do you reckon? Twenty-five feet?'

'Thirty, more like.'

'Enough, anyway.'

They were looking at two lengths of white plastic cord, loosely coiled. The last time they'd seen anything like that, it was tight round Jocelyn Steel's neck and she was hanging from it.

43

Of all his colleagues, Diamond least wanted to see
Georgina when he returned. At this time in the
evening she should have been off the premises,
singing her socks off in some rehearsal hall.
Instead she stood with a commanding view of the
staff car park at the back of the nick. The bust
that wouldn't be ignored was straining the silver
buttons again. No way could anyone slide past and
pretend she wasn't there.

'You've got things to tell me, Peter,' she
boomed.

'Not really, ma'am,' he said. 'It's a bit
premature.'

'But you arrested a man for the murders. They
brought him in twenty minutes ago.'

'On suspicion.'

'He's the killer, though?'

'Put it this way. I want the truth out of this
scumbag before it's too late.'

'No violence, Peter.'

'We haven't found Martin Steel. His chance of
survival is running out minute by minute.'

'I'm serious about that.'

'I thought it was one of your choir nights
tonight.'

'It is, but I've sacrificed it. What have you got
on this man?'

'Can I tell you later? There's a heap of work to
be done, people to see, things to check.'

'Be mysterious, then,' she said, pink with
annoyance. 'Personally, I've always believed in

335

holding nothing back.' Her chest swelled even more.

Diamond averted his eyes.

'Things have been happening here,' Georgina went on. 'I'll walk upstairs with you and fill you in.'

'If you like.'

She made just enough space in the doorway for him to ease past without physical contact. For a moment they were toe to toe and he had a memory of the ladies' invitation waltz at Jim Middleton's tea dance with little Annie steering him with her thighs. With practice he might take to ballroom dancing. Maybe Georgina saw the look in his eye because she set off along the lower corridor as if pursued by a bear. He had to wait for the stairs at the end before she spoke again. 'This afternoon it was all Harry Lang.'

'At this stage I'm ruling no one out.'

'And he ended up in hospital.'

'His own fault, ma'am. Has he recovered consciousness?'

'Allow me to finish, Peter. You're like a coiled spring. He's still too confused to interview, but the doctors are optimistic. Quite properly—and I give credit when it's due—you ordered forensic tests on the Ballance Street flat and they are still going on. I can tell you that the early results are promising.'

'Oh?' She'd surprised him. He'd been on autopilot up to now. The evidence against Monnington had pushed Harry Lang way down the list of priorities. Now a sliver of doubt pierced his thinking.

'Yes,' she said in a throwaway voice, 'the

336

fingerprint team gave me a call. They lifted a mass of prints from the living room and kitchen area and some of these have been compared with the national database. They found three good matches.'

'Anyone I know?' Diamond said, trying to sound cool about it.

'Two of them are cousins, little more than juveniles.'

'From Kosovo?'

'I don't think so. They sound quite British to me. Craig Curly and Hugh Short.'

'Or Short and Curly?'

Georgina clicked her tongue and let out a sharp, angry breath. 'I hadn't thought of that. I suppose they could be made-up names.'

He thought so, too. He wouldn't mind betting they were also known as Romney and Jacob, those woolly extras in Operation Fleece. Someone in this scam had a twisted sense of humour. 'You said there was a third?'

'Gary Jackman, who runs a car repair business. He did a six-month stretch for changing the plates on stolen cars.'

Young Paul Gilbert's unreliable informer. Georgina had wandered into a minefield. How much did she know? 'He's known to us already. Pondlife.'

'The point is, Peter, it doesn't take Sherlock Holmes to tell us that Ballance Street was being used to plan robberies. We haven't yet discovered Harry Lang's true identity, but we now know why he took flight when you arrived with a squad car.'

'You're thinking these are the ram-raiders?'

'It adds up, doesn't it? Lang clearly has a source

of money. He owns a good car. You don't expect a council-house tenant to be driving a brand new Subaru.'

'Ill-gotten gains?'

She nodded. 'I'm not against immigration. It brings this country many talented and decent people, but you're going to get some crooks as well. Lang could be the ringleader. We can't be certain until we question him. Meanwhile Gary Jackman will do for starters.'

He swallowed hard. 'You want to question Jackman?'

'He's waiting downstairs.'

'What—have we pulled him in?'

'On my authority. Don't look so alarmed, Peter. I'm not taking over. Which of you is running the ram-raid inquiry now?'

He had to think. 'DI Halliwell, ma'am. He's been helping me this afternoon, seeing that not much was happening on the ram-raid front.' Halliwell knew Jackman was on the payroll. He'd handle this with kid gloves.

Georgina drew herself up again. 'Tell Mr Halliwell that when he can drag himself away from other duties he has the little matter of an interview to conduct.' She swaggered off like the gunslinger who has just cleaned up the town.

*   *   *

Clive the computer man was at work in the incident room when Diamond looked in. Halliwell had already handed him Dalton Monnington's laptop.

'Have you cracked the password?' Diamond

338

asked.

'Working on it. What exactly am I looking for, Mr D?'

'If I knew the answer to that, I wouldn't have brought you in. A list of his clients would be good.' He called across to Halliwell, 'Did you fetch the plastic cords from Monnington's car?'

Halliwell held up an evidence bag.

'Good. What we want now is the cord used to hang Jocelyn Steel. Should be in the evidence store. We compare them, of course, and if they're similar we look at the ends and see how they were cut. If we're really lucky they join like two halves of a loaf and bingo, we've got him.'

'I'll see to it, guv.'

'No, you won't.'

Halliwell frowned. He wanted to be in at the kill. Deserved it.

'Give it to DC Gilbert. I'm afraid the ACC has other plans for you.'

*   *   *

So it was John Leaman who joined Diamond in interview room one and cautioned Monnington.

The amorous sales rep was sitting with arms folded. His mouth was set in an inverted U-shape, defiance writ large. 'I want my solicitor and I want to speak to him in private.'

'Noted,' Diamond said. 'The custody clock has started. Let's get this under way.'

'Didn't you hear? It can't start without my solicitor.'

'Sorry, my friend. You're entitled to ask for your brief, and I'm entitled to delay him for up to thirty-six hours.'

A glare. He didn't know if Diamond was bluffing. He was in no position to find out.

'Police and Criminal Evidence Act. I'll confirm that in writing if you wish. At this stage I'm giving you a chance to earn some goodwill. Where can we find Martin Steel?'

'No comment.'

'Don't be awkward, Dalton. This is one life you can save. Where's he being kept?'

'I want my solicitor.'

'I told you. You must wait.'

'In that case, so must you.'

'Is Steel dead already?'

'No comment.'

'Because if he isn't and you cooperate, we can make this whole experience less uncomfortable. Do you smoke?'

Monnington shook his head.

'Coffee? Clears the brain.'

Another shake of the head.

'You see, this thirty-six hours allows us time to check the evidence. We've got DNA from your comb. We're looking at your laptop. The plastic cord from your car boot is being minutely examined. It's all over for you really.'

Monnington didn't look unduly worried.

Inside, Diamond was seething. He turned to Leaman. 'We've got a silent one, John. No point in running the tapes when nobody is speaking. Why don't you turn them off for a bit?' This was meant to alarm Monnington, and did, the more so when Diamond stood up and took off his jacket.

'No,' Monnington said. 'Leave them running.'

'Why? Have you got something to say?'

'I'm protecting my rights.'

'Stuff your rights,' Diamond said, coming round the table. 'What about the rights of that poor sod you've got trussed up in some godforsaken hole?'

'You're mistaken.'

'Where is he, then? Sitting at home with his feet up? I don't think so.'

'I know nothing about this.'

'Did you fit a jacuzzi at the Steels' house in Midford? Jocelyn and Martin Steel?'

'In point of fact, no.'

'Oh, come on, Monnington. Let's not split hairs. You may not have installed it, but you sold it to them. We found the invoice in their filing system. Give it a Whirl. That's your company, right?'

'It wasn't a jacuzzi. It was a hot tub.'

This, at least, was progress. He remembered the job. The link to the Steels was admitted.

'Tell me the difference,' Diamond said with an effort to be patient.

'A jacuzzi uses an air system. Bubbles. A hot tub works on a different principle altogether, using jets of water.'

Diamond glanced at Leaman. 'The things you learn in this job.' He went back to his chair and nodded to Leaman to resume the tape-recording. 'So you don't deny visiting the Steels to sell them their hot tub?'

'Two years ago,' Monnington said. 'That was all of two years ago.'

'We're getting somewhere. You admit they were clients?'

'That's no crime.'

'Taken together with your attempts to start a

341

relationship with another of the victims, Delia Williamson—'

'*Relationship?*' he broke in. 'I flirted with a waitress.'

'Gave her your hotel room number. If she'd come knocking on your door as you planned, would you have let her live? You like them begging for it like Lottie Brown, don't you? You're a sexy devil. But you get nasty when they ignore you.'

He looked away.

'We've got your number, Dalton. You can't take rejection. Killing them isn't enough. You have to punish them, make an example of them by stringing them up. And when the boyfriends and the husbands come looking, they get the same treatment.'

Monnington shook his head and said nothing. But his hands were shaking.

'All right,' Diamond said. 'Let's leave your twisted thinking for later. Where can we find Martin Steel?'

'I've no idea.'

'I told you, it's over, Dalton. The killing is over. No way are you going to string this man up. Is he dead already?'

'No comment.'

'Did you work with someone else? Are you trying to protect anyone?'

Silence.

'What do I have to do to get the truth? Will your partner Angie help us? You must have some regard for her, because she survived. We can pick her up and bring her here, but it's a two-hour drive.'

He shook his head again.

'Don't worry, she knows all about you and your playing around. I've spoken to her. I keep telling you, it's common knowledge what you are. You're finished. If you've got a shred of decency you'll tell me where to find Martin Steel. That's all I'm asking at this point. Tell me, and we'll give you a break. You want some sleep tonight? You can get it.'

Monnington sighed and looked up at the clock.

Diamond made a grab for his hair and shoved his face hard against the table.

He yelped, more in shock than pain.

Leaman said, 'Guv, don't do this.'

Diamond jerked the face upwards. 'I haven't marked him.' With his free hand he slapped Monnington sharply on both cheeks. 'This is pit-a-pat. I haven't started. Stand up.'

Monnington obeyed. He'd gone dead white, but red patches were forming on his cheeks.

'Has anyone ever roughed you up?' Diamond said, staring. 'I mean really given you a workover?' Without moving his eyes he said to Leaman. 'Leave us alone for a bit.'

Leaman said, 'Guv, I can't do that.'

'It's an order.'

'I think he might be ready to talk.'

In fact, Monnington was opening and closing his mouth without giving voice to anything at all. Then he fell back onto the chair and started making a series of animal-like sounds.

'That's all I bloody need. Hyperventilating,' Diamond said. 'Get him sorted.' He marched out of the room.

He met Ingeborg coming fast downstairs.

'Guv.'

'Out of my way.'

She grabbed his arm. 'Guv, I was coming for you. DI Halliwell needs you.'

He'd sacrificed Halliwell for the ram raid. The bloody ram raid. 'He can get stuffed.'

'He says it's personal.'

'Does he want out? Is that what it is? You can tell him I want out as well, but it ain't going to happen.' He brushed her arm aside and marched on, he didn't know where. He needed to cool the fire raging inside his head.

She wasn't giving up. She shouted after him, 'He sticks up for you whatever anyone says and you treat him like shit.'

He stopped and turned. 'Would you care to repeat that?'

She was white and shaking. 'No, but I meant every word. People who toe the line get nowhere with you.'

'You could find yourself in front of a disciplinary board.'

'All right, but will you speak to Keith? I've never seen him so serious.'

If Ingeborg was risking her career, something was badly wrong.

'Where is he?'

He found Halliwell in interview room two sitting across the table from a skinny young man with a shaved head. Gary Jackman was wearing a scuffed leather jacket flecked with paint. His hands were oil-stained. There was smouldering resentment in his brown eyes.

'I'll come out,' Halliwell said.

'This had better be good.'

Out in the corridor, Halliwell was twitchy. He waited for a uniformed sergeant to get out of earshot. 'Something came up in here, guv. He's saying he was double-crossed by the gang, which is why our stake-out came to grief.'

'Well, he would. He gave us crap information. If this is all you've brought me here for—'

'No, listen,' Halliwell cut in. 'You recall that he runs this vehicle repair shop and does up stolen cars? He's insisting the gang didn't use the vehicles he'd worked on, except for the decoy. He says the getaway car they used for the raid in Westgate Street was a blue Nissan Pathfinder and the owner is the brains behind the raids, planned the whole thing and torched his own car up at Lansdown the same night.'

Diamond's shoulders twitched in a reflex action. How could this be true?

44

He recalled the heart-to-heart he'd had with Halliwell—blurting out his feelings about Paloma—on the drive back from the Ballance Street flat. My big mouth, he thought. This silly story about the ram raid could have been dealt with routinely, Jerry interviewed and cleared without anyone finding out who was dating his mother. Instead Halliwell feels in honour bound to tell me about it and I'm in honour bound for

Paloma's sake to deal with it myself. What will that do for our relationship?

Halliwell was backtracking fast. 'Guv, I don't believe Jackman. He's giving us this bullshit to shift the blame.'

'How does he know about the burned-out Pathfinder?'

'He's in the car-repair business. Spare parts. They can spot a dead one like vultures.'

'Why would he make this up?'

'He's between a rock and hard place. He's going to get hammered by the ram-raiders if he gives evidence against them, yet he owes us something for the fiasco the other night.'

'So he fingers Jerry Kean, who has sod all to do with it? If that's so, he's an idiot. We check it out and find he's lying. He's worse off than before.'

'Do you want to talk to him?'

'Jackman? No, I don't.'

'Do we follow this up, or not? '

Diamond sighed, weighing the options. Absurd as the allegation was, it would have to be investigated. He looked at the time. 'Leave this with me. I'll get the truth of it.'

'But you're wanted here. The hangings.'

'I said I'll do it.' He walked away, leaving Halliwell staring after him.

Time was bearing down, but the questioning of Dalton Monnington had come to a temporary halt. How long did it take to get over a hyperventilation attack? Twenty minutes? Half an hour? Or longer?

The other main suspect, Harry Lang, was still semiconscious.

If there was a right time to see Jerry Kean, it

346

was now. He took out his new mobile and called the only number in the directory.

Paloma's voice lifted his spirits, for all the awkwardness he felt. 'Hello.'

'This is Peter.'

'Peter? How nice.'

He was tempted to say not nice, not nice at all. Instead he asked if she knew where Jerry was.

'Right here with me.'

That simplified matters. 'In your home?'

'Sainsbury's, as it happens, late-night shopping. Where it all started, really. Do you want to speak to him?'

'I'd rather see him in person. It's sort of ... delicate.'

'Where are you? Still at work? You're overdoing it.'

'You caught me on a bad day.'

'You'd better speak to Jerry. I'm handing this across.'

Jerry's voice asked what the problem was.

'It's to do with your stolen Pathfinder. I need to clarify a couple of things with you.'

'How can I help?' Jerry said in such a civil tone that Diamond was tempted to deal with the matter over the phone.

But when the call ended, Jerry would be annoyed he'd come under suspicion. He'd sound off to Paloma and she'd be hurt, as any parent would. Better, surely, to deal with it face to face. 'What are your plans for the next twenty minutes?'

'Back home to unload the shopping.'

'Paloma's?'

'Mine first. Her car is at my place.'

'I'll see you there? It won't take long. Where

347

exactly do you live?'

*   *   *

He told Leaman he would be out of the building for the next half-hour. 'Time out for all concerned,' he said with a weary smile that left Leaman in no doubt that his boss was as much in need of a break as the hyperventilating suspect.

*   *   *

Jerry's flat was in Cavendish Mansions, a converted hotel in Laura Place, just across Pulteney Bridge. No doubt Paloma's money helped him live at a smart address, just as she subsidised his cars. This young man had no need to get involved in criminality, Diamond told himself. The ram-raid charge just didn't stick.

They were ahead of him after he'd parked the car, carrying bags of shopping into the building. He stepped out and caught up with them in the entrance hall. Jerry was collecting his post from the pigeon-hole system near the lift. Paloma turned and kissed Diamond. He was aware how tense and tight his lips had become. He was shaking a little. This interview would be about as stressful as any he'd done.

He took over Paloma's bag of shopping. Strictly, it was Jerry's shopping. No doubt of that, because it was one of those Hosannah totebags. All the shopping was bagged like that. He had no use for Sainsbury's carriers. The ecology was safe with Jerry.

'We did a joint shop,' Paloma said. 'My stuff is

348

still in the car. At least, I think it is. I hope Jerry hasn't got my wine.'

'Mother, if I have, you know it's safe with me,' Jerry said as he joined them.

' "Eat, drink and be merry," ' she said, winking at Diamond. 'That's somewhere in the good book, isn't it?'

'And you know how it goes on?' Jerry said.

'Never get into a quoting contest with my son,' she said to Diamond.

'All I can quote is the official caution,' he said, 'and I try not to do it among friends.'

Jerry let them into his flat. The first impression was that it could do with some lighter wallpaper. The heavy maroon in the hall set off a couple of pictures to nice effect, but only after the lights over them were switched on. They were views of cathedrals. That figures, Diamond thought. They wouldn't be reclining nudes.

The kitchen where they took the bags looked as if no one used it. Every surface was clean and uncluttered.

'Put your frozen stuff away and then Peter can ask you his questions,' Paloma said. 'He's still working, unlike you and me.'

'Listening to you,' Jerry said, 'anyone would think I was still about nine years old.'

'Darling, you are, to me,' Paloma said, winking at Diamond.

The fridge-freezer, when opened, was a miracle of arrangement, everything sized and sorted. The newly purchased items went into slots that were the only possible places for them.

'Cup of tea?' Paloma said.

Diamond said he hadn't time, so they went into

the living room and sat on padded upright chairs with ornate wooden backs. There was a piano, and it was easy to imagine a Victorian musical evening here, with polite guests watching the chiming clock on the mantelshelf and wishing the chairs were more comfortable. A bookcase and sideboard completed the furniture. The books were of the sort those Victorians would have called 'improving'—biographies of Mother Teresa and Anne Frank shared the space with *Pilgrim's Progress* and Golding's *The Spire*. The CDs were mostly of church music. It takes all sorts, Diamond decided.

'So is there some query about the love of my life?' Jerry asked.

Diamond, his mind on higher thoughts, was thrown until Paloma said, 'His Pathfinder.'

'Got you.' It was a rare moment of humour from Jerry.

'My late lamented Pathfinder,' Jerry said.

'The night after you reported it missing a ram raid took place—a jeweller's in Westgate Street.'

'Westgate Street? I saw the shopfront all smashed in. Did my car do that?'

'I'm asking you, Jerry.'

He vibrated his lips, more puzzled by the question than upset. 'How would I know? I wasn't at the wheel.'

'Someone says you were. He was involved in the raid and says you planned the whole thing.'

Paloma said, 'Peter, that's crazy.'

Jerry shook his head slowly and curled his lip in disdain.

It was easy to understand how this was an affront to both of them. 'That's why I'm here,'

Diamond said, 'to get Jerry's side of the story. Where were you on Sunday night?'

'Easy,' Paloma said, folding her arms defiantly. 'Evensong.'

'Perhaps Jerry would like to speak for himself.' This sounded like a put-down, and was. He'd have said it to anyone interrupting. But it pained him to see how Paloma turned pale and then shrank into herself.

'She's right,' Jerry said. 'I never miss evensong.'

'But that's early, isn't it?'

'True. It wasn't me who mentioned it.'

Paloma was red-eyed, her mouth shut tight.

Diamond tried to focus. This was one of the toughest situations a policeman is ever faced with, questioning close friends about a serious crime, yet he had to press on. 'So it doesn't cover the time I'm interested in.'

Jerry was answering with confidence, as if he'd heard the questions already. 'After the service several of us went for a fish-and-chip supper.'

'Where?'

'Spike's, in Railway Street, just across the street from your police station.'

Diamond knew Spike's. He'd taken many a warm packet home from there. 'These were people from the church?'

'The young crowd, anyway.'

'What time did you leave?'

'I suppose about nine thirty.'

'The thing is,' Diamond said with an effort to match the buoyant mood of Jerry's answers, 'the raid took place about one in the morning.'

'That's all right, then,' Jerry said. 'Virginia can vouch for me, if that's all you need to know.'

There was a momentary break in the flow.

'You have a girlfriend?' Paloma said, recovering some of her sparkle.

'No, mother. This was our Save the Sinner Group. We had a meeting at Virginia's house in St James's Square. There's a mission month coming up and we have to plan it.'

Saving sinners was a far cry from ram-raiding if it was true. 'What time did this meeting break up?' Diamond asked.

'Close to one in the morning. Why don't you speak to Virginia?' Before any more was said, Jerry took out his mobile and pressed a couple of keys. He held it to his ear. 'Virginia? Jeremy. I've got a policeman here asking where I was after midnight last Sunday evening. You can tell him, can't you?' He handed the phone to Diamond.

The speaker at the other end sounded suspicious. 'Is this a practical joke?'

'No, Miss.' Diamond told her who he was. 'Jeremy tells me he was at your house. Is that correct?'

'Let's be crystal clear, officer,' Virginia said, and the frost was tangible, 'it wasn't only Jeremy. Seven of us were here. And we were on the Lord's business.'

'And what time did you finish?'

'At five past one. With a prayer.'

'You're certain of the time?'

'Absolutely. It's in my report of the meeting.'

'And that's written down somewhere?'

'Jeremy has a copy of the minutes. I sent them out yesterday.'

'Really? That's all I need to know.'

'The Lord be with you, then.' The blessing

352

came over as just a tad conditional, but no doubt sincerely meant.

'Thanks.' He returned the phone to Jerry. 'She says you were sent a report of the meeting.'

'Could be in the mail I just picked up,' he said, reaching for the letters he'd placed on the piano. 'Yes, this is one of her envelopes.' He opened it and handed the folded sheet to Diamond to open.

The summary of the meeting began with the list of those present, including J. Kean, and ended with the words: *The meeting ended at 1.05 a.m.*

In his mind Diamond added the words *Thank the Lord*. 'That clears it up, then.'

Jerry shrugged. 'If I'd opened this first we needn't have troubled her.'

'Thanks, anyway.'

'Who was it who tried to set me up?' Jerry said.

'You wouldn't have heard of him. He's a lowlife, desperate to shift the blame. He's made it worse for himself.'

'So it wasn't one of those personal trainers you asked me about?'

'No, someone else.'

Jerry frowned. He didn't want to leave this. 'How would he have heard of me?'

'I'd rather not get into that.'

'Be mysterious, then.'

Paloma said, 'Peter's got to be discreet, Jerry. He's doing a sensitive job.'

Diamond gave her a grateful smile. Her loyalty had been under severe strain. It was remarkable that she was seeing things from his point of view. 'And I'd better get back to that sensitive job, much as I'd like to stay on.'

Paloma said she was leaving, too.

Alone with Diamond, waiting for the lift, she said, 'I was falling apart in there. For a bit I believed my son was about to be arrested.'

'I know,' he said. 'Perhaps I should have talked to him alone.'

'He's my own flesh and blood, and I know robbing shops would be against all his Christian principles so I shouldn't have had any doubts. It's hard to describe, being a mum. I'm so relieved that's over.'

'If it's any help, I didn't think he was mixed up in this. But I had to make sure.'

'Of course. And Jerry—being Jerry—doesn't make things easy. I love him as only a mother can, but even I can see he's his own worst enemy.'

'In what way?'

'Self-righteous.'

'It's called the courage of his convictions.'

In the lift, she reached out to Diamond and kissed him. 'I could tell how difficult that was for you. You're a sweet man.' As the doors opened, she squeezed his arm. 'Spend the night with me.'

He felt a surge of happiness he hadn't known for a long time. 'It could be late, I mean really late.'

'Doesn't matter.'

45

Only now would Diamond admit to himself what pressure he'd been under. The relief was like the passing of a migraine attack, the moment it was safe to draw back the curtains. Jerry was in the

354

clear. For a time common sense had been suspended. Suspicion had seeped through Diamond's veins, creating pain and confusion. It hadn't counted that Jerry had proved his good intentions day after day as a hospital volunteer, that he was a committed Christian who would baulk at breaking one of God's clearest commandments. Bringing the young man in and exposing him as a criminal had become a real prospect. Paloma would have been devastated; the fragile relationship between them shattered.

He had just found out how much he valued that relationship.

Back at Manvers Street, he sought out Keith Halliwell and told him Jerry was not involved in the ram raid and explained why. 'A church meeting, and I defy anyone to find a more wholesome alibi than that.'

'At one in the morning?'

'Young people are just waking up when you and I are ready for bed.'

'Clubbers, maybe, but this was a church meeting, you say? What time did it start?'

'Late. They went for a fish-and-chip supper first. I've seen the minutes and I know when it broke up.'

'So it was minuted?'

'All typed up nicely, praise the Lord, as they say.'

'Gary Jackman lied to me, then. Scumbag,' Halliwell said, angry he'd been strung along. 'He's messed up big time. We'll nail him now.'

'Later will do,' Diamond said. 'He's a minnow. Where is he now? In the cells? Let him cool his heels for a bit.'

'Guv, this is personal.'

'I said leave it, Keith. Get your priorities right. Find out what's going on at the hospital. If Harry Lang is able to talk, go up there and take a statement. The clever money's on him.'

For all his strengths, Keith Halliwell sometimes got his focus wrong. He was capable of sorting out the ram raids now he was back on track.

But the bloody ram raids were a minor issue.

Diamond went looking for Leaman and found him in the incident room chatting earnestly with Ingeborg. 'You're back, guv,' Leaman said, raising his voice for her benefit. Ingeborg hadn't seen who had come in and could have said something she regretted. It was obvious they were discussing Diamond and he had a fair idea that it was about the bullying of a witness.

'How's Monnington?'

'I left him with the doctor. He seemed to be recovering.' Leaman signalled something problematic by clearing his throat. 'He was complaining about the treatment.'

'Oh? What did she do to him?'

Ingeborg stifled a giggle.

'Not the doctor's treatment,' Leaman said.

A halo would not have looked out of place over Diamond's head. 'I barely touched him. There isn't a mark on him.'

They knew better than to challenge him.

But Leaman had his own agenda. He said as if floating a theory, 'No disrespect, guv, but do you think it would be an idea if I took over the questioning when we go back?'

Diamond could have erupted and almost did. Instead he reined back his annoyance, realising it would have confirmed that he was out of control. 'And what would you ask him?'

'Where he's got Martin Steel.'

'He's stonewalling. You heard me try.'

'Yes, but he has to understand he can't bluff his way out of this. I can get through to him. I'm sure I can.'

'With sweet reason?'

Leaman shrugged. 'Something of the sort.'

'Nice cop replaces nasty one, is that it?'

Now he turned crimson. 'Nothing so crude as that.'

'Give it to me straight, John. How will you handle this?'

In effect, he'd already conceded Leaman would take over the questioning. Something might be gained from sitting in as the observer.

Encouraged, Leaman said, 'We've got a trump card now.'

'And what's that?'

'Like you suggested, I went to the evidence room and collected the plastic cord used to hang Jocelyn Steel. It's identical to the pieces you found in Monnington's car. Same colour, same diameter.'

The nasty cop felt a flutter of excitement.

'Did you look at the ends to see if it was cut from the same piece?'

'You can't tell with the naked eye. That's a job for forensics. But I've measured them, and what we have are two lengths of cord, one at twenty-two feet, the other twenty-eight foot three, just about right to haul a body over a beam. The cord used on Mrs Steel was just over twenty-three.'

He rested a hand on Leaman's shoulder. 'OK,

John. Give it your best.'

*   *   *

Monnington's jaw dropped and his brown eyes opened wide when the two detectives returned to interview room one carrying evidence bags. What was he anticipating? Torture?

Leaman asked if he was feeling better. Monnington gave a shrug. Diamond checked the clock and spoke the preamble for the tape. Then nodded, and Leaman took over.

'The reason we're doing this is that a man's life depends on it. No one has seen Martin Steel for three days. We think you can tell us where he is.'

The predictable shake of the head.

Leaman said in a measured voice, 'The killing has to stop, Dalton. It's over now. Time for you to think about your situation.'

He said, 'I've thought. I want my solicitor.'

'That can be arranged, and will. Cooperate now and we'll all feel more agreeable.'

Silence.

'I don't think you appreciate how much we've got on you. Your laptop is being examined at this minute.'

This got the response. He sounded panicky. 'You'd better not damage the files. I need them for business.'

'You may not be in business much longer. We expect to find some names we recognise, like Martin and Jocelyn Steel.'

He tried to appear indifferent. 'I don't suppose they're on file any more. I haven't spoken to them for two years.'

'But you got to know them quite well?'

'I wouldn't say so.'

'Come on, Dalton, any half-decent salesman makes a relationship with his clients.'

His professional skills were in question and he was spurred into saying, 'All I remember is that they fitted the profile of our customers. High-flyers, professional people, singles or couples, generally with no kids. They're the ones most interested in spending money on leisure items for their homes.'

'Did you ever come across a wealthy couple by the name of Twining, living out at Hinton Charterhouse?'

A shake of the head.

'That's in your area, isn't it? We're going back to 2004 now. It seems to me they were just the sort of people you would target.'

Monnington's eyes narrowed. 'What do you mean—target?'

'As potential customers. Like you say, well-heeled professional people living in a big house in the country.'

'Never heard of them.'

'They died the same way as Jocelyn Steel. And Delia Williamson and Danny Geaves. Strangled first, and then suspended as if they'd hanged themselves.' Leaman let that sink in. He was handling this well. 'The thing is, all these people were found in Bath. That's one common factor. And another is this.' He reached for the evidence bag and took out the coil of plastic cord. 'White plastic cord used to string them up. Have a good look at it. This was used on Mrs Steel.' He pushed it across the table. 'For the tape, I'm now showing

Mr Monnington the cord found attached to body five.'

Monnington swayed back in the chair.

'Feel free to handle it,' Leaman said. 'It's been forensically examined.'

Monnington made no move at all.

'It's identical to the two lengths of cord we found in your car.'

A look of panic passed across his features.

'Same quality, colour, diameter. Even the length would be similar if we added the portion of cord we had to cut that was tight round the victim's neck. About twenty-three feet, by my estimate. The lengths in your car'—Leaman reached for the other evidence bags and slid them towards Monnington—'were twenty-two feet and twenty-eight foot three.'

The eyes still looked alarmed, but Monnington was making a huge effort to appear unaffected, deliberately ignoring the coils of plastic, fixing his gaze somewhere neutral between Leaman and Diamond.

Leaman persevered, determined to get a response. 'It's obvious they're not tow-ropes. The plastic is strong enough to string up a corpse, but you couldn't pull a car with it. It's not long enough for a washing-line. Anyway, why would you want a washing-line in your car?'

Monnington remained silent.

Diamond stole a look at the clock. The cord was supposed to be the trump card and it was in danger of being ignored.

Leaman said, 'If there's an innocent explanation, you'd better tell us.'

After another uneasy pause, Monnington said,

'Take them away from under my nose and I'll tell you.'

The breakthrough? Diamond's pulse beat faster.

Leaman leaned forward and scooped up the cords and bags and dropped them on the floor beside him. 'Well?'

Monnington sniffed and said as if to a persistent child, 'If you really want to know, I use them in my work.'

'How?'

'For demonstration purposes.'

'Oh, yes?' Leaman couldn't have sounded more sceptical.

Monnington went on as if such details were too obvious to explain, 'To mark out the shapes of the spa baths so that customers can visualise them. I lay them out in a circle, right? My company supplies two sizes of bath. One is seven feet in diameter, the other nine feet. If you do your maths, you'll see that the twenty-two-foot cord is the circumference of the seven-foot bath. And the twenty-eight-foot-three cord is for the nine-foot bath. Twenty-two over seven is the approximate value of pi, the ratio between a diameter and a circumference.'

Leaman was drowning in a virtual jacuzzi.

Diamond took over. 'Let's get this right. You lay down the cord in the shape of a circle at the place where the bath will be installed?'

'To show the client how much room it will take.'

'And the cord is pre-cut to the two sizes?'

'You could try it here, but you wouldn't have room for a whirlpool, and why would you want one in an interview room?'

'Take a wild guess,' Diamond said.

*   *   *

Clive the computer expert was waiting when they emerged in their deflated state. Clive had better news, but it was short-lived. He'd cracked Monnington's password and the files were accessible. 'There's masses of stuff about plumbing and water pressures and ceramic tiles.'

'E-mails?' Diamond said.

'Not many. He's a deleter.'

'Is that bad?'

'It doesn't help you much.'

*   *   *

But the incident room was buzzing when he returned there with Leaman. A call had come in from Express Fit, a vehicle service centre on the Upper Bristol Road. The CAD room had received what they described as a garbled phone message about twenty minutes ago and the caller seemed to be in some distress.

'He gave his name,' Ingeborg said, 'and the woman at the garage—she's an office cleaner who picked up the phone—said it was very faint, but it sounded like Marcus Teal.'

'Martin Steel?'

'That's what we're thinking.'

'He's alive? What did he say?'

'He kept repeating, "Help me." She asked him to speak up and he couldn't. She asked where he was and he said he didn't know, except somewhere near Bath. She thought he said he was tied up and

362

lying on the floor.'

'This has got to be Steel. Has the call been traced?'

'They're trying. It's not so simple.'

'Why not? Did you tell them it's life and death?'

'It's automated. Long-distance calls are logged, but local calls are not. They can't retrieve them so easily. Something to do with the billing system. They're doing all they can.'

'Oh, great! Was there anything else he said? You got it all down?'

'I spoke to the cleaner myself and went through it twice.'

'Why would he call a garage?'

'We're thinking certain numbers were keyed into the phone and he managed to press the button that called Express Fit. If he's tied up he may have touched the button with his foot.'

'So we have a phone that is pre-set to call this garage. Could be private, or some office. We need a printout of all the Express Fit customers.'

'I've asked for it. Someone is coming in specially. They're closed, you see. He was lucky the cleaner picked up the phone.'

'He needs more luck than that.'

*   *   *

He returned to his office and called Paloma on the mobile. 'I'm sorry, but I'll have to cancel tonight. Things are happening here.'

'Good things?' she said.

'Not really. I can see myself spending the night here.'

'Peter, that's awful.'

'Sorry.'

'For you, I mean. You looked tired when I saw you. Couldn't you call it a night and go back refreshed in the morning?'

'No, there's too much stuff going on.'

'About those ram raids? It's only property.'

'No, the other thing.'

'The hangings?' She hesitated. 'Has there been another one?'

'Not yet, but there could be.'

'Ghastly. What sort of monster ... ? Forgive me, I'm not helping. Listen, I know you'll say it's a silly thing to do, but before I go up to bed I'm going to leave my front-door key under the mat just in case you do sort everything out. You can let yourself in at any time.'

'That's not a wise thing to do.'

'That's the policeman talking, not the man I know.'

'Both.'

'It's a deal, then. Promise?'

'Paloma, I can't promise anything.'

But if he needed an extra incentive to finish the job he had one now.

*　　　*　　　*

Paloma was right. He was dog tired. He wished she hadn't said it, because he felt more woolly-minded than ever. His brain was trying to pick up on something said during the questioning of Monnington, some detail that had been passed by. The harder he tried to grasp whatever it was, the more it eluded him.

'I want to listen to the tape of that interview,'

364

he said to Leaman.

'Rubbing my nose in it, guv?'

'Not at all.'

'I really thought we'd got him. I couldn't see any other explanation for those bloody lengths of plastic.'

'Nor me.'

'He's right,' Leaman said. 'I've done the sums now. The two cords from his car make circles just the size he says. And the laptop hasn't given us a single name we know. It's a lost cause. Shouldn't we let him go?'

'Fetch the tape. I want to hear it.'

In the incident room a few minutes later they ran the interview. Leaman, Ingeborg and Paul Gilbert huddled with Diamond over the machine. They were alert for Monnington's responses, but Diamond had a curious feeling it was something Leaman had said that was significant.

After a couple of minutes, he said, 'Stop it. Now play that sentence again.'

'That was me, not Monnington,' Leaman said.

'Play it.'

Leaman's voice came over: *The thing is, all these people were found in Bath. That's one common factor.*

He nodded. 'Common factor. That's the cue. Now go back a bit further, to where Monnington was telling us about the kinds of people he targeted as customers.'

Leaman pressed the rewind. Now it was Monnington's voice: *All I remember is that they fitted the profile of our customers. High-flyers, professional people, singles or couples, generally with no kids.*

Diamond snapped his fingers. 'Stop there.' The adrenalin rush was starting and his brain was making connections. 'He's talking about the Steels, right? Equally, he could have been talking about the Twinings.'

'Except he claims not to have heard of the Twinings,' Leaman said.

'That's not the point. Forget Monnington for a moment. Think of our victims and the common factor.'

'But they weren't all his customers.' Leaman's logical mind couldn't follow Diamond's free association of ideas.

'I said forget him. It's what he said. *Professional people, singles or couples, generally with no kids.*'

Next Ingeborg sounded sceptical. 'That may be true of the Steels and the Twinings, but Delia Williamson wasn't a high-flyer. She was working as a waitress.'

'Maybe,' Paul Gilbert said, 'but don't forget she lived with that muso in a big house in Walcot.'

'He wasn't the one who was killed,' Ingeborg pointed out. 'It was Danny Geaves, her ex, and he can't be described as a professional. What's more, she had two kids by him, so that doesn't fit the profile either.'

Diamond nodded. 'Two little girls.' But he wasn't shaken. His thoughts were slotting into place. 'I'm trying to remember stuff. I need to look at some witness statements. Can we get them up on the computer?'

'No problem,' Leaman said, ever ready to showcase his efficiency. 'Who, in particular?'

'Let's start with that skiving teacher you and I met in the George.'

'Harold Twining? He's on file for sure. I logged everything he said.'

'Find the bit about children—the children they didn't have.'

Leaman used the mouse to bring up the report he'd written. 'He mentioned it several times. Here's what he told us, the exact words: *No kids, no ties, not even a budgie to look after.*'

'I remember him saying that.'

'Then he comments on what the coroner said. *He said if they'd had children, or even a dependent relative, they might have felt their lives had more purpose.* Then you asked if they wanted a child and couldn't have one and he said—these were his actual words—*Another misguided theory. She had a baby stopped a year after they married. They slipped up.*'

'Right. Christine Twining had an abortion.' Diamond's gaze shifted swiftly from the screen to his team. 'And so did Jocelyn Steel. Now who told us that?'

Paul Gilbert said at once, 'The friend, Agnes Tidmarsh. I took down the witness statement. May I?' He brought up another document on the screen and scanned rapidly to the sentence: '. . . *a couple of years before they moved down here she had a termination. She was in that high-pressure government job and it wasn't the right time. Neither of them was ready for a family then. She kept it quiet from everyone, including her mother.*'

'That's two couples out of three,' Diamond said. 'Now, am I dreaming this, or did Amanda Williamson tell us her daughter had an abortion at some stage? Bring up the file.'

Gilbert returned to the list of files. 'Williamson,

Amanda? I don't see it here, guv.'

'Where the hell is it, then?'

'Is the name exactly right?'

'Of course it is.'

'Well, who would have typed up the statement?' Leaman asked.

'Don't know,' Diamond said, his patience snapping. 'I can't remember every bloody thing. Who was with me that morning in Bradford on Avon?'

Nobody spoke.

He thought hard, gave a deep sigh, and said, 'I was alone.' As the full catastrophe dawned on him, he said, 'Oh, buggery.'

Furious with himself, he sank his face into his hands and muttered more obscenities.

The rest of them were silent. Nobody knew what to say.

He struggled to recall the interview, but so much had happened since. He could picture the scene, seated on the bench in Amanda Williamson's small garden overlooking the town, but the words she'd spoken eluded him. He could visualise it all with ease: the church spire, the cars crossing the old town bridge with its quaint lock-up, the landscape stretching right across to Westbury. Then another detail came back to him: the tape-recorder on the bench between them.

He'd taped the conversation.

'Wait.' He got up and went to his office. The recorder was there on his desk half buried under all the other clutter. He brought the thing back in triumph and declared that he'd meant to ask one of them to transcribe the interview. In a moment they were listening to Amanda Williamson's voice.

368

He fast-forwarded and picked up his own voice asking, *So what went wrong? Why did they split up?*

Amanda answered, *Who can tell what goes wrong in a relationship except the people involved? I made a point of not interfering.*

He fast-forwarded a little, and she was saying, *She went through a bad patch, needed lifting emotionally, and Danny didn't see it, or was too busy to notice. He was doing all the caring for the girls.*

He switched off. 'What does that mean—"a bad patch"?'

'Depression, obviously,' Ingeborg said. 'Can we hear some more? Does she say what caused it?'

'That's as much as I got,' he was forced to admit.

'It's not what you said, guv. Amanda doesn't mention her daughter having an abortion.'

He refused to be downed. 'But it crossed my mind at the time. I could sense she was holding back. Do we have her phone number?'

'It's here on file with all the other contact numbers,' Gilbert said. 'Do you want me to call her?'

In a moment they were listening to the amplified voice of Amanda speaking live. 'What is it? Do you have some news for me?'

'I may have soon,' Diamond said. 'First I need your help. When we met, you spoke of your daughter going through a bad patch in her marriage. You didn't specify what it was and I didn't ask.'

The voice altered, becoming taut and defensive. 'That was a private matter. If it had any bearing on what happened to her I would have told you.'

'You'd better tell me now, ma'am. It's crucial to the case.'

'I don't see how.'

'For pity's sake,' he said. 'You may think you're protecting her reputation, but I'm trying to stop her killer from murdering someone else tonight. Why was she depressed?'

There was a silence. Then: 'She got pregnant again, disorganised as usual, poor darling. Stopped taking the pill for some days and wondered why she was putting on weight. It was a shock when she found out. She'd had a difficult time when Sophie was born and she didn't want to go through all that again.'

'And Danny wanted the child?'

'No, it wasn't like that. He supported her. So did her GP. He arranged for her to have the abortion at the Royal United.'

'That's all I need to know.' He looked round at his team.

They had found the common factor.

46

Early in the Diamonds' marriage, Steph had been diagnosed with something the medics called RSM, Recurrent Spontaneous Miscarriage. She had lost four babies altogether. That word 'lost' is a euphemism that tries to downplay the grief, but can't. He'd been amazed how she had found the courage to try again after each bereavement. She had wanted children with increasing desperation, and so had he, and her gynaecologist had said there was 'no physiological limitation', but after the fourth, the expert changed his opinion. She was given a hysterectomy.

So it was difficult to feel neutral about abortion. The result is the same—a pregnancy that fails—but there is a gulf between those who miscarry, the 'have nots', and those who seek abortions, the 'haves' who would rather be 'have nots'. In their low moments he and Steph envied friends with children, and resented those who confided that they had 'slipped up' and gone for abortions.

He didn't see it as a debate between the pro-choice and pro-life camps. He couldn't side with either. Personal experience had convinced him that each case had to be judged on merit. In his job he'd seen abused and mentally handicapped women unable to cope with pregnancy and he would have argued strongly for their right to a termination. This was a profoundly complex issue.

Ingeborg was the first to react. Any intelligent woman would question what had been suggested. 'Let me get this right, guv. Are you saying these couples were killed because they had abortions?'

'Could have been.'

She fixed him with her wide blue eyes and her words came with the force of someone who has thought through the issues. 'But it's not logical. The people who oppose abortion are pro life. That's their argument, that a foetus is a living human being and we have no right to kill it. They're not going to murder anyone.'

Of all the team it was Leaman who rallied to Diamond's defence. 'They can and they do,' he said in his blunt style. 'There was a case in

America a couple of years ago. A Presbyterian minister shot and killed a doctor who performed abortions.'

'A *minister*?'

'He's the best known example, but there have been others. I don't know how they square it with the sixth commandment.'

Ingeborg stared at him for a moment, frowning, thinking. Then her expression changed and her hand went to her mouth. 'You're right. I remember. He killed twice. It was in Florida and he was executed for it. I can't believe this is happening here.'

'These are emotive issues,' Diamond said. 'The logic can get pushed to one side.'

Paul Gilbert spoke up. 'I may be out of order here, but couldn't these abortions be a coincidence?'

This struck a more harmonious note with Ingeborg. 'I agree, Paul. If you look hard enough—and God knows we have—you're going to find something the victims have in common. That's light years from proving it was the reason they were killed.'

Diamond was trying to keep this from getting heated. 'OK. Let's see what we've got. Three couples. Three abortions. So far as we know, not one was medically essential. They made a choice. The Twinings because they didn't want their careers interrupted. Delia and Danny because they had two kids already and she'd had a difficult time with the second one. The Steels for the career reason again; they weren't yet ready to start a family.'

'How on earth could the killer have been aware

372

of any of this?' Ingeborg said.

'He'd need to know each of them extremely well,' Gilbert said.

'Or their gynaecologist,' Leaman said.

Ingeborg shook her head. 'Medical ethics.'

'A rogue nurse, then? An anaesthetist?'

'They aren't told the patients' history.'

'A medical secretary?' Leaman said. 'That stuff is written up in the records.'

Ingeborg digested that and nodded. 'I suppose you could be right about that.'

'Staying with what we know for certain,' Diamond said, 'the victims are taken from their homes to some secret location and kept there. The woman is strangled and taken by night to some city park and strung up to make it look like a hanging.'

'Execution?' Leaman said. 'A life for a life?'

'Maybe. A couple of nights later, the man is hanged. In Danny's case, it was literally a hanging.'

'Why wait?' Leaman said. 'Why doesn't he string them up together?'

'Logistics,' Paul Gilbert said. 'A double hanging would be almost impossible for one man to carry out.'

'Agreed,' Diamond said. 'The transportation, rigging up the gallows. Too much.'

'So he does it in stages.'

'Yes, and taking big risks. The majority of murderers hide their crime by disposing of the body. He could bury his victims or dump them on a refuse tip. Instead he has the weird idea of displaying them. At great risk. Why?'

'To make some kind of point?' Gilbert said.

'That's how it looks to me. The bodies are left hanging as if an old-fashioned judicial execution has taken place.'

'Except this is in public, not behind a prison wall,' Gilbert said.

'There was a time when they were hanged in public.'

'And left for people to see, like that highwayman we heard about,' Leaman said.

Ingeborg was nodding and her voice was more animated. 'Guv, I wasn't willing to believe you, but this is making sense now. This is about retribution. The killer casts himself as judge and executioner for what he perceives as the taking of life.'

Diamond heard her, but his reasoning had come to a grinding halt as the intuitive part of his brain leapt ahead. A pulse throbbed in his temple. He sensed with a horrid certainty that his world was about to implode.

Meanwhile Leaman was agreeing with Ingeborg. 'There's a kind of logic here, even if it's misguided.'

'Can we save Martin Steel?'

Another of Ingeborg's unanswerable questions. If nothing else, it underlined how little time was left.

Diamond had to function, whatever was going on in his head. He mobilised his team. 'We find out which hospital or clinic each of them attended. If it's the same one, we're not whistling in the dark.' He assigned them people to contact. Leaman would call Harold Twining; Gilbert, Agnes Tidmarsh; and Ingeborg, Amanda Williamson.

374

Eager to begin, they didn't notice the state he was in. They saw him step into his office and must have assumed he was leaving them to get on, declining to breathe down their necks. In truth, he was having difficulty moving his limbs. He was in turmoil. The nightmare he dreaded had come back to haunt him. He thought he'd banished it, but here it was, more stark than before.

He slumped behind his desk and snatched up Jerry's black totebag and took out Steph's Agatha Christie book. The bookmark was still there at the page he'd inscribed for her. The throbbing in his head was a drum-beat. He felt as if Steph herself was communicating with him.

He looked at the bit about times of services and the invitation to 'join us and be joyful'. Then he noticed the words printed along the bottom edge. It was the credo of the Hosannah Church. *We believe in the power of prayer, the sanctity of life and the Lord's commandments.*

The sanctity of life.

47

Twice he lifted the phone and twice he put it down. He could not be certain. Not one hundred per cent. He needed Paloma's help if it was true that her son had killed five people and was about to kill a sixth.

He didn't believe she knew Jerry was a murderer. Mothers can forgive and excuse almost anything, but the Paloma he knew couldn't bottle up such knowledge. The pressure would be unstoppable.

Without realising why it was so vital, she might say where he was holding Martin Steel. She probably knew the places where Jerry hung out, where he relaxed and spent time alone. From childhood on, we find our hideaways, the sanctuaries where we escape for a time and brood and dream: garden sheds, garages, basements, attics, derelict buildings, caves. Somewhere like this must have been used to house the victims until they were despatched.

His hand moved towards the phone again. His duty to help that innocent man outweighed all personal considerations. But how would he tell Paloma what he suspected? You can't wrap it up in kind words. It's still devastating. His fingers bunched.

The phone wouldn't do. This needed to be face to face.

He got up and stepped into the incident room.

Leaman looked up. 'Guv, I've got the dope on Christine Twining. She went to a private clinic called the Sheridan, up near the university at Widcombe.'

'Get onto them, then, and see if they have any record of Jocelyn.'

'What about patient confidentiality?'

'The patients are dead.' If nothing else, his brain was working again. 'John, I need to check something. I'll be twenty minutes, maximum. You're in charge. Any big news, call me at once.' He scribbled his mobile number on a memo pad.

Leaman said, 'Guv, would you do me a favour?'

'What's that?'

'Turn the bloody thing on.'

376

*   *   *

After crossing Churchill Bridge to join the roundabout he drove under the viaduct where Danny had been hanged. He knew this killer never used the same place twice, but he couldn't resist a glance upwards.

Nothing.

Nothing except that a transit van to his right almost veered into him. The brakes screeched. His own fault. In this mental state he shouldn't have been driving. The van driver thought the same and pounded his horn.

Good thing the roads south of the river were less busy. He got to Paloma's just before eleven. The lights were on. No other car was on the drive.

He reached for the doorbell and then hesitated. Instead, he stooped and found the key under the mat. Anything that would soften this blow was worth doing.

He let himself in. 'I Can't Get No Satisfaction' was playing in the room she used as a living room. Words she'd written in that first letter came back to him, the list of things she said she had in common with him. Rock music was among them. He took a deep breath, spoke her name and pushed open the door.

The Stones were playing to an empty room.

The kitchen, then. Maybe she was getting something to eat.

Lights on. Kettle faintly warm. Two of the Hosannah bags on a hook behind the door. She'd unpacked her shopping. Where was she?

He called to her again and tried two other large

377

rooms downstairs.

A petrifying thought gripped him. What if Jerry had been by and attacked his own mother to silence her?

'Paloma, are you there?'

No response.

Heart pounding his chest wall, he ran up that fancy staircase to the landing where her bedroom was.

The bedroom door was shut. He put his ear to it and listened. Nothing. Turned the doorknob and looked inside. Dark. He touched the light switch and let out a slow breath on finding she wasn't lying dead.

A movement in his own pocket made him start. The damned mobile was vibrating. He put it to his ear and listened.

'Guv?'

Leaman.

'What's up?'

'I thought you'd want to know. We've now checked all three women and they had the terminations at different hospitals. Christine Twining at the Sheridan, like I said. Delia at the RUH. And Joss Steel at another private place, the King Steven, at Prior Park. She was living in London at the time, but she must have come down here for privacy.'

He was silent, but his brain was racing.

'Are you there, guv?' Leaman said. 'It knocks our theory on the head, doesn't it? The killer can't be a medical professional unless he kept changing his job.'

'Right,' he said, more to himself than Leaman. His worst suspicions had taken root. The medical professionals might be in the clear, but what of a volunteer visiting a different hospital each evening of the week?

He couldn't let personal loyalty subvert his duty.

Decision time.

'John, I want you to bring a man in for questioning. His name is Jeremy Kean and he lives in Cavendish Mansions, up at Laura Place. We want prints, DNA, his clothes and we'll need a search warrant.'

'Now?'

'At once. And send a car to the Hosannah Church on Green Park Road in case he's there. Have it searched. He could be holding Steel there.'

So much for Jerry. But what of his mother?

Her study, or whatever she called it—the place where she kept her library of costume designs— was at the far end of the landing.

Again he hesitated at the door. Called her name and repeated it.

Not a sound came back.

He went in. The lights were on, but she wasn't there. In dread of what he would find, he crossed the room and opened the door between the shelves.

Paloma was sitting at her computer wearing earphones. She looked up, smiled and removed them.

'Some notes I recorded and wanted on file,' she said. 'Peter, what a wonderful surprise. I didn't expect you so soon after what you said on the phone.'

He had an urge to wrap his arms round her

before he said a word, but he remained in the doorway. 'Still on duty, I'm afraid.'

'Well, you shouldn't be. You're look ghastly.'

'Has Jerry been here?'

'No. Why?'

'Have you spoken to him since we were at his flat?'

'On the phone, you mean? No, I haven't. What's this about, Peter?' She caught her breath. 'Has something happened to him?'

'Nothing like that.' He stared at her for a moment in silence and then shook his head. 'Paloma, I wish there was a way of breaking this gently.'

Her hand went to her mouth. 'He's in trouble, isn't he?'

'He could be. When you were shopping did he say what his plans are for this evening?'

'I didn't ask. It's always one hospital or another with the books, but that's early. He should be home by now unless there's another church meeting.'

'If there is, he's in the clear.'

'What do you mean—"in the clear"? You don't have to be so mysterious.'

He took a step towards her, suffering with her, hating what he had to tell her, wanting to take her in his arms and promise everything would be all right, he'd make it right, whatever happened. But the policeman inside him was adamant. You don't conduct yourself like that. You hold your emotion in check.

He moistened his lips. A muscle was twitching at the edge of his mouth. 'That evening when I first came here, after the meal we had in the

Italian restaurant, I talked about my marriage to Steph and the miscarriages and we got on the subject of abortion.'

'And I told you about mine,' she said.

'You said Jerry is pro-life and you take the opposite view.'

'Well, I would.'

'Does he know about the child you aborted?'

'I've never discussed it with him. He may have heard from his father, I suppose. Now that he's so anti I wouldn't risk telling him myself. Call me a coward, but he doesn't need to know, does he?'

'This Hosannah Church makes the sanctity of life one of its main issues, doesn't it?'

'No doubt of that. Where's this going, Peter? What are you trying to say?'

He spoke in a low, undramatic tone. 'We know the medical histories of these women who were murdered. Each of them had an abortion.'

Her face convulsed with horror as she made the connection. Then she covered her eyes. 'Oh my God, say it isn't true.'

He knew he must tell her the rest. 'He visits hospitals with his library trolley. He has the opportunity to see where they keep the patients' records. He's known to the staff. No one is going to suspect a volunteer of doing anything underhand. But this pro-life issue is a crusade. People who choose to have an abortion for no good medical reason are murderers in the eyes of extremists. It's possible Jerry has taken it a stage further.'

A cry came from Paloma, a long, agonised wail of despair. She dipped forward and her face slammed on the keyboard in front of her. Her

381

back shook. She sobbed uncontrollably.

He couldn't watch this without responding. He bent over her and gripped her shoulders. 'Paloma. I can't begin to tell you how sorry . . .'

She didn't answer. She was inconsolable. She had the shakes now.

He took off his jacket and wrapped it round her. Shock is a dangerous condition. The blood pressure falls dramatically. First-aid training tells you the best you can do is calm the patient. But how?

Of all things, the phone in the jacket pocket started vibrating and Paloma felt it against her. She jerked and gasped. He grabbed it out and stuffed it in his trouser pocket.

There was a bottle of water on the filing cabinet. He uncapped it and said, 'Drink a little of this.'

She turned to face him, tears coursing down her cheeks.

He handed her the water and she took some. 'You came here to tell me?' she said.

He nodded.

She drank some more of the water. 'Answer your phone. You've got a job to do.'

He took out the mobile and pressed the key to make contact. He knew it would be Leaman.

'Guv?'

'Go on.'

'Two lads on patrol just reported in from Kean's place. Negative. One of his neighbours saw him go out about nine thirty. That's two hours ago. It looks bad.'

'The church?'

'Also negative.'

'I'll get back to you shortly.' He returned the phone to his pocket and asked Paloma if she had any idea where Jerry would be. 'If we can find him we may prevent another tragedy.'

Her face was a mask of pain. She shook her head. 'I can't think. I can't think.'

His own thought process had stalled as well. 'What does he drive now?'

'He rented a Mitsubishi Shogun. Black.'

'D'you know the registration?'

She didn't.

He frowned, struggling to get those thoughts functioning again. Something important. He tried running through Jerry's routine: the personal training, the hospital visits, the church. He pictured him pushing his trolley of books.

'When he visits the hospitals, how does he transport the trolley? It wouldn't fit into the Shogun.'

'He uses the church van. It's dark blue, with Hosannah written on the side.'

This was the breakthrough.

'Where's it kept?' He raised his palm. 'Hold on. I know. You told me there's a depot for the books on some trading estate. *That*'s where he's gone.'

48

Paloma sat beside him as he drove down Lyncombe Hill. She wasn't speaking, but she'd stopped crying. She had insisted she wanted to help, and Diamond could see the usefulness of having her with him. An arrest is the ultimate

383

confrontation. Her presence might be a calming influence. She had a good rapport with her son.

The Brassmill Trading Estate, off Brassmill Lane, was familiar territory, almost his own back yard, just down the road from Lower Weston. Raffles the cat had once gone missing for two days and turned up there at a printer's, where they had a tabby of their own on a diet of gourmet beef fillet in sauce. Raffles, used to cheap chicken chunks in jelly, climbed up the curtain and claimed sanctuary when it was time to go home.

When last there, Diamond hadn't noticed a book depot on the estate. Easy to overlook, though. Every building looked the same.

He'd called Leaman and cars were converging on Brassmill from several points of the city. There was still a hope that Martin Steel was alive. It had turned midnight already, but the MO suggested he would be taken out and executed later in the night.

'Not far now,' he said—the sort of bland remark that gave Paloma the chance to say something if she wished.

After a pause she said, 'I wouldn't have thought of this place.'

'Tucked away, isn't it?'

'I've never seen it. He scarcely ever speaks of it.'

'Everything closes down at six. Tailor-made for keeping a hostage.'

That drew a line under the conversation.

The streetlights dwindled when they turned off the Upper Bristol Road at Weston and headed into trading estate country, where functional 'units' were rented at a fraction of city-centre prices. The Locksbrook Estate came up first. Brassmill Lane was just a continuation on the road. A police car with lights turned off was parked at the first entrance.

He braked and lowered his window. 'Anyone gone in?'

'DI Leaman and two RRVs, sir. Take a left by the tyre-fit place and you'll see them.'

He drove in and located the other police vehicles parked in front of a carpet outlet. Leaman came to meet him, stooped at the open window and saw Paloma, but didn't get introduced.

'What do you reckon?' Diamond asked.

'The book depot is right behind this warehouse, guv. There's a Shogun Warrior parked outside.'

'That's his motor.'

'We've disabled it.'

'Good. What sort of back-up do we have?'

'A rapid response team. The place is surrounded.'

'Let's go in. I'm not expecting a shoot-out. He isn't that kind of animal.'

He got out and so did Paloma. He asked her to stay well back unless she was needed. Then he walked round the side of the carpet warehouse and saw the Shogun parked in front of a row of three small cabin-style buildings with flat roofs.

Leaman pointed to the one on the left. The windows were screened with slatted blinds. A light was on.

Diamond signalled with palms down that he wanted no action from the armed back-up. With Leaman at his side he walked up to the door, looked for a bell-push, found none and rapped with his knuckles.

No response.

He eyed Leaman, shrugged, and tried again with more force.

Same result.

'It has to be the fifty-pound door key, then.'

Leaman motioned to one of the men in Kevlar body-armour. An enforcer, a police battering ram, was brought over.

'It's a crime scene inside,' Diamond warned. 'I don't want you going in like the SAS.'

The locks must have been stout because three swings were needed to gain entry.

A foul smell hit them when the door swung inwards. Diamond pressed his hand to his face.

His way in was blocked by Jerry's trolley. He had to trundle it to one side, and even then he was faced with a fully stacked bookcase reaching almost to the ceiling. To get further in you had to sidle around it.

He took a step in and spoke Jerry's name. Trying to sound reasonable with a message that suggested the opposite, he said, 'There are armed men with me. I want you face down on the floor.'

No sound came back, and he had a strong sense that the place was empty.

He edged round the bookcase.

No one.

But if any doubt lingered about Jerry's guilt, this scene removed it. The bookcase was literally a front that screened off a primitive cell, with slop bucket, mattress, plastic plates and water bottles. Scraps of food were scattered about the floor along with shoes, Kleenex tissues and Hosannah totebags.

Leaman came in behind him.

'Don't ask.'

'But his car's still outside, guv.'

'Hole in one, John. He drives here in the Shogun and uses the van to transport his victims. He's already on his way to another hanging.'

49

'What do we do now—wait for a shout from uniform?' Leaman asked, making it sound like an accusation. The stress was getting to everyone.

'What you do, Inspector, is inform all units they're looking for a dark blue van with Hosannah written on the side.'

'Do you know the make and registration?'

'If I did, would I keep it to myself?'

'Is there any way to work out where he's heading?'

'You think that hasn't crossed my mind?' He left Leaman using his personal radio and went back to Paloma. He wanted her to see the interior of the book depot. Not to rub her nose in it, but to remove any scintilla of doubt about her son's recent actions.

Her mouth quivered, but she drew in a sharp breath and got control. They walked over to the building. At his suggestion she held a tissue to her face when he took her in. She stood looking for a couple of seconds and then needed the fresh air. Outside, she swayed a little and he thought she would faint, so he took her back to his car. There was a bottle of water in there.

He waited for her reaction, but she was numb. Her eyes were opaque and her shoulders sagged. All her vitality had drained away.

'You did the right thing, making me look,' she said finally in a low, flat voice. 'There's no escaping that.'

'And you had no suspicion?'

Her eyelids closed a moment longer than was natural. She gave no answer.

'Any thought where we can find him now?'

She shook her head. 'Dear God, I wish I knew.'

Sensing the turmoil within her, he kept to practicalities. 'Must be somewhere he's familiar with. He'll have visited there a number of times, staked it out. There are only so many places he can know that well.'

She pressed her hands to her face as if to hold her emotions in check. 'He knows the church and the hospitals he visits. Laura Place, where he lives. The Pulteney Bridge area.'

Diamond had already gone through these possibilities in his mind. Pulteney Bridge would be a spectacular place for a hanging, but it would entail breaking into one of the shops built into the structure and that would add to the complexity of the crime.

'He evidently knows the parks,' he said.

'Yes, he enjoys a walk.' She'd missed the point, and perhaps it was a mercy.

'Where does he do his shopping?'

'Waitrose is the nearest. Sometimes like today he'll do a big shop with me over at Sainsbury's.'

'Green Park, where you and I met.'

She glanced at him, bit her lip and looked away. The tears were not far off.

He went back to direct operations. Some of the rapid response team could be stood down. Four would remain in case Jerry returned to collect his car. But if he did, he would already have committed a sixth murder.

Leaman had broadcast a description of the van. 'There aren't that many commercial vehicles moving around the city after midnight,' he said. 'With so many officers on duty we must stand a chance of intercepting it.'

'By now it won't be moving,' Diamond said. 'It'll be stationary, and close to the place he's selected.'

'Even so.'

Diamond nodded. 'But there's so little time. My guess is that he leaves his victim tied up in the back of the van while he rigs up the gallows. Unrolls the plastic cord, slings the end over the crossbeam or whatever, secures it, makes a noose, cuts it. Ten minutes maximum. He left here at least an hour ago.'

'There are people about. He may have to wait a while to pick his moment.'

'We can hope.'

To his credit, Leaman was trying to contribute ideas. 'He's never used the same sort of structure more than once. A kid's swing, a viaduct, a tree, Sham Castle, the arch in Victoria Park.'

'Where does that take us? The possibilities are endless. A crane, scaffolding, a multistorey car park, a floodlight tower.'

'He hasn't used a bridge over the river.'

Diamond pulled a face. 'Do you know how many there are? I can think of ten. I left instructions that each one was obboed.'

389

'Would he have driven out into the country?'

'If he has, we're sunk. But there's a certain arrogance at work here. Up to now he's found sites within the city and I'm sure he means to get away with it again. Where do you look for a parked car in a city?'

'Car park?'

'Get them all checked. We've got the manpower.' He thought of what he'd discussed with Paloma, and added, 'The one behind Sainsbury's.'

Leaman spoke into his radio.

Diamond kicked at some weeds growing through the asphalt. Then he returned to Paloma and sat in the car with her.

She asked if there was any progress and he shook his head.

'I'd better tell you,' she said without looking at him.

'Tell me what?'

Mental pain has its own vocabulary. From the depth of her being came a moan primal in its intensity. A mother's lament. People say there is nothing worse to endure than the death of your own child. Maybe something is worse, Diamond thought, and that is to discover that your child has grown up into a cold-blooded killer.

The sound died away. Her eyes were still squeezed shut and her head was shaking.

'It's all right,' he said, knowing it wasn't. He was at a loss.

She reached for his hand and gripped it with extraordinary force. Then the words came, haltingly, each one as if it hurt. 'You asked just now if I'd had any suspicion about Jerry. Well, I

390

don't know what you call suspicion, but I'm his mother and I see him a lot, and I've had a horrible feeling for weeks that he was getting into something bad, something illegal, though nothing so terrible as this. How could anyone imagine . . . ?' A sob jerked from her chest. 'I'm sorry. I can't go on.'

'Try,' he said. 'I need to know.'

She drew another long breath. 'I could tell he was on edge a lot of the time, ever since he became so involved in this church. But they're church people and they shouldn't be doing bad things, so I kept telling myself I must be mistaken.'

'Did you raise it with him?'

'Quite a few times. That is, I didn't say he was up to no good. I said I could tell he was under pressure. I didn't think it was the job, or a woman. I wondered if he had money problems, but he knew I could help him out and sometimes did.'

'What did he say when you spoke to him?'

'That I was fussing and ought to treat him like a grown-up. It's so hard.' The tears streamed from her eyes again. 'You've got to let go, I know that. But as his mother I could sense he was in some kind of trouble and it was getting worse all the time. Little things you notice, like if we were shopping he'd move into another aisle to avoid people he recognised. Or he'd jump if the phone rang. And he changed his address about five times in two years for no good reason.' She swung to face Diamond and her voice broke up as she said, 'That's why I wrote you the letter.'

'What letter?'

'That first letter asking to meet you in the Saracen's.'

Ambushed yet again. *That* letter. 'The one I ignored?'

'Yes, it was unforgivable what I did. I had this stupid idea that if I started a friendship with a policeman, a senior policeman, and invited you home, Jerry would be shocked into stopping whatever he was doing that was making him so furtive.'

He'd taken one low punch before, when she'd told him he was virtually entrapped. He'd ridden that one, telling himself he should be flattered to get the attention. Now he'd found out she'd picked him because of his job, not who he was. He was just 'a senior policeman'.

Paloma's next words came in a burst, as if to stop him saying anything. 'I'm sorry, Peter. I deceived you. I used you. I read about you and knew you'd lost your wife three years ago. I thought you were probably lonely. Once I'd got this idea, I pursued you. I was driven. It was the only way I could see of getting through to my son.'

He couldn't speak. It was his turn to be numb. He closed his eyes, absorbing it all. What a mug. All the soul-searching about starting a relationship, the guilt about Steph, the belief that someone found him sexually attractive—overweight and middle-aged as he was—all this was down to vanity. Pathetic. Even after learning that the affair had been plotted by Paloma to reel him in, he'd forgiven her. Deep down, he'd been flattered that she cared enough to go to all the trouble she had.

Now he knew she hadn't wanted him at all

392

except to make a point to her shithead son, as evil a killer as he'd come across.

Conned.

'And none of it succeeded,' he managed to say finally. 'He didn't give a toss.'

'That's wrong, Peter. When he met you and learned I was going out with you he was shocked to the core. I could tell.'

'He carried on with the killing.'

'Peter,' she said. 'I just want to say—'

'Don't say anything. Not now. I can't take any more.'

He got out of the car and started walking to where Leaman was speaking to someone on his radio. He felt betrayed.

But at this low point he still had to function. A killer was out there. Another victim was about to die.

One thing made sense. Paloma's last remark—about Jerry being shocked to the core—linked up with a real event. Jerry must have torched his own car, the precious Nissan Pathfinder, in panic that it would be searched and reveal DNA from his recent victims, Delia and Danny.

There seemed to be something happening. Leaman flapped his hand to him to hurry.

'We've got the shout, guv. The Hosannah van is in Sainsbury's car park, just like you said.'

50

After telling Paloma where he was driving, he was silent. He didn't trust himself to say more.

The trip was a short belt into the city along the Upper Bristol Road and then south to Green Park. Unusually for Diamond, he put his foot down. Not much was on the move at one twenty in the morning. Sirens and beacons were not being used. This would make the inrush of police vehicles conspicuous, so he'd ordered a discreet operation. He didn't want Jerry Kean alerted and making a run for it.

Back in 1966, after nearly a century of railway history, the last train pulled out of Green Park station. It was decided not to demolish the fine Palladian facade built by the Victorians. It fitted in with the rest of Bath and hid the train shed behind. Now the site was regenerated as a shopping precinct with car park, shops, superstore, restaurant and covered market. Diamond wished he'd thought of this place as a likely site for the next execution. The arched interior with its cast-iron ribs was in the classic style of St Pancras and other great stations. Crucially for Jerry Kean, there was open access. Once the market stalls inside were closed for the day, the old train shed was deserted. Ample opportunity to sling a cord over a girder and rig up another spectacular hanging.

Not many cars were parked overnight in the space where rail tracks had once run. In his private car Diamond drove past the police vehicles and right up to the end where the great arched shed was. It was difficult to see much, but he picked out the Hosannah van and stopped a few spaces away.

He'd expected Leaman the keeno to be ahead of him. Instead, when he got out, the first to come up was Georgina. Seeing the triumphant look in her eye, he would have settled for Leaman.

'Glad you made it, Peter,' she said. 'My tactics seem to have paid off.'

'Your tactics?'

'Pulling out all the stops. The massive surveillance exercise.'

'That was your idea?'

'My decision.' She was taking any credit that was going. Such is the privilege of assistant chief constables.

'Have you made the arrest, then?'

'Good Lord, no. I've only been here three minutes, straight from seeing the organiser of the ram raids. The man who calls himself Harry Lang, would you believe?'

He didn't trust himself to comment.

Georgina added, 'DI Halliwell interviewed him in hospital with me sitting in. He admits to everything.'

'Congratulations. Are you sure he isn't in your choir, singing like that?'

She gave an uneasy laugh. 'I don't think so.'

'Shall we get on with this, ma'am? Has the van been searched?'

'I gather DI Leaman has had it open and found nothing.'

'They're somewhere in the station, then.'

'Apparently not.'

395

He gave her the quizzical look she seemed to expect.

'No joy so far,' she said and leaned closer. 'Who's the lady in your car, if it isn't a personal question?'

'Ah, but it is.' Bloody cheek, he thought. Spotting Leaman, he turned his back on Georgina and went over.

'I don't get it, guv,' Leaman said. 'The van's been parked for some time. The engine's almost cold. No one inside. They've vanished.'

He didn't believe that for a moment. Taking a few steps into the shed, he peered up at the arched girders. By day, the glass roof gave plenty of light. At this late hour it was impossible to see what was up there. 'Let's have some lights. If he's still about he knows we're here.'

He wanted to see if the tell-tale plastic cord had been drawn over any of the girders and tied to one side, ready for the hanging.

Powerful flash-lamps probed the roof. A vehicle equipped with rotating lights was driven in. In the next five minutes numerous pairs of eyes stared up at the ironwork and sighted nothing.

'I don't get it,' Leaman said for the second time.

'Shut up, then.'

Diamond was near the end of his tether. He walked to the far end, the former booking hall. By day and evening it was in use as a brasserie, sometimes with live jazz, but at this hour it was in darkness. There were no signs of a break-in. He rattled the door. 'Let's have this open.'

'What with?' one officer asked.

'What do you think? Your magic wand?'

396

A kick did the job. They went in, switched on the lights and made a swift search of the seating area, bar, kitchen and toilets. Nobody was in there.

'What's upstairs?' he asked.

'The Bath Society meeting room.'

He felt movement in his pocket and took out the mobile and looked at it. Who on earth knew his number besides Paloma and Leaman, who were both near by?

He slapped it to his ear. 'Yes?'

'Guv.'

Ingeborg. She'd shown him how to use the thing.

'Guv, he's here, round the front entrance. You'd better come fast, but try not to panic him. There's a noose round Martin Steel's neck.'

His skin prickled. He ran to the door that led on to the street and kicked it open. He was among a cluster of metal tables and patio heaters. He ran on across the cobbled forecourt to where he saw Ingeborg standing beside a police car parked in James Street West to block the traffic. She was pointing.

He turned to look at the station front with its six columns above the metal canopy that had once protected passengers waiting for taxis. He couldn't see Jerry Kean or Martin Steel. 'Where are they?'

'On the roof,' Ingeborg said. 'He must have seen the activity. I'm sure he knows we're here.'

He stared up at the balustrade extending along the whole facade of the building. The roof was flat and about thirty feet high. 'I can't see anything.'

'He's pulled back out of sight. He's definitely there. Look.'

As she was speaking, a figure came into view, silhouetted against the sky, edged towards the parapet and stopped. From the reluctant movement, this person could only be Martin Steel, hampered by some kind of restraint. His hands were fastened behind his back and there was something odd about his head.

A voice at Diamond's side said, 'Oh God, no.'

It was Paloma. She'd got out of the car and followed him.

'We need people up there,' he said. 'And lights, and a hailer.'

Ingeborg already had her personal radio out and was calling for the back-up.

Diamond's eyes adjusted to the conditions and he picked out more detail. A long cord was lashed to one of the balusters and hung down in a loop. The other end was tied in a noose around Martin Steel's neck. The strange shape of the head was explained. He was hooded, as if for a judicial hanging.

'You know what that is over his head?' Diamond said, more to himself than anyone else. 'One of those totebags he uses for shopping. We found some grains of sugar in one victim's hair. Now we know why.'

A sob came from beside him.

'Paloma, you'd better not watch this.' He felt a pang of sympathy for her. This killer had been her child.

'I want to be here.'

He didn't argue. He turned to Ingeborg. 'Tell them I reckon the way up is through the meeting room. There must be a hatch to the roof.'

He was trying to be positive in the face of

imminent tragedy. One shove from behind and Martin Steel would topple forward and dangle dead on the end of the line. Somewhere out of sight was his executioner primed to act. In truth it would take a miracle to stop it happening.

He cupped his hands and shouted, 'Martin, the police are here. We'll get you out of this.'

There was no response from the hooded man.

But Diamond guessed this would bring Jerry Kean into view to check the situation below, and he was right. The second figure materialised.

'Jerry, this is Peter Diamond. Do you hear me? It's all over. We can end this peacefully if you do as I say.'

Jerry shouted back, 'Go to hell.'

Paloma took a sharp breath, on the point of appealing to her son, but Diamond gripped her arm and said, 'No.' He called up, 'You've made your point five times over. It'll all be written up in the papers. There's no sense in taking another life.'

From the roof came the riposte: ' "Before I formed you in the womb, I knew you." '

'What on earth are you on about?' Diamond called back.

'He's quoting from the Old Testament,' Ingeborg said.

'If he's going to give us a sermon, we might gain some time.' He shouted back at Jerry, 'Would you repeat that? I didn't catch what you were saying.'

'Jeremiah, one, five. They're the words of the Lord,' Jerry called. ' "Before I formed you in the womb, I knew you." Proof positive that human life begins at conception. These people have been murdering their unborn children. They deserve to die.'

'But you didn't know these people. You stole their case notes from the hospitals, but you didn't know them personally until you kidnapped them.'

'Judges don't know the people who appear before them, but they decide on their guilt.'

'You're judge and executioner, are you?' Diamond was working at full stretch to prolong this. 'What are your qualifications?'

'It's my mission. "The Lord called Samuel, and he answered: Here am I." '

'You've been talking to God?'

'He spoke to me, just as he spoke to Samuel.'

Diamond turned to Ingeborg. 'He's crazy. Did you get through?'

'They should be on their way, guv.'

'All right, Jerry,' he returned to the debate, 'and is this action of yours supported by your church?'

'They don't know what I'm doing. But like me they believe it's a mortal sin to murder the unborn.'

'Are you saying you're all in it together? Who was it I spoke to on the phone? Virginia. Is she an accessory to murder?'

'Of course she isn't. You're twisting my words.'

'What's Virginia's second name?'

'She's nothing to do with this.'

'What I don't follow, Jerry, is how you feel so passionate about the lives of unborn children, yet you don't find it morally wrong to take the lives of their parents.'

'They made their decision and that made them murderers, so they forfeit the right to live.'

'I think you've missed my point,' Diamond called back, and then muttered in an aside to

Ingeborg. 'I can't keep this going indefinitely. Why aren't they up there by now?'

She used her radio again.

Jerry was holding forth again. 'The Book of Exodus tells us, "If men strive and hurt a woman with child so that her fruit depart from her, and yet no mischief follow, he shall be surely punished ... Life for life, eye for eye, tooth for tooth, hand for hand, foot for foot."'

'Yes, but we're not living in Old Testament times, Jerry. There's all kinds of stuff in there that doesn't apply any longer.'

'I know what you're doing,' Jerry shouted. 'You're trying to distract me from my duty, but you won't succeed. This sinner shall pay for his wickedness.' He stepped closer to the hooded man and gripped his shoulders.

'Jerry, your mother's here,' Diamond yelled, at the limit of invention.

Jerry hesitated. 'You're lying.'

Paloma cried out, 'It's true, Jerry. Don't do this. You might as well kill me, too.'

What do you mean?'

'I had a baby stopped when you were a child. There was no medical reason. I just didn't want another one. If you think the man you're holding is wicked, then so is your own mother.'

He didn't respond for several seconds. Then he said in a barely audible voice, 'Is that true?'

Paloma said, 'I swear to God it is.'

Jerry went silent again, taking it in. He removed his hands and stepped away from his prisoner. His mother's words had stunned him. He covered his eyes. He was making involuntary movements, as if convulsed. Then he spread his arms and stepped

401

towards the balustrade, poised to leap to his own death.

Paloma screamed.

Those on the ground could only watch. Diamond put his arm round Paloma and she turned away and pressed her face against his chest and sobbed.

Ingeborg said, 'They're on the roof, guv.'

Figures in black sprinted across the roof and grabbed Jerry and pulled him down and out of sight. Others grasped Martin Steel and helped him away.

Diamond muttered, 'About bloody time.'

*   *   *

Much needs to be done after a major arrest. Martin Steel was brought down. Before being driven off in an ambulance he told Diamond the salient facts of his ordeal. He and his wife had been abducted at knifepoint by Jerry, tied up and driven to the trading estate. In the book depot they were kept pinioned for days and put through a quasi-judicial procedure, accused of murder by abortion, with Jerry as judge and jury. He had told them they were sentenced to death and would find out what it is like to await execution. 'He's fanatical,' Steel said. 'He would only quote scripture each time he brought us food and water. He took poor Joss out one night and I didn't see her again.' At this point he was too distressed to continue. He would be kept in hospital overnight and sedated.

Jerry was driven to Manvers Street and put through the process of fingerprinting and DNA testing. He spent the night in the cells in a zipper overall. The questioning wouldn't start until next day.

The crime scene people sealed off the station roof ready for examination. Georgina, who had missed the main action, came out to the front to bond with Diamond on the success of the operation she had masterminded, but he had gone.

He was driving Paloma back to Lyncombe, answering her questions about what would happen to Jerry. After he'd explained each stage of the process, she said, 'It's kind of you to do this.'

'I wasn't going to send you home in a police car,' he said. 'What you did tonight took courage. You saved a man's life.'

'Not just me.'

'Just you,' he insisted. 'I'd run through my repertoire. It was what you said that stopped another killing.'

They drove up Lyncombe Hill in silence, each in a hell of their own.

Outside the house he stopped and the engine idled and something needed to be said. It was Paloma who spoke. 'I'm ashamed of myself. I was a scheming bitch, the way I used you. You gave me nothing but kindness.'

'I'm not complaining,' he said. 'I understand your motives. Too bad I wasn't the deterrent you hoped for.'

'You're more generous than I deserve.'

'Not so. Meeting you was good for me. No regrets.'

He meant this. She'd befriended him under false pretences, but the friendship had grown into something real and worth preserving. He'd learned things about himself. He'd moved on. This wasn't a time for looking back. She was going to need massive support in the weeks to come.

She opened the door on her side. 'I guess it's goodbye, then.'

He put his hand over hers. 'It doesn't have to be.'